CUMBRIA LIBRARIES

3 8003 041

KT-408-121

ANNA DEAN lives in the Lake District with a husband and a cat. She sometimes works as a Creative Writing tutor and as a guide showing visitors around William Wordsworth's home, Dove Cottage. Her interests include walking, old houses, Jane Austen, cream teas, *Star Trek* and canoeing on very flat water.

www.annadean.co.uk

By Anna Dean

a&b

A Place of Confinement

ANNA DEAN

Allison & Busby Limited
12 Fitzroy Mews
London W1T 6DW
www.allisonandbusby.com

First published in Great Britain by Allison & Busby in 2012.
This paperback edition published by Allison & Busby in 2013.

Copyright © 2012 by ANNA DEAN

The right of ANNA DEAN to be identified as the author
of this work has been asserted by her in accordance with
the Copyright, Designs and Patents Act 1988.

All characters and events in this publication,
other than those clearly in the public domain,
are fictitious and any resemblance to actual persons,
living or dead, is purely coincidental.

All rights reserved. No part of this publication may be reproduced,
stored in a retrieval system, or transmitted, in any form or by
any means without the prior written permission of the publisher,
nor be otherwise circulated in any form of binding or cover
other than that in which it is published and without a similar
condition being imposed on the subsequent buyer.

A CIP catalogue record for this book is available from
the British Library.

10 9 8 7 6 5 4 3 2 1

ISBN 978-0-7490-1316-5

Typeset in 12.75/16.1 pt Adobe Garamond Pro by
Allison & Busby Ltd.

The paper used for this Allison & Busby publication
has been produced from trees that have been legally sourced
from well-managed and credibly certified forests.

Printed and bound by
CPI Group (UK) Ltd, Croydon, CR0 4YY

For my sister, Elizabeth Jane, with love

Chapter One

Charcombe Manor, Saturday 18th April 1807

My dear Eliza,
I am in prison and I do not know how much longer I can bear my confinement. The crime I have committed does not merit such a severe punishment. I <u>must</u> find some method of escape, or else run mad . . .

Miss Dido Kent ceased writing and looked with disgust at the words on her page. They were marred by ink running from an overloaded, careless pen – and with all the selfishness of an overburdened mind.

She was thoroughly ashamed of the momentary weakness which had led her to write what must distress her sister. She drew in a long breath, wiped clean her pen and sat for several minutes composing herself before taking another sheet of paper from her desk and beginning the letter afresh.

My dear Eliza, (she wrote in a neat, restrained script)
Aunt Manners and I have at last arrived at our destination, and we are both well. At least, I have suffered no great injury in our journey and our aunt, though racked

with 'indescribable pains' and 'so weak she can scarcely stand', is, you will be very glad to hear, quite _determined_ upon not mentioning these facts — for she does not wish to trouble anyone. I know this because she tells me so — a _dozen_ times _every_ day . . .

She stopped again. It seemed impossible for Dido, once she had a pen in her hand, not to express what was on her mind. But dwelling upon her aunt's offences would not do at all.

She lifted the dangerous instrument from the page and looked about for some unexceptionable topic; something which might amuse Eliza and raise her own spirits.

I like Charcombe Manor quite as well as I anticipated, she wrote. _It has all the solidity, charm and beauty which I have heard described by other visitors. We found the house already full of company upon our arrival yesterday, but our host, Mr Lancelot Fenstanton, made us very welcome indeed. A whole hour's speech was insufficient to express the vast debt of gratitude which our visit to his humble abode inspires._

My aunt's letter informing him of our visit had arrived only the day before. And a mighty fine surprise it'd been. D— him if he hadn't been smiling about it ever since! It was thirty years since she'd set foot over the threshold and he didn't know how he'd make enough of her and her charming young friend.

'Young friend', Eliza — did you mark that? I like Mr Lancelot very well indeed! His gallantry is a little *extravagant, I grant. And if he did not look so handsome and laugh so much over his own nonsense, I <u>might</u> find him ridiculous. But one simply <u>cannot</u> mock a man who mocks himself continually.*

I am writing now from the great hall. I sit here at my writing desk surrounded on all sides by old Flemish tapestries of hunting scenes; there is a broad hearth with black firedogs, a harpsichord which looks as if it may be a hundred years old, an ancient carved screen shutting out the doors to the offices, and a staircase with wide, shallow treads worn smooth by generations of Fenstanton feet. It is a very nice hall; but at present it has for me something of the nature of a prison. For 'I cannot get out', as Mr Sterne's starling complains.

Aunt Manners is taking her afternoon rest, but is so very apprehensive of the indescribable pains returning that she has forbidden me to stray beyond the possibility of an urgent summons. Oh Eliza! I confess that the confinement of the past two weeks is beginning to tell upon my spirits – and my temper . . .

Dido stopped again, read over the letter, and decided that this, more moderate expression of misery might be allowed. If she was to be permitted no honesty at all, completing the letter would become impossible.

She continued as rationally as she could . . .

When Margaret devised this attendance upon Aunt Manners as punishment for my recent offence, she chose very well indeed. It is a heavy penance. Since our setting out upon this journey, I do not believe I have been permitted to stir

9

fifty yards from our aunt's side — except upon errands for her convenience. And there is no term fixed for my imprisonment. I have asked again and again how long we are to remain here, but cannot obtain an answer. Catherine has invited us to pay her a visit when we leave Charcombe and I am <u>longing</u> to go to Belsfield . . .

The pen halted again. Dido had now strayed onto ground which was *much* too dangerous. She had better not dwell on thoughts of Belsfield Hall, nor her reasons for wishing to be there.

What was needed, she decided, was a subject which would engross her and make her forget, for a while at least, her present state of exile — and the terrible cause of that exile. She laid down the pen and looked about.

Before her, the vast front door (thick enough — by its owner's account — to withstand a cannon's blast) stood open upon a sunny garden of dark clipped hedges and bright flower beds. Warm scents of gillyflowers and box made their way into the cool hall, together with the faint salty breath of the sea which was little more than a mile away.

On the lawn beyond the flower beds, Charcombe Manor's other visitors could be seen walking about and sitting upon the green benches. Dido rested her chin in her hand and fell to watching them, for all the world as if she were sitting in a theatre looking out onto a stage.

Now here might be matter to distract her thoughts from her own ills!

She took her penknife from the desk and sat for

several minutes thoughtfully mending her pen. Then she laid down the knife, turned once more to her page – and began upon a new topic.

Eliza, I believe that there is something amiss among the other people gathered here at Charcombe Manor. This is not a house at ease with itself. I had begun to suspect it even before our delightful host had completed his speech of welcome.

You see, for all Mr Fenstanton's fine words and compliments, there has been a coldness in our reception – a grudging silence – among the other guests. I hardly know how to describe the feeling which hangs over the house. But if you have ever inadvertently walked into a room in which people were making love, or else quarrelling with one another, you may be able to imagine the sensation. We are supernumerary; we have intruded. This house is filled with unfinished conversations and anxieties which must be hidden from us.

One cannot help but feel uncomfortable . . . And one cannot help but feel curious too . . .

Dido's eyes travelled back to the bright garden beyond the open door. She would dearly love to walk out into the sunshine – but dared not attempt it for fear of her aunt's summons. However, though she was denied fresh air, exercise and society, she might at least observe the unfolding of the household's drama. When a woman is in a state of disgrace and exile, she is well advised to snatch at amusement where she can . . .

And, as she looked out, the guest who immediately

caught her attention – the figure which, as it were, held dominion over the green stage – was Mrs Augusta Bailey, marked out by the brilliance of her scarlet shawl and the dramatic clasping of her hands to her breast as she addressed Miss Martha Gibbs who strode restlessly beside her.

. . . *Mrs Bailey,* wrote Dido, *is, of everyone presently gathered here, the most discomposed, the most nervous – and the most resentful of our arrival.*

Mrs Bailey is the wife of Mr Lancelot Fenstanton's 'very oldest friend'; but Mr Bailey is away at present on business overseas. Mrs B is rather a pretty woman with a very high opinion of herself and her consequence in the world. She is a little rouged and powdered, and possessed of a figure which is <u>almost</u> youthful. However, there is a certain stiffness in the way she walks, a slight creaking when she sits down, which suggest there may be a little more to Mrs Bailey than is allowed to meet the eye. I am sure there is ten years more to her age than she is willing to allow.

And, whatever the secret may be which is being concealed here, I am <u>sure</u> it concerns Mrs Bailey rather nearly . . .

Dido tapped one finger upon the table as she considered . . .

In point of fact, I believe the mystery to be all about the ward of Mr and Mrs Bailey – a Miss Letitia Verney: a young lady I have not yet met, but have heard talked of. When my aunt enquired after Miss Verney upon our arrival yesterday, Mrs Bailey turned as red as her shawl and became most <u>remarkably</u> interested in our journey hither and in

12

*describing to us the extremely fine weather we are to enjoy
during our stay.*

*As you know, it is not in Aunt Manners' nature to notice
or be pained when her remarks offend others, which is
fortunate for her – else she would live in a continual state of
suffering. But I could not help but notice that her question
was unwelcome, and I began immediately to take a great
interest in the name of Letitia Verney. I soon found out that
Miss Verney is a very beautiful young lady of nineteen who
has been in the care of Mr Bailey since she was a child. She
is the particular friend of Miss Martha Gibbs – who has
been invited here on that account. I understand that Miss
Gibbs, Miss Verney and Mrs Bailey all arrived together at
Charcombe Manor about a fortnight ago . . .*

The pen stilled once more as Dido gazed out into the
bright garden, this time turning her attention upon Miss
Gibbs who was loping awkwardly beside Mrs Bailey. She
was holding on to her bonnet with one hand, for the
breeze was almost dislodging it – though it did not appear
to be stirring her companion's hat at all. And it seemed all
of a piece with the hapless Miss Gibbs' character that the
wind should vent its spite upon *her* bonnet and nobody
else's . . .

*. . . I found myself seated beside Miss Gibbs at dinner
yesterday, so I took the opportunity of expressing the – very
understandable – hope that we shall meet her friend Miss
Verney during our stay at Charcombe.*

Oh Lord! But she did not know about that! For there was
no knowing was there? And her spoon was dropped into her

soup plate and the conversation was lost in a great mopping up of soup with a napkin – which ended in the overturning of a flower vase.

Yes, all in all, I am <u>almost sure</u> that it is Miss Verney who is making the company uneasy. Or perhaps I should rather say that it is the <u>lack</u> of Miss Verney which is making the company uneasy. For she has not yet appeared, and her whereabouts are <u>never</u> mentioned . . .

I should dearly love to know what has become of her – and why her absence is causing so much anxiety . . .

Dido's pen was halted yet again – this time by an urgent drumming of hooves upon the high road.

Out in the garden the shadows were beginning to lengthen and the spring day was growing cool. The company was gathering upon the upper lawn now, preparing for a return to the house.

From her seat in the hall, Dido could look past the lawns, along the length of the carriage drive which rose gently to tall iron gates shaded by beech trees which were just breaking into leaf. The gates stood open and, on the road beyond, she could now see a horse approaching – and turning into the drive at a speed which set the gravel dancing about its hooves.

Everybody on the lawn turned to look, and Lancelot Fenstanton began immediately to run towards the house. He joined the rider as he dismounted at the foot of the steps, and the two men fell into an earnest conference.

Dido would have dearly loved to know their subject, but their voices were pitched inconsiderately low. The rider drew a letter from his pocket and handed it to Mr

14

Fenstanton, remounted and started off along the carriage drive.

Mr Fenstanton remained upon the step, broke the seal of the letter with a quick movement and began to read. And he proved to be one of those people who *must* read aloud. Dido could see his lips moving, hear the rhythm of the words. So eager was she to catch the meaning too that, insensibly, she had risen from her chair – taken a step towards the door – when Mr Fenstanton ceased reading and turned about.

She sat down with her heart beating rapidly, earnestly hoping that her impertinence had not been detected. But the gentleman was in the hall now and he looked so very anxious that she felt authorised to cry out, 'I hope you have received no bad news, Mr Fenstanton.'

'Ha! Bad enough!'

'I am very sorry to hear it.'

Lancelot Fenstanton stood a moment beside the door, beating his hat against his leg and gazing out along his carriage drive as if he had never seen it before. Then he crossed the hall in long strides, threw himself down in the chair opposite Dido and tossed his hat onto the table.

He bowed his head with something of the air of a good-natured little boy puzzling over his lesson. He was a well-looking man of about forty and his countenance seemed made for smiling. He was not above average height, but powerfully built; his black hair was only touched with grey at the temples and the lines in his rather tanned face seemed all fashioned by laughter and an outdoor life.

He looked up, caught Dido's watching eye and smiled

broadly. 'I'll tell you what, Miss Kent,' he cried, 'I think you are suspicious of us all!'

Dido coloured and disclaimed immediately, but he was not to be put off.

'Yes, yes, I see how it is,' he said. 'Dear Mrs Manners may have noticed nothing, but *you*,' he waved the letter in his hand, 'I fancy *you* have been taking the measure of things ever since you arrived. I am right, am I not?'

Dido was not used to being understood so very easily. She would have to be a little careful of Mr Fenstanton . . .

'I am very sorry if I have seemed impertinent,' she said, 'but I confess that I have detected a certain . . . uneasiness in the house. I hope there is no great trouble.'

'Ha! Yes, we are uneasy enough, I should think! And, do you know, I said to dear Mrs Bailey yesterday that we might as well tell you all about it. For it's damned awkward keeping secrets within the house, and I'm sure you won't breathe a word of it.'

'No, indeed I shall not,' said Dido virtuously. 'Am I to understand that it is a rather delicate matter?'

'About as delicate as it can be! The long and the short of it is,' he said, picking up his hat and turning it about in his hands, 'our Miss Verney has disappeared.'

'Disappeared?'

'There is no other way of telling it, Miss Kent. Two days ago a young man called upon her here. A gentleman she has known for some time and who was come to stay with friends ten miles away. Mrs Bailey had already hinted to me that she was a little uneasy about the acquaintance. But we did not any of us think there was any *great* danger.

However, Miss Verney went out walking with this young man – and she has not been seen since.'

'You fear that she has—'

'It seemed plain that they were off to Scotland together and we've had men searching for them along the turnpike – making enquiries at the inns. We have traced a carriage to the Bristol road.'

He looked so very dejected that Dido very much wished to help him. She watched him compassionately as he began to tap a finger fretfully upon the table. 'The young lady's going must be a very great worry to you,' she said.

'It's the very devil!' he cried. 'For poor old Reg Bailey – he's Miss Verney's guardian, you know – he asked me particularly to watch over the girl while he's away settling his affairs in Antigua.' He sighed extravagantly. 'But I thought Miss Verney was a sensible girl; high-spirited, certainly, but never foolish. I had no idea of her getting into this kind of scrape. And I'm damned if I know how to get her back.'

Dido smoothed the soft barbs of her pen. 'Is Miss Gibbs not able to supply any information?' she suggested. 'A young lady's intimate friend is often a party to such a scheme.'

'No, poor little Martha Gibbs knows nothing at all. She is as shocked as the rest of us.'

Or so she claims, commented Dido internally. 'And what of Miss Verney's maid?' she asked aloud. 'For I understand that in cases of elopement the young lady's maid is generally the first to be enquired of.'

'A very wise practice, I don't doubt. But, unfortunately,

no use in our case. For the maid is gone with the mistress. She – the maid – seems to have engaged a chaise from the Bull at Old Charcombe.'

'And Miss Verney went away in that chaise?'

Mr Lancelot rubbed unhappily at his brow. 'Why, I think she must. For the postillion reports taking up a lady not far from our gates at some time about five o'clock.'

'Only a lady? There was no gentleman with her?'

'No, only a lady and her maid. Which is damned odd, ain't it? I suppose she meant to meet with her gallant again upon the road, but it's a very strange way of carrying on.' He studied his companion a moment as she sat thoughtfully brushing her pen across her cheek. 'It's a puzzle, ain't it?' he said. 'And I'll tell you what – I fancy *you* are rather partial to a puzzle, Miss Kent!'

Dido blushed; he was certainly too keen an observer for comfort.

'Now, now, there is no need to look so bashful. For I do not mind your being interested at all. Why,' he cried, throwing wide his arms, 'I hereby authorise you to be as impertinently curious as you wish. Ask what questions you will! Pry into anything you choose!'

'Thank you. You are very kind, sir.'

'I only condition for your finding out in the end what has become of Miss Verney.'

'I wish I might. But I doubt I can succeed where others have failed.'

'Hmm.' Fenstanton tapped a finger meditatively upon the table and considered his companion very closely. Her little round face was, as the saying goes, 'past its first youth', and the plain white cap *ought* to signify sedate spinsterhood. But there was something about the way in which Miss Kent wore her cap – something in the way the bright brown curls could not be contained within it, but spilt out onto cheek and brow – which was not sedate at all. And, though the fine green eyes were at present demurely downcast, there was in them a mixture of lively calculation, inquisitiveness and downright deviousness which is by no means usual in ageing maidens . . .

Perhaps Mr Fenstanton was tempted to hope that she *might* succeed in the task. He leant closer across the table. 'I should be very glad of your assistance, Miss Kent. And I understand that we are to have the pleasure of your company some weeks. Mrs Manners has promised me that she will stay at least until the end of the month—'

Dido's dismay must have been writ clear on her face, for he stopped short. 'Ha! But I think you are wanting to return home.'

'Oh no!' She turned away in confusion – dreadfully aware of his keen gaze – and, between the fear of seeming ungrateful for his hospitality and all the painful remembrances which the word 'home' called forth, she did not know how to look or what to say. For, in point of fact, Dido was a true exile: wretched in her state of wandering, yet knowing that there was no safety in returning. Life as her aunt's companion might be dull and humiliating; but at home, back in Badleigh, a far worse fate awaited her . . .

'I am very happy here, Mr Fenstanton,' she assured him. 'And you are quite correct in thinking that mysteries interest me. I confess that Miss Verney's absence had already begun to exercise my mind.'

'That's good! Now,' he said with a confiding air, 'I shall tell you the strangest part of the story.' He looked down at the letter in his hand. 'You see, all my previous ideas have been stood upon their head. I have just now received the oddest message.'

'And is the message from Miss Verney?'

'No. It is from the young man.'

'Is it indeed? And where is he? What does he say?'

'He is still here in Charcombe. And he says he don't know where the young lady is any more than we do.'

'But that is not possible! Miss Verney walked out with him and has not been seen again. What does he say became of her? Did she leave him to go away in the chaise?'

Mr Lancelot shook his head. 'He *says* he knows nothing about a chaise. He says they returned together to the house at five o'clock – or just a few minutes after. He says he stood beside the gate and watched her walk along the carriage drive and in through the front door.'

'How very odd!'

They had both turned now to the door and were gazing out at the sunny gravel drive which was no more than a hundred yards long and had not so much as a bush to obscure it.

'It is more than odd,' said Mr Fenstanton, 'it is impossible. For at five o'clock the whole company was gathered here in the hall. This room was not empty from four o'clock until the dinner bell rang at half after five. And Miss Verney did *not* walk in through that door. The fellow is lying.'

'But how strange that he should tell such a very poor

sort of lie. Why has he not invented a more believable tale to hide his villainy?'

'I'm sure I don't know, Miss Kent,' said Mr Fenstanton, gazing out at the gravel and the gates. 'But he is lying. Young ladies cannot simply vanish while walking along a carriage drive and through a door.'

Chapter Two

. . . Young ladies cannot simply vanish, can they, Eliza? Mr Fenstanton is in the right there. If a lady disappears from one side of a door she <u>must</u> appear upon the other side of it. We live in a rational age and cannot tolerate anything which goes against nature.

But why does the young fellow tell such an unbelievable story? And why is he still in Charcombe? Has the world come to such a pass? Are young men grown so very indolent that young ladies must now abduct themselves?

I do not like this business at all. It must be put to rights.

But I rather wonder how this latest news will be received by my fellow guests. Will it surprise them as much as it surprises me? Or is there <u>someone</u> here within the manor house who knows more than they are telling about Miss Verney's disappearance?

I rather think that there is. Such a sudden, mysterious removal argues for an accomplice . . .

Dido stopped writing and watched Mr Lancelot Fenstanton as he hurried down the steps to share the news with Mrs Bailey and Miss Gibbs, who were still walking together on the upper lawn.

She had her eye fixed upon Miss Gibbs, for as the

'intimate friend' she must be the one most suspected of complicity. How would she look when the letter was shown to her?

The girl looked up anxiously as Mr Fenstanton approached and moved towards him – as if wishing to escape her companion. But Mrs Bailey caught at her arm and the gentleman addressed them both with his news.

Mrs Bailey began to remonstrate before he could even finish talking. She was shaking her head, clutching the red shawl dramatically to her bosom. Mr Fenstanton handed the paper to her – as if to prove he had been telling the truth. But all the while Miss Gibbs stood unmoving, one hand still tethering the wayward bonnet as its long ribbons flapped about her face, her eyes fixed intently upon the stout figure of Mrs Bailey. She seemed to be interested only in her companion's behaviour. There was no sign of shock upon her own account.

In fact Dido could not escape the impression that the contents of the letter had been no surprise at all to Miss Martha Gibbs . . .

But no sooner had she reached this very interesting conclusion than she was distracted by the approach of a third lady.

In a dainty flutter of white muslin, Miss Emma Fenstanton – Mr Lancelot's young cousin – came running along that part of the carriage drive which led away to the stables at the back of the house. She moved with such energy and elegance that she seemed almost to dance across the lawn. She had a parasol in one hand and a book beneath her arm. She immediately drew the master of the house away from the others and the two fell into a lively conference.

Perhaps he was telling her about the letter. They were walking away together; they had almost gained the terrace before the house and Dido was in hopes of hearing their conversation – Miss Emma seemed distressed. She was clinging now to her cousin's arm. And she seemed to be pleading with him.

In her eagerness to hear what was passing, Dido leant towards the door, but the light, girlish voice was lost in the breeze. And when Mr Lancelot replied he spoke quietly. The genial look was gone from his face: he looked stern.

What, Dido wondered, was little Miss Fenstanton asking that displeased him so much? Was she making some plea on behalf of the vanished Miss Verney? She was shaking back her short black curls; there was a look of entreaty upon her pale face as it turned up gracefully.

But the gentleman was immune to her charm. He spoke briefly with every appearance of firmness, and walked away, leaving Emma gazing after him, her arms crossed about her book. She stamped a small foot in irritation. Then stood for several minutes, lost in thought.

At last she seemed to take some decision and began to walk purposefully towards the house.

She stopped a moment in the darkness of the porch, and looked about with the quick little movements of a hunted animal. It appeared that she might have private business to conduct in the house which she did not wish to be overlooked. Perhaps, thought Dido, that private business related to the vanished lady . . .

Miss Emma was running into the hall now. She crossed to the library door, unaware of the silent observer in the shadows. But then, with her hand upon the lock of the library door, she looked about – and saw the inquisitive figure sitting with her writing desk at the hall table. 'Miss Kent!' she cried. 'Why, I thought everybody was in the garden!' She moved away from the door – as if she did not wish to be suspected of having any interest in it.

'But why, why, why do you sit inside on such a delightful day? Whatever are you up to?' Emma skipped across the hall and laid her parasol and her book on the table. (The book, Dido noted with some surprise, was the dry and worthy *Dr Gregory's Advice to his Daughters*.)

Dido pleaded her aunt's indisposition as her reason for not joining the company in the garden, and Miss Fenstanton sat down beside her with a look of sympathy on her merry little face. 'Ah dear,' she said, 'how delightful it must be, to be as rich as Mrs Manners and able to torment all one's relations! I hope that I may be as rich one day – and then I shall be *horribly* tyrannical.' She gave a little laugh – in any other girl it might have been a giggle, but in Emma it was a laugh, musical and gentle on the ear. 'I shall make a dozen different wills and threaten everybody with not leaving them a penny! It will be such fun!'

Miss Fenstanton did not mean to be unkind. Such flights of fancy were common with her. But Dido blushed; any reminder of her own situation – her enforced attendance upon her aunt and the mercenary motives which must be imputed to it – was painful. She said nothing, and studied her companion so that she might provide a description for Eliza.

Though she was but sixteen, there was a look of good health and high spirits about Miss Emma; an air of blooming womanhood. And so it was a shock to look close and find that there was little actual beauty in face or figure. Her complexion was good, but her nose was insignificant and her eyes, though bright, were rather small. But, pleased with herself and with the world, Emma Fenstanton had never considered the possibility that she was not pretty. And, possessed of such certainty within herself, she carried her point with all observers. She passed everywhere for a beauty.

At the moment there was one decided flaw in her looks which appeared as she drew off her gloves and laid them beside the book on the table.

'Your hand is scratched,' remarked Dido solicitously.

'Oh!' Emma laughed again and looked down at her hand. An angry red mark ran across the white skin, beaded with blood which was but recently dried. 'I scratched myself on a rose bush while I was gathering flowers this morning.' She indicated a large vase which stood near the hearth.

Dido made a civil remark upon the prettiness of the flowers' arrangement; but all Emma's attention was now fixed upon the open door, beyond which could be seen the small plump figure of her father, Mr George Fenstanton.

He was hurrying purposefully across the lawn towards the house.

Emma jumped up, took her parasol and book from

the table and ran out onto the steps – as if she did not wish to be discovered within doors.

'Now then, miss!' boomed Mr George as he all but ran against his daughter on the front steps. 'I'll thank you to stop a moment and listen to me.'

He took her arm and paused a moment, struggling for breath after his brisk walk across the lawn.

He was a short, round, oddly smooth-looking man in a tight green coat. His pink scalp showed through the sparse white hair of his head and his busyness and self-consequence showed through every movement that he made, every word that he spoke. And when Mr George was feeling particularly self-important, some odd arrangement of his teeth made a whistle of his breath.

'What are you about?' he demanded, still holding his daughter's arm.

'Nothing, Papa.'

He snatched the book from under her arm, read its cover and handed it back to her without a comment. 'Now, I don't like the way things are carrying on,' he said, whistling loudly. 'Did I see you just now quarrelling with your cousin Lancelot?'

'No, Papa. We were not quarrelling, merely talking.'

'Well, miss. I'll thank you to remember your duty. This is a fine opportunity for you to catch Lancelot – while the Verney heiress is out of the way. And I expect to see you *smiling* at him – not quarrelling.'

'Yes, Papa. I shall smile.' Miss Emma turned up her face and displayed a dazzling – but mischievous – smile that was all made up of dimples and white teeth and sparkling black eyes.

George Fenstanton seemed blind to the danger of the smile. Looking pleased with himself for having resolved this little matter, he linked his arm firmly through his daughter's, and steered her back to the company on the lawn.

Left alone in the hall, Dido indulged herself with some rather suspicious thoughts about the lively Miss Emma. Why had she come into the house? And why had the discovery that she was not alone prevented her from completing her purpose?

And it was very doubtful that Emma had been telling the truth about the scratch on her hand. The vase by the hearth contained lilacs, and lilies aplenty – but there was not a single rose. In fact, as well as Dido could recall, there were as yet no roses blooming in Charcombe Manor's garden. Miss Fenstanton would have had little reason to approach a rose bush . . .

Chapter Three

. . . Well, perhaps Miss Emma Fenstanton has some knowledge of Miss Verney's plans and is pleading her cause with Mr Lancelot . . . Or perhaps Mr George Fenstanton has quietly disposed of Miss Verney in order that his daughter may have a better chance of marrying Mr Lancelot.

By the by, Eliza, the existence of this Mr George burst upon me when we arrived at Charcombe Manor. He is the brother of our Aunt Manners and also of Mr Lancelot's late father. I had no notion of her possessing a surviving brother, for I have never heard one word of him from her lips – unlike 'my dear nephew, Lancelot,' about whom we have all been hearing for ever.

And I notice that she has little more to say to Mr George than she has of him, scarcely ever addressing him unless she has the opportunity of contradicting him.

I confess that I can feel little regard for the man myself. He is a pompous, prosing fellow – and I have noticed that he is very much attached to Charcombe Manor in a jealous, younger brother sort of way. I do not doubt that it would suit him <u>very well indeed</u> to see his child married to the present owner (though I do not believe the child herself has much enthusiasm for the scheme) . . . Perhaps he has taken extreme measures to bring about a match! Perhaps Mr George is at the heart of Miss Verney's odd 'elopement' which appears to be no elopement at all.

I declare, when one comes to consider the matter there are all manner of interesting possibilities!

I watched very closely this evening to see the effect of this latest news – the young man's claim to have escorted the lady safely home. All the older members of the company – Mr Lancelot, Mr George Fenstanton, Mrs Bailey and my aunt – are united in a disbelief of the young man's account. He is a thorough-going villain in their eyes.

As one might expect, the two young ladies are less inclined to condemn, youth being always predisposed to trust and excuse.

Martha Gibbs and Emma Fenstanton, I should say, have such a friendship as two young ladies thrown together in a country house – without possessing a thought or feeling in common – may be supposed to have. They are confederates in working a chair cover and sit over it every evening, conversing very comfortably; in no danger of ever understanding one another on any subject beyond the choice of threads and patterns.

Merry little Miss Fenstanton considers it 'a great lark' that the young man knows not where Letitia Verney is. And she doubts not he is 'as foolish as other men – even though they do say he has a handsome face'.

To which Miss Gibbs solemnly replies, 'Lord yes! It is just as you say. He has a _very_ handsome face indeed and one cannot believe such a fine man is a liar.'

I cannot help but wonder about Miss Martha Gibbs – I am _sure_ she was not surprised to hear that the young man denies all knowledge of abduction . . .

You will probably find my enthusiasm for this mystery unbecoming, Eliza; but I know you are too kind to begrudge me a little diversion from the duties of a niece. Life as a lady's 'companion' is excessively dull. I may not walk abroad for fear of my aunt being 'seized suddenly'; if I am detected with a book in my hand, she is immediately taken with the desire of having 'a comfortable chat'; and I am scarcely allowed to be in company.

I am writing now in Aunt Manners' bedchamber; she is unwell and has retired early. I am required to sit with her until she sleeps, to guard against the possibility of her being seized so very suddenly as to make her unable to ring the bell. It is an acute sickness of the 'enervating' sort which overcame her at teatime – just after she was disappointed in the forming of a whist table when all the young people vetoed cards and decided that dancing was to form the evening's entertainment.

She has taken a glass of wine and a particularly large dose of the brown medicine which is generally of use in cases of 'enervating' seizures. And I hope that she is on her way to sleeping now . . .

She stopped writing again, and raised her head to listen. The sound of a lively Scotch air came very faint from below. The dancing was yet in progress.

Dido had been surprised that the company should be so very merry while Miss Verney's fate remained uncertain. But Mr Fenstanton and Mrs Bailey were determined that no rumours of elopement should begin to circulate. For the sake of the young lady's reputation everything was to be smoothed over – and her absence explained by that convenient cover-all of 'visiting friends'.

The Parrys, a family of neighbours who knew nothing of the business, had walked up to the manor after tea. And since there were three grown-up young Mr Parrys, and not one inconvenient daughter, there were probably gentleman enough in the hall that even Dido might be asked to dance . . .

Of course, at six and thirty, such calculations *should* be beneath her notice. And besides, why should she expect to be entertained at Charcombe? The very purpose of her being here was that she might suffer every pain of neglect and insignificance, until she had learnt her duty to her family . . .

But there is something so very *inviting* about a Scotch air – even when it is rattled out upon an old harpsichord.

She looked across the wainscoted chamber – very gloomy beyond the candle's light. In the high bed with its four posts and its dark crimson curtains, her aunt lay very still, her fingers just clutching the edge of the sheet, her eyes shut tight, her soft little face composed beneath her starched white nightcap.

Was she sleeping? Might it be possible to creep down and join the dancing? A little company, a little exercise would be delightful . . . And it might be possible to learn more about Miss Verney's disappearance . . .

Dido laid down her pen, rose very quietly and began to tiptoe about the room, putting to rights her aunt's possessions. She folded the dressing robe which had been left across the bed's foot and put it away in one of the pair of closets that flanked the fireplace. Then she took from the side of the bed the pretty new slippers of green silk which the maid had but just finished sewing in their journey thither. She noticed that the backs were already trodden down, and shook her head over the damage as she put them away, for she never could bear to see good shoes injured needlessly.

Mrs Manners did not stir as she worked and Dido began to hope that escape might be possible. She crept slowly towards the door . . .

'My dear?' The voice was weak: the voice of a woman barely alive and about to whisper a parting benediction. 'Are you there?'

'Yes, Aunt.' She sighed and went to the bedside.

'Oh, I wondered where you were got to. I feel so very *unwell*.' Mrs Manners peered up short-sightedly at her niece. One hand released the covers and fastened itself upon Dido's wrist. It was a dry little hand, heavily burdened with rings. The bones in it were as delicate as a bird's; but its warmth and strength were strangely at odds with the weakness of the voice.

'Shall I send for an apothecary?' suggested Dido.

'No, I do not wish to be a trouble to anybody.' The hand tightened, the thick gold of the rings bit into Dido's wrist.

'But if you are unwell . . .'

'I am not one to make a fuss over a little illness,' whispered Aunt Manners, closing her eyes. 'I am too much used to suffering! But—' Her eyes opened again suddenly. 'I recall there is scarcely any brown medicine left and we shall not be able to get any tomorrow for it is Sunday. You must go to Charcombe *early* on Monday,

33

Dido, and find a medical man who can make some more.'

'Yes, Aunt.'

'You must seek out the best physician in Charcombe.'

'Yes, Aunt. And shall I ask him to visit you?'

'No. I do not wish to have any clumsy country apothecary about me. You must find out all you can about the man . . . And then I shall decide whether I wish to employ him.'

Mrs Manners lay back upon her pillows; her blue eyes – slightly clouded by the influence of physic – were fixed upon the carved oak tester of the bed with such an air of patient suffering as Dido believed would have irritated a saint. Though she could not but admit that the attitude was gracefully done. Selina Manners was now well past fifty, but her famous beauty was not entirely worn away, for it went deep into her bones, her very being; and the features beneath the lace and ribbons of her nightcap had still an arresting perfection in their form, though the enchanting eyes which had once enslaved the wealthy Mr Manners were faded and weak; the lips thinner, less red.

'Now, my dear,' she said in a voice blurred by oncoming sleep, 'you and I shall have a comfortable chat.'

'Oh!' Dido was tormented by the sound of the dance still seeping through the uneven floorboards.

But there was no escaping the chat and, unfortunately, at such moments Mrs Manners found no subject more comfortable than the offences of all her relations who were, by her account, intent upon 'getting money off me. Between my kin and poor Mr Manners' own family, I am worried to death!'

'Yes, Aunt,' murmured Dido, miserable with boredom

and an obscure kind of guilt. It was a common refrain. She could have supplied every word of it herself and she well knew that she was expected to contribute nothing to the conversation. 'Yes, Aunt, very true' was all that was required.

Mrs Manners' lids flickered sleepily, peeling up oddly and revealing rather more white of the eye than is usual. But she continued to struggle against the narcotic.

'But I am too clever for them all,' she gloated sleepily. 'They shall not get the better of me. They shall see!'

'Yes, Aunt, I am sure they shall.'

'My brother George is the worst of them all. And he thinks he has got the better of me.'

Dido began upon another anodyne reply, but as she spoke she noticed that her aunt's sleepy eyes had come to rest upon her own hand – where there was a ring missing; the great ruby from the middle finger was gone, leaving in its place a deep white groove to testify to the many years it had been worn.

'Aunt, where is your ring?'

'It is nothing. Do not say anything about it.'

'But—'

'It is nothing.' The little white hand fluttered briefly in a regal gesture of dismissal. 'George may have it if he wishes. He thinks he has got the better of me . . .' She gazed up at the tester for a moment, nodded very wisely in its direction. 'I do not care about it, however. I have not come here to oblige *him*.' She shook her head wisely. But the brown medicine had won at last. Her lids flickered and closed. A moment later her lower lip dropped slightly and a thin snore rattled out.

Dido breathed a sigh of great relief, but found that the hold upon her wrist was not relaxed. Through the old, uneven floorboards came the tormenting sound of the dance; the candle burnt still beside the writing desk, but even her letter was beyond her reach while that hand confined her wrist. There was nothing to be done but to settle herself as comfortably as she might upon the narrow bedside chair and wait to be released.

She gazed down for a moment or two at the delicate finger with its telltale groove. The missing ring was of considerable value. Why should Mrs Manners give such a generous gift to a brother she did not seem to like?

It was another intriguing puzzle.

But, despite her efforts, Dido found that she was too tired and dispirited to dwell for long upon intriguing puzzles. Thoughts of her own wretched situation were rising up to engulf her weary brain . . .

Chapter Four

The cause of Dido's punishment and present exile from the home of her brother and sister-in-law at Badleigh Vicarage was a certain Doctor Jeremiah Prowdlee. It was on Doctor Jeremiah Prowdlee's account that she was fixed here at her aunt's side, doomed to an indefinite sentence of measuring out medicine and listening to a litany of complaints.

Doctor Prowdlee was the new rector of Upper Marwell – a parish adjoining Badleigh. He was a large man with a high, white, shining dome of a head which did not seem to have lost its hair so much as allowed it to slip down about the face, where it clung on tenaciously. He had a puritanical turn of mind, a pompous air – and a family of children which filled a pew and a half in his church.

There was no longer a Mrs Jeremiah Prowdlee. She had died (possibly of exhaustion and depressed spirits, in Dido's opinion) some months before her husband came to Upper Marwell.

When the doctor arrived in their midst during the previous autumn, Dido had, perhaps, been insufficiently alert to the danger of a man with a dead wife and a pew and a half full of children. For she was at that time very much occupied with other concerns.

Retrospectively she was keenly aware of how very often Doctor Prowdlee had, at Margaret's invitation, intruded upon their evenings with his wheezing breath and his awkward compliments. ('I hear that it is to your fair hand that I may attribute the excellence of this seed cake, Miss Kent.' And 'Your sister has been telling me of your invaluable assistance in sewing for her little boys.') But, at the time, it had not seemed alarming at all. And, even when her neighbours began to enquire rather often after 'dear Doctor Prowdlee' as if she had some privileged knowledge of the man's state of health, she attributed it to nothing more than that kind of solidarity which is generally supposed to exist among clergy families.

But the true peril of her situation had burst upon her one fine spring morning when her brother, Francis, was struck down by a bad sore throat and Doctor Prowdlee (most obligingly) rode over to Badleigh to 'do the duty of the day'.

The sermon had been very long and of that sort which suggests the speaker only is in accord with the will of God and all the rest of the world in error. The doctor's text was taken from the Book of Proverbs. 'Who can find a virtuous woman?' he intoned solemnly, his eyes sweeping the assembled bonnets and upturned faces. 'For her price is far above rubies.' And then he was launched upon an impassioned condemnation of the 'independence of spirit' which was abroad in young women today, the result, apparently, of their reading 'disgusting and revolutionary books' – and dancing too much. By Doctor Prowdlee's account, the men of today were as hard-pressed to find a virtuous woman as the patriarchs of the Old Testament . . .

Though, mused Dido as she listened with but half an ear, today's men had the advantage, for they had only to find one virtuous wife apiece, whereas the patriarchs had had to secure two or three — to say nothing of concubines . . . But perhaps virtue was not required in a concubine . . .

She blushed and upbraided herself for the thought. Such ideas were, no doubt, the product of excessive dancing and reading – though she could not recall ever having read anything *very* dangerous or revolutionary.

She was watching a bumblebee blundering about the stained-glass sandals of a saint in the window beside her, and thinking that its stout body, thin black legs and persistent self-important drone made it rather resemble the doctor, when she became aware that her sister-in-law was looking at her – and smiling. Margaret rarely smiled – and never in Dido's direction.

Rather alarmed, Dido looked about for a cause and discovered Doctor Prowdlee leaning over the pulpit, his broad face pink and shining with emotion above his black whiskers and white surplice. 'A virtuous woman,' he was saying, in a rather softened tone, '"looketh well to the ways of her household, and eateth not the bread of idleness". Fortunate is the man, my friends, who finds such a woman!'

And he was looking directly at Dido.

'In point of fact, the entire congregation was looking at me,' she cried distractedly to her sister-in-law afterwards. 'At least, the female half of the congregation was looking at me.'

'But of course it was,' said Margaret impatiently, 'for everyone has noticed his attentions to you this past month. They have all been waiting for him to make you an offer – and have been crying out upon your good luck! As well they might!'

She need not say more – she need not remind Dido of her age, her poverty, her dependence upon Margaret and Francis for a home. It had all hung, palpable but unspoken, in the chill air of the parlour, where the bright bars of the grate were unsullied by fire (because there was a gleam of sun in the March sky and it was, by Margaret's account, 'a wicked waste to burn coal while the sun shines').

Shivering with cold and emotion, Dido still hugged her worn pelisse about her shoulders as she laid down her prayer book and, with a great effort, suppressed her horror of the pew and a half full of children, the vigorous black side whiskers and the very notion of being such a ruby as had been described in the sermon. 'I am sure,' she said, seeking refuge in the forms of propriety, 'I am very flattered by Doctor Prowdlee's good opinion of me. But I do not think that he and I would suit one another.'

Margaret's lips thinned with fury. 'Do you mean that you will refuse him?'

'You forget, dear sister,' said Dido repressively, 'that the gentleman has not made me an offer. He has only paid me a – rather public – compliment.'

'But he will offer,' protested Margaret. 'And you will refuse him? At six and thirty! I call that very selfish indeed when you know—' She stopped herself. Even

Margaret's scanty notion of good breeding would not quite allow her to say outright that Dido was a burden upon her brothers. 'You know that your entire family would rejoice to see you so respectably provided for.' She pulled her gloves slowly from her hands, finger by finger, and added quietly, 'It would, Dido, be a great relief to all your brothers to know that you were *settled.*'

Dido shrank into painful silence. She hoped with all her heart that her brothers loved her too well to wish her *unhappily* settled. But there was no denying that the fortunes of the family were very bad at present: the collapse of her brother Charles's bank had been a blow to them all, and her brothers would be very glad to be relieved of the burden of her maintenance. But would they wish her to sacrifice herself?

Of course, the main point was that *Margaret* would rejoice to see Dido settled in Upper Marwell with Doctor Prowdlee, the children and the abominable whiskers. So there was nothing to be gained from further discussion. She resolved upon waiting quietly for the proposal – and refusing it quietly when it came.

But she had been denied the opportunity of refusal. For, within a very few days of this extraordinary sermon, a letter arrived in Badleigh parsonage from the widow of the wealthy Mr Manners – Dido's mother's brother. Mrs Manners was setting off upon a journey to visit her own relations in Devonshire and, requiring a companion, she had selected Dido from among her multitude of nieces.

Margaret had immediately accepted the invitation upon her sister-in-law's account and seen them off with very great satisfaction. For Mrs Manners was childless, and, consequently, her fortune – and its future disposal – were of great interest to her entire family; she was a lady who must be sedulously courted.

And besides, attendance upon an elderly relative promoted that very picture of domestic womanhood which Margaret was most anxious to foster in Doctor Prowdlee's mind. While the gentleman could not make his offer, he could not be refused; and, in the meantime, it was to be hoped that Dido might be made so utterly miserable – might be brought to loathe the condition of dependent spinsterhood so much – as to view Upper Marwell's crowded rectory in a favourable light.

It was certainly not intended that she should be released from her present servitude until she was willing to accept the honour of becoming Mrs Prowdlee.

Dido roused herself at last, cold and cramped, from her desponding thoughts and found that Aunt Manners' hold had relaxed. She was sleeping now, her mouth hanging slightly open, her lower lip trembling with her snores. The candle by the writing desk had burnt out and the only light came from the dying embers in the grate; no sounds rose from below. It would seem the company was all abed.

Dido's spirits were severely depressed by the remembrance of Doctor Prowdlee, and she was worn down by close attendance upon an uncongenial companion. And yet, she reminded herself, there was *one* comfort.

In exiling her sister-in-law to Charcombe Manor, Margaret had unwittingly bestowed a blessing. For Charcombe was but ten miles from Belsfield Hall. At Belsfield Hall there resided a certain Mr William Lomax; and it was, in point of fact, the many charms and perfections of this gentleman which rendered the sermons and the side whiskers of Doctor Prowdlee particularly repulsive.

If only Dido could get to Belsfield, then perhaps she might find a solution to all her problems . . .

'It won't do at all,' said Mrs Manners suddenly and her hold reasserted itself.

Dido started and looked down at the faded, perfect little face sunk in the pillow. The eyes were wide, but unnaturally dark in appearance, and they seemed to be fixed upon some distant object. 'Aunt Manners, are you feeling unwell?'

There was no reply for several minutes. The eyes continued to stare upon the distance, persuading Dido that her aunt was not quite awake – though she did not seem to be quite sleeping either. This half-and-half state was perhaps some effect of brown medicine. At last Mrs Manners continued, in a confiding tone. 'A woman cannot escape, you know. Once they have chosen who she is to marry, she *must* do her duty by her family.'

Dido shifted uncomfortably in her seat, for the words touched rather closely on her own musings. 'Are you talking of Miss Verney?' she said.

'Letitia is a poor foolish girl.' Mrs Manners moved her head restlessly upon the pillow. A long white curl escaped from her cap and unravelled across her cheek. 'She will be at Birmingham now,' she said.

'Birmingham?'

'Yes. She will have lain at Bristol last night and reached Birmingham today if they drove the horses hard. In three days' time she will get into Scotland – and then it will be too late.'

'You must not worry about it, Aunt,' Dido soothed.

And then an idea occurred.

Mrs Manners seemed to be asleep – or at least only half sensible – and yet she heard, she answered questions. Perhaps this was the moment for obtaining information she would not give when she was in her senses.

Dido leant closer and spoke very quietly, but clearly. 'Aunt Manners, when shall we leave Charcombe?'

There was a pause. The little face on the pillow creased, the lips worked together a while, making a tiny rustling sound. Then: 'I cannot leave Charcombe until Letitia is got back.'

'Ah!'

'Lance must get her back – and then everything can be settled.'

Well, thought Dido, sitting back in her chair, if the finding of Letitia Verney was the necessary preliminary to Mrs Manners' removal from Charcombe, then Miss Letitia Verney *must* be found without delay.

It was refreshing to discover that there was something to be done. Dido's was an active disposition, better suited to struggling against her imprisonment than quietly accepting the punishment which had been laid upon her. She would help Mr Fenstanton to recover Miss Verney, and then she could escape from here and pay her visit to Belsfield. Her days of suffering and penance might soon be over.

Chapter Five

Where was Miss Letitia Verney?

Dido awoke very early next morning with this question uppermost in her mind, and escaped from her own little room while her aunt was still sleeping in the next chamber. She was yawning and heavy-eyed as she tiptoed onto the landing, for she had had barely five hours' rest. But the chance to be alone, to be, for an hour or so, free from the orders and impertinence of her aunt, amply repaid the loss of sleep.

She needed air and exercise – and a chance to consider the business of Miss Verney's disappearance.

It would seem, she thought as she crept along the creaking gallery and down the stairs, that Aunt Manners had also anticipated a marriage between Letitia Verney and the master of Charcombe. What was it she had said? 'I must know that the foolish girl is got back and everything is settled.'

Dido paused in the great hall where a newly lit fire was just roaring and spluttering into life, sending out blue threads of smoke and little showers of sparks which fell harmlessly on the flagged floor. It would be a suitable alliance, she thought. For Miss Verney – by Mr George's account – was 'an heiress', and Mr Fenstanton was a substantial landowner. At least, it would be suitable to *mature* eyes. To a lively young woman of nineteen it might present a rather different aspect. Mr Lancelot was a fine man, but he could no longer claim to be *young* . . .

Was it possible that Miss Letitia herself resented the wishes of her elders; and could resentment have played a part in her sudden removal from Charcombe?

As Dido tugged open the heavy front door and stepped out into the sunshine, an uncomfortable thought occurred. Supposing the unknown Miss Verney felt herself to be as much oppressed by her family as she, Dido, did? Was it fair, or kind, to join in the poor girl's pursuit?

But then, she reassured herself, elopement was such a *very* dangerous course. A girl of nineteen put herself in such grave danger by removing herself from her friends. It could not be wrong to promote her return.

The air in the garden was still and damp, the grass was silvered with dew, and a thin mist was lying over the lower lawn; but the sun was just breaking through, gilding the mist and filling the world with the promise of another warm day. Wood pigeons murmured in the trees by the gates and a thrush was singing above the hall door.

And Dido was not the only one to have been drawn out early by the beauty of the morning. Mrs Bailey was already walking along that part of the terrace which fronted the east wing of the house.

Reckoning that improving her acquaintance with Mrs Bailey might be a suitable beginning of the great quest, Dido turned along the terrace and came upon the lady just as she paused to look in through one of the house windows. She was shading her eyes against the sun and pressing her nose to the glass in an effort to see within, in a very odd, impertinent manner.

'Good morning, Mrs Bailey.'

'Oh!' The lady turned with both hands clasped dramatically to her heart. 'Oh, Miss Kent! *Vous me surprenez!* And then, with pale shock rapidly giving way to blushing consciousness: 'I was just . . . looking in upon the east wing, you know,' she said, as if it were the kind of thing which anyone might do.

'Oh!' Dido could not help but look over Mrs Bailey's shoulder at the window – catching a glimpse, through a half-closed blind, of gloom, uncarpeted floor, and a few articles of furniture obscured by dust sheets.

'This part of the house is all closed up, you know,' ran on Mrs Bailey hurriedly. 'This wing is not used. And so, I thought I would just take a little look . . . to see what kind of repair it is in. I wonder that dear Lancelot has allowed it to fall into such a bad state.'

Dido felt her own acquaintance with the gentleman to be too slight to allow any comment, but, peering into the half-empty apartment, she noticed that the plaster was, in places, darkened by damp, and she was inclined to agree with Mrs Bailey. Perhaps, she thought, Mr Fenstanton, though rich in land, was rather poor in cash. Such a circumstance would make 'an heiress' particularly lovely in his eyes . . .

But, before she was able to pursue this train of thought any further, her companion claimed her arm with alarming familiarity, turned her away to the lawn and compelled her to walk. 'I wish most particularly to talk to you, *tête-à-tête*, my dear Miss Kent.'

Seen close – as Dido was now obliged to see her – Mrs Bailey was less pretty than one at first supposed. She was extremely well painted, but her features were large, slightly coarse. She was a woman who was at her best when viewed from a distance. Her lips pursed now into an exaggerated rosebud, she paused, gave their linked arms a vigorous shake, and added, with the air of a superior bestowing a delightful favour, '*Dido*. I am sure you will not mind if I call you so.'

'Well—' began Dido, who did mind a great deal.

'Now, Dido, I have been quite longing to talk to you ever since yesterday when Lancelot told me that he had been frank with you on the subject of our *petite difficulté*.'

'I hope you do not mind Mr Fenstanton's telling me about Miss Verney.'

'Well!' cried Mrs Bailey with an arch look. 'I declare that at first I was just a little bit cross with him! For it was very, very naughty of him – and so I told him. For I should warn you that I always speak my mind. My friends are always rebuking me for my candour. But no.' She put her head to one side and looked condescending. 'No, upon reflection, I do not mind such a steady, sensible little creature as *you* knowing it.' She gave a trilling laugh. 'Why, who would you tell about it? No one of any importance. A lady's companion does not mix much in society!'

Dido frowned at this and walked on in resentful silence as the sun gained power, dissolving the mist from the lower lawn. Birds sang extravagantly on every side and the walk was a prisoner's brief respite which she was determined to enjoy; her aunt would awake all too soon. But she must also begin upon her quest . . .

'Miss Verney's going is a very upsetting business . . .' she began cautiously.

'Dear me! I beg you will not concern yourself with it, Miss Kent!' cried Mrs Bailey with energy. '"Cudgel thy brains no more about it" – as Shakespeare says. For I am sure you have more than enough to occupy you in attending upon your aunt. You must not, for our sake, run the risk of offending her, you know. It is very kind of you to wish to help us I am sure, but I cannot allow you to neglect your own *interest*.'

Dido was too taken aback to reply.

'Oh, there is no need to look so uncomfortable, my dear,' trilled Mrs Bailey. 'We are all friends together here, you know! And I have heard all about your aunt from Lance.' She lowered her voice a little. 'He tells me that Mrs Manners now has possession of all the fortune which her husband made in the City.' She patted Dido's hand with a great show of compassion. 'It must have been a heavy blow to your family when it fell out that way; and I understand entirely that your first duty must be to please your aunt.' She stopped, smiled brightly, and under the ridiculous – but common – misapprehension that words can be rendered less offensive by quietness, she mouthed almost inaudibly, 'For the sake of the will.'

Dido longed to contradict, but knew herself to be too shamefully enmeshed in Margaret's schemes. For a moment all the beauty of the morning was snatched away by this ugly representation of her own situation. But then, fortunately, she remembered that she had sought this interview for the sake of being impertinent herself, rather than suffering the impertinence of another.

She returned to the attack. 'The young man – the gentleman whom you believe is the cause of Miss Verney's disappearance – do you have cause to doubt his character?' she asked boldly. 'Do you believe that the young lady's fortune, rather than affection, is his motive?'

'Oh!' cried Mrs Bailey, her large cheeks reddening. 'There can be no two opinions upon that point! Our poor girl's situation is *très dangereux*. *Très dangereux!* All the world knows that Tom Lomax is an unprincipled and greedy young man. I am only sorry that dear Letitia—'

Mrs Bailey was compelled to stop walking, for her companion had come to a standstill and was staring at her in a state of silent shock.

'My dear Dido,' she cried, keenly searching her face, 'whatever is wrong? Have I said something amiss?'

'No, no . . .' Though in fact the garden with its mists and flowers and beech trees had become for a moment quite indistinct as this new, startling piece of information was borne home. 'No, it is merely that I had not known the name of the young man concerned until this moment.'

Mrs Bailey's lips were smiling – but her eyes were shrewd and sharp. 'Are you acquainted with Mr Tom Lomax?'

'Oh . . . yes,' replied Dido a little unsteadily. Then, strengthened by the realisation that her connection might be explained without betraying a very near interest, 'He is a friend of my niece and her husband. His father – Mr William Lomax – is their man of business at Belsfield Hall.'

'Is he indeed?' said Mrs Bailey coolly. She released Dido's arm. 'I did not know about that.' It was clear that the acquaintance did not recommend Dido to her. 'And what, pray, is your opinion of Tom Lomax?'

'I believe he is a rather *thoughtless* young man,' said Dido cautiously. In point of fact her opinion was probably as low even as Mrs Bailey's own. But affection for the father checked her condemnation of the son. 'How did Miss Verney become acquainted with him?' she asked.

'Oh! The damage was done in Worcestershire last autumn when Letitia visited the Hargreaves.'

Dido, struggling to make sense of this shocking turn of events, recalled that she had herself heard a rumour last autumn of Tom Lomax being in hopes of marrying an heiress. 'And who are the Hargreaves?' she asked, her voice still a little unsteady.

'The Hargreaves are very suitable acquaintances, I assure you,' cried Mrs Bailey as if defending herself from an accusation. 'For Mr Hargreaves has a cousin that is married to a baronet. And Mrs Hargreaves was a Miss Jennings before she married – from a very respectable family . . . Though they have no titles that I know of . . .' Mrs Bailey pondered for a moment, but seemed unable to produce even a noble great uncle or a knight-by-marriage with which to dignify the Jennings race. 'I assure you, I have never had any cause to regret Letitia's friendship with Amelia Jennings – unlike some other unfortunate connections . . .' She broke off with a significant raising up of the eyes.

But it was not Dido's business to settle for half-spoken opinions – she wished to know everything about everybody at Charcombe Manor, and caught at this hint immediately. 'Dear me,' she said with a look of concern,

'I hope that you have no reason to disapprove Miss Gibbs as a companion for your ward. She seems a very good-natured girl.'

'Well! Her father cannot give her more than a thousand pounds, I believe. And,' the rosebud lips pursed themselves again, the voice became a whisper, 'the family resides in *Birmingham*, you know.'

'I know nothing of Birmingham. I have never been there.'

'Neither have I, I assure you!' declared Mrs Bailey triumphantly and, having thus disproved any claim the place might have to gentility, she walked on and resumed her tale – determined to tell it in such a way as would prove herself to be entirely innocent and only imposed upon by others.

'Letitia, Miss Jennings and Martha Gibbs all became friends while they were at school together in Taunton,' she explained. 'And so, when she married, Amelia Jennings entreated Letitia and Martha to pay her a long visit. For, *entre nous*, I rather fancy she did not expect to find much pleasure in the society of Mr Hargreaves.'

'And it was at this lady's house that Miss Verney met Mr Tom Lomax?'

'Yes. Perhaps I should not have let her go, but . . .' Mrs Bailey shot Dido another suspicious look '. . . I had no idea of Mr Hargreaves having such very *unsuitable* acquaintances.' She sighed extravagantly. 'I blame myself for it!' she said, with the air of a woman who blamed everybody but herself. 'I am too mild and confiding. I declare my friends are always rebuking me for it. But I thought Letitia too sensible to be a prey to ambitious men. And it is a bad thing to be always thwarting the young, is it not? For as the Great Bard says, "youth's a stuff will not endure."'

Mrs Bailey sighed pathetically – very much oppressed by this last melancholy truth. And, feeling, no doubt, that she had now explained and excused herself sufficiently, she turned towards the house.

Dido fell into a reverie of pity for the absent Miss Verney. She knew Tom Lomax to be extravagant, selfish and quite determined upon making his fortune by marriage. Any young woman who had – through love or folly – placed herself in his power was to be pitied indeed. Concern for the young lady must be her first thought. But it was not long before her mind turned with even greater compassion to the suffering of someone else – someone much dearer.

Tom's father would be terribly hurt by the business.

Chapter Six

As Dido attended her aunt, and prepared herself for church, her mind was full of foreboding. The mystery of Miss Verney's disappearance touched her more nearly now. Its speedy solution was more necessary than ever, but there was added the need for the *right* solution. Nobody in Charcombe Manor could now be more determined than Dido to prevent the business being bruited abroad, or more anxious to avoid disgrace and shame.

Mrs Manners noticed — and strongly resented — her niece's preoccupation. Dido, she declared, was 'as dull as a cat'.

'I cannot get two words from you this morning, miss!' she complained as she was helped from her carriage at the church gate. 'I am not accustomed to such sulky silence.'

'I am sorry,' said Dido, hurriedly, as she climbed back into the carriage to retrieve her aunt's salts and spectacles, shawls, cushions, walking stick and parasol, 'but I have a great deal on my mind.'

'On your mind! Why, what can *you* possibly have to worry about?'

'Well,' Dido began a little breathlessly as she balanced one last cushion upon her burden, tucked two prayer books under her arm, 'I am worried about—'

She stopped because her aunt's attention had now been drawn away by the approach of her brother, Mr George Fenstanton, who bounded up, officiously offering his arm.

'Go away, George!' Mrs Manners put such an emphasis of hatred into the three words that Dido dropped a cushion. She drew back into the shadows of the carriage and watched Mr George's face redden. Beyond him she could see the little crowd of parishioners gathered in the sunny churchyard – all eyes turned towards the arrival of the manor party.

'Now then, now then, Selina,' he whispered, smoothing back his thin white hair and looking about him uncomfortably. 'We must put a good face on things, you know. People are watching. Take my arm.'

'No.' Mrs Manners' voice was low, but firm. 'You may take my jewels from me, George, but I see no reason to pretend to anyone that I *like* you. Ah, Lancelot!' She turned to her nephew as he approached and made a great show of taking *his* arm, bestowing upon *him* the privilege of supporting her into the church.

As Dido stepped slowly from the coach with her burdens she was almost inclined to pity George Fenstanton's red-cheeked embarrassment, for there was quite a crowd assembled among the grass mounds, mossy stones and daffodils of the churchyard to witness his humiliation.

The return of the beautiful Selina Fenstanton to her family home would seem to be a matter of great interest to neighbours who had been content to know nothing of her for thirty years. They bustled about her now, eager to see how marriage, time and widowhood had influenced her, and exclaimed that 'she was not changed at all!', and that they 'could scarcely believe it was thirty years since she had been married here in this very church!'

And more than one curious eye was cast in the direction of the rejected brother, walking alone through the crowd to the church door; head down, hands clasped behind him. But Dido found she could not quite feel compassion. There was about Mr George such an air of self-importance, such an ill-judged determination to impose his authority on all about him, that she could not but hold him responsible for his own discomfort.

It was well that she had such very interesting thoughts to occupy her, for she soon found herself jostled aside to stand quite disregarded against one of the sandstone buttresses of the little church. Other members of the manor party were stopping frequently in their progress from chaise to pew, hailing friends and exchanging remarks upon the weather. But no one spoke to Dido. Once burdened with the paraphernalia of a companion, a woman becomes invisible to society. Over the last weeks she had been reminded many times of this horrible truth, but it had not yet lost its power to hurt her.

However, invisibility provides an excellent situation from which to observe one's fellow men. Dido bit her lip, clung to her burdens and watched. She watched Mrs Bailey attempting to avoid the attentions of a stout man in a canary-yellow waistcoat – watched her take refuge behind the scrubby yew bush which grew from the tomb of Mr Barnabas Finch ('released from this vale of tears'). She watched Mr Lancelot Fenstanton – stepping away from his aunt now and talking with an air of benign patronage to a short pockmarked lad. The boy was twisting his cap constantly in his hands. He passed a note to Mr Fenstanton . . .

'Miss Kent, may I speak with you?' The voice was hissing so close to Dido's ear that she felt its warmth on her cheek and took an instinctive step back.

Martha Gibbs was beckoning urgently at her side and, as Dido stared in bewilderment, she stepped away behind the buttress. There seemed to be nothing to be done but to follow her.

When they were both standing in long grass, pressed between the damp wall of the buttress and the slanting gravestone of Mrs Elizabeth Fosset ('she wore her virtues like a crown of glory'), Miss Gibbs whispered, 'She mustn't see me talking to you.'

'Who?'

'Why, Mrs Bailey of course. She says I ain't to say a word to you.'

'That is rather inconvenient.'

'I mean I must not say a word about Tish going and everything.'

Dido merely raised her brows and waited for her companion to explain herself; but the girl stood in silence for a minute, as if struggling to find a beginning.

Martha Gibbs' awkwardness of manner was, unfortunately, not relieved by much beauty. Her face was long, her features heavy and, at present, her appearance was further marred by some remarkably ill-made curls which peeped from under her white straw bonnet – their ends frizzled from the hot poker having been applied too long.

'Mrs Bailey is afraid you mean to interfere, you know,' Martha began. 'She thinks you mean to try to find Tish.'

'And why should she be *afraid* of my . . . interference?'

Martha glanced about her, and seeing that there was no one by – excepting, of course, Mrs Fosset – she whispered, 'I don't believe she wants Tish found.'

'I beg your pardon? I do not quite understand—'

But now she was begun, Martha seemed determined to have her say as quickly as possible. 'I beg you, Miss Kent, to find her. I am so afraid for her, but I dare not do anything.'

'But why should Mrs Bailey not wish to recover your friend? It is not much to her credit if a girl in her care disappears.'

'It would make her and Mr B rich, though, wouldn't it?' said Martha bluntly. 'Tish is always telling me Mrs B would get her fortune if she could. She says she is a wicked, jealous woman. And now she has been proved right. Tish has twenty thousand pounds, you know. And if she is never heard of again, what do you suppose will happen to the money?'

'I hardly know.'

'Why, it'll stay in the hands of Mr and Mrs Bailey, won't it?'

'I suppose it might. But, my dear Miss Gibbs, I am sure your very natural concern for your friend is getting the better of your judgement. You cannot believe that Mrs Bailey wishes harm to come to Miss Verney . . .' She stopped, for the look upon Martha's face declared that she *did* believe it.

'If she wants Tish back, why has she not had her

pursued?' Martha ran on hastily. 'Ain't that what a girl's family is supposed to do when she goes off to Gretna Green? They chase after her and bring her back, don't they?'

Though Dido could not help but smile at Miss Gibbs' belief in a kind of protocol governing these events, she was forced to admit that there was some weight in her argument. 'Has there been no one sent in pursuit of Miss Verney and Mr Lomax?'

'No. Mr Lancelot behaved very odd from the beginning. I thought he would ride after her immediately. But he did not – for you and Mrs Manners were to come, you know, and he said he must stay for his guests. And now he *talks* about searching for her, but he don't *do* anything. And Mrs B has never insisted on someone else being sent off to Gretna Green. Lord! Do you not see, Miss Kent? Tish was right: that wicked woman really does want to be rid of her!'

Dido stirred uncomfortably in the long grass as the damp began to penetrate her Sunday shoes. 'It does seem a little strange that no very definite steps have been taken to avert a marriage.'

'Oh Lord!' cried Miss Gibbs. 'They are going in.' She seized Dido's arm so violently the parasol fell down on Mrs Fosset. Miss Gibbs picked it up and balanced it hastily on top of the shawls and cushions. 'You will not speak a word about what I have said, will you?'

'No, though I do not know . . .' But Martha had already rounded the buttress and was striding off after the rest of their party – skirts held inelegantly high to display sturdy black boots.

Dido paused a moment. Was it possible, she wondered, that Mrs Bailey was herself the greatest danger to the girl placed in her care? It was a shocking and melancholy thought. In more cheerful surroundings she might have discounted it entirely; but here in the gloomy shadow of church and gravestones, the thought seemed to take hold of her and chill her being. Young women – indeed women of any age – were so very much at the mercy of those placed in authority over them . . .

The chill deepened as Dido followed the manor party through the porch into a small, plain church of whitewashed walls, cramped benches and broad pillars, under a roof curved like a barrel.

There was a holy smell of cold stone, hymn books and candles – and an air of bleak austerity. The high pulpit was backed by painted boards on which were written the Creed and Ten Commandments in the hand of a century past. The windows were filled only with plain glass; and a marble monument in a side chapel showed a sleeping knight with his nose, his sword and half of one leg broken away.

Dido was looking about as she walked, and thinking that the church had perhaps suffered at the hands of Cromwell's Ironsides, when her eye fell upon a familiar gentleman close beside her in a pew – and all at once the day began to wear a brighter aspect.

She stopped abruptly and the parasol, which was still balanced precariously upon the cushions, clattered to the ground again. The familiar gentleman turned quickly to retrieve it – revealing the face, and the smile, of Mr William Lomax.

She received the parasol in a nerveless hand; he bowed, his grey eyes half laughing, half indignant, as they took in the burdens in her arms and glanced at the retreating back of her aunt. He reached out. With some difficulty she shuffled the bottle of smelling salts into the crook of her arm, and his hand closed about her fingers, warm and firm. They both spoke together:

'I did not know you were at Charcombe—'

'I am come about this odd business of Tom's—'

They stopped, smiled and stood looking upon one another, quite content to be silent for a moment as the sounds of the congregation shuffling into the pews echoed about them. He looked as handsome as ever, she thought; the same well-made figure and very distinguished profile. But he looked a little tired, or worried perhaps; the fine bones of his cheeks were rather more prominent than she had ever known them before – giving his face a sad, bruised appearance.

He began to speak again, but just then Mrs Manners – who had now reached the Fenstanton pew at the front of the church and was waiting for her cushions to be placed – turned back impatiently. She creased up her eyes and peered imperiously. There was a moment of recognition.

He bowed.

Aunt Manners stood stiff, unbending. 'Dido!' Her voice cut sharply along the crowded nave. 'What are you doing, dawdling about *again*? I am not accustomed to being kept waiting.'

Dido was forced to hurry away, but her mind raced

with a dozen half-connected thoughts. That the news of Tom's escapade should bring him here was not surprising – she might have foreseen it . . . He had seemed glad to see her . . . Her aunt's conduct was unpardonable . . .

Mrs Manners was now pointing imperiously at the place where her cushions were to be arranged and, as Dido hurried forward, she said, in a whisper so audible the bats hanging in the bell tower were probably able to hear it, 'I am surprised at you for speaking to that man.'

'I beg your pardon, Aunt?'

'I am astonished that you should acknowledge acquaintance with a family which has used *my friends* so ill. Not there . . . *there*,' stabbing with an impatient finger. 'The red cushion is to go at my back.'

Dido bent to her task in resentful silence. But, as the church music men struck up the first psalm and the congregation rose to sing, she stole a look back along the aisle, her eye seeking out the firm, upright figure which appeared to particular advantage among the bulky forms of the surrounding farmers. Her cheeks burnt with indignation at his being blamed for the faults of his son. She looked until some sense told him that she was looking. He glanced up, caught her eye, and could not prevent himself from smiling affectionately before hurriedly returning his attention to his hymnal.

It was a delightful smile. A smile to lift her spirits to the barrel roof with the swelling voices, in a rush of pleasure which even the sour looks of her relative could not diminish. She would certainly not slight him on anyone's account. Affection and justice both cried out against it.

Up in their gallery above the nave, the fustian-clad fiddlers plied their bows with enthusiasm and the old church rang with song. Dido Kent praised her maker and sang for joy that the man who loved her was close by. After two weeks of penance and insignificance his look of admiration was an exquisite pleasure, and she would not allow anything to intrude upon it – certainly not the disapproval of such a woman as Aunt Manners.

The truth was that silent looks across a church suited Dido rather well, for had she and the gentleman been allowed only a few minutes' more conversation she would certainly have found something upon which to disagree with him, something to remind her of the reason why – for all her admiration of the figure and the profile – she had not yet said 'yes' to his offer of marriage.

In point of fact, theirs was a rather singular affection, strong enough certainly to withstand Aunt Manners – and the delay to marriage which Mr Lomax's present lack of fortune occasioned. But Dido's regard for the gentleman had not yet created that humility of spirit, that willingness to adopt her beloved's opinions which is almost universally considered a necessary condition of marriage. Nor had she even that talent for keeping silent which will sometimes make up for a wife's lack of real agreement with her husband. What Dido thought, she spoke – even to the man she loved; in fact, most especially to the man she loved.

This was a difficulty. But Mr Lomax had now ceased to hope for a change in her. Courageous man that he was, he declared himself resigned to a life of dispute; he understood her character and yet he wished her to be his wife. He believed – he had told her after their last great disagreement – that trust and mutual confidence might, in their case, take the place of deference and silent acquiescence.

But could a happy marriage be built upon such very unusual foundations? Over the last months Dido's mind had veered alarmingly between the yes and the no. But now, watching him across the crowded church, her heart swelling with indignation and music – and admiration – the yes was very much in the ascendant.

Why restless, why cast down my soul?
Hope still and thou shalt sing . . .

Dido closed her hymnal at last and sat down to the sermon with a heart full of hope.

Beside her Mrs Manners settled into her cushions – and a comfortable doze – while Mr Lancelot drew out a pencil and paper and began to make notes upon the sermon.

For a short time Dido felt at peace with all the world; in charity with everyone. And, fortunately, Doctor Jeremiah Prowdlee was very far from her thoughts at that moment. Otherwise she might have been obliged to confess that Margaret's predictions had been accurate: just two weeks acting the part of companion were enough to make any woman look upon matrimony with a favourable eye . . .

Chapter Seven

'Dido, I forbid you to speak to that man.'

It was another discreet whisper for the listening bats.

Many eyes turned towards Aunt Manners as she made her dignified progress through the crowded church at the end of the service. It was, perhaps, something about the way she walked, an awareness of her own importance and dignity, which gave such significance to her small figure.

Dido followed, clutching her burdens in mutinous silence and dawdling so that the rest of her party might leave her behind. Aunt Manners reached the west door, stopped and waited with a look of haughty expectation. The aisle was rapidly filling with people now: young misses in fresh muslins for the fine spring weather, red-faced farmers with their hats crushed beneath their arms, and matrons guarding flocks of children as they looked about them for a gossip. Dido let the crowd hurry past her and slowly drew level with the pew where Mr Lomax remained alone.

He had considerately turned his face away at the sound of her aunt's words. He was now pretending to read the Commandments on the board above the pulpit – as if he were suddenly in need of advice about the coveting of his neighbour's ox and the making of graven images. Dido stopped; still he would not look at her. The fine profile was infuriatingly impassive: as stiff as the crisp cravat which supported it. She could not accost him forcibly – but if she walked on, her aunt would have been obeyed. And that would be intolerable.

There was, she determined, only one thing to be done.

She opened her arms and let everything that she was holding slip away – retaining her hold only on the fragile bottle of salts. Shawls and cushions tumbled down on the rushes of the aisle; the parasol clattered against the pew's end, and, as if to make quite certain of gaining Mr Lomax's attention, a prayer book bounced hard against his knee.

At the back of the church, Aunt Manners turned red with anger and hurried out of the west door.

Mr Lomax, being too well bred to leave a lady unassisted, began immediately to gather books and shawls and cushions. 'But you should not have acknowledged me,' he said quietly as he picked up the spectacles and shook dust from them. 'It is only reasonable that your aunt should resent me.'

'No.' Dido took up a shawl and folded it slowly. 'It is not at all reasonable. You are not your son, and whatever he has done to offend, you are guiltless. The whole family should not be held responsible for one man's sins.'

'It is the way of the world, Miss Kent.'

'Then the world is wrong,' said Dido with quiet conviction.

He retrieved the prayer book and smoothed out the

creases from its pages. 'And would you seek to change the world's opinion on the matter? It would be a revolution far beyond anything the French and the Americans have achieved between them.'

'I do not presume so far.' She laid down the folded shawl on the pew, took up another and slowly picked fragments of rushes from its fringe. 'I seek only to act as my conscience dictates. It is a matter of integrity, Mr Lomax, not revolt.'

He looked down at her busy little fingers and shook his head. 'I do not think we shall ever agree upon this point,' he said.

'But upon another point I am sure we are in complete accord: the necessity of finding your son and Miss Verney.'

He rested his hand upon the pew's end. 'That is what has brought me here,' he said quietly as the last footsteps echoed away through the west door, leaving them alone in the little church. 'Mr Fenstanton wrote to enquire whether I knew anything of the business. I did not; but I hoped I might be able to talk some sense into Tom.'

'And have you met with any success?'

His face clouded. He beckoned Dido into the shelter of the pew and they sat down side by side. 'No, I have had no success at all,' he confessed. 'Tom continues to tell this nonsensical tale of returning the young lady to the house. You have heard it?'

She nodded.

'It is a lie, of course!' he cried, then shook his head. 'And yet he insists that it is true. He will not be shaken from the foolish story.'

Dido gazed silently into his grave, troubled face. She was so close to him that her hand rested against the sleeve of his coat; she could see the troubled little furrows between his brows. 'And what is your opinion?' she asked gently. 'Do you believe that your son has persuaded Miss Verney to remove herself from her friends' protection?'

'I think he must have done.' He looked at her very directly. 'Unfortunately, my knowledge of Tom's character makes me believe him very capable of guilt . . . And yet . . .'

'Yes?'

'The business has been carried on so very oddly. Why is he not with her? I cannot understand what he would be about.' He shrugged up his shoulders and sighed.

'Do you think it possible,' suggested Dido, 'that he believes his own tale to be true; that he has somehow been mistaken . . . or deceived?'

Lomax looked at her in surprise. 'I cannot see how that might be—' he began.

But just then they were interrupted by the sound of footsteps in the aisle. Mr Lancelot Fenstanton had returned to the empty church and both Dido and her companion were suddenly aware of how very close they were sitting – and what an odd appearance their private conference might have to an impartial observer.

She jumped up with a quick farewell and hurried forward to meet the gentleman, wishing with all her heart that she had been allowed a few minutes more to pursue the very interesting idea of Mr Tom being deceived.

* * *

Mr Lancelot insisted upon taking some of Dido's burdens into his own hands as they left the church together. 'I have been commissioned by our aunt to seek you out, Miss Kent,' he explained with a smile. 'There is some arrangement of the carriage windows, or some order to be given to the coachman which only you can properly accomplish.'

Dido suppressed an answering smile. 'I am very sorry to keep her waiting,' she said quietly.

'But,' he continued, as they stepped out of the cool, damp porch into sudden sunshine and birdsong and the fresh, clean smell of daffodils, 'I am a selfish fellow, you know, and I'm hoping to snatch a moment to talk to you myself. I have something to tell you about.' He laid the parasol down upon the final resting place of Mr Barnabas Finch, and drew a letter from his coat pocket. 'The pot boy from the inn at New Charcombe delivered this to me before the service.'

'Oh,' cried Dido deeply interested. 'Is it from Mr Tom Lomax? Has he changed his account?'

'No, it ain't from young Tom at all. It's from some fellow I never heard of in my life before.' He gave the letter a puzzled look. 'Fellow by the name of Brodie,' he said. 'Do you know him?'

'No, not at all.'

He looked down thoughtfully at the page again, then handed it to Dido.

She took it eagerly and read:

Sir,

Although no acquaintance subsists between us, I hope you will forgive my intruding myself upon your notice. I am

70

reluctant to take such a liberty, but flatter myself that I have two claims upon your indulgence: first, an acquaintance with a guest currently residing in your house, and second, the possession of some very important information concerning Miss Letitia Verney, the ward of Reginald Bailey. The young lady is in very grave danger.

The business upon which I wish to consult you is delicate and complicated, concerning, as it does, the danger of elopement and secret marriage. So I shall say no more of it here – except to observe that I have in my possession papers of the utmost importance to you. I shall wait upon you tomorrow morning and hope that you will be at liberty to receive me. It will certainly be to your advantage to do so – and to attend very closely to everything which I have to say.

Your humble servant
James Brodie.

'What an extraordinary letter!' cried Dido. 'Whatever can be the danger threatening poor Miss Verney? And who is this Mr Brodie?'

'Well,' said Mr Lancelot taking the letter back into his own hands. 'That last is a question which someone in my house will be able to answer. Someone is acquainted with him.' He stopped and looked at her with concern. 'What is it, Miss Kent? You look quite queer.'

'Oh, it is nothing.' She turned away from him and began to hurry towards the little gate of the churchyard and the carriage from which she could see the angry features of her aunt peering.

But it had occurred to her that if someone in the house

was indeed complicit in Miss Verney's disappearance, then it might be from that person that Mr Brodie had gained his information. In short, the man or woman at Charcombe Manor who acknowledged Mr Brodie's acquaintance must be suspected of playing a part in the young lady's disappearance.

Chapter Eight

. . . But Eliza, this business becomes odder and odder. For when Mr Lancelot read Mr Brodie's letter to the whole company at tea, <u>nobody</u> would admit to knowing the man at all!

Which raises the very interesting possibility that somebody is lying.

Dido paused and recalled the scene in the drawing room.

Mr George Fenstanton became quite indignant over the business and it was all: 'Now then, Lance, my boy, I make no doubt he was just a common little fellow wanting to claim acquaintance in good society. No need for you to bother us all with it, no need at all . . .' Until my aunt – who never loses an opportunity of contradicting her brother – interposed with, 'But we aren't any of us bothered, George. It is only you who is making yourself ridiculous about a trifle.'

In point of fact, the only member of the company to express any doubt about knowing the man was Mrs Bailey.

She does not <u>think</u> that she knows any James Brodie; but it would seem that the unfortunate Mrs Bailey is frequently finding her acquaintance claimed by people she has no memory of! And she is often obliged to draw back from introductions, for she has quite a horror of forming 'second-rate' connections . . . In short, we were given to understand that it is quite _impossible_ for Mrs Bailey to remember everyone who might wish to claim her as a friend.

But I was unable to observe Mrs B for long, for our aunt was now calling out, 'Can that girl not even drink tea safely!' And I was obliged to rescue an overturned teacup. On the sofa beside me, Miss Gibbs was mopping at her gown with her handkerchief, choking upon her cake and anxiously enquiring, 'Does this man say what it is he knows about Tish? What kind of danger is she got into?'

She was _very_ worried. Perhaps she is worried because she is the one who wishes her association with Mr Brodie to remain secret; but maybe she is simply worried to hear that her friend is in 'grave danger'.

Aunt Manners has been in an ill mood all evening – the kind of mood in which she insults and contradicts everybody. She has now retired to bed overcome with 'enervating' symptoms; I have administered a particularly large dose of the brown medicine and she is sleeping soundly. Though she was restless for a long time – in that strange state between sleeping and waking which brown medicine seems to induce – and her mind ran a great deal upon Letitia. She insists that Miss Verney lies at Manchester tonight – and will be married at Gretna Green in only two days' time. The continued presence of the bridegroom in Charcombe does not seem any impediment to her.

The house is all abed, the clock down in the hall has just struck one and, _at last_, I am able to return my thoughts to the mystery of Miss Verney's disappearance.

I wonder whether Miss Gibbs is correct in believing that

Mrs Bailey does not wish her ward to be found. I believe Miss Martha to be very much influenced by her friend's ideas. There was a great deal of 'Tish says' in her account. I do not think Miss Gibbs is much in the habit of forming opinions of her own and suspect that she has rather fallen under the spell of the rich and beautiful Miss Verney.

But I cannot help but agree that Mr Lancelot's not pursuing Letitia is very strange indeed. Of course (despite our aunt's assertions) an anvil marriage is not possible while Mr Tom is in Charcombe – but Mr Lancelot did not <u>know</u> that the young man had remained here until he was informed of it yesterday. So why did he not ride after Miss Verney immediately? For, besides the interest he might have as a suitor himself, there is the responsibility laid upon him by the guardian.

I cannot make it out. And I cannot even guess at the information which Mr Brodie will bring tomorrow . . .

It was a noise which had stilled Dido's pen; not a loud noise, but an oddly disquieting one. She held her breath, listening hard.

The candle flame swayed on its wick, throwing light around Mrs Manners' chamber, lighting, in turn, the high bulk of the great bed, the grey ashes on the hearth, the crewel work curtains drawn close across the window. There was nothing to be heard now beyond the faint creak of a settling floorboard and the snores of the sleeping woman.

And then it came again – a small desolate wail which struck directly at the heart. Surely it was the crying of a baby? And yet Dido had not heard of there being an infant in the house. She rose cautiously, went on her toes to the window, and lifted an edge of the heavy curtain.

Outside, the light of the moon lay across the old-fashioned garden of low clipped box hedges, and trim beds of flowers and herbs.

Charcombe Manor had been built during the reign of Elizabeth and, like many houses of its time, its front had been fashioned in the form of a giant E in compliment to that monarch. From this window in the west wing – at the extreme end of the bottom leg of the E – Dido had a view of the entire house front, looking beyond the shorter central leg, which contained the great hall, to the looming outline and blank, dead windows of the deserted east wing.

At first all seemed still down in the garden – but then there was a movement almost directly below Dido's window. A stooping figure in a deeply hooded cloak resolved itself out of the shadows and made its way along the path, walking rapidly, but stooping forward slightly – for all the world as if it held something cradled in its arms and concealed within the folds of the cloak.

The figure disappeared in the shadow of the creeper which grew in the angle where the east wing joined the main part of the house. Dido watched until her eyes grew weary, but it did not reappear.

Chapter Nine

The next morning found Dido awake early and walking on the terrace before the house – once more stealing time in which to pursue her investigations.

The memory of the cloaked figure had disturbed her dreams and she had woken with a strange notion: perhaps the figure was Miss Verney returning for some reason in secret to the house. She had laughed at herself for the fancy – and yet it had been strong enough to bring her here to the place where the figure had appeared.

She followed a path of sandstone slabs worn smooth by centuries of rain and passing feet, until she was beneath the window of Mrs Manners' room. Here she stopped and looked about. This was the point at which she had first seen the figure. From whence had it come?

The paved path ended here, but the carriage drive swept away around the end of the west wing. She followed it, even the tread of her feet in the gravel sounding loud in the stillness of the morning.

She passed through a screen of laurels, under which a noisy blackbird was scuffling for worms. Beyond was the back door of the house, standing open upon a cavernous kitchen. Within, a housemaid was pouring hot water from a great black kettle into jugs for the bedchambers, and behind her a cook was turning chops on the griddle. The housekeeper, Mrs Matthews – a tall woman in black with a look of perpetual bereavement about her – was standing close beside the door with a small bowl in her hands.

'Can I help you, miss?' she called and stepped out into the sunshine. It was the kind of 'can I help you?' which is a thinly veiled 'what are you doing here?'

'Oh! No, thank you. I am just looking about me.' Dido hurried on towards the stables, but felt the woman's eyes upon her all the way.

The stable yard was tidy, its cobbles newly washed and gleaming in the slanting sunlight. Beyond the yard Dido could see a large kitchen garden and one end of a stew pond, backed by a rising slope of grass and wild flowers, topped by a little round summer house with a brightly tiled roof and a weathercock shaped like a fish. To her left, stalls and haylofts enclosed two sides of the yard. A white-faced clock set high up in the walls announced that it was almost eight o'clock; a stable door stood open and, within the building, two grooms were working and arguing.

'They can't be gone,' cried one impatiently. 'Take another look.'

Dido crept quietly to the doorway and peered cautiously into the warm, horse- and hay-scented gloom.

A broad-shouldered lad with a red neckerchief and shirtsleeves rolled above the elbow was standing with his back to her, examining the foreleg of a little grey mare. His companion – a younger boy with cropped hair and pimples – was standing beside the partition of a neighbouring stall and shaking his head vigorously. 'I've *looked*, Charlie. They ain't there!'

'Look again!'

The younger boy disappeared around the partition. Charlie lifted the mare's hoof, gently probed the fetlock and cursed under his breath. The horse shifted restlessly and he patted her. 'Poor old girl,' he soothed. 'Some great lump's been riding you, hasn't he? And now we'll have you laid up for weeks.' As he set down the hoof, his companion reappeared.

'S'no good, Charlie. They're gone for sure.'

'Damn! What am I to do? Mr Lancelot will string me up when he finds out.'

The younger lad looked sly. 'Then don't tell him,' he said.

'What if he asks?'

'Just tell him you've done what he told you. He'll never know the difference.'

'Aye, maybe you're right,' said Charlie. He picked up his coat which was hanging over the stall's partition and turned towards the door.

Dido retreated hastily to the front of the house, coming to a standstill on the path beneath the window of her aunt's room.

She stood for a moment regaining her breath and wondering what was missing from the stables. But, unable to find any satisfactory answer, she turned her mind back to the figure she had seen in the night.

Slowly, looking about as she walked, she followed the course that the figure had taken to the angle where the east wing joined the main body of the building. This part of the house was thickly hung with clematis, the leaves upon it lush and green, the flowers as yet but tight buds. The path before it was cool and shadowy and thickly fringed with moss.

She looked about for the cause of the figure's disappearance; and there, half hidden among the brown tangle of the creeper's stems, she found a little 'Gothic' door, shaped to fit a pointed arch of stone. The door was old, its planks dry, cracked and bleached; its latch was rusted and the growth of the clematis across its upper half declared it to be seldom used. However, it had been lately opened, the stems about it were broken; a handful of fresh leaves lay upon the moss-covered path.

So, she thought with satisfaction, it was through this door that the figure had disappeared. But where did this door lead?

She stepped forward to try the latch and trod on something soft which squashed unpleasantly beneath her thin shoe. She started back and saw a sticky, flattened slug among three others which were still whole and fat and shining as blackly as well-polished boots. They were, she noticed, all gathered about a round depression in the moss which was about a hand's span in diameter. But there was nothing to show what might have created the mark.

Taking care to avoid the slugs she lifted the latch of the door – and found it locked.

There was a moment or two of very respectable hesitation, a little looking about to be sure she was not watched; then – curious and vexed with herself in about equal measure – she stooped down and put her eye to the large old-fashioned keyhole below the latch.

Gradually her squinting eye made out orderly rows of leather-bound books and a table upon which was spread the morning's newspaper . . . In short, she was looking upon nothing more remarkable than Mr Lancelot's excellent library . . .

Disappointed – though she would not have admitted it – that the door did not lead to some secret passageway or hidden chamber, Dido retired to continue her deliberations in the breakfast parlour. Here she found sun streaming through the mullioned windows, lighting up oak-panelled walls and a vast old dresser laden with silver dishes. A burnished breastplate and two crossed broadswords hung above the chimney piece of carved stone.

The two Mr Fenstantons – uncle and nephew – were alone at the long table and deep in the discussion of business.

'The cost is damnably high,' Mr Lancelot was protesting as she entered.

'But worth it, my boy, well worth it!' said Mr George. 'For nowadays, the sea is the very thing for making people healthy. Before the season is even begun we will have more folk wanting our cottages and boarding houses than we can accommodate.'

'It is all very well for you,' murmured Mr Lancelot discontentedly. 'You seem to have found a way of holding off your creditors. But as for me—'

He stopped abruptly as he saw Dido at the door

and, replacing his frown with a smile, began upon an explanation. 'We are discussing our new town, Miss Kent. George and I, and Parry and a few others are building a new town here at Charcombe . . .'

But his uncle immediately took the interesting topic out of his hands. As Dido settled to coffee and French bread, Mr George – who had not previously troubled to speak three words to her since her arrival at the house – informed her that the air about Charcombe was so remarkably fine that the place seemed 'meant by Providence, don't you know, to be a place of Great Resort. There's not such another place on the whole coast from Cromer to Dawlish. And soon it will be all the fashion to come here.'

Mr George Fenstanton, it seemed, had great faith in the curative powers of the sea. He was a thorough enthusiast who drank his pint of seawater and milk every morning and who – no matter what the weather – took his 'dip' promptly at three o'clock every afternoon. Whistling importantly through his teeth, he continued his little discourse by explaining to Dido that no one could be very unwell within a mile of the sea, nor completely healthy without spending at least six weeks of every year breathing its air and bathing in its waters. And, finally, contrived to suggest that the very pinnacle of health was only to be achieved by renting one of his own new-built houses . . .

His concern for the health of his fellow men and the health of his own purse seemed to be about equal. But, as he talked, Dido's attention was drawn away from his pink-faced enthusiasm to Mr Lancelot, who was gazing silently upon the chops on his plate. She was wanting to know *his* opinion.

'Well,' she cried politely as soon as she had an opportunity, 'this new town seems a delightful scheme and I wish it luck with all my heart.' She took care to include both gentlemen in her smile.

'Ha!' cried Mr Lancelot. 'It will be very delightful indeed, if only it pays us for our trouble. I confess, Miss Kent, that I would never have entered into it myself. But my father had begun upon it before he died not much more than a twelve-month ago. And—'

'And it would be a damned discredit to his memory if you should give it up!' said Mr George, his head positively glowing through his thin white hair.

He would no doubt have said a great deal more, but they were interrupted by the arrival of Martha Gibbs and Emma Fenstanton.

Miss Gibbs entered the room yawning and continued to yawn over her toast. 'Lord!' she said, 'I ain't slept a wink! There has been such a noise of crying all night. I did not know you had got a baby in the house, Mr Fenstanton.'

All eyes turned upon her immediately.

'Did you not hear it?' she asked in surprise, her knife suspended above the butter dish.

The gentlemen shook their heads.

'I heard nothing at all,' said Emma daintily lifting a chop from its heated dish. 'I slept like a log – as they say. Though personally I have never supposed logs to be very sleepy sorts of things. Have you, Miss Gibbs?'

'Oh Lord! Yes indeed. I wish I had slept like a log.'

'I believe I heard something,' said Dido. 'Just once – a very faint little cry. But perhaps it was no more than the wind, or something of that sort.'

'Ha! It was not the wind,' said Mr Lancelot, smiling broadly, though he did not raise his eyes from his plate. 'There is indeed a baby in the house! And I apologise to you if he kept you from sleeping, Miss Kent . . . and to you also, Miss Gibbs.'

'The poor child sounded very distressed,' said Dido.

'I don't doubt he was. He has been distressed for more than a century now.'

'A century?' repeated Martha; the knife with which she had been spreading butter clattered out of her hand.

But Dido caught the meaning of his smile. 'Are you telling us that there is a ghost in the house, Mr Fenstanton?'

'Oh no!' cried Emma, yawning prettily. 'You are going to tell one of your ghost stories, are you not, Cousin Lance?'

The gentleman made a great show of ignoring her and turned courteously to Dido. 'But of course there is a ghost, Miss Kent. We Fenstantons could not hold up our heads in the neighbourhood if we had not a ghost in the house. And, of course,' he added, smiling at Miss Gibbs, 'it is Her Ladyship's chamber – the haunted room – that *you* are lying in.'

'Oh Lord!'

Emma laid a friendly little hand on Martha's arm. 'Do not mind him, Miss Gibbs. He is only teasing you.' She threw a little grimace in her cousin's direction. 'Lance can be very cruel sometimes.'

Mr Lancelot caught her eye and made a mocking little bow. 'Thank you for that kind reflection! But,' turning back to Miss Gibbs with a smile which Dido could not entirely excuse of teasing, 'I fancied you already knew that your chamber was haunted. For when you arrived, Letitia asked that you and she might share the haunted room. It has been a whim of hers to sleep there ever since she was a little girl.'

Martha paled. 'Tish never said a word to me about there being a ghost in our room.'

'Well, you need not look so very frightened. For our ghost is a harmless little fellow. He died a very sad death during the civil war.'

Martha stared in wide-eyed silence. She licked the butter from her fingers and picked up her knife – leaving a trail of grease across the white tablecloth.

'I believe Miss Fenstanton is right, you *are* about to tell us a ghost story,' said Dido, as she briskly buttered her own toast.

'Now then, now then,' interposed Mr George firmly. 'There is no need to repeat Francine's foolish old tale, Lance. My poor sister had a wild and melancholy fancy. She read too many old books in the library – and said a great many things which are better forgotten.'

But Lancelot was not to be dissuaded. 'Do not listen yourself if you do not wish, George. But don't prevent the rest of us from enjoying a good fright!'

Mr George assumed a tone of rather ill-judged authority – as if he believed his nephew to be still no more than twelve years old. 'Come now, my boy, there is no need to distress the ladies.'

Lancelot's smile did not falter as he met his uncle's eye. 'But I am determined,' he said, 'for I am very proud to have a ghost in *my* house.'

The emphasis upon the possessive was very slight, but Dido did not fail to catch his meaning – and nor did Mr George; he threw down his napkin, excused himself to the ladies, and stalked out.

Mr Lancelot laughed at his retreating back. 'Well, it is a dreadful tale!' he said, leaning back in his seat and hooking his fingers around the buttons of his waistcoat. 'The little boy's parents, you see – Sir Mortimer Fenstanton and his lady – were loyal through and through to King Charles.' He had lowered his voice to that sort of trembling half whisper which is universally acknowledged to be the proper delivery for a tale of terror.

'And so Cromwell's soldiers attacked the house,' he continued. 'They carried away the knight and his wife. But, before she was taken, Lady Fenstanton's last act was to conceal her baby son from the Roundheads. Only one other person – an old and trusted servant – knew where the child was hidden . . .' He paused dramatically.

'Yes?' urged Martha breathlessly.

'And that one old servant was so overcome by the attack that she died of a seizure within an hour of the soldiers leaving the house.'

'Oh!' cried Miss Gibbs in a kind of refrain.

'And so no one could find the baby – though they could hear him crying fit to break a heart of stone!'

'Oh!'

'And,' he added, raising his finger, 'his poor little skeleton was not discovered until many years later.'

Little Miss Emma ostentatiously smothered a yawn with a very large handkerchief, and reached for another chop. Her disapproval seemed to be making her remarkably hungry. She leant towards Miss Gibbs and in the pretence of a whisper – which in fact carried easily along the length of the table – she said, 'Of course, my cousin speaks of what he understands. Lance knows all about the killing of little innocents.'

That was a remark to cloud even Mr Lancelot's sunny countenance and he immediately demanded an explanation.

'I mean, of course, your shooting of innocent woodcock and pheasant,' Emma replied composedly. 'What else do you suppose me to mean?' She raised her little face in a dangerous challenge and a rather uneasy silence filled the breakfast room.

Dido considered the tale, quite refusing to shiver over it, though the temptation to do so was great. And she wondered why it was that, while a child dead now, a fortnight ago, even a year ago, would be sad and shocking, there was something about the distance of a century and a half – assisted no doubt by the addition of Mr Cromwell's name and all the panoply of history – which gave the account a kind of dark fascination. 'And now,' she said, breaking the silence, 'this sad little ghost keeps the household awake with its weeping?'

'It does,' cried Mr Lancelot putting aside his frown. 'And sometimes, Miss Kent, there is another sound – the sound of footsteps. And some people say that they have seen the dark shape of the poor mother returning to find her lost child. Now, what do you say to that?'

'I say that I do not believe in ghosts.' Dido looked him in the eye and shook her head.

He began to protest and might perhaps have attempted to persuade her into belief. But his attention was drawn away first by the arrival of Mrs Bailey and then by the bringing in of the morning's post.

There was a small heap of letters for Mr Lancelot. He gave them no very welcoming look, and left them unopened beside his plate. Mrs Bailey, Dido noticed, received no letters at all, which was perhaps a little odd for such a very popular woman. For Miss Fenstanton there was a book – a copy of *Blair's Sermons* sent fresh from the bookbinders – which she opened eagerly.

For Dido herself there was but one letter and, as the cramped hand immediately declared it to be written by Margaret, she did not hurry to break the seal. Instead she sat for a moment or two drinking her coffee and considering the events of the night, events which resembled rather closely the haunting which her host had just described . . .

She would not believe that the figure in the garden was the long-dead Lady Fenstanton, any more than she would allow the crying to be produced by a ghostly infant; so her thoughts were necessarily complicated – and not a little suspicious.

She studied Mr Fenstanton as he sat brooding over his unread letters. One hand rested on his coffee cup and his first finger beat an impatient rhythm on its rim, as if he were displeased with his correspondents; the dark hair fell forward over his eyes and the morning sunlight brought forward gleams of grey which were not usually to be seen.

Was it possible, she wondered, that he had told her this tale in order to explain away a scene which he feared she had witnessed? Had he so far mistaken her character as to think she could be persuaded into a belief that any odd appearances in his house were of a supernatural origin?

It was impossible to tell, she thought, as she reluctantly opened her letter; she must know *his* character a little better before she could determine his motives.

Margaret's handwriting was not easy to read. It was designed to fit as many words as possible on only one sheet of paper, for she was violently opposed to either the stationer or the post office profiting from her correspondence. This morning's letter began with an assurance that the family were all in good health, moved rapidly to a complaint upon the cost of butchers' meat, with an enquiry as to the price of shin beef in the Charcombe neighbourhood, and proceeded to minute instructions upon the purchase of calico – if Dido should chance to visit the shops in Exeter and there was anything tolerable to be got for less than three shillings a yard, which she (Margaret) doubted, for drapers were all become so very greedy these days . . .

Dido sighed, turned the page and began to make out that part which had been written crosswise.

. . . Well, I daresay you pass your time very pleasantly indeed at Charcombe Manor, for I understand that Mr Fenstanton keeps a good table and everything is very comfortable there. But I am sorry – and very surprised – that we have not yet heard one word from you. For you must know that we

are particularly anxious to hear how dear Mrs Manners bore with her journey – and whether she keeps in tolerable health. And whether you have yet been able to discover <u>why</u> she has gone to Charcombe Manor; for, as I have told you, I see no reason for her to visit a place which she has not been near these <u>thirty years</u>. Unless it is because of the Fenstantons' persuasions and hypocritical attempts to win upon her affections. I do so hate encroaching people! I have no opinion of the Fenstantons; they are all for what they can get. I have no doubt but that they have some scheme to get money from the poor lady; and so, Dido, you must be upon the lookout and see what they are about. For it would be a great disgrace to us all if they should succeed in imposing upon her. As everybody knows, her fortune was all her husband's and the Fenstantons certainly have no rights in it. And I consider their behaviour to be very suspicious indeed . . .

Dido laid down the letter, looked thoughtfully along the breakfast table, and found herself for once in agreement with Margaret. There was every reason to doubt the behaviour of Charcombe's residents. There was not a person here against whom a suspicion could not be raised.

There was Miss Gibbs with her heavy sleepless eyes – and those curls which, Dido noticed, had been burnt again; why had she been the only person kept awake by the weeping of the 'ghost'? And beside her was the merry Miss Fenstanton bowing her little head with truly remarkable eagerness over her dry tome of sermons, though looking up from time to time to throw an odd little look of disdain in her cousin's direction. Then there was the popular Mrs Bailey, trying to busy herself with an egg and pretending that she did not care about receiving no letters. And at the head of the table their host was still scowling at his correspondents – very much as if they were pressing him for the payment of debts . . .

Chapter Ten

. . . It pains me to confess it, Eliza, but I cannot help but think Margaret is in the right. The Fenstantons are certainly in need of cash. Their building scheme is costing them dear and I think it very likely indeed that they are seeking a reconciliation with our aunt for the sake of her fortune. The ring has already been given up – though I cannot understand at all why it should have been given to Mr George, when it is her nephew to whom our aunt shows a degree of affection.

But I fear I lack Margaret's nice discrimination in all this and find myself quite unable to distinguish between the <u>mercenary schemes</u> of others and the <u>prudential concerns</u> of my own family. Are we not all equal in guilt? Do we not all court Mrs Manners for the sake of her money?

Are we not, every one of us, 'all for what we can get'? And every time I place a cushion or pour a draught of medicine am I not tainted by interest? Oh Eliza, I despise myself for being poor! And I despise myself even more for being dependent upon the poverty of my brothers. For I find I cannot, for their sakes, neglect our aunt – or even speak my mind to her. I fear to injure their interest as well as my own.

And, after all, I think we debase ourselves for nothing. For, quite apart from the 'encroaching' claims of the Fenstantons, we – I mean my Uncle Manners' family –

are so very numerous that I doubt any portion of the money he has left will ever fall to you or I, or our brothers. I calculate that there are, surviving our uncle, three brothers and a sister (all senior to our mother), sixteen nephews, twenty-one nieces and two great-nephews. In all this tribe I do not rate our chances very high; in short, Eliza, there are a great many other devoted relations who have a stronger claim and are able, I do not doubt, to place cushions and measure medicine with much more grace than I can ever achieve.

And yet, what am I to do? Insult and neglect my aunt? But then you know, when the will is read and all those dearest to me are left as poor as ever, will I not always wonder how far I am to blame?

And rudeness is never excusable. And the rich are as deserving of kindness as the poor . . .

Oh dear, Eliza! I shall torment myself – and you – no more with this. I shall return instead to the much more agreeable subject of someone else's poverty, and consider Mr Lancelot's debts – for debts I am sure he has.

That he should be embarrassed for money argues for his need of Miss Verney's fortune. Has he been pressing her too hard for an answer?

Perhaps the 'elopement' is not what it appears at all. Perhaps Miss Verney was reluctant to make the match with Mr Lancelot, had refused – or was upon the point of refusing – and this removal was either an escape, or else a part of some plan to coerce her into acceptance . . .

All in all I think escape more likely. I do not feel justified in harbouring such dark thoughts against my host . . . Though his cousin hints at his cruelty . . . But I believe that must be *some secret jest of Miss Emma's. Her statements are mostly fantastical . . .*

No, I cannot believe Lancelot Fenstanton such a thorough-going villain as would shut away a young lady in some distant farmhouse until he can bend her to his will . . .

Mr Lancelot has not the look of a character in a horrid novel. And besides, I cannot comprehend how he could have accomplished such villainy . . . Nor how he could convince Mr Tom Lomax that there had been a return to Charcombe Manor . . .

But if it is only an escape on the part of the young lady – one in which Mr Tom <u>might</u>, I suppose, be complicit – why have Mr Fenstanton and Mrs Bailey been so very dilatory over pursuit?

I cannot hit upon a satisfactory theory; and all in all I can only agree with Margaret – there is suspicious business carrying on here and, for once, I intend to do exactly as she orders: I intend to be very much 'upon the lookout'.

And I only wish that I might remain here this morning looking out for the arrival of the mysterious Mr Brodie. I wonder very much what he shall have to say about Miss Verney. And who among the company here he will claim as an acquaintance.

But I must set off now for Charcombe village to search out brown medicine and discover whether the town's physician is such a man as my aunt might approve . . .

There was no brown medicine to be had in the village of Old Charcombe – for there was no longer a medical man there to make medicine of any colour.

'Doctor Sutherland has gone away up the hill,' Dido

was told when she made enquiries. And at first she supposed this to be some local method of softening the discussion of death; but at last she was given to understand that the doctor was not deceased but had only moved his business a half mile away, onto the cliff top where the Fenstantons' new town was building – 'on account of all the sick people that are to come there.'

Her informants – two elderly women selling fish from a stone bench in the village square – laughed heartily at her mistake.

'You're not from these parts, then?' said one of the women boldly as she chewed on a nasty-looking black pipe.

'No,' confessed Dido rather distractedly, 'I am visiting Mr Fenstanton.' She was not pleased to discover that she must continue her journey. All her thoughts still centred upon the manor house where Mr Brodie might be arriving at this very moment.

She looked back – beyond the busy little square with its low grey buildings, ancient mounting block, marketing women and gleaming silver fish open-mouthed on the wet stone – to the inland road which wound through the village over a single arch of stone bridge. She was sorely tempted to turn back along that road immediately and report her mission a failure. Then she would be able to witness Mr Brodie's arrival, discover which of her fellow guests he claimed as an acquaintance – and hear his news of Miss Verney . . .

She became aware that the women were laughing again. 'Staying at the manor, are you?' said the pipe smoker and she turned to her friend – a smaller woman in a vast and ancient leghorn bonnet. 'Well, well, she'd better take care, hadn't she?'

The lady in the leghorn screeched delightedly at this exquisite piece of wit. 'Aye,' she said shrilly, wiping blood and fish scales from her hands onto a grimy apron. 'That's not a safe place for young ladies, is it, Sarah? Why, she'll be carried off to Gretna Green before she knows it!'

'I beg your pardon?' cried Dido, dismayed to find that rumours were spreading despite Mr Lancelot's caution. 'I do not quite understand you.' She looked all innocent bewilderment.

The two women laughed louder. Sarah took her pipe from her mouth. 'You ask Mr Sutherland about it!' she said, pointing the short black stem at Dido. 'Aye, you ask him,' she said again before turning away to serve the next customer.

Dido stepped away from the jostling crowd around the bench, glad to escape from both the shrill wit and the stink of fish, and wondering very much why she should be referred to the doctor for information.

She turned reluctantly in the direction of the new town and her eye followed the dusty white road which she could see leading out of the cluster of cottages, and zigzagging on up an open slope of grass and gorse, towards such a wide, bright expanse of sky as always signals the presence of the sea. And she wished again that she might return directly to the house.

She had already lost a great deal of time, for Mrs Manners had found other errands for her to perform which 'would be no trouble at all since she would be in the village anyway'. And she had been obliged to seek out a laundress suitably versed in the science of washing good lace, as well as delivering several letters to the post office and helping the young postmaster to distinguish the directions in her aunt's careless, old-fashioned hand, deciphering for him the tangled letters of Worcestershire on one cover and convincing him – with some difficulty – that another was directed to Bristol, not 'Beef-tea' as he had averred.

Now she was almost overwhelmed by impatience.

And, in point of fact, brown medicine was not even wanted today; her aunt's symptoms were no longer of the 'enervating' sort. This morning there were 'sharp palpitations' and a 'frantic throbbing' of the temples – the illness, it would seem, had turned 'hectic'. And only red medicine was of use against hectic symptoms – unless there was an outbreak of 'fluttering biliousness' – in which case the white variety would be required. But Dido had not quite courage enough to return empty-handed, lest the very absence of the antidote precipitate an enervating attack.

So she started up the road towards New Charcombe. The sun grew stronger, warming the gorse bushes until they smelt of freshly baked cake, and making the white dust of the road dazzling. As she walked Dido puzzled over many things. She puzzled over why someone at the manor might wish to deny being Mr Brodie's friend – and how the lie might be sustained after the gentleman's arrival; she puzzled over the fishwives' cryptic information; she puzzled over Miss Gibbs' lack of rest and Mr Fenstanton's fondness for horrid tales . . .

But she arrived at the top of the hill and the beginning

97

of the new town with glowing cheeks, a dusty petticoat –
and no answers to any of the puzzles in her head.

Before her, a street or two of good white stone had
been laid down across the turf of the cliff top and there
were a few dozen completed houses. There were some
people of quality determinedly taking the air, but a great
many more workmen building houses to accommodate
the visitors and invalids who were yet to find their way
here. Wherever Dido looked there were scaffolds and
barrows; grimy young lads mixing mortar, and solemn
masons in their caps and aprons dressing stone.

She smiled at the memory of Mr George Fenstanton's
panegyric on the place. But, as she started along the
broad mall which topped the low cliff, she felt the power
of the seaside in a lifting of her spirits. A pleasant breeze
was ruffling the tops of the waves and setting the bright
awnings of the bathing machines a-flapping down on the
beach. Gulls wheeled overhead. The sun sparkled on the
water, and also upon the clean white stones of the new
buildings, making them appear as bright and fresh as the
waves themselves.

About halfway along the mall there was a space for
benches laid out. A heap of stone and several lengths of
wood declared that the masons and carpenters had not yet
completed their work; but there were two or three seats
already built and these were occupied by some retired
military men and dowagers such as frequent watering
places in the unfashionable times of the year.

And then, as she approached the spot, Dido discerned
another figure – young and long in the leg – a figure
which had an unpleasantly familiar look . . .

Her pace slowed. There was no mistaking the gentleman sitting there with his legs sprawled across the pavement, one hand resting upon the silver head of a cane as he thoughtfully perused a letter. It was none other than the man who had lately caused such a stir at Charcombe Manor – Mr Tom Lomax himself.

She faltered, half determined upon hurrying away; but at that very moment he turned his head and saw her. He jumped immediately to his feet, sweeping off his hat, putting up the letter and making a hurried bow.

'Miss Kent! Why, of all the birds of the air, you are the very one I have been hoping to fall in with!'

Dido made her curtsey and approached him warily. His thick, pale hair shone in the sunlight; his features were certainly well-looking, though rather marred by scrubby sidewhiskers and a small, wet, sulking mouth. And the stare he was presently turning upon her was unpleasant – sly and uneasy. It was a year and a half since their last encounter, and they had not parted on the best of terms, for Dido had then taken it upon herself to save two other young ladies from his heartless scheming.

His impudent, familiar manner irritated her exceedingly, yet she could not help but wonder why he wished to talk to her – and what he might have to say about Miss Verney.

'I suppose,' he said abruptly, returning his hat to his wind-ruffled head, 'that the Fenstantons and Mother Bailey have been all making me out to be a scoundrel.'

Dido made no reply, but cast down her eyes. One of the dowagers – seeing all and hearing nothing – smiled indulgently upon them as if she suspected a romantic encounter.

'Ah!' cried Tom. 'I see that they have.' He shrugged up his shoulders in a pretence of ease and indifference. 'Well, I am sure I don't give a damn what they think of me at Charcombe Manor. They can go to hell for all I care! But,' he added anxiously, 'I would wish *you* to know that I am innocent.'

She looked up in surprise.

'I know no more about what's become of Miss Verney than you do,' he said with a kind of impatient pleading. 'I returned the girl safely to the manor. I *saw* her walk in through the house door. You must believe me, Miss Kent.'

'Why, Mr Lomax, I am surprised to find that you should wish for *my* belief.'

'But I do,' he said, leaning upon the back of the bench. Dido recalled that he was a young man who always avoided the exertion of the perpendicular if he could. 'At least,' he added after a moment's pause, 'I wish for your assistance.'

'You wish me to help you . . .'

'. . . find Miss Verney.' He smiled and tapped his stick against the leg of the bench. 'Well, there is nobody quite like you for poking about. That is, Miss Kent,' with an elaborate bow, 'there is no one quite like you for solving puzzles.'

She coloured – a circumstance which did not go unnoticed by the watchful dowager, who now touched her companion upon the arm and pointed out the couple with a very meaning turn of the eyes.

'I thank you for the compliment, sir,' said Dido. 'But, I fear I must decline the commission.' She would not, for the world, have him think that any trouble she took in the business was undertaken for his convenience.

'Damn it!' he cried fretfully. 'I need someone to help me. I am *persona non grata* at Charcombe Manor now. I cannot even set foot over the threshold. I can do nothing to prove my own innocence.'

'Hmm.'

'You do not believe me!' he cried resentfully. 'You think I am lying about taking Letitia back to Charcombe Manor.'

Dido looked out over the cliff's edge, beyond the sands and the bathing machines to the sea and a distant ship with its gleaming white sails and circling retinue of gulls. 'In point of fact,' she admitted, 'I am rather inclined to believe your account of the young lady's return. Or rather, I think that *you* believe it to be true – I do not think that you are deliberately lying.'

'Why, I am glad to find I have your good opinion!'

She kept her eyes upon the ship. 'I certainly have a very good opinion of your prudence.'

'By which, you mean to say that you think me selfish and scheming.'

'I have certainly had the pleasure of your acquaintance long enough to know that you are no fool. And I am quite sure that if you *had* persuaded Miss Verney into an elopement you would have found a better method of concealment.' She met his eyes. 'Something safer than this extraordinary story of her returning to the house – a story which seems to cry you out a liar to the whole world.'

'Now that,' he said, 'is a point well made.' And, just for a moment – for no more than the space of a heartbeat – he brought the tips of his fingers together in a considering gesture; a gesture which was so very suggestive of his father that Dido drew back, confused and uncomfortable. 'So, you will help me prove my innocence?' he urged.

'Ah! Pardon me, sir, but I did not quite say that I believe in your *innocence*.'

'But if you do not think—'

'I do not think you are lying. But – if I may be frank upon this matter—'

'Oh, I beg that you will!' he cried. 'There should be no secrets between you and me.'

'Very well, then. I confess that I remain uneasy about your behaviour towards Miss Verney. In the past, Mr Lomax, I have found myself unable to approve some aspects of your conduct. I have had reason to suppose you mercenary in your search for a bride.'

Tom threw back his head and laughed.

'Do you deny it?' she asked. 'Do you deny that you are trying for a match with Miss Verney, for the sake of her fortune?'

Tom prodded thoughtfully at a broken fragment of stone with the tip of his cane. 'I deny that I have abducted Miss Verney.'

'But you do not deny that you are pursuing her fortune?'

'No, I don't deny it.'

'Well, then, you will certainly get no help from me in your scheme. But I may attempt to seek out the facts surrounding Miss Verney's odd disappearance – in order that she may be found and restored to her friends.'

He smiled at that.

Dido did not like his seeming so happy. Mr Tom's happiness was too often secured through the suffering of someone else. 'But,' she added firmly, 'I shall do nothing at all to promote your marriage to Miss Verney.'

He sneered and rattled his cane against a leg of the bench. 'That might be a little ill-advised, Miss Kent.'

'I beg your pardon.'

'I only mean to say,' he continued, watching her closely, 'that in promoting *my* marriage, you would be furthering the cause of your own.'

Heat flooded Dido's cheeks. She could neither speak, nor look at him; she turned her eyes away to watch a herring gull gliding up the breeze above the stark ribs of a new roof.

'It will not do to be so very disapproving,' he laughed. 'For you and I both know that it is my little difficulties with my creditors which keep my father from marrying again. He thinks himself too poor to take a wife. But let me get an heiress to settle my debts and *you* could be a married woman by Michaelmas!'

'I do not understand your meaning, sir,' she said, exerting herself to speak calmly.

He only laughed.

Shocked and shaking, she could trust herself to remain no longer. She turned and began to make her way blindly along the mall. But he raised his cane, pointed it at her retreating back and called, 'You understand me,

Miss Kent. And you know that you and I are natural confederates in this business.'

She fled against the salt breeze, her hands shaking as she clutched her pelisse about her. She wanted only to escape, to get beyond the cruel gaze of his eyes.

All at once the open mall which had, minutes ago, seemed all cheerfulness and refreshment was become a place of torture. It was too straight, too wide. There was no avoiding that terrible stare; she seemed to feel it as an ache upon the back of her head.

She was now passing the broad steps which fronted the town's newly built public rooms, and she saw that a large wagon was drawn up on the road. Like a hunted fox seeking cover, she hurried forward and escaped to stand on the steps, where the sides of the wagon hid her from Tom's view.

She stood quite still in the deep shade, trembling with relief as the pain upon her neck eased. She pressed a gloved hand to her mouth.

What did he know – what did he suspect – of how matters stood between her and his father?

She could not bear that he should know – and laugh. The vulgar sneer seemed to pollute what was most dear to her. But was she also doubting herself? Did some part of her pain spring from the suspicion that he had guessed aright?

Dido stood for several fugitive minutes in the shadow of the wagon – whose gaily painted sides declared it to belong to the travelling theatre company of one Mr Isaac Mountjoy. And, in the shelter Mr Mountjoy provided, she forced herself to face her own schemes – to name them to herself. What was it, exactly, that she had planned as she sat beside her aunt's bed?

To find Miss Verney, and so get herself to Belsfield. And once there she hoped to . . . reach an understanding with Mr Lomax? To achieve an engagement public enough to relieve her of Doctor Prowdlee's attentions?

Yes, she confessed it to herself, that *was* her plan.

But there was no denying that it would be a long engagement. No marriage could take place until the debts which Mr Lomax had assumed for his son's sake were all paid. Two or three wretched, interminable years must be waited through. Two or three years spent as a 'visitor' in Margaret's house, becoming every day more contemptible in the eyes of the world.

Tom's marriage to a wealthy woman would certainly be to her advantage. But she was not quite so unprincipled as to sacrifice another woman's happiness in the cause of her own.

At least, she hoped that she was not. And, after all, she told herself, once she was returned to her family, it would be for Miss Letitia herself to decide whom she married, would it not? In searching for Miss Verney, Dido was by no means directly promoting her marriage to Tom.

Chapter Eleven

'Ah! Fair damsel, what is it that troubles you?'

Dido looked up in alarm as the voice boomed over her head, and saw a man as large as his voice hurrying down the steps from the colonnaded front of the rooms. He was wearing a canary-yellow waistcoat and had a slightly familiar look.

'Ah me!' he cried, pressing his hands to his brilliant breast, 'I would give the world to ease the sorrow from your lovely countenance!'

Dido stared.

He came to a standstill on the step beside her, and bowed deeply. 'Isaac Mountjoy at your service, madam. May I be of any assistance to you?'

'You are very kind, sir,' she replied, and at the same moment remembered where she had seen him before: it was in the churchyard. He had been talking to Mrs Bailey. 'But I have only stopped to catch my breath. I am in no need of assistance . . . Unless you could direct me to the house of Mr Sutherland.'

'Indeed I may, for I am familiar with the physician of that name. If you will but step this way, madam.' He beckoned her out of the wagon's shelter and pointed along the street to a substantial house which stood alone near the end of town, and close beside the path leading down to the beach. There was – as yet – only one building beyond it and that was the town's inn, standing very new and fine and white-fronted where the ground began to rise up to the downs.

Dido thanked the gentleman for his help. He bowed again more extravagantly than ever and intimated that his day – perhaps his whole existence – had been rendered meaningful by the privilege of being allowed to be of use to her.

As she fled from his compliments, Dido wondered a little that such a man as this should be a member of Mrs Augusta Bailey's wide circle of acquaintances . . . Or perhaps he was one of those 'second rate' persons who sought continually to connect himself to the unfortunate woman . . .

The physician's house was so new built that the little plot before it was still choked with stones and shavings of wood, and Dido was obliged to employ her knuckle upon the door for it yet lacked a bell. But a fine new board above the door informed her that the premises were occupied by Doctor Angus Sutherland, 'qualified and experienced practitioner in all modern systems of medicine'; which modern systems included 'the methods of Electricity, Animal Magnetism and the Medicinal Application of Mud'.

As she noted this information in compliance with her aunt's instructions to find out all she could about the town's medical advisor, Dido fervently hoped that with all his modern systems Doctor Sutherland was also conversant with the mysteries of old-fashioned brown medicine; for she was more anxious than ever to complete her errand and escape the town. Even now, from the very corner of her eye, she could see, far back along the straight terrace, the figure of Tom Lomax; he appeared to be watching her and she wished very much to get beyond his reach.

The house door opened, letting out a fine scent of broiling chops and sausage, and revealing an elderly, indeterminate female in black who might have been a rather grand housekeeper, or a slightly shabby relative. She shook her head sadly. She was very sorry, but Mr Sutherland was not here. He had been called away from his breakfast more than two hours ago to a gentleman who'd been took sudden up at the inn. Dido might step into the parlour and wait if she wished, but she did not know how long the doctor would be, because there was no knowing, was there, when folk were took sudden?

No, Dido agreed regretfully, there was no knowing; and she said that she would walk up to the inn to search for the elusive Mr Sutherland.

But, just as she turned away from the house door, she saw Tom again. He had taken a seat upon one of the benches and, with his long legs stretched across the pavement and his hands folded upon the head of his cane, he had every appearance of sitting it out until she was obliged to pass him again.

'I wonder,' she said quickly, before the woman could close the door, 'whether there might be another way back to Charcombe Manor – rather than the road through Old Charcombe.'

'Why? Are you from the manor?' The tone was more genteel than that of the fishwives – but there was the same air of impertinent curiosity. The doctor's relative (surely a relative, or she would not presume so far) peered at Dido with weak blue eyes as if wondering whether she had seen her before.

'Yes,' said Dido, 'I am come on a visit.'

'Oh!' It was a long drawn-out exclamation. 'Well he don't go there, you know.'

'I am sorry, I do not quite understand you.'

'My brother, Mr Sutherland, he's not been to the manor for thirty years. Not since Miss Francine Fenstanton died. So it will be no good you asking him to visit, because he won't.'

'I see, but . . . why?'

'The why is his business not mine,' was the brisk answer. 'I am just telling you he don't go there. Now, if you want another way home, that's easy enough.' She stepped out into the dusty little garden and pointed. 'If you just go up behind the inn there you'll find a track that will lead you straight over the downs to the manor and that'll take a good half mile off your walk.'

'Thank you. That will be a great help to me. But is there some trouble between Mr Sutherland and Mr Fenstanton?'

'No.' The woman retreated within her door. 'No trouble. Angus just don't go there.'

The door closed abruptly.

Dido walked on slowly up the slope, feeling Tom's gaze upon her back at every step – and wondering about this remarkable doctor who contrived to know of Miss

Verney's disappearance although he had not set foot in the manor for thirty years . . .

As she approached the new hotel she noticed a little bustle about the place – one or two folk hurrying about, exchanging eager words and meaningful looks; but the daily coach from Plymouth was drawn up on the gravel before the door and she supposed it all to be no more than the usual business of arrival.

She mounted the steps and, under the pillared porch, met the little pockmarked lad she had seen in the churchyard, with such a very long white apron tied about him that he seemed in momentary danger of tripping over it. Her enquiry after Mr Sutherland produced a round-eyed stare. 'Is he still engaged with his patient?' she asked.

'Oh no, he's done with poor Mr Brodie. He's in the parlour now – if you'd like to come with me, miss, I'll take you to him.'

'Mr Brodie? Is that the name of the gentleman Mr Sutherland has been attending upon?'

But the boy was off and Dido had no choice but to hurry after his retreating back into a sunny apartment which was very different from the usual sort of inn parlour – for it had not an inch of dark panelling in it, nor even a low beam. In fact it was so new it smelt still of plaster; Venetian windows cut almost to the ground displayed a view of the sea to great advantage; all was light and airy and, though the tables and chairs were a little sturdier than those required for family use, they would not have appeared entirely out of place in a gentleman's drawing room.

Three ladies – coach passengers perhaps – were gathered about the fireplace drinking a hasty dish of tea. And, standing close beside them, was a tall, lean man with a shock of white hair, who could be no other than the town's medical man, for he was gently haranguing one of the ladies upon the subject of her health, as he bent over the hearth with a poker in his hand.

'. . . Aye, madam,' he was saying in the warm, comfortable growl of a Scotch man, 'I can cure you. I can cure you. If you will but remain with us here in Charcombe for a month or two – and submit yourself to my *infallible* system of cure – I will guarantee to rid you of all your nervous complaints. The sea air, a little bathing, combined with my new system . . .' He straightened himself as he saw the boy approaching and laid down the poker with great care, as if it were particularly important that it should lie exactly in parallel with the fender.

'If you please, Mr Sutherland,' ventured the pot boy, 'there's a lady here wishes to speak with you.'

'Is there, is there?' Mr Sutherland turned to Dido – revealing the narrow, bony face of a robust man of sixty or more, thick black eyebrows which were rather startling beneath a white head of hair, and a pair of sharp blue eyes which were even more alarming. 'And how may I be of service to *you*, madam?' he asked, bowing attentively and contriving somehow to suggest an invisible queue of applicants for his attention.

Dido hastily introduced herself and brought forward the subject of brown medicine, describing its usual effects and the symptoms it relieved. 'My aunt, Mrs Manners, is most anxious—'

111

'Mrs Manners?' The doctor's black brows gathered like storm clouds over the sharp blue eyes. 'Mr George Fenstanton's sister? She is here in Charcombe?'

'Yes – she has come on a visit to the manor.'

'Och! Has she indeed!' The man turned away and began fastidiously to sweep up a tiny amount of ash which his recent attentions had shaken from the fire. Recalling his sister's objections, Dido suspected reluctance. He seemed about to refuse his help.

But in a moment he laid down the hearth brush in exact parallel with the poker, and straightened himself smiling broadly.

'Your aunt,' he said, 'is an old acquaintance and I believe I had better wait upon her directly.'

'Oh no,' cried Dido much surprised and rather alarmed, for she doubted Mrs Manners would welcome an unsolicited visit. She pressed instead for the immediate supply of medicine and succeeded at last in carrying her point.

He agreed that she should return with him to his house where he could provide the physic; but he hoped she would have the goodness to carry his card to her aunt, to give her his compliments – his *warmest* compliments – and impress upon her the extreme desirability of having *proper medical attendance* during her stay at Charcombe.

When the matter was thus far settled, and the tea-drinking lady had also been supplied with a card, the pot boy was dispatched to fetch Mr Sutherland's bag and hat. And, as they left the inn together, Dido felt entitled to turn her mind to Mr Brodie.

'May I ask if the gentleman you have been attending is

112

recovered?' she said as they stepped out of the inn porch into the sunshine and salt breeze. 'For I know that Mr Fenstanton is expecting to see him at the manor today – and perhaps, if he is to be delayed, I might carry a message for him.'

Mr Sutherland stopped upon the steps, his black brows gathering again over the brilliant eyes. 'Mr Brodie was to visit Mr Lancelot Fenstanton? Do you know why?'

'No . . . That is . . .' Dido recollected herself and continued more cautiously. 'I do not know. I only know that Mr Brodie had written to announce his arrival. It was a matter of business, I suppose.'

'What manner of business?'

'I do not know.'

The doctor looked troubled for a moment. Then: 'Och! Well,' he cried, 'it's business that won't be transacted now!'

'Oh?' said Dido, stopping short as she detected in the finality of his tone a whole new meaning of *taken sudden*. 'Do you mean . . . ? That is, I hope poor Mr Brodie is not . . . dead?'

'Aye, lassie, he's dead. For that's generally the case, you know, when the illness is a bullet through the heart.'

Dido looked so alarmed that Mr Sutherland immediately detected nervousness and opened his bag in search of a restorative (a new and particularly efficacious concoction of his own). 'Mr Brodie was murdered?' she cried. 'But how? Why? Was he set upon by robbers?'

'No, no. There were certainly no robbers, for there were banknotes and a watch still in his pockets when he was found.'

'Then how was he killed? And when?'

113

'Well, it would seem to have happened last night,' said Sutherland, still peering into his bag. 'Sometime after eleven o'clock, for certain, for I was with Mr Brodie myself until about that time. I was here in the parlour playing cards with him and another gentleman.'

'Oh! And do you know how he might . . . ?'

Mr Sutherland sighed as he continued to search systematically for his remedy among the neat rows of phials and bottles in his bag. 'I regret it is all too clear, what happened, Miss Kent. The folk here at the inn say that my two companions continued with the game after I left – and a disagreement started. The two gentlemen left the inn together about midnight, and . . .' he shrugged up his shoulders '. . . Mr Brodie never returned.'

'And so, everybody is quite sure that this . . .' Dido hesitated. A terrible suspicion was laying hold of her. 'Everybody is quite sure that this *other gentleman* is to blame?'

'Aye,' said the apothecary comfortably. He drew a small phial from the bag. 'The constables have been sent off to find him.'

Dido began immediately to run away from the inn, down the green slope and out onto the terrace, her heart jarring fearfully at every step. Raising her hand against the sun which was glaring under the brim of her bonnet, she gazed anxiously along the straight walk, past strolling gentry and dusty workmen. Two dark, sturdy figures were striding briskly towards the bench upon which Tom Lomax still lounged.

When they were about fifty yards from him, Tom looked up and saw them approaching. He jumped immediately to his feet, stumbled against the pile of stones that the builders had left beside the bench, and half fell. The constables, seeing that he was attempting escape, began to run. Tom recovered himself and seemed to recognise that flight was impossible. He remained where he was; when the men reached him and laid their hands upon his shoulders, he was nonchalantly replacing the scattered stones, as if he had not a care in the world.

'Och! That's a shocking sight,' said a voice close beside Dido. Mr Sutherland was now approaching, shaking his head solemnly. 'It's a very shocking sight to see a young fellow of decent family taken for such a crime!'

Dido nodded, too overcome for speech. For her mind was ahead of him in anticipating the suffering of that 'decent family' – and of one dear man in particular whose heart would surely be broken if his son was convicted of murder . . .

Chapter Twelve

'I cannot believe it,' said Dido; but her voice shook as she spoke. She tried again, willing herself to be firm, to convey that certainty which she was quite determined to feel. 'I *will* not believe it. I know that Mr Tom Lomax is indolent and selfish and yet I *cannot* believe him capable of murder.'

There was a kind of comfort to be found in stating her conviction – even though Mr Lancelot Fenstanton and Mr Parry were both looking at her very doubtfully and showing no sign of sharing her opinion. She felt still inside her the heavy blow which had fallen as she saw the constables take Tom. A jarring chord of shock was yet vibrating somewhere within her and she quite ached to be alone; but that was a privilege which was many hours distant.

On her return from Charcombe she had found Mr Parry already arrived with news of the murder and everyone in the house eager to hear her account. She had only escaped to hurriedly change her dress as the dinner hour approached. Now everyone was gathering in the hall – and Mr Lancelot had drawn her away into the seat beneath the great window, to talk the business over again before Mr Parry.

Charles Parry, it seemed, was in the Commission of the Peace and it had fallen upon him to make enquiries into Mr Brodie's death. He listened courteously to Dido's protests, but continued to look very grave. Though perhaps little could be imputed to this, for gravity was the gentleman's common expression. Indeed his face was so heavily folded and lined that one could no more imagine him smiling than a bloodhound.

'It is a very terrible thing to be forced to acknowledge that any acquaintance is capable of murder, Miss Kent,' he said with dignified concern. 'And I am sorry, very sorry indeed, that you should have had it forced upon you.' He folded his hands behind his back and took a ponderous little turn about the bay of the window. 'Upon my word, I should not like any daughter of mine to find herself acquainted with a *murderer*.'

He stopped and looked down upon Dido regretfully. 'But there can be little doubt of young Lomax's guilt. The folk at the inn heard him quarrelling with the gentleman that is dead. And,' with a look towards Mr Lancelot, 'my friend here has now told me all about the disappearance of Miss Verney – and the note which he received yesterday from Mr Brodie.'

'Oh!' Dido's hands were trembling in her lap so that she was obliged to still them by wrapping a corner of her shawl about them. She had been thinking of nothing but Tom's danger since she had first detected it in Mr Sutherland's words, and yet it was a shock to hear it on another's lips. 'You believe that Mr Lomax killed Mr Brodie in order to prevent him reaching Charcombe Manor with his information about Miss Verney.' She stated the worst of it as calmly as she could; but she could hear the tremor in her own voice and could not prevent her fingernails driving into her palms under cover of the shawl. 'You believe that he has abducted the young lady and has now committed murder in order to hide his crime?' She raised her eyes and looked from Parry to Fenstanton, desperately hoping – all but pleading – that they would contradict.

The gentlemen exchanged looks of compassion.

'It is the most reasonable conclusion,' said Mr Parry, his words slow and precise as the ringing of a death knell.

'Oh, but there are a great many reasons for its being a false conclusion!' she cried, even as her distraught mind sought out those reasons. For his father's sake she would not believe Tom guilty. There *must* be arguments for his innocence. 'We are by no means certain that Mr Tom Lomax is responsible for Miss Verney's disappearance. If only we could discover what has become of the young lady – then we would know whether or not the young man had any motive for murder. Remember that he strongly denies any knowledge of her whereabouts.'

'But that is entirely of a piece with his being guilty,' put in Mr Lancelot. 'I don't doubt the damned fellow has got the girl hidden away somewhere.'

'But why has he not devised a better excuse?' Dido turned eagerly from her host to the magistrate. 'Mr Tom Lomax is a clever man,' she said. 'Cunning, perhaps you would rather call him; but in this case cunning and cleverness must count for the same thing. And, throughout this whole business he has not behaved as a

118

guilty and cunning man might be expected to behave.' She thought for a moment and found she liked the argument. 'He must have known that he had been heard exchanging heated words with Mr Brodie. I cannot think that he would have been so foolhardy as to shoot that gentleman immediately afterwards and not a quarter of a mile away.'

'Regrettably,' said Parry, 'murder is not always a rational act. But I beg you will cease to trouble yourself, Miss Kent—'

'Ha!' cried Fenstanton, striking his hand against the stone frame of the window. 'I see it now! What I think happened was young Tom tried to dissuade Brodie from coming to me and, when he failed, he became desperate: ceased to think quite sensibly. Do you see? I daresay he had had a little too much to drink – the fellow at the inn says he was pretty free with his calling for whisky. And so he shot Brodie – almost in a moment of madness.'

Mr Parry nodded solemnly.

And Dido herself could not help but admit that it was all horribly plausible. But she persisted. 'Was there a weapon in Mr Lomax's possession when the constables seized him?'

'No,' said Parry.

'But a pistol is very easy got rid of,' added Mr Lancelot. 'Tossed out into the sea, most likely.'

That was true enough – and she remembered that Tom had been very near the cliff top when she met him. But, as she recalled that meeting, the desperate hope of innocence revived – and with it the spirit of argument.

'When I spoke with Mr Lomax this morning,' she said, 'he seemed so very much at ease. He was, of course, concerned about Miss Verney's disappearance. But, for all that, he seemed easy – not at all like a man who had recently committed murder and left the body lying close by.'

'Now then, my dear, are you qualified to make that judgement?' asked Mr Lancelot with a gentle smile. 'I mean, are you much in the habit of talking to murderers?'

'I will not be teased out of my opinion!'

'Forgive me.' He sat down on the window seat beside her. 'I do not mean to tease, my dear Miss Kent, I only wish to say how very strong the evidence appears against the young fellow.'

She began upon another protest, but it was cut short by the approach of Mr George Fenstanton, who was looking more than usually red about the face and pink about the scalp. He addressed himself to the gentlemen, seeming not to notice Dido at all and making no apology to her for his interruption. But his words drove even her own arguments from her head.

'Now then, Lance, my boy,' he said speaking again to his nephew in the authoritative tone which had ceased to be appropriate more than twenty years ago. 'What's this you were saying about Parry here wanting us all to look at the dead body at the inn? I don't think we can allow any such thing.'

'Ha!' cried Mr Lancelot. 'I regret that I *must* allow it. And I mean to speak to everyone about it after dinner.' But, looking around, he found that his uncle had left him no opportunity of delay. Dido was not the only person waiting for an explanation. Every head was now turned in his direction.

Martha Gibbs was positively staring, and the ball of yarn which she had been rolling had escaped from her fingers to unravel a long pink strand across the grey flags of the hall floor. Mrs Bailey, meanwhile, was clasping her hands to her breast as if posing for a tableau entitled 'Innocence Surprised'. Even Aunt Manners had roused herself from her doze in the place of honour beside the fire; and Miss Fenstanton – who was just returning from one of her many visits to the library – had paused in crossing the hall and had gone so far as to lift her eyes from the book in her hand, though one finger still rested at her place on the page.

'Well then,' said Mr Parry, clasping his hands firmly behind him, leaning his long body forward and pacing out into the room. 'I had better explain.' The company waited in silence. 'And first I must apologise, especially to the ladies, for being the cause of such an unpleasant inconvenience. Upon my word, I would not wish any daughter of mine to look upon a murdered man.'

There was a little pause as he gathered his thoughts – during which, unfortunately, the whole company heard Aunt Manners mutter, 'The old fool hasn't got a daughter.' Miss Gibbs giggled.

'Well now,' said Mr Parry loudly, his folded cheeks blushing red. 'As you may imagine, there is a great deal of business to be settled over Mr Brodie's death. For, besides bringing a case against the young man who killed him . . .' He caught Dido's eye and bowed courteously. 'The young man who *seems* to have killed him,' he amended. 'Besides all that, we must find out just who Mr Brodie was. His friends must be found and informed of his death. And there is . . .' he cleared his throat with a great show of delicacy '. . . there is the little matter of the *funeral costs* to be settled.'

'But I daresay the landlord at the inn can supply all the information you need,' said Mr George, and he attempted to dismiss the difficulty with a wave of his hand.

'But it seems that he cannot. All that is known in that quarter is that Mr Brodie came up on the Plymouth coach two days ago, engaged a bed for a few nights, and . . .' he paused and turned his head from side to side, surveying the company and looking for all the world like a bloodhound seeking the scent. 'And the only other thing that is known about the unfortunate man is that he intended to come here, where, by his own account, an old acquaintance of his was paying a visit.'

There was a short silence before everyone burst out with fresh denials of knowing the dead man. Dido looked eagerly from face to face, trying once more to determine who it was that was lying.

Lancelot rose from his seat and held up a hand. 'Well, well,' he said soothingly, 'it is all a very great mystery. But Parry, you see, wishes to make quite certain; he thinks perhaps someone may recognise the fellow if we go to look at him; that perhaps someone *does* know him and the name only has been forgotten.'

The whole company now began to cry out at the idea of looking at the dead man.

'Lord!' declared Miss Gibbs with some enthusiasm, 'I

ain't ever looked at a murdered man before! And I don't know how I shall like it.'

Miss Emma was philosophical. '"The sleeping and the dead are but as pictures",' she quoted, with a grin, '"'tis the eye of childhood that fears a painted devil".'

But there was a sharp intake of breath from Mrs Bailey's quarter of the room. And Dido was extremely interested to see that lady looking red and anxious – and hurrying to hide her right hand beneath the needlework in her lap. And, before the fingers were entirely obscured, she noticed that they were crossed – very much as if Mrs Bailey was frightened and felt herself to be in urgent need of good luck.

Dido was instantly possessed of the idea that this was the culprit – the liar who wished to deny a knowledge of the dead man – but she was, unfortunately, prevented from making any further observation by a coming on of enervating symptoms.

The mention of a murdered man had proved too distressing for the delicate nerves of Mrs Manners – she was now half prostrate. And Dido could stay no longer in the hall; she must attend her aunt to her chamber and administer a large measure of brown medicine. It was exceedingly inconvenient to be called away at this most interesting juncture – and she had no wish to hear her aunt's opinion of recent events.

'It is too bad of Mr Parry to put us all to so much trouble,' she said fretfully when Dido and the maid had at last settled her in her bed. 'I am not accustomed to looking upon murdered bodies!'

'No, Aunt.'

The dainty little hands plucked at the edge of the sheet. It was an unpromising sign; Dido was apprehensive of a 'comfortable chat'.

'It is all the fault of this wicked young man,' complained Mrs Manners, 'this Tom Lomax, as he calls himself. He has stolen away Letitia and hidden her and, I daresay, ruined her, and now he has killed this man at the inn. And I do not see why *I* should be made to look upon a dead man on *his* account.'

'It is by no means certain,' said Dido as calmly as she could, 'that young Mr Lomax is guilty.'

'Not guilty? Why I should say he is! Why should you think otherwise?'

It was a pertinent question. Why should Dido think otherwise? Had she any cause other than her own wishes? 'He is of such a very respectable family,' she said.

'No, he is not,' said Mrs Manners with decision. 'A family is only respectable if it behaves respectable. These Lomaxes, are *not* respectable at all if they have a murderer among them.'

Preserving a suitably submissive silence cost Dido dear. She was longing to protest. But she knew that this was not only her aunt's prejudice; it was the opinion of the world.

However, as Mrs Manners composed herself to sleep with a look of triumph on her face, Dido did find an argument for Tom's innocence – or at least an argument for the guilt of someone else . . . She remembered the figure which she had seen creeping in secret into Charcombe Manor on the very night of the murder.

Mr Brodie, it was supposed, had been killed at about

midnight. And the clock, she remembered, had struck one just before the figure appeared. Time enough for a murderer to have made the journey back from New Charcombe.

And someone among the guests at the manor had known the dead man – but had not wished to acknowledge the connection.

Chapter Thirteen

. . . *I am become a pariah, Eliza. The company of Charcombe Manor looks askance at me. I am not to be trusted! My association with the guilty name of Lomax makes them all uneasy, I believe, and some among them find it impossible to hide their disgust.*

At dinner Mr George Fenstanton was so good as to indulge me with a little discourse upon the merits of summary hanging, which Mrs Bailey immediately improved with a few choice comments upon the likely role which 'bad blood' must play in producing extreme vice in one so young as Tom Lomax.

It was a painful meal, relieved only by the watchful courtesy of Mr Lancelot. I have made my aunt my excuse now and escaped from them all. So — while she sleeps restlessly — I shall snatch a precious opportunity of 'talking' to you, Eliza.

I hardly know where to begin. But I shall not attempt to describe to you the anxiety, the dread which I feel of the misery impending over Mr Lomax. I know that your feelings are there before me — that you share every anxiety, every fear. And, besides, it is not a subject upon which I dare allow myself to dwell.

I shall turn my thoughts instead to a consideration of what is to be done to avert the evil. How is Mr Tom's innocence to be proved?

His presence at the inn, his arguing with the dead man, are both beyond doubt and I believe the best way of coming at the problem is by considering his motive. Everybody agrees that Tom's reason for killing Mr Brodie was to prevent his reaching Mr Fenstanton with news of Miss Verney.

So the motive rests upon Mr Tom having abducted Letitia Verney. The greater crime depends entirely on the lesser. If it could be proved that he played no part in the girl's disappearance, then the case of murder must fall.

And I am convinced, Eliza, that Tom Lomax has no more idea where Letitia Verney is now than you or I have. He cannot know where she is. Else why did he remain in Charcombe? Why was he not at her side, pressing his suit; pursuing her fortune; carrying her away to a blacksmith-priest in Scotland?

And why – if he is privy to her whereabouts – should he solicit my help in finding her?

No, no. Tom Lomax is not the cause of Miss Letitia Verney's removal from Charcombe. That is an explanation which makes no sense at all.

So two possibilities remain. Either Miss Verney is the author of her own disappearance, or someone else has contrived to carry out an 'abduction' and throw the blame upon T.L.

Dido read through the argument with some satisfaction. The neat, orderly lines of script were remarkably comforting; all her worry and misery compressed into clear thought and rational words. Now she could see her way forward . . .

The first puzzle to be solved must be how Tom was deceived into thinking Miss Verney returned safely to the house. How can he have seen her walk through a door when all her friends declare that she never arrived upon the other side of that door?

I must begin to investigate this question without delay.

My aunt has been very unhappy since retiring to her chamber. Letitia's sins run very much upon her mind. In her half-dreaming imagination she has placed the fugitives in the Westmorland town of Kendal tonight and, since this is but 'half a day's hard riding' from Gretna Green, she is very apprehensive indeed.

However, she seems at last to have fallen into a calmer state. And I think I shall attempt to steal away. There is company come to tea below and dancing is once more under discussion. I hope that I shall be able to creep out into the grounds undetected and look about me.

Dido laid down her pen and rose as quietly as she could, but it was not quietly enough.

Before she could reach the door of the bedchamber, a tremulous voice spoke from within the closed curtains of the bed. 'I shall see Doctor Sutherland,' said Aunt Manners, in the precise tones of a drunkard attempting to prove his sobriety.

Dido parted the curtains cautiously and leant over the high, crimson-covered bed. The light from the candle by the writing desk caught the pale little face within. The eyes were staring blankly into the distance, proving that the lady remained in a half-sleeping state.

'I am a very sick woman,' she continued argumentatively. 'Why should I not see a physician?'

Dido turned away hoping her aunt was insensible of her presence.

'And he is a very clever man, you know. He was a great help to my sister, Francine, with all her nervous complaints.'

Dido stopped – turned back to the bed.

Mrs Manners tossed her head restlessly on the pillow; her voice became more argumentative than ever. 'It was all lies the things they said about him . . .'

'What did they say?' asked Dido quickly.

'They said he came here too often. They said that his motives were mercenary. But Francine was sick – and he was her physician. It was only natural that he should call every day.'

'Indeed . . .'

'I shall send for Doctor Sutherland tomorrow,' said Mrs Manners. 'George will not like it . . . But I shall not be put off by George . . .' Her voice faded as she slipped away into true sleep.

Dido stood a moment beside the bed staring down thoughtfully at the sleeping figure – until the striking up of a dance tune below roused her to a recollection of her intended visit to the grounds.

What had really happened on the afternoon of Miss Verney's disappearance? Dido wondered as she closed the great front door on the noise of the company and stepped out into a chilly but tranquil evening.

Around her, the flower beds and lawns were darkening and the trees in the valley cast a purple dusk, but above the woods rose the downs, glowing in the last of the ruddy sunlight, and over all was spread a glorious red-streaked sky, filled with a promise of fair weather. The stillness sharpened Dido's mind. It almost seemed as if the answers to all her difficulties might be hanging here in the air with the scents of woodsmoke and damp grass.

How had Letitia Verney disappeared while only walking a hundred yards along this gravel carriage drive and into the house? The driveway ran straight between the smooth lawns, offering no possibility of concealment even now in the gathering dusk.

Dido had descended the steps and begun to pace slowly towards the gates, when the great door behind her opened and Emma Fenstanton stepped out, her white gown gleaming in the dusk.

'Miss Kent, I *must* consult with you!' she cried running down the steps.

'Oh!'

'I have something very *important* to tell you.' She drew her shawl about her – and it immediately fell into exactly the right, the most becoming, folds. 'I know what you are about,' she said turning up her bright little eyes to Dido's face. 'You are trying to determine how Mr Lomax's extraordinary story might be true, are you not? You want to prove that he did not run away with Letitia.'

Dido looked at her in surprise.

'Oh, it was very plain in your face at dinner that you want him to be innocent,' said Miss Emma, 'so I thought what a great laugh it would be if you and I could puzzle it all out – for I am sure we are as clever as any man.'

'I see.'

'And then, all at once, I saw what had happened!'

They had now begun to walk side by side along the drive. Miss Fenstanton was shorter than Dido – who had always been considered an inch or two short of elegance herself. But the young lady's air was so assured that, walking beside her, one immediately believed her height to be perfection.

Dido felt over-tall. 'And what do you believe happened?' she asked, bending her head.

'Letitia deceived Mr Lomax. She made him believe that she had returned to the house, when, in fact, she had not.'

Dido looked curiously at her companion, wondering what she would be about. Her face was all smiling certainty; her eyes danced with the enjoyment of her own genius. 'Why should you think that Miss Verney would trick the poor man?'

'Because,' said Emma, her voice thrilling with the importance of her information, 'Letitia was not pleased with Mr Tom Lomax. He had offended her.'

'Indeed! And are you in Miss Verney's confidence? Has she told you of his offence?'

'No,' admitted Emma. 'Letitia Verney and I are not exactly *intimate* now. We were once. When we were little girls we spent a great deal of time playing together in this house.' She paused a moment and looked back fondly at the old grey manor house. 'No, Letitia and I are good friends now, but,' she said, slipping her arm through Dido's and walking on towards the gates, 'the time is gone when she and I shared secrets. However, I

131

did overhear her telling Miss Gibbs that Mr Tom Lomax was not to be trusted.'

'Did you indeed?' said Dido, deeply interested. 'When did you hear it?'

'Just two days before she went away. She said that his motives were mercenary and she did not believe him to be disinterested.'

'Indeed!' This made excellent hearing! It rendered an elopement very unlikely. 'Are you quite certain that that was her opinion?'

'Oh yes.' Miss Fenstanton smiled up at Dido, as self-possessed and sure of herself as a cat.

'And were you surprised to hear her talk like that? Would you say that in general she is a suspicious person?'

'Well, I would say that she is *cautious*. I tell you honestly, Miss Kent, I do not think she is at all the kind of girl to be running away to Gretna Green.'

This opened up new vistas of possibility. Until this moment, Dido had not doubted that Miss Verney was in love with Tom Lomax. But if she were not . . .

'Now,' said Emma. 'You *must* allow me to tell you what happened on the afternoon Letitia disappeared. For I have reckoned it all out – which I think proves what a woman's mind is capable of. Women are as capable as men of thinking rationally, you know, and it is very *unphilosophical* of men to suppose we are like children—'

'What do you believe happened?' asked Dido quickly before her companion could be taken with one of her flights of fancy.

'I believe a trick was played upon Mr Lomax.'

132

'A trick? You think that this disappearance of Miss Verney's might be a species of revenge upon the gentleman – because she was angry with him for his mercenary ambitions?'

Emma paused and frowned. 'No, I think it was more in the nature of a test.'

'A test?'

'Yes, Letitia often talks of "testing" suitors. Like the fairy stories, you know – when men must accomplish great tasks to prove themselves worthy of the princess's hand. She would be cold, demanding – that kind of thing – just to see whether a man would bear with her patiently.' She shook her head, half admiring, half disapproving. 'Once she "tested" cousin Lancelot by insisting that he missed a whole day's shooting in order to accompany her to the shops in Exeter.'

'And did Mr Fenstanton complete his "test" to her satisfaction?'

'Oh yes! He is quite determined to marry Letitia.' She glanced up smilingly. 'Papa will be disappointed, you know. Lance will never marry *me*. Even if I would have him – which I certainly never shall! Indeed I do not think I shall ever marry.'

'Then how are you to gain that fortune with which you will torment your family when you are old?'

Emma laughed delightedly. 'That is a difficulty, is it not? I see I shall have to give a little more thought to the matter.'

Dido smiled and shook her head. She found herself rather liking Miss Emma. 'But, in the meantime,' she said, 'you must tell me more about this "test" upon

133

Mr Lomax. How was it to operate; and what was to be "proved" by it?'

Emma shrugged up her shoulders. 'His constancy, perhaps,' she said. 'Or his intelligence. Perhaps she meant that he should find her out. Perhaps he had to discover how he had been deceived – solve the mystery.'

'I see.' Dido walked on in silence for a moment, not sure whether to believe or not. Then, putting aside the motive, she turned her attention to the greater puzzle. 'But how was the trick accomplished?'

'Well, Letitia must have given him the slip. And this,' coming to a standstill, 'is the place where it was done.'

They had arrived at the spot where three well-grown beech trees stood beside the carriage drive, within yards of the gates. The smooth grey trunks towered up against the evening sky; bright green leaves were unfurling on the overhanging branches and bluebells were just pushing through the carpet of old brown leaves, among roots spread like giant grey claws.

'This,' said Emma firmly, '*must* be the place at which she disappeared. There is nowhere else it could have been done. She slipped away and hid behind one of these trees.'

'It is not possible!'

'Is it not?'

'There are two very strong objections. Firstly, Mr Lomax is quite sure that she did not slip away. He assures me that his eyes were upon her the whole time. Gazing devotedly, I don't doubt.'

'And is Mr Lomax so *very* devoted?'

'He is a great deal too devoted to Miss Verney's fortune to neglect any detail in his role of lover.'

Miss Fenstanton's pale face puckered into childlike disappointment. 'Perhaps,' she suggested, 'he was distracted for a moment – and in that moment she slipped away.'

'Even if I could believe that possible, there would still be another, stronger, objection remaining. Mr Lomax stood just there, beside the gate, until Miss Verney entered the house door. He saw her walk beyond these trees. He saw her walk the length of the carriage drive.'

'Ah! No, no!' cried Emma eagerly. 'I had thought of that. You see, Letitia had an ally in her plan – Miss Gibbs.'

Dido could only look at her in wonder.

'And Miss Gibbs,' Emma continued, 'was already concealed behind the tree before Mr Lomax and Letitia returned. It was all prearranged. As Letitia stepped behind the tree, Martha stepped out. It was the work of a moment.'

'And it was Miss Gibbs that Mr Lomax saw walk into the house?'

'Yes. They are of a similar height – and if they were seen only from the back . . .' Emma held up her hands with a smile as if she had herself accomplished the clever trick. The dimples flashed in her cheeks.

But Dido shook her head. 'Were the two young ladies in similar gowns that day? What of their bonnets? Their cloaks? The dressing of their hair?'

'As to all that, I confess, I cannot remember. But,' Emma continued, brightening, 'I rather think that Martha *did* come in around the time that Miss Verney is supposed to have returned. She came in from the garden

135

rather late. She said that she had been misled as to the time by the stable clock being slow.'

'Did she indeed?' Dido looked thoughtfully down the sloping drive to the manor house, lying like a crouching beast in the dusk. But, even from here, at the top of the gentle rise, it was not possible to see the buildings grouped behind the house and the face of the stable clock was not visible.

Emma seemed encouraged by her companion's considering expression. 'You begin to believe me, do you not?'

'Oh, I am not sure . . . Not entirely. But what do you suppose Miss Verney did next?'

'She waited here, of course – behind the tree – until her maid came with the chaise.'

'But would not Mr Lomax have seen the chaise taking her up?'

'No, no for I suppose he went away along the path over the downs.' Emma beckoned Dido to the gates and pointed across the dusty high road to the deep, well-worn track which led away through overarching hazels, crossing a small stream upon stepping stones before rising gently towards the uplands. 'That would be the nearest way back to the inn at New Charcombe,' she said, 'and if the gentleman took that path he would be beyond sight and hearing within a few minutes.'

'I suppose he might.'

This notion of Miss Verney playing a trick upon Tom Lomax was, in many lights, a pleasing explanation. And Miss Emma was certainly determined to make it out to be possible. Dido looked thoughtfully at the little white figure beside her. The girl was all energy and smiles as usual, but what was her motive? Why should she be so very determined upon Tom's innocence?

Dido turned back to the driveway with her hand resting on one of the iron gates. 'The trees,' she observed, 'are so very close to the spot upon which Mr Lomax was standing. The exchange would have had to be performed within ten yards of him. How could he have been so very inattentive as not to notice that one young lady had been substituted for the other?'

'Oh! I have just had an idea about that,' cried Emma. 'Miss Kent, are you familiar with the tricks of mountebanks?'

'A little. I have seen them carrying on at fairs, and my Uncle Manners used to delight in performing little tricks which he called "magic" when I was a child. I believe he meant to entertain me.'

'And were you not entertained?'

'No. I confess the performance most often ended in tears and disgrace – on my part, of course, not my uncle's. I never could take pleasure in being deceived. If only he would have told me how the trick was accomplished then I might have been delighted. But a trick without an explanation was as unsatisfactory as a story without an ending.'

'And I think that your feelings are unchanged. You still must have an explanation.'

'Oh yes.'

'Well, I believe the explanation usually lies in distraction. The watcher is made to look away while some little sleight of hand is carried out.'

Dido looked doubtfully about her at the gates and the drive and the house front. 'I will grant,' she said, 'that it is possible to make a child look away for a moment while one card is substituted for another, or a sixpence is concealed beneath a handkerchief. But I cannot believe in a grown man allowing a woman to disappear before his eyes!'

'Is it not because such performances *seem* impossible, that they are given the old superstitious name of "magic"?'

'And you believe that Miss Verney performed magic that afternoon?'

'Yes,' laughed Emma, 'I am quite certain of it.'

Dido looked suspiciously at her pale little face in the gathering dusk. 'You are very eager to see Mr Lomax acquitted,' she said.

Emma only blushed and drew the shawl closer about her shoulders.

'Are you at all acquainted with the young man?' said Dido.

'Oh no. Not at all.'

'But you met him on the day that he called here?'

'No. I was with Mrs Bailey in Exeter that day.'

'You are very concerned about the fate of a young man you have never met.'

'Oh,' cried Emma, 'it is nothing. It is only that I never can bear to see any fellow creature condemned unjustly.' She shivered as if she had but just discovered the evening to be cold, and began to walk back towards the house.

Dido pursued her. 'And where do you think Miss Verney is now?' she asked.

'I do not doubt she is in Worcestershire with her friend Mrs Hargreaves. From all I have heard of that lady, she is the very sort to take part in such a scheme.'

'I sincerely hope you are right. I know that Mr Fenstanton has written to Mr Hargreaves – and every other friend that he knows of . . .' Dido stopped talking as she realised her companion had ceased to listen.

Emma had come to a standstill on the gravel and was staring towards the house.

'Is something wrong, Miss Fenstanton?'

'Oh, no. It is just a light.'

'A light?'

There was, in fact, a great deal of light. The vast window of the hall blazed brightly, throwing its beams out onto the terrace, turning the clematis stems into a delicate, dark tracery, and the box hedges into long solid blocks of shadow. The faint sound of music reached them on the still evening air, proving that dancing was yet in progress.

But Emma was not looking at the hall window or the terrace. She raised a finger slowly. 'There,' she said, 'there in the east wing. Do you see a light?'

Dido's gaze followed the pointing finger, and she saw a faint light in a window on the first floor of the east wing, the window closest to the main body of the house.

'Now why should anyone go into that part of the house at this hour of the night?' said Emma. 'Those rooms have not been used since my aunt Francine died.'

The two women stood side by side in the dusk and watched as the light disappeared from the first window and appeared a moment later at the next window along.

They watched it move slowly to a third, before finally coming to rest in the fourth – the last in the wing. 'Those were my aunt's apartments,' said Emma. 'But they are all shut up now. Who would want to go there?'

The question stirred Dido into life. She took her companion's arm. 'Let us see who is missing from the company in the hall,' she said.

Chapter Fourteen

The great hall appeared very bright after the gloom of the garden. Extra candles had been set up on the instrument, where one of Mr Parry's sons was obliging the company with a lively Irish air; and the light showed up faces flushed with dancing, the tumbled curls and bright eyes of the ladies – and young men with their cravats awry. The exercise had made everyone warm. Two casements had been opened in the great window and the old tapestries on the walls stirred slightly in the draught of night air, making the shadowy huntsmen and stags appear to move among the woven trees. Moths had found their way into the room and were executing their own dances about the candle flames.

Dido's eye moved quickly over the five couple of dancers. Mr George was manoeuvring the particularly large and unwieldy Mrs Parry down the set. Mrs Bailey was standing opposite the youngest of the Parry sons – who looked painfully embarrassed by his situation.

And there was one lady disengaged. Miss Gibbs was sitting glumly in the window seat, plying her fan and endeavouring (unsuccessfully) to look as if she did not care about dancing.

As Dido skirted round the set and made her way to the

window, she took another rapid survey of the room – and found one gentleman missing.

'Oh,' she cried, approaching Martha with a look of sympathy. 'You are out of luck to have no partner! Where is Mr Lancelot Fenstanton?'

'He went off just before the dance began,' sighed Martha. 'A servant came and whispered something to him and he was off saying he must look at a sick horse. But he said he would be back before the dance was finished.' As she spoke, Martha cast no very friendly look at Emma who had now curled herself like a basking cat into the window seat. Poor Miss Gibbs was no doubt calculating that her dance was lost entirely. When the gentleman returned he would ask his cousin.

Dido's eyes strayed from the look of resentment to the wide staircase. But the hall was so well lit as to render the gallery above all darkness. She was just wondering whether, on the pretence of visiting her aunt, she might escape and look into the east wing, when Mr Lancelot himself appeared from behind the carved screen and hurried towards them.

Both girls turned to him and Dido noticed that, beyond the bulk of his partner, Mr George was watching too, very eager for his daughter to enter the dance on her cousin's arm.

Mr Lancelot stopped, bowed and surveyed the girls with a smile – and then he turned to Dido. 'Miss Kent, I have not yet had the pleasure of dancing with you since you have been at Charcombe. I hope you will indulge me now.'

He had succeeded in surprising everyone. Martha looked mortified. Emma was smiling good-humouredly;

142

but her father appeared to be upon the point of exploding with rage. Dido offered her hand in confusion, her mind momentarily distracted from the pressing question of why anyone should wander about a disused part of the house in the hours of darkness.

But, by the time he had handed her across the set, she was sufficiently accustomed to her position of honour to say: 'I hope your horse is recovering, Mr Fenstanton.'

'Ha! My horse?'

'The sick horse that you were called away to look at,' she said – her suspicions all alive again.

'Oh no!' he cried cheerfully. 'I shall not bore you with talk of my horse. All the world knows that ladies despise gentlemen who soliloquise upon their horses. If you find me such a dull partner, you may never consent to dance with me again.' And he began immediately to talk of Devonshire: of its beauties, its castles and its fine prospects, and of the many places which he hoped she would be able to visit during her stay at Charcombe.

It was all very delightful. But, before Dido gave herself up entirely to the pleasure of dancing with a charming (and remarkably sure-footed) man, she did spare time to consider that although the passage behind the screen might have brought Mr Lancelot through the back of the house from the stables, it might also have furnished a route from the backstairs and the first floor of the east wing.

And then, as they joined hands and danced down the set, she looked at the dark shoes flying beside her across the flagged floor. They were remarkably clean. They certainly did not give her partner the appearance of a man who had been called away to hurry into a stable yard.

Chapter Fifteen

. . . I am quite determined to look into the east wing this morning, Eliza. I shall do it just as soon as the housemaids have finished their work upon the stairs and the gallery. It is not long after seven, but I have already been walking in the grounds. I hope that my aunt will sleep another two hours – it may be three, for she was remarkably restless last night. I found her awake and full of complaints when I came up from the dancing in the hall.

Now, what is your opinion, Eliza? Why should Mr Lancelot – or anyone else – go into a deserted part of the house in the dark? What business there could be so very urgent as to call a host away from his guests?

That is the most <u>pressing</u> question in my head this morning. Though it is by no means the <u>only</u> one. For my thoughts run a great deal too upon Miss Emma and her theories and information.

Emma Fenstanton is an odd, contradictory little creature, with her pretty ways that seem calculated to ensnare lovers, her avid reading of such very <u>worthy</u> books, and her strong opinions which deride the entire male sex. She is an intriguing mixture of the frivolous and the serious. I cannot make her out at all, and so it is very difficult to judge exactly what she would be about.

144

Why did she come out to join me yesterday evening? Why was she so very determined to tell her unlikely tale of Miss Verney's deception? Perhaps it was no more than the pleasure of exercising her fancy. But somehow I think it was more than that. Her whole heart seemed to be in the attempt to prove Tom Lomax innocent — and yet she says that she has never met the man for whom she was pleading so earnestly.

Can I trust her? In particular, can I trust the information which she supplied about Miss Verney?

The character which she gave the absent young lady is, I believe, of the first importance. And this I have some cause to rely upon. For Miss Emma's description of 'cautious' accords very well with the opinions of Mr Lancelot and Mrs Bailey — both of whom have described Miss Verney as 'sensible'. They have both — in their own ways — expressed to me the same surprise that the young lady should run away. And so it would seem that in suddenly removing herself from Charcombe Manor, Miss Verney was acting against her character.

So, what might have prompted a normally cautious girl to behave so very incautiously? Did love overpower her reason?

Miss Fenstanton, of course, has assured me that Miss Verney is <u>not</u> in love with Tom Lomax — that she doubts his character, believes him to be mercenary. But upon this point Miss Emma's testimony stands alone . . .

And it is rather contradicted by Mr Tom's own behaviour. When I spoke to him upon the promenade, everything about him declared his belief in the young lady's affection . . .

Has she deluded him?

Such a delusion would accord well with Miss Fenstanton's tale of a trick, though it does not make the execution of that trick any less impossible.

Well, I must seek further information on this point. I shall apply to Miss Gibbs; I shall ask _her_ opinion as to whether her friend is genuinely attached to Tom Lomax.

I have already pursued one little enquiry which Miss Emma's information suggested. I was particularly struck by her account of Miss Gibbs complaining that the stable clock was slow. When I walked out just now I visited the stable yard and found that the clock was indeed telling the wrong time. I asked young Charlie about it and he confirmed that 'it's almost allus slow, miss. I puts it right every Thursday morning but by Friday that's starting to get behind agin.'

I consider this information to be of the greatest significance – but I do not yet know exactly what to make of it.

Well, it is half after seven now and I am in hopes of finding the stairs and gallery empty. But, before I leave you, I shall just mention another little problem which is disturbing my poor brain: the fishwives.

During our dance I broached this subject with Mr Lancelot – suggested to him that a rumour of Miss Verney's disappearance might have spread despite his best efforts. But he was sanguine, quite certain that the matter had not been bruited abroad. So I cannot help but wonder how those two women in Old Charcombe came to know about it.

Well, I must be about my business. But I shall leave this letter open so that I may tell you of anything I find in the east wing . . .

* * *

When Dido crept along the passageway from her room and stepped onto the gallery, she saw that the hall below was deserted – except for Miss Fenstanton who was just disappearing once more into her favourite room: the library.

She paused for a moment leaning on the rail of the gallery, wondering – and not for the first time – just why Miss Emma visited the library so very often. She never seemed to take any book from it . . .

But the sounds of wakening in the bedchambers behind her roused her abruptly from this rather interesting consideration, reminding her to make the most of the opportunity for getting into the east wing unobserved.

She hastened forward, moving as quietly as she could. She had almost reached the door which led into the deserted part of the house, when a voice called from the hall below.

'Ha! Miss Kent. I thought I heard the sound of your little feet!'

She turned with a sinking heart to find Mr Lancelot Fenstanton just emerging from his business room at the back of the hall.

'I wonder if I might intrude upon your valuable time,' he said, and there was nothing to be done but to smile and descend reluctantly.

Mr Lancelot stood for a moment in the shadow of the stairs and ran a troubled hand through his hair. His face was once more that of a little boy unhappily engaged upon his lesson. 'I have a visitor in my room,' he said, almost in a whisper.

'It is very early for callers.'

'But this caller does not wish to be seen by my guests. Nor,' he added hastily, 'do I wish it. For I think they would be angry with me for admitting him.'

Dido was intrigued. 'But you do not fear my anger?' she said.

'No, no. For I'll tell you what, Miss Kent, I rather fancy you and I understand one another. I am sure *you* will agree that it's only humane to talk to the gentleman.'

Dido was wondering a little about this confidence which he seemed to place in her, when he swept all such thoughts from her head by adding, 'My visitor is Mr William Lomax.'

She was dimly aware of Mr Fenstanton explaining that Mr Lomax had come to talk over the danger in which his son presently stood; and that, understanding Dido to have met the young man yesterday, he had asked particularly if he might speak with her. But the greater part of her attention was taken up with the thought that Mr Lomax was here, now, in the house.

'You do not wish to see him?' asked Mr Lancelot, misunderstanding her hesitation. 'Please do not distress yourself! You need not be bothered by him. Why! Just say the word and I'll have the footmen throw the fellow bodily from the house!'

Laughing in spite of herself, Dido assured him that there was no need to summon his men – she was, in fact, very happy to talk to Mr Lomax who was 'an old acquaintance. And,' she added more seriously as they both turned towards the door of his room, 'I am very grateful for your liberality in admitting him.'

She entered the untidy, masculine little room, with a multitude of emotions boiling within her. But, from the moment she saw Mr Lomax rising hastily from the high-backed chair beside the hearth, everything else was swallowed up in concern. There was such a pallor to his well-cut features, such suffering gravity in the solemn grey eyes as inflicted an almost physical pain upon her.

Hardly knowing what she was about, she hurried forward with hands outstretched. She recollected herself and made her curtsey just in time; but never before had she wished so fervently that she had consented to their engagement – for only such a connection could authorise her to go to him now, to comfort him as she longed to do.

She held out her hand, he folded it firmly in his own.

'It is very kind of you to agree to see me, Miss Kent,' he said with a formality which was all for their host, while the pressure of his hand spoke a warmer greeting.

'I am in my way to visit my son – in the village lock-up,' he said when they were all seated. 'And Mr Fenstanton has told me that you saw him yesterday – before the constables . . . that is, before we learnt of Mr Brodie's death.'

'I did.'

'And how did he seem?' The words burst out of him. 'Did he seem worried? Apprehensive? Did he seem as if . . . ?' He stopped, unable to continue.

There was a silence, broken only by the cracking of sticks in the newly lit fire.

Mr Lancelot rose to his feet. 'Perhaps,' he said courteously, 'this painful discussion would be easier without a looker-on.' And, when neither of his guests opposed the suggestion, he withdrew.

As the door closed behind him, Dido abandoned propriety – and her chair. She drew a footstool close beside Mr Lomax, and, sitting down upon it, looked up into his eyes. They were fearful and wretched, clouded with pain. In the leaping light of the flames, the muscles of his throat moved. He swallowed hard, sought her hand and held it tightly. 'Tom has but four days,' he stammered. 'On Saturday the judges will arrive in Exeter to hold the county assizes. He will be tried . . . and . . .' He was unable to go on.

'He is innocent,' said Dido with every ounce of certainty she could find within her, abandoning every doubt, determined to make him believe it; determined almost to *make* Tom innocent – if that was what was needed to ease his father's pain. Because this pain *had* to be relieved. She could not bear to look upon it. The near approach of the trial was a great shock to her, but she was determined to give no hint of it in her manner. 'I know he is innocent,' she said calmly. 'We shall prove that he is.'

'No,' he said quietly. 'No, *I* shall prove it. I do not wish you to be concerned in this business any more than is absolutely necessary.'

'You are too cruel!'

'Cruel?' His brows shot up as surprise pierced through his misery.

'Yes,' she said. 'Could *you* bear to stand by and do

150

nothing if you saw *me* unhappy? Would you not wish to do all that you could to put things right?'

He simply shook his head – unwilling to argue with her.

'You know you would.'

'And *you* know,' he said, succumbing to dispute in spite of himself, 'what my reply must be. Our roles cannot be reversed. It is only natural that a man should face danger and exertion for a woman he esteems. But no man of honour would allow a lady to be drawn into trouble on his behalf.'

'And what if the lady wishes to be drawn into trouble?'

'In that case, the gentleman must protect her from her own poor judgement.'

'Then the gentleman is a blockhead!'

'I thank you for the compliment.'

Their eyes locked and they sat for a minute in uneasy silence.

'If you do not require my help,' she asked at last, 'why have you come here?'

He made no answer, but only put his hand to his brow.

'I have you there, have I not?'

'Ah! But I did not actually deny that I wished for your *help*,' he attempted. 'I only said that I would take upon myself the entire *danger* of proving my son innocent . . .'

'This is sophistry!' she cried. 'Admit that you need me!'

He only smiled and shook his head. He had never yet admitted that she had won an argument – and she doubted that he ever would (though she was determined not to cease trying for it).

'I will admit,' he said, 'that your *information* might be very useful to me. Will you tell me about your meeting with Tom yesterday?'

She gave up the point (for the time being) and began her account – taking care to dwell upon every detail which showed his son to have been at ease and completely unsuspicious of the calamity which was about to befall him. Lomax listened with lids half veiling his eyes, his chin set firmly – like a man enduring pain in silence. She noticed the bruised appearance of his cheekbones again and it hurt her badly. She made up her mind to avoid quarrelling with him if she possibly could.

As she at last faltered into silence, he turned a searching look upon her. 'Tom asked for your assistance?'

'Yes.'

'In God's name! My son is the most selfish—' He broke off and sat for some time with his hand to his brow, and such a look upon his face as must silence Dido. So very painful a combination of anger and concern was something which only a parent could comprehend, and she could only watch it with silent respect.

'Tom has placed me in an impossible situation,' he confessed at last. 'Against all my wishes I have no choice. I *must* ask a further favour of you.'

'Oh?'

He spread his hands helplessly. 'He will not see me. He will not allow me to visit him unless . . .'

'Unless?'

'Unless I bring you to him.'

Though she did not doubt that Tom's reasons were

selfish, she was exceedingly grateful for his insistence. But she looked down demurely – it would not do to exult. He was quite capable of changing his mind and denying Tom's request. 'Then I shall come with you straightaway,' she said.

'No!' he cried, aghast. 'I do not yet know how he is housed – what manner of place the gaol is. I must at least be sure it is fit for you to visit.'

The impulse of romance was to cry out that she did not care – that she would go into the darkest, most wretched prison in the world for his sake. But romance is not always kind. Such a statement would only exalt herself at his expense – and do nothing at all to make him comfortable. Upon this point it was better not to argue.

'I shall make enquiries about the gaol directly,' he said, jumping to his feet with an air of renewed purpose. 'And then I must continue the search for the young lady.' He paused with his hand upon the back of the chair. 'I understand that Mr Fenstanton has written to the intimate friend in Worcestershire. So I think I had better seek out Miss Verney's other acquaintance. This morning I shall ride to Taunton and speak to her teachers and fellow pupils at the school there. Perhaps one of them may have information to give.'

'That is a good thought,' said Dido, rising from her stool and accompanying him to the door. But, before they parted, she laid her hand upon his arm. 'Perhaps,' she said, 'it might be as well to make enquiries about Miss Verney's *character* too.'

'Her character?'

'Yes. I hear such very contradictory accounts of her within this house. I fear that some of my informants are not telling the truth. But her teachers in particular – if they have had charge of her for some years – should be able to say whether she is the kind of young lady to elope; or to tell what other cause might make her run away.'

Chapter Sixteen

Dido understood Mr Lomax too well to press for an immediate visit to the gaol; but the waiting was painful. After he was gone – hurrying away before the other house guests were stirring – she found it absolutely necessary to pace about the hall, railing inwardly against the inconveniences which delicacy places upon the female sex; though her rational mind could not help but concede that, of all the hardships endured by womankind, this sort of anxious protection was the most kindly intentioned.

She was longing to talk to Tom. She wished to be 'getting on', as she expressed it to herself. There was so little time, and what could she do, shut up here in the house . . . ?

By chance, as this impatient thought crossed her mind, she found that she had come to the foot of the staircase and, looking up it, she remembered her plan for visiting the mysterious east wing.

She looked about; the hall and gallery above were both deserted.

She ran once more up the stairs and this time reached the end of the gallery and the interesting door which led into the deserted part of the house. Her hand was actually upon the latch, when again a voice called out to stop her.

'Lord! Miss Kent! You are up and running about very early!' Miss Gibbs was just emerging onto the gallery from her chamber. She yawned widely and approached the door. 'I declare I have not slept a wink again, there was such a crying in the night! And I could not run a step until after I have ate my breakfast!'

Dido said something rather foolish about the beauty of the morning making one energetic; but Miss Gibbs was not to be got rid of.

'Where are you going?' she asked bluntly. Her eyes were red with sleeplessness and the curls about her face were once more singed. (How, wondered Dido, could any woman – even one as clumsy as Miss Gibbs – make the same mistake again and again when dressing her hair?)

'I confess that I was attempting to creep into the east wing unobserved. For I have a great curiosity to see the whole house.'

'Oh well! Then I shall come with you,' said Martha and, without waiting to hear whether her company was wanted, she threw open the door, crashing it loudly against the wall. Martha Gibbs was certainly not the ideal companion for a covert mission.

And it soon appeared that she had her own reasons for seeking a private conference, for she stepped forward eagerly, preventing Dido from passing through the door. 'Have you found out anything about Tish?' she said in her flat, forthright way.

'I do not yet know what has become of her,' Dido replied cautiously. 'But I have made one or two discoveries. And,' she added, thinking that since she could not rid herself of the young lady's company she might as well take advantage of it, 'there is a question or two I should like to ask of you, Miss Gibbs.'

'Oh, but—' Martha looked wary.

'For example,' said Dido, looking about to be sure they were not observed and speaking low, 'what is your friend's opinion of Mr Tom Lomax? Does she admire him? Or does she . . . distrust him?'

Martha frowned immediately. 'Why should she think bad of him?' she demanded.

'Perhaps she might suspect that he was pursuing her for the sake of her fortune.'

'Oh, but Miss Kent, he ain't like that at all!' cried Martha. 'He is the most delightful young man in the world!'

'And does Miss Verney—' Dido began, but Miss Gibbs was not to be stopped.

'And it is all nonsense, you know, what they are saying about him wanting Tish's money. For he ain't mercenary in the least – he is all for love.'

'Is he indeed? And may I ask how you are able to speak of it with such certainty?'

'Oh!' Miss Gibbs blushed furiously and looked down upon the floor. 'Oh, I overheard him telling Tish about it – quite by accident, of course. I was not meaning to listen, Miss Kent. I would not for the world have you think bad of me.'

'I understand. As a chaperone sometimes one cannot help but hear . . .'

'Yes! That's just how it was! And so you see, I heard him telling Tish that he loved her so much he did not care about the money one jot and . . . and he said that he would want to marry her just the same if she had not a penny in the world! So you see—'

But just then there came the sound of Mrs Bailey's voice, the tread of her feet upon the stairs. Seizing Dido's arm, Miss Gibbs hurried her through the door, into the east wing and across the dark lobby beyond. She paused, listening as if she feared pursuit. Her face was still red, her eyes wide in the sudden gloom, and the air of a thing pursued was compounded by her rather rapid breathing.

Dido waited in silence for an explanation of this strange urgency.

To the right there stretched an uncarpeted passageway. The passage windows were all shuttered, but, upon one side, three doors stood open at regular intervals, admitting pale oblongs of daylight from the three rooms beyond. There was a musty smell of a place long shut away, and a slight smell of damp and decay besides. The plaster of the walls and ceiling had crumbled in places, dusting the uneven floorboards with white. Dust motes floated in the shafts of light and the silence of the place reasserted itself as the echo of the closing door faded.

'I must know what has happened to Tish,' whispered Martha at last. 'Papa has writ to say I must go home straight away. But I *can't* leave Charcombe now . . . Not before I know that Tish is safe.'

Dido looked levelly at her companion. 'Miss Gibbs,' she said quietly, 'what do *you* suppose is the cause of Miss Verney's disappearance? Do you suppose that Mr Tom Lomax—'

'He ain't got anything to do with her going,' said Martha quickly.

'But how can you be so very certain?'

'Because I know it is some scheme of Mrs Bailey's. Tish says Mrs B has been wanting rid of her these last two years.'

Dido could only stare in surprise and wait for more information.

Miss Gibbs bit furiously at her lip. Her eyes rolled about and her fingers twisted in the chain of a locket she wore about her neck. At last she burst out with: 'Mrs B has been against Tish ever since she married Mr B.'

'And their marriage took place two years ago?'

'Yes. Till then, Tish says, everything was very pleasant. Mr Bailey was always very kind to her. But then he married – and Mrs B was jealous of Tish being so pretty, you know, and was always making trouble for her. And then last autumn they quarrelled.' Martha hesitated, her hand twisting her necklace so tight she seemed to be in danger of breaking it. 'Did you know there had been a great falling out between Tish and Mrs B?'

'No. What was the cause?'

'It was about us going into Worcestershire to visit Melia. Mrs B didn't like it at all. She don't like Tish going anywhere without her. She watches her like a hawk.'

'But Mrs Bailey permitted the journey into Worcestershire?'

'Yes, she did,' said Miss Gibbs with a strangely suspicious shake of the head. 'Though I was quite sure she never would. It was all very odd. It happened very sudden when we was all in town together. I had a headache and stayed at our lodgings; and Mrs B and Tish went off to dine with the Whittakers and on to the theatre afterwards. And when Tish got home that night she comes to me laughing and says it's all settled, but I must not ask how. We was off to Worcestershire next day and Mrs B sent us the whole way in her own coach. But she's been in a great rage ever since . . . And Tish has always said Mrs B would get her own back if she could . . . and now Tish is gone. And Lord! I don't know what to think!'

Dido stood in silence for a moment, struggling to comprehend. From beyond the closed door could be heard footsteps on the stairs and the voices of the household gathering for breakfast.

Martha turned fearfully towards the sounds. 'I can't say any more. She mustn't know we've talked. But you will find out things, won't you? You'll find Tish – and prove to everyone that Mr Lomax ain't done her any harm. But I mustn't seem to help you.'

'Why? Why is such caution necessary?'

Martha only shook her head like a startled horse.

'Miss Gibbs, why are you so very frightened?'

But Martha was already opening the door and peering about its edge. 'I must go to breakfast before I'm missed.' Then she was out through the door and striding hurriedly along the deserted gallery.

Left alone in the east wing, where every movement of her feet echoed about the crumbling walls, Dido fell to wondering about Martha Gibbs. Why was the girl so very frightened? Had she been threatened? Were her suspicions of Mrs Bailey well founded, or was she too much influenced by her friend's account of her stepmother? Nothing about Miss Gibbs suggested a very deep thinker and it was obvious that she had been used to defer to the more forceful Letitia. She had, perhaps, a little too much of a plain girl's trust and respect for beauty.

For several minutes Dido stared along the gloomy passage with its dusty patches of sunlight. The only thing she could be sure of was that Miss Gibbs knew more than she was prepared to tell. Fear was certainly keeping her silent upon some very material points.

Well, she must look for another opportunity of gaining the girl's confidence. But now she must complete her exploration, before she was missed at the breakfast table.

She started cautiously along the passage, the boards creaking and the fragments of fallen plaster crunching under her feet at every step . . .

She stopped abruptly and studied the dust upon the floor, making out the vague shape of footprints. Someone had walked here recently. Whoever it was had walked rather lightly and it was not possible to see the prints clearly; but they *might* be the prints of Mr Lancelot's dancing shoes . . .

Except that those dancing shoes had been perfectly clean when he returned to the hall! She remembered searching them for evidence of the stables.

She looked down at her own feet in the block of light falling through one of the doors. There was already a layer of plaster dust covering the toes, turning the dark, serviceable leather grey. There had certainly been no such dust on the feet of her dancing partner.

Frowning thoughtfully, she looked into the first room of the wing. It was a dismal sight: a bedchamber stripped of its smaller furnishings, leaving only a mouldering bed and an oak linen press – items too large to be easily moved.

And it was the same in every room. In the next room a bird had fallen down the chimney at some time, soiling the bed hangings and covering the floor with feathers in its frantic efforts at escape. But the third, and last, room was the most desolate of all. Here so much plaster had fallen from the ceiling that the canopy of the bed had collapsed beneath its weight, skewing the curtains and spilling a great heap of rubble and white dust onto the fine yellow silk of the coverlet.

Dido stood in the doorway, quite at a loss to understand why anyone should come here by candlelight. There was nothing in this room that could be of use, or interest, to anyone. And yet she was sure that it was here, to the last room, that the candle had been carried. She remembered the light's faint journey along the wing and imagined someone carrying a candle down the passageway, the light falling through the open doors and illuming each window in turn until it came here, to the end . . .

Except this was not the end. It could not be. She now had a vivid memory of counting the windows – there had been *four*. It was in the fourth window that the light had come to rest, not the third.

She stepped back into the passage. But there was no door beyond this one. She moved into the room – the

162

floorboards groaning alarmingly beneath her. There was certainly only one window in this room – as there had been in all the others. She turned to the far wall of the chamber which was half obscured by the bed hangings. The door to the fourth room must be there.

She drew aside the torn, dirty silk, sending gritty dust into her hair and eyes. And there was the door. An unremarkable little door, such as one might find in any old house leading from a bedchamber into a dressing room. But there was one very remarkable thing about this door. There were three bolts fixed to it; sturdy bolts, slightly rusted, but still sound.

Two of the bolts were undone, the third half closed to hold the door in place. When Dido set her hand to draw this last bolt, it moved smoothly as if it had been recently released.

The door creaked open and there was the last room of the east wing: a narrow dressing room, bare, but a little cleaner than the outer room. Some of the plaster dust had been brushed from the floor; the counterpane on the small bed shaken. The only other furnishings were a table and a chair beside the tiny fire grate, and they had likewise been cleared of dust; rather roughly – the arc of a swiping hand or cloth was still visible. But it was the window which drew Dido's eye. It was a casement window in solid stone embrasures. And into the old grey stones had been fastened a thick set of iron bars.

The little room was, in fact, a prison.

Dido sat down upon the bed; for several minutes she was too shocked for rational thought. But her head was full of a great many impressions. She felt the desolation of this deserted wing and the contrast that it made with the inhabited portion of the house, where the company was drinking its chocolate and coffee and eating its toast and chops. She felt the oddness of a hidden, empty place in the midst of life and bustle . . . And then her heart chilled at the wretched evidences in this room . . . evidences of restraint . . . imprisonment . . .

She looked from the bolts upon the door to the bars at the window and gradually reason began to assert itself over the horror of the moment.

This room had been made secure, and made secure for a purpose. The existence of a prison argued for a prisoner. She went to the window and set her hand to the bars. They chilled her hand and, as she slowly uncurled her fingers, she saw that they had left a red stain of rust. Rain had made its way in through the old window leads and, from the base of the bars, a thin red trickle lay, like blood, across the grey stone . . .

And there, beside the rust stain, was something scratched in the stone. She peered more closely at the place where daylight fell on the window sill. There were a great many scratches which looked like letters unsuccessfully formed. She studied them, but could make out nothing until she came at last to a pair of initials carved – as one sees such things sometimes scratched by tourists upon castle walls or druid stones. Two letters . . . She looked closer; traced the marks with a finger. FF? Yes, that was what it appeared to be. And four straight lines had been cut to enclose the letters. She looked along the window ledge and saw the same two letters, framed in the same manner, again – and again. And then, upon the stone mullion, she found them repeated three more times.

The repetition spoke of the monotony of a confined life. But the engraving was not freshly cut. It appeared to be years old – as old perhaps as the rusted bars. And yet, someone had recently been here. The dust had been disturbed – and the bolts upon the door had been drawn . . .

Chapter Seventeen

. . . The existence of this prison room is excessively disturbing! For whom was it designed? Francine Fenstanton? The carved initials suggest it. And Miss Emma seemed to identify the chambers in the east wing as belonging to her . . .

But the room has been visited recently. And I confess that the discovery has raised an alarming notion in my head. It has revived my idea of Mr Lancelot acting a part from a horrid novel. But now I am not imagining him consigning an unwilling Miss Verney to a remote farmhouse, but contriving instead to shut her away in his own home. It would be a more convenient and economical villainy. And – upon the evidence of fiction – one not infrequently resorted to; though it is a stratagem more often employed by the lords of castles in the Alps and Pyrenees than by country gentlemen in modest English manor houses.

But the idea that Miss Verney is still within the house haunts me. Eliza, I wonder whether this is the secret which Miss Gibbs is keeping, the information which she dare not share. I <u>must</u> talk with her alone again – and find out all I can about the circumstances of Miss Verney's disappearance. I hope I may manage it when the dressing hour arrives . . .

But, for the time being, I am confined to our aunt's chamber. She has been restless and ill at ease since I returned from Charcombe yesterday with tidings of the murder; and this morning she is suffering from a headache of the 'squeezing, throbbing' variety. She has insisted upon Mr Sutherland being summoned and he is now in consultation with her.

Dido looked across the chamber. The blinds were closed – for sunlight was a great aggravation of the squeezing and throbbing – and it was extremely gloomy. On the other side of the single candle sat the elderly maid, Benson, straining to see her thread as she stitched away at a new pair of green silk slippers for her mistress. Beyond her, Mrs Manners lay gracefully upon her sofa, her hands clasped upon her breast. The long, lean figure of the physician loomed attentively over her, murmuring in sympathetic tones . . .

Mr Sutherland is at present applying 'electrical tractors' to the palpitations in Aunt Manners' temples. And, much to my astonishment, he seems to be having some success in relieving her symptoms.

When this novel treatment was first mooted, I imagined some large, extravagant machine such as one sometimes sees demonstrated in Bath and Tunbridge. But the electrical tractors are in fact nothing more than two tapering metal rods, rather like short, thick knitting pins, which must, according to Mr Sutherland, be applied to the seat of pain to 'draw off the poisonous electrical fluid which is causing the poor lady's suffering'.

He is busy about it now. The doctor sits beside the sofa, talking constantly in a low, soothing voice and passing the 'tractors' to and fro across my aunt's brow. He has been engaged upon the process for above a quarter of an hour, so I suppose there is a great deal of noxious fluid to be disposed of. Alarmed by his description of the process, I sent Benson to the kitchen to fetch a bowl in which this poisonous substance of pain might be collected. But I notice that it has not been needed; the electrical fluid would seem to be entirely invisible . . .

Dido looked again towards the sofa where Mrs Manners lay, with an expression of unusual tranquillity on her face. The doctor was leaning intently over his patient – the useless earthenware bowl on the table at his elbow. The medical process seemed to be reaching its end; he was talking ever more quietly, the metal rods were moving more slowly.

'Och, now,' he was saying gently, 'the troublesome pain has all been drawn off. You had better sleep. Sleep peacefully and when you wake you will feel rested and refreshed.'

He ceased speaking, there was a long sigh from Benson and a snap as she broke off her thread, followed by slow steady breathing from Mrs Manners – who would seem to have done just as the doctor advised and fallen asleep. Which was quite remarkable, there having been no medicine of any colour consumed.

The doctor rose slowly and wrapped the electrical tractors in a square of white silk, folding in the corners with neat, meticulous movements and admirable precision.

'She will probably sleep now for an hour,' he said

quietly to Dido, stretching his long body which was stiff with stooping over his patient. 'A little tea when she awakes, perhaps. And – as I have explained to her – a little gentle exercise would do her a great deal of good. I shall call again tomorrow. The tractors must be applied daily.'

Dido, who was by no means at ease with invisible fluids and odd devices, opened her mouth to say . . . she hardly knew what. But then she caught Mr Sutherland's sharp eye, and looked at her peacefully sleeping aunt . . . And was silenced.

She accompanied him out of the room, along the passageway and onto the gallery which ran above the hall. Here, where the light was stronger, Sutherland stopped and turned to her, his blue eyes disconcertingly sharp beneath the fall of white hair and the beetling black brows. 'I think, Miss Kent, that you do not believe the tractors have any power.'

Dido coloured uncomfortably.

'Aye!' He shook his head with a smile. 'You do not deny it, do you? And yet, neither can you deny that Mrs Manners' symptoms have been relieved.'

'I am very glad that my aunt's headache is cured, but . . .'

'But?'

His look was inviting; she could not resist speaking her thoughts. 'But imagination is a powerful force, Mr Sutherland. It has long been observed that in the matter of health imagination will always play its part, and whether we regard ourselves as well or ill may depend a great deal upon our expectations.'

'You would argue that her faith in the tractors was enough to work her cure?'

'I am not sure that her faith rested in the electrical devices,' admitted Dido with a smile. 'I think perhaps it was vested in the man applying them. You are an old acquaintance of my aunt's, and she was delighted when I delivered your card to her; she immediately felt that you would be able to help her.'

'Och, I see what you are about, Miss Kent! You mean to flatter me out of my argument! But perhaps you can explain to me how this powerful force of imagination and expectation operates upon the constitution.'

'I hardly know . . .'

'And yet you do not doubt its effect! You cannot see this imagination. You cannot,' he added with gentle mockery, 'gather this imagination in a bowl. But you prefer to believe in *its* mysterious operation rather than in the force of electricity, the existence of which has long been proven.'

'But . . .' She stopped and stood for a moment gazing into his brilliant eyes, noticing how the black centres were oddly small – and yet seemed to contain within them tiny images of her own face. She could find no argument against him; though it was not in her nature to believe that there was no such argument.

'Well, well,' he said at last. 'We are at least agreed that *something* is giving dear Mrs Manners relief from her headache. And I am sure you wish the treatment to continue.'

'Oh, yes, of course,' said Dido – suddenly very aware of how much a quietly sleeping, pain-free aunt was to be preferred over a querulous, irritable one. 'Yes I quite agree.'

'Then,' he said with a bow, 'I shall wait upon the lady again tomorrow. But I shall not come until the evening, for I understand that you must all look at Mr Brodie's body in the morning.'

He started down the stairs, but his mentioning Mr Brodie had turned Dido's thoughts from electrical treatments.

'You mentioned to me, Mr Sutherland,' she said, trotting down the stairs after him, 'that you were with Mr Brodie on the last evening of his life.'

'Yes, I was.' He stood still, looking at her rather curiously. 'I took my dinner at the inn that night and stayed until about eleven o'clock.'

'Was Mr Brodie an acquaintance of yours?'

'No, it was merely a chance meeting at an inn. We played a few hands of cards together – drank a little whisky. I confess,' he added with a wink, 'that a wager and a dram are my two great vices.'

Dido paused, her fingers tapping on the banister. 'Then you do not know who in this house was a friend to Mr Brodie?'

'No.' And, though he had answered freely when her questions related to himself, there was something repressive in his voice now. He seemed . . . offended . . . no, not quite offended, but evasive . . .

His manner made Dido curious; and the opportunity of talking to someone who had met the dead man was not to be missed. 'What kind of a man was Mr Brodie?' she asked. 'For you know, one cannot help but wonder about him. Dying always makes a person famous for a while.'

'Aye! And being murdered raises a fellow's fame even further!'

'You blame me for being inquisitive?' She searched his face; but it was utterly still, impossible to read. All she seemed to see were those disconcerting little reflections of herself staring out of his eyes.

'No, lassie,' he said at last, 'I don't blame you.' He turned away and began to walk rather briskly down the stairs. 'But I cannot tell you much. I was scarcely in the man's company an hour. He seemed . . . unpolished and argumentative.'

'And what did you and he – and Mr Tom Lomax – talk of over your cards and whisky?'

'Chiefly cards and whisky as I recall. Och, yes!' He stopped only three steps from the bottom of the stairs and looked back with a smile. 'I remember – we talked of electricity and animal magnetism.'

'Oh?'

'Aye. Brodie had as poor an opinion of my methods as you have yourself, Miss Kent! He wanted to know whether such treatments were to be trusted. Said he'd heard fellows like me could put a kind of spell on folk and make them do as we wish.'

'Did he indeed? What a horrid idea! And how did you reply to him?'

'I told him if I had power such as that I'd have made folk give me all their money long ago and I'd be set up comfortably on my own estate now – not toiling away in Charcombe.'

He held out his hand and began to take his leave, but just then the outer door opened. Mr George Fenstanton walked into the hall and started up the stairs with little bouncing steps, saw Dido and Sutherland – and stopped abruptly. His breath whistled through his teeth. 'You . . . ?' He glowered at the physician, his face and scalp reddening. 'Why are *you* here?'

Mr Sutherland bowed and explained his attendance upon Mrs Manners – his tone cool, but civil.

'In this house,' whistled Mr George, 'medical men use the *back*stairs.'

'Do they?' replied Sutherland calmly, with a great appearance of interest. 'How very unusual.' He said no more, only stood waiting for Mr George to speak again, his brilliant stare fixed steadily upon the smaller man who was obliged to tilt his head up to meet it.

Dido waited for an angry explosion – but none came. George Fenstanton did not speak another word. After a short silence – filled by the insistent ticking of the hall clock – he turned away with lowered eyes, and, seeming to forget that he had intended to mount the stairs, he moved towards the breakfast room instead.

. . . Well, Eliza, wrote Dido rapidly when she had returned to her aunt's chamber and her writing desk, *what do you say to Mr Sutherland for a murderer?*

If he left the inn at eleven o'clock, it is <u>possible</u> that he returned to meet Mr Brodie behind the inn – and shot him. A doctor's bag would provide an excellent means of concealing a weapon, would it not?

The chief obstacle to this very convenient explanation of

events is a thorough absence of motive. Mr Sutherland says that he had never met Mr Brodie before that night; and it would seem unlikely that he should – in the course only of a card game – conceive such an antipathy as to make the man's death essential to his happiness . . .

But, though I cannot – as yet – find any cause for him being a murderer, I do have reason to suspect that Mr Sutherland knows something of Miss Verney's disappearance. The fishwives' information suggests that he has been the cause of that business being bruited abroad; and his cold meeting with Mr George – together with the remarks of the lady who keeps his house – give a reason for his gossiping.

It would seem there is some animosity between him and the Fenstanton family. And my aunt's rambling remarks under the influence of brown medicine rather suggest that that animosity arose from his attendance upon her sister Francine thirty years ago . . .

Chapter Eighteen

When the dressing bell rang that afternoon, Dido approached Miss Gibbs with a very friendly smile – and an offer of assistance.

'Assistance?' repeated Martha blankly as they climbed the stairs together. 'What kind of assistance?'

'Well, I hope you will not mind my mentioning it, but I have noticed that you have lately had some ill luck in dressing your hair . . .'

'Lord!' Martha's hands flew to cover the burnt curls. 'Does it look so very bad?' she whispered.

'No, no. But,' Dido took her arm, 'I cannot help but wonder *why* you should have the same mishap again and again.'

'I am sure I don't know why, Miss Kent. Lately it just seems to happen so.'

'Well, I hope you will allow me the office of a friend.' They walked together along the gallery and approached Miss Gibbs' room. 'With Miss Verney and her maid gone you have no one to help you – and my sister tells me that I have some skill in arranging hair.'

Martha pushed open the door of her room. 'It is very kind of you I am sure,' she said, running an anxious finger through her hair.

'No trouble at all.' Dido hurried forward into the bedchamber – and came to a sudden standstill.

There was something wrong with the room.

It was very like the room occupied by Mrs Manners. There were the same panelled walls, and a curtained bed facing a casement window. Beyond the bed was a grate with a small fire in it, the flames pale in the afternoon sunshine; there was a closet set into the wall on one side of the grate, and beside that – against the back wall of the room – was the toilette table. Strewn about was all the flotsam common to a young lady's bedchamber: a pair of silk stockings hung over the carved oak footboard of the bed, a shawl had been dropped upon a chair, a length of yellow ribbon was knotted about one of the bedposts, a garter and an open novel lay upon the window sill. There was a smell of face powder and rose water – and burnt hair. It was all remarkably ordinary. And yet . . . something about the place made Dido acutely uneasy. 'What a very . . . *strange* room,' she said.

'Lord, it certainly is!' cried Miss Gibbs. 'Mr Fenstanton is in the right to call it haunted, I'm sure. And if you could hear the odd crying in the night, Miss Kent, you would believe it too.'

'Crying?' repeated Dido, looking about her and trying to understand the cause of her unease, quite determined not to submit to a supernatural explanation.

But Martha was now looking remarkably suspicious and businesslike. 'Was you wanting to ask me more questions about Letitia?' she said. 'Is that why you wanted to come here?'

'Oh no,' said Dido, ashamed that her stratagem had

been so easily seen through. And a little ashamed too of the prejudice which had led her to suppose that because the young lady lacked elegance she must lack penetration too. 'That is . . . Yes, I should like to ask you one or two things. I am sure you will not mind – for it is all in the cause of finding your friend. And we may talk it all over as I arrange your hair.'

Martha protested once more that she had told everything she knew, but she sat down before the toilette table willingly enough and allowed work to commence upon her ruined curls. And, as Dido brushed the hair up and forward to cover the burnt parts, she started upon the subject of Miss Verney's last day at Charcombe Manor.

'What – exactly – can you remember about the day your friend went away?' she asked.

'Nothing. I have told you . . .'

'Who was in the house when you set off for your walk?' Dido paused in her brushing and looked very directly into the eyes of her companion reflected back in the looking glass. The gloomy corner of the room, and the dark, spotted old surface of the glass, gave poor Martha's stare a white and haunted look. 'Miss Fenstanton and Mrs Bailey were gone to Exeter that morning, I believe,' she prompted.

'And Mrs B was all for Tish going with them.'

'But Miss Verney chose to remain at home?' Dido resumed her brushing.

'Yes. We had got a note from Mr Lomax and knew he was to come here that day. So, of course, we were mighty glad to have the others go away because we wanted to see him by ourselves. But there was a fine carry on

177

about it, for I think Mrs Bailey suspected Tish was up to something. And she got awful cross and insisted she go with her to Exeter. But in the end she gave it up and went off in a fine old temper.'

'And only Mr George and Mr Lancelot remained in the house?'

'Yes, but they was in the hall with a lot of papers talking about the new town and how much it is costing and how they are to get funds.'

'I see.' Dido searched with one hand for pins among the ribbons and the court plasters and the phials that cluttered the toilette table. 'And you and your friend received Mr Lomax in the drawing room? You did not talk to the gentlemen in the hall?'

'No.' Martha joined in the search for pins, and found three at last after some hard peering into the gloom. 'Except,' she said, 'just as me and Tish went upstairs to fetch our bonnets, Mr Lancelot looks up. I think Mrs B had set him on to spy on us, you know. "Where are you going?" he says. And Tish was very angry at that, for her spirit is pretty independent.'

Dido pushed home the pins and stood back to observe the effect. 'And what answer did Miss Verney make?'

'Oh, she tossed up her head and said she was going to show Mr Lomax the view from the top of the downs. "Do you mean to go alone with this young fellow?" says Mr Lancelot. All disapproving, you know. "Oh yes," says Tish, as bold as you like, "for it would be beyond Martha's strength to walk so far." And she gave him such a look, as if she would say, "You cannot stop me. *You* are not my guardian."' Martha gave a long, admiring sigh.

'Tish has a very fine spirit. She does not care how she talks to *anyone*.'

'Twenty thousand pounds can give a woman a great deal of spirit,' said Dido as she unwound the ribbon from the bedpost. 'But why should she wish to anger Mrs Bailey – or Mr Fenstanton?'

'Oh, it has been her way lately to defy Mrs B,' said Martha. 'I told you, they have not been friends since Tish persuaded her into letting us go to Melia's house . . . Oh, that *is* clever!'

Dido had wound the yellow ribbon into a bandeau about Martha's head and was now tucking the burnt hair out of sight, while bringing forward some little natural curls brushed up from the back. She finished the task, peered into the glass and – as well as she could judge in the poor light – decided the effect was not unpleasing. 'Well,' she said, sitting down upon the edge of the bed, 'I suppose running away is a fine way of discomposing her guardian. But it is an unusual motive for elopement.'

'No, no!' insisted Martha. 'She has not eloped. I *know* she has not. You must believe me. I cannot tell you how I know it; but I am quite certain that Tish has not—' She stopped abruptly, for she had turned now to plead her cause and saw that her companion was not attending to her. 'Miss Kent? Whatever is wrong? Lord! You look like you have seen a ghost.'

'Oh! No,' said Dido, continuing to stare about her. 'No, there is certainly not a ghost. That is not what is wrong at all.' She jumped up. 'It is not that the room is haunted – that is not what struck me as wrong when I

179

came into it. It is something in the arrangements . . . The toilette table!'

'I beg your pardon.'

Instead of answering, Dido walked to the window and – much to Miss Gibbs consternation – knelt down and fell to studying the carpet. 'I understand now,' she said at last, sitting back upon her heels. 'I understand why you have been burning your hair.'

'My hair? But it was only an accident.'

'An accident repeated again and again.'

'Yes . . .'

'Because you cannot properly see what you are about! Why, I found it myself just now. I could not find the pins because the light was so poor – and I could barely make out your reflection.' She pointed an accusing finger at the inoffensive table. 'Why,' she demanded, 'is the toilette there? No lady should dress her hair with her back to the light. This,' she said, pointing to the floor before her, 'is where it *should* stand: beside the window where the light is good. And until very recently it did stand here. I can see the marks which its legs have left upon the carpet.'

'Oh, yes,' said Martha, 'it did. But Tish did not like it there and had it moved.'

'Why?' Dido jumped to her feet. 'Why would she not let it stand in the light?'

'It was just one of her whims. There is no arguing with Tish when she gets an idea into her head.'

'Indeed.' Dido pressed a knuckle thoughtfully to her lips. 'Perhaps she did not wish to see her own reflection clearly,' she mused. 'Miss Gibbs,' she asked slowly as her

180

mind struggled for understanding, 'has your friend been *unwell* lately?'

'No!' The answer came too quick. Martha had turned her head away – Dido could see nothing but the white neck with little wisps of curls, and the vague image of her face swimming in the dark glass. 'No, Tish has been quite well.'

'Then has she seemed careless of her appearance – depressed in her spirits?'

There was a pause. Martha picked up a piece of court plaster from the clutter on the table and worked it nervously through her fingers. 'Perhaps,' she admitted at last, 'she has been a little low-spirited and unhappy since our coming back from Worcestershire. But she has not been ill. Everyone has said she is in good looks and quite plump.'

Chapter Nineteen

... *Why should any young lady move her toilette table into an obscure corner in which she can scarcely see her face in the glass? I have known some vain women veil their mirrors when the pimples are too terrible to look upon; but Miss Gibbs reports that her friend has lately been in good looks.*

And why was Miss Gibbs so very reluctant to admit that her friend has been unhappy? It almost seemed that she was ashamed to speak of it.

Did this lowness of spirits make Miss Verney wish to escape Charcombe Manor? Or was it the cause of someone else wishing to remove her from the house?

Eliza, I find myself continually drawn in two opposing directions. Sometimes my thoughts are all in favour of an escape, and sometimes I am persuaded that someone else is the author of the young lady's disappearance.

The story of the maid and the chaise <u>might</u> be a fabrication by the guilty party.

And there are three possible 'guilty parties' in my head. Mr Lancelot might be employing some unfair means of persuasion; Mrs Bailey might have designs upon the fortune of a ward for whom she seems to feel little affection; and Mr George might wish to dispose of the inconvenient heiress in order that he may marry his own daughter to the master of

Charcombe. Mr Brodie and his 'information' might have cut across the schemes of any one of them. Perhaps desperation turned one of them into a murderer.

But I cannot approach Mr Parry with accusations against them _all_. I must find out more – and quickly too for it is but four days until the assize judges arrive to hold court in Exeter.

And, unfortunately, I find myself very inconveniently placed for investigation this evening – separated from the rest of the company by two floors!

And this is all on account of Mr Sutherland who, I find, is a remarkably _persuasive_ man. His suggestion of 'a little gentle exercise' carried such force with my aunt that this evening she and I and her maid must climb up here to the long gallery at the top of the house so that she might make use of her father's old chamber horse . . .

I confess that I cannot but find a chamber horse comical, Eliza, particularly when it is employed by such a very _dignified_ woman as our aunt. She sits so very straight upon its springs, holding the high handles so hard that her knuckles are white and she rises and falls in a pretence of riding so very solemnly that I must look away for fear of laughing out loud.

A turn or two about the drawing room might, I am sure, have provided gentle exercise just as well. And I wish we had stayed below so that I might talk with my fellow guests.

But the long gallery is a pleasant enough place. It runs the length of the main house, and has a sloping floor of ancient boards. A pious-looking Fenstanton lady with a rosary and a fine Elizabethan ruff looks down upon my aunt from her picture frame – and disapproves of her activity, I think. There is old woven matting of rushes on the floor which gives

the place a remarkably church-like smell, and the light of the
setting sun is shining through the western window. Benson
sits in its light, sewing upon the green silk slippers . . .

Dido stopped abruptly and looked in wonder at the last three words she had written – as if they were the revealed wisdom of Holy Writ. She laid down her pen and stared at the little maid whose full-moon face was bent industriously over her work. The light of the sunset laid a slightly reddish sheen across the material in her lap; but there was no doubting that it was *green silk*.

There was something wrong here. Here was another of those odd little details – like the placing of the toilette table in the haunted chamber – which made Dido uncomfortable. Details which could no more be left uninvestigated than a pebble in a shoe.

She put aside her writing desk and stood up. 'Benson,' she said – speaking quietly and trusting to the creaking of the springs in the chamber horse to screen her words from her aunt. 'Why are you sewing those slippers?'

The maid started and looked up anxiously, her little hands dropped her work and twisted together. Many years' attendance upon Mrs Manners had made her constitutionally apprehensive of rebuke. 'My mistress has need of them, miss.' She spoke in a whisper – not from fear of being overheard, but because whispering was a habit with her.

'But why?' persisted Dido. 'I mean why *green silk* slippers? Has she not just such a pair which you made on our journey here? She wore them for the first time on the day after we arrived at Charcombe. I remember noting when I put them in the closet that she had already begun to tread down the backs of them.'

'Oh yes, miss!' Relieved understanding flooded across the little round face. 'I did make a pair just last week; but those are spoilt now. They became covered all over in white dust and my mistress said I was to throw them away.'

'White dust?' said Dido trying to sound as if an interest in dust was the most natural thing in the world. 'Do you mean white *plaster* dust?'

'Why yes, miss, I think it was plaster dust.'

Dido was about to ask more but was prevented by a sudden, ominous silence. The creaking of the chamber horse had ceased.

'I have exercised enough,' announced Mrs Manners.

'Oh!' Dido turned and hastily gathered her thoughts. 'Shall we return to the drawing room?'

'No,' said Mrs Manners sitting very erect and eying her niece as if she wished to know what she was about. 'I shall go to my room and rest.'

'But—'

'I shall rest and you shall read to me.'

'But I have no book.'

'Well, I daresay, Miss Dido, you have the wit and the strength to get one from the library, have you not?'

'Yes, Aunt.' Dido stood up and turned to the stairs.

But her aunt seemed to wish to torment her particularly this evening. 'Be sure to bring a *respectable* book,' she said. 'Something sensible. Sermons – or a history perhaps.'

'Yes, Aunt.'

'Providing it has not too many battles in it.'

Dido bit her lip. 'Yes, Aunt.'

'Nor folk having their heads chopped off,' she insisted, still watching closely – almost as if she were deliberately testing. 'I am not accustomed to that sort of unpleasantness.'

'Yes, Aunt.'

'And I do not wish to hear about foreign parts. And none of your novels, please!'

Dido finally reached the stairs and began to run down them with her mind in turmoil.

White plaster dust! Her aunt's slippers had been spoilt with white plaster dust. And there was only one place in Charcombe Manor which could inflict such damage. The east wing!

Dido arrived in the hall rather breathless and found it deserted. But bright light and voices spilt through the half-open door of the drawing room. The door of the library was also ajar and, when she entered, she found one candle burning on a table by the window, with a little Tunbridge-ware workbox beside it.

She took up the candle and began to search the serried rows of books. The gilt lettering of each volume glimmered into prominence as her light passed. *Culpeper's Complete Herbal*, volumes of Shakespeare and Edmund Spenser's *Faerie Queen*. There was nothing very new. Mr Lancelot did not seem to be a great collector of books; there was nothing here which would please her aunt, no sermons or histories.

And Dido's mind was soon wandering from sermons to slippers. She sat down upon the set of steps which gave access to the higher shelves, and thought . . .

On the evening that she had seen the light in the east wing she had made a serious error in her calculations. She had reasoned that the only person who was absent from the hall was Lancelot Fenstanton. But that had been a foolish mistake. *Mrs Manners* had not been in the hall. And, now that she gave the matter some thought, she remembered that her aunt had been particularly restless that evening – that she had, in fact, been still awake when the dancing ended.

But why should Mrs Manners exert herself to walk so far as the east wing? What could be there to interest her?

Dido was suddenly shaken from her reverie by the entrance of Benson – sent by Mrs Manners to enquire why the choosing of a book was taking such a very long time. She jumped up, raised her candle high and looked about desperately for something suitable. The light fell at last upon a chair beside the window on which had been laid aside Miss Fenstanton's new volume of *Blair's Sermons*.

This would serve the present purpose very well – and Dido hoped that Miss Fenstanton would not object to her borrowing it.

She picked it up and ran up to her aunt's chamber, still puzzling over what there could be in the east wing to draw Mrs Manners from the comfort of her bed.

In the bedchamber Dido drew a chair close to her aunt's sofa and began to read. Mrs Manners clasped her hands in her lap, closed her eyes and lifted up her face with that expression of virtuous expectation which is proper to sermon-listening.

Dido started upon a rather dull-looking chapter entitled 'The Rights and Duties of Mankind'.

Grandmama Kent had had a similar taste for having improving books read aloud, and Dido had very early acquired the trick of mechanically producing sounds from a page without the engagement of any part of her brain. Her mouth, once set in motion, could continue well enough. Expression was not possible, but expression was not required. One aimed rather for that soothing monotony which most swiftly produces sleep.

And the long sentences and ponderous tone of this book were well suited to use as a soporific. 'In the present state of society,' she read, 'it seems necessary to go back to first principles in search of the most simple truths . . .'

She yawned and thought how very refreshing it would be to read for once a moralist in charity with his own age. Then, as she continued to pronounce the words insensibly, her mind wandered back to the east wing . . .

It would seem that the apartments at the end of the wing were those of Miss Francine – Mrs Manners' dead sister. Was it sentiment which now took the lady to that ruined chamber? It must be a powerful emotion which could draw such a fastidious woman into that place of dirt and decay; and an uneasy emotion which must be satisfied in secret . . .

Dido turned a page of the book.

'Men . . .' she found herself reading, 'appear to me to act in a very unphilosophical manner when they try to secure the good conduct of women by attempting to keep them always in a state of childhood.'

She stopped reading as a slight familiarity in the words broke upon her consciousness.

Her first thought was that Emma Fenstanton had used remarkably similar words in their talk upon the drive. And her second thought was that Mr Blair would not express such an idea.

There was a small snore from the sofa. Mrs Manners was contriving somehow to sleep soundly with an expression of righteous attention still upon her face. She seemed to have detected nothing amiss in the sermon.

Dido turned the book over. Its cover certainly declared it to be '*Sermons* by Hugh Blair DD FRS (Edinburgh) One of the Ministers of the High Church'. Everything about the cover was severe and respectable; from the old-fashioned lettering with its long, straight *S*'s, to the plainest of plain black board bindings.

And yet . . .

She glanced back at some of the passages she had insensibly read:

'Men complain, and with reason, of the follies and caprices of our sex . . . Behold I should answer the natural effect of ignorance!'

These were not quite the sentiments Dido had expected of Doctor Blair. And besides, whatever could be meant by 'our sex'? As far as she knew, the Scotch Church did not admit *women* to the ranks of its ministers . . .

She turned back again and this time referred to the title page – which told a very different story from the cover. It read: '*A Vindication of the Rights of Woman with Strictures on Political and Moral Subjects*, by Mary Wollstonecraft.'

It would seem that Dido had in her hands – that she had

189

for the last half-hour been reading aloud – the opinions of one of the most scandalous women of the age! This was, in fact, one of those shocking and revolutionary books which Doctor Prowdlee had so thoroughly condemned!

It was very interesting that Miss Fenstanton should have such a book in her possession.

The silence seemed to have penetrated Mrs Manners' half-sleeping brain. She stirred upon the sofa. 'Yes, yes,' she murmured, 'it is all very right and true,' and fell back into a comfortable doze, without any notion of what she was approving.

Dido laughed quietly to herself as she began to understand the strange construction of the volume – and Miss Fenstanton's ingenious arrangement with the bookbinder, which would allow her to read whatever she wished without raising any protest from her father. It was a clever stratagem.

And, from these thoughts, she soon fell into her own considerations of 'moral subjects'. She turned the book over, studied again it's very unexceptionable cover and reflected upon how, in other ways, appearances might be deceiving. The outward show, the identity presented to the world, might be as effectively disguised in a person as in a book . . .

Mrs Manners was sleeping soundly now, and Dido could not resist temptation. She seized the opportunity of exploring further the book which would never have been allowed in Badleigh Parsonage. It was a chance which might never fall in her way again . . .

Chapter Twenty

. . . I confess myself rather surprised by the book's content, Eliza. I have always understood – from everything I had heard of it – that it is revolutionary and improper. But there is a great deal of sense in it; unexceptionable sense which any intelligent woman – or man – <u>must</u> approve. Miss Wollstonecraft's style is awkward and, at times, indelicate; but one cannot disagree with her when she argues for a more rational education of girls. There is weight to her argument that they should learn more than those accomplishments suitable to marriage, for, as she observes, marriage is neither universal, nor eternal; spinsters and widows are frequently called upon to make their own way in the world – and all too often find that their education has left them ill-equipped to do so. A woman may find herself a burden upon her family and obliged almost to beg her bread from her more fortunate relations, because she has no respectable means by which to provide for herself . . .

Dido compelled herself to stop writing. The argument had begun to heat her cheeks and send the ink spattering from her pen. There was much more she would have liked to say upon this subject, but she doubted Eliza would wish to read it and, besides, she had sat down to write about something quite different.

She struggled a moment for composure, then turned resolutely to a new subject.

The dust upon my aunt's shoes argues for her being more closely involved in the secrets of this house than I had previously supposed possible. It is a rather disconcerting discovery for I have always supposed that lady to be mundanely inconvenient; a source of common irritation rather than intriguing mystery.

But I cannot help but wonder whether her visit to the prison room is connected with the giving away of valuable jewels to her brother.

For I must tell you, Eliza, that there are more jewels gone. This morning brother and sister were closeted together for two hours in earnest conversation. And now there is but one ring left upon my aunt's fingers (a poor plain little thing of scarcely any value) – and again I am told that I must make no mention of the matter.

Perhaps Aunt Manners has some secret to hide and pays her brother to hold his tongue. Maybe that secret centres upon the east wing and its barred and bolted chamber – and maybe it has to do with Mr Brodie.

For I think I have been a little remiss in my suspicions there too. I have considered the possibility of everyone in this house lying about their knowledge of the man – except my aunt. Blinded by my prejudice that the inconvenient and irritating can not also be mysterious, I have failed to take into account some very salient facts. Firstly, that Aunt M has been particularly troubled with hectic headaches since she learnt of the murder; and second, that she was thrown almost into a fit when the looking upon Mr Brodie's body was first broached by Mr Parry.

Is an acquaintance with Mr Brodie the cause of her brother's power over her? And if it is, might Mr George Fenstanton have committed murder in order to safeguard a secret which is peculiarly profitable to him?

I have no very high opinion of Mr George's character. He is resentful even of that universal and lawful injustice which has bestowed his father's estate upon his nephew; and he has a high opinion of himself which does not appear to be shared by anyone around him. His nephew, his sister, and even his daughter are contemptuous of the authority he feels entitled to impose upon them.

It may be he has turned to devious methods to achieve his selfish aims and is demanding money from his sister with a threat of revealing her friendship with the dead man . . .

But am I even justified in thinking our aunt was acquainted with Mr Brodie? I should dearly love to ask. But the question would certainly produce a great many words on the subject of impertinence and duty – and no information at all. Perhaps I should do better to ask at a time when the brown medicine has power over her!

I confess that it is rather a comfort to have _any_ new possibility to consider; for I have lately been obliged to give up another, rather satisfactory, theory – that of Mr Sutherland having murdered Mr Brodie.

Mr Parry called again this morning and – as I was for two hours excused from attendance upon my aunt – I was able to take the opportunity of talking a little with him about his own investigations into the murder. And I find that he has been by no means dilatory. Though perhaps not quite so _inquisitive_ nor as _universally suspicious_ as he ought to be, he has exerted himself so far as to enquire into Mr Sutherland's movements on the fateful night.

And it appears that that gentleman must be blameless. For he was called away from the inn at eleven o'clock to attend upon a dying woman at a farmhouse five miles distant from Charcombe. And, since poor Mrs Wardle did not take her leave of this life until six in the morning, he remained there in the house. Mr Wardle and his daughter were both watching by the deathbed all night, and are willing to swear that the physician did not stir from the house until half after six.

This is a heavy blow. It would have been a great deal more agreeable _not_ to harbour suspicions against my acquaintances here within Charcombe Manor. But then, you know, _that_ cannot be entirely avoided, for they will persist in behaving so _very_ suspicious.

And, in point of fact, I am, at this very moment, engaged in laying a trap for Miss Emma Fenstanton. I am in the library with the intention of ambushing her.

You see, I now have a much more _decided_ opinion of Miss Fenstanton's character. The nature of her reading, and her arrangement with the bookbinder, point to an intelligence and guile which I had only half suspected before. I am now quite _certain_ that her attempt to clear Mr Tom of the charge of abduction was more than a flight of fancy. She is not, by nature, a silly or a trivial creature. She has a reason for promoting his innocence. I am sure that she has.

And I cannot help but wonder whether that reason is connected with her other strange behaviour. On my very first day in this house, I observed Miss Fenstanton escaping from *the rest of the company and creeping away into the library. It is a trick which I have since seen repeated . . .*

I must know what she is about! It may of course be something entirely unrelated to the murder, but I must be sure. I must understand <u>everything</u> which is carrying on in this house.

And that is why I am here now. My aunt is sleeping and everyone else is out of doors. I am in hopes that Miss Emma will again attempt to return here unobserved . . .

Dido laid down her pen and looked about her, wondering very much why this room tempted the young lady. No one else cared for the place; this was not in general a reading family.

All the books upon the shelves were old and large, magnificent in leather and gilt. They provided an air of solemnity and learning; but it was a gloomy, old-fashioned room. The few expanses of wall not clothed in bookcases were panelled in fine polished oak, the colour of which almost exactly matched the dark bindings of the books. The wide fireplace was adorned with a vast and ancient overmantel of carved oak, complete with coats of arms and the large head of a rather ugly ram – in compliment to the flocks which had long ago made the fortune of the Fenstantons. The air was filled with the scent of dust and leather and aged paper.

What was there here to draw Miss Fenstanton from the enjoyment of fresh air and company?

I hope that she will come here soon, wrote Dido, *for I cannot wait long. Today we are all to go to the inn at*

*New Charcombe to look upon poor Mr Brodie. It was all
arranged by Mr Parry during his visit. I must walk thither
in order to perform some errands for my aunt. And I intend
to take the opportunity of meeting Mr Lomax in the old
village so that we may visit his son. I have sent word to
him and . . .*

Out in the hall – beyond the door which had been
purposely left ajar – there was the sound of a light,
tripping step. Dido bent her head over her letter and,
with her pen resting on the last word, waited.

But the door did not open. The footsteps passed away
across the hall.

She set down her pen and went to the door. Miss
Fenstanton was running across the hall from the front
door to the screens passage; her bonnet was hanging back
from her curls, her shawl was slipping gracefully from her
shoulders, and there was a little workbox tucked under
her arm. For a moment it was doubtful what she was
about; then Dido made out that she had come there to
meet someone. Matthews, the grim housekeeper, was
waiting for her beside the screen.

Emma held out her hand, she seemed to be thanking
the housekeeper – who answered rapidly, saying
something in which was included the name of her master
and also the need to 'be mighty careful' about something.

She handed a little package to Emma, who put it
away quickly in her workbox, before turning towards the
library.

Dido had only just time to resume her seat and look
up in great surprise as Miss Emma and her workbox burst

through the library door. The door slammed and the girl leant against it in a moment of relief.

'Good morning, Miss Fenstanton.'

Emma started, her cheeks coloured and she could barely manage a greeting. She dropped into a chair and put her box – a pretty little thing of Tunbridge-ware with a pink silk lining peeping from its lid – on the table.

And Dido, quite cruelly, hastened to increase the poor girl's distress. 'I am glad of this opportunity of speaking to you alone,' she began pleasantly, 'for I have been wishing to return your book. I hope you do not mind my borrowing it.' She pushed across the table the extraordinary copy of *Blair's Sermons* which had been lying ready beside her writing desk.

Emma Fenstanton stared at it, and seemed for a moment as if she might deny possession. Then: 'Oh!' she said. Dimples flashed into existence for a second, her bright eyes darted to her companion's face. 'I wondered where it was got to. Did you . . . did you happen to look into it, Miss Kent?'

'Yes. I read a whole chapter to my aunt yesterday.'

'To your aunt?' The last vestige of Miss Emma's usual self-possession was lost. Her hands flew to her face. 'And . . . and what was Mrs Manners' opinion?'

'Oh, she approved it heartily – if sleeping soundly throughout may be counted approval.'

Emma sat in stunned silence – until she caught at the smile which was spreading across Dido's face. In a moment both women were laughing loudly.

'She suspected nothing,' Dido reassured. 'And your secret is quite safe with me. I shall not say a word to anyone about the surprising sentiments which Mr Blair expresses in this particular volume of sermons.'

Emma answered with very promising gratitude. Then, with a little of her playfulness returning she added, 'And what did *you* think of these *sermons* Miss Kent?'

'Well, I did not find Miss Wollstonecraft's style of writing pleasant, but many – indeed most – of her opinions I considered very sound indeed.'

'And that,' cried Emma, 'was what everyone thought – when this was first published.' She crossed her arms over the disguised book and continued eagerly. 'When the *Vindication of the Rights of Woman* first appeared it was not thought shocking at all, you know – well, not so *very* shocking. It was thought to be just another book about the education of girls.'

'It is certainly a subject which often exercises the female pen,' agreed Dido.

'But then – after her death – the circumstances of Miss Wollstonecraft's life came to be known.' Emma's dark eyes glinted wickedly in the library's gloom with the spice of gossip. 'She loved a man to whom she was not married, you know,' she whispered. 'And she *gave way* to her passion.'

'Yes, I had heard that there were . . . irregularities.'

'And it was *that* which turned the world against her book. It was the scandal of her life which made men like Papa forbid their daughters to read her work.'

'And so,' said Dido, lowering her own voice to suit the very convenient atmosphere of confidence and intimacy which was gradually taking possession of the library, 'you believe it is on account of her character, rather than her opinions, that the lady is despised?'

'Yes.' Emma sighed extravagantly. 'And is it not the way of the world, Miss Kent?' She shook back her curls and lifted up her eyes. 'Is it not the fate of every woman to be judged by her character . . . by what she *is* rather than what she *thinks*?'

'Indeed. Reputation is everything to the female sex,' agreed Dido. 'I believe it always has been – since we ceased to live in a state of complete savagery.'

'But do you not sometimes wish to defy the world and behave quite shockingly?' sighed Emma.

Dido chose not to consider the question. 'And yet,' she observed quietly instead, 'you have *not* defied the world, Miss Fenstanton.' She indicated the book. 'You proceed by subterfuge, and read in secret what is proscribed.' She smiled. 'It is a stratagem of which Miss Wollstonecraft would certainly not approve. She denounces as beneath us all those little tricks and subterfuges which we women use to gain our ends.'

'Oh!' cried Emma. '"Behold the natural effect of ignorance!"' She shrugged up her shoulders. 'In short, you know, I cannot help but be devious. It is my faulty education – and the denial of my rights and liberties – which has made me so!'

'This is poor morality and you know it,' laughed Dido. 'I would be quite worried about you if I did not believe your little trick to be harmless.' She paused. 'If I did not believe *all* your little tricks to be harmless.'

Emma's smiling dimples disappeared abruptly. She dropped her eyes, ran a finger around the edge of the book's cover. 'I do not understand you, Miss Kent.'

'Your little arrangement with the bookbinder is not your only secret, is it? You have other schemes in hand?'

'Now, why should you suspect me?' cried Emma, clutching her book to her as if it were a breastplate to ward off attack.

'Because,' said Dido looking at her levelly, 'you have shown yourself to be quite determined to prove Mr Tom Lomax innocent of the crimes charged against him. And I cannot help but wonder why you are so very concerned about a young man you have never met.'

Emma's dimples returned. She cast up her eyes to the finely moulded plaster of the library ceiling. 'Perhaps you suspect me of being secretly acquainted with Mr Lomax,' she mused playfully. 'Perhaps you suspect me of being in love with him.'

'Perhaps I do.'

'Why, what a very interesting woman you think me, Miss Kent! I am quite flattered! But in fact I am very dull, you know. I give you my word that I have never met the young man. And – being so very dull as I am – I have not the knack of falling in love with gentlemen I do not know.'

'But I will not believe that you are dull at all, Miss Fenstanton. I *know* that you have some other secret to hide. Come now, I have obliged you with the quiet return of your book. Will you not oblige me by satisfying my curiosity.' She smiled invitingly. 'Please tell me why you like to come alone to this room.'

Emma looked uncertain. Dido began to hope . . .

But her hopes were cruelly dashed by the opening of the library door.

'So this is where you are hiding, Emma!' Mr George's perspiring face appeared around the door's edge. 'Make haste! Make haste and come into the garden. Lancelot is asking for you.'

Emma rose quickly, threw one mischievous smile in Dido's direction, and was gone. Father and daughter could be heard crossing the hall; he in full flow of disapproval of her 'hiding herself away indoors, and spoiling her eyes with too much reading . . .'

As his complaints faded away into the garden, Dido railed inwardly against her ill luck, and wondered whether another ten minutes might have produced anything of interest. Perhaps they might; but Miss Fenstanton was a difficult subject for investigation. She seemed to delight in subterfuge for its own sake . . .

So absorbed was Dido in these considerations that it was several minutes before her eye fell upon the workbox which had been left behind on the library table.

She stared at it a moment as if she feared that it too might be snatched away from her. Then she went to the door and looked out into the hall. She wished to be quite certain of privacy. Only when she was sure that she was alone did she return and cautiously lift the lid of the workbox.

Inside, the housekeeper's paper-wrapped package lay among the coloured cottons, the scissors and the needle cards. A little grease had seeped from it and stained the pink silk lining.

Dido drew back a corner of the paper – and revealed a freshly cooked chicken leg.

Chapter Twenty-One

. . . Well, Eliza, why should any young woman go to such trouble to convey a chicken leg into a deserted library? I had not put Miss Fenstanton down for a secret eater! I <u>have known</u> girls who seek to satisfy in private an appetite which they consider indelicate to reveal at table, but I am quite sure that Miss Emma has no such overstrained notions of refinement.

So I cannot doubt that it was her intention for the chicken to be consumed by someone else. But who is this eater of roast chicken? I can see for myself that there is no one here in the library . . .

Dido stopped and looked about rather uneasily – almost expecting to see this hungry person watching from among the books. But the shelves and the panelled walls stretched blankly about her. The only watching eyes were the distinctly malevolent ones of the ram above the fireplace.

She got to her feet and made a slow circuit of the room, running her hand carefully over books and wooden panels. There was no sign of any hiding place . . . And yet, she thought, considering the style of the room . . . and the age of the Charcombe Manor . . .

An idea darted into her brain.

Pausing only to lock her letter away in her writing desk, Dido ran out of the room. She sped across the hall, took the shallow stairs two at a time, and did not stop until she had cleared the second flight and arrived at the very top of the house.

The long gallery was silent and deserted; the sun shone in through the south-facing windows onto the worn matting, white walls – and the disapproving Elizabethan lady. Dido approached her slowly over gently creaking boards and was gratified to find that she had remembered correctly – there was, indeed, a *rosary* in the white tapering fingers.

She peered up at the picture, and found it an old, indistinct thing; an indifferent likeness of a forgotten ancestor, such as hang by the dozen upon the walls of country houses everywhere, grimed over with the dust and smoke of more than a century, turning slowly to the uniform colour of chocolate and disregarded entirely by family and visitors alike. The lady seemed to be fading into her background, her broad skirts now barely distinguishable from the dark room in which she stood.

Dido clambered onto the chamber horse in her eagerness to read the picture and, swaying precariously on its protesting springs, brought her face close to the canvas. From here it was just possible to make out a little of the background – though it all seemed to swim in a brownish fog. Beyond the broad blue sleeves and the crimped white edges of the lady's ruff, the corner of a chimney piece could just be made out. There was an overmantel of dark wood – with the head of a ram carved upon it.

'Exactly as I thought!' she cried, just before losing her balance and stumbling backward onto the floor.

But even the fall could not diminish her spirits. She sat down upon the chamber horse and gave several little bounces of triumph. Her mind was rapidly filling with ideas about Miss Fenstanton and her secrets. She began – like a woman sewing patchwork – to fashion a very serviceable theory from bits and scraps of observations which had individually seemed to be of little value.

She thought about a little ghost crying in the night; the mysterious figure creeping from the garden to the library; she thought about a round depression in the moss of the path; she thought of thick black slugs, and of the Elizabethan lady's piety; she thought about the scratch upon Miss Fenstanton's hand and the concern of that young lady to prove Tom innocent; and she thought about the rather weak excuse given for that concern . . .

At last she paused to consider her fine new piece of patchwork. The pattern of it was remarkably satisfying. But there was yet one detail missing. There was one enquiry to be made without delay. She rose from the chamber horse, determined upon risking her aunt's displeasure and escaping the house for a few minutes.

For it had become absolutely imperative that she consult with young Charlie and his assistant in the stables.

'I have been thinking about the story of Charcombe's little ghost,' Dido remarked to Mr Lancelot later that day as they were walking together along the shady road which led beside the river to the village of Old Charcombe. 'In particular I have been wondering where exactly Lady Fenstanton is reputed to have hidden her child.'

'Ha! I am sure I don't know.' He considered a moment. 'No, I never heard *where* the child was put.'

Dido was a little disappointed in drawing a blank here for, in general, the gentleman seemed in the mood for confidence. He had insisted upon accompanying her on her walk to the village and seemed to be taking pleasure in her company. They had been talking very comfortably about his house and grounds, and she was in hopes of learning a little more about his family. For recent discoveries (in particular the spoiling of the silk slippers) had led her to suspect that the mysteries surrounding her might be rooted in the past of Charcombe Manor.

'I wonder,' she pursued, 'whether there is any record of the story written down. I remember Mr George saying that his sister, Miss Francine Fenstanton, read old books in the library. Perhaps she found it written in a book there.'

'Perhaps she did. The library was certainly a valuable resource to poor Aunt Francine, for she led a very *confined* life.' He frowned – as if painful memories had been awakened.

'I am sorry,' said Dido quickly. 'It is a fault of mine – when I am very interested in a subject I become impertinent. Please forgive me.'

'No,' he said gently. 'There was no impertinence.' But his thoughts seemed to have become fixed upon his aunt and he shortly broke out with: 'It is thirty years since Aunt Francine died, you know. Thirty years since Charcombe

Manor had a woman's civilising presence! It is a period, is it not?'

'It is indeed.'

'It is too long for a house to be without a woman's gentle influence. I fear the old place has suffered for it.' He regarded her very seriously, pushing back his hat with a thick, strong finger. 'And perhaps I too have suffered,' he suggested. 'I have not – since I was eleven years old – enjoyed the daily companionship of a woman.'

He stopped walking and laid his hand diffidently over hers, in a manner which must have been suspected by any woman whose mind was not entirely occupied with the pursuit of a murderer.

But, as they stood close together beneath a great oak with the sunlight twinkling through the leaves, the sound of the river and birdsong filling the air, Dido was thinking rather more about Mr Fenstanton's family and the mysteries carrying on in his house than she was about the gentleman himself. The earnest look of his brown eyes was entirely lost upon her.

'Miss Francine Fenstanton was sickly, I believe,' she said.

'Oh! Yes, she suffered from a great many nervous disorders.'

'As my Aunt Manners does?'

'Yes, but in those days – when she was young – Aunt Selina was quite well. I believe all *her* illnesses began with her marriage. As a girl she was always stout and confident – much more easy with the world than her poor sister.'

'But,' continued Dido, starting to walk busily forward and forcing her companion to do the same, 'despite their different characters, the sisters were attached to one another?'

'They were devoted. Why do you ask so particularly about it?'

'Oh!' She looked up into his face, and, receiving an indistinct impression of intimacy, decided upon a direct question. 'I cannot help but wonder,' she confessed, 'whether the cause of my aunt's disagreement with her brothers – the reason why she has been so long absent from Charcombe – was some dislike of the way her sister was treated.'

'Ha! You have the right of it there!' he cried. 'My father and uncle were very stern guardians of their sisters. Very determined that they should make good marriages, you know. And Aunt Selina believes that their unkindness was an aggravation of Aunt Francine's illness.'

'I see.' Dido began insensibly to walk faster as she pursued her own thoughts, and the unfortunate Mr Fenstanton was obliged to lengthen his own stride.

'It is an old story,' he said, with the dismissive air of a man who has subjects of his own to pursue. 'My dear Miss Kent, I would not have you think I share their philosophy. Mercenary marriages! I ain't got patience with them. Affection is the thing to my mind. Happiness in marriage is more important than fortune, ain't it?' As he spoke he again laid his hand over hers and attempted to draw her to a standstill. But he saw that he had now lost her attention entirely.

For they had just turned the last corner of the lane, and the village was before them: a cluster of grey cottages lay beyond the high curving back of the bridge; there were a few thin blue spires of smoke ascending from the chimneys, and the hot red glow of a forge reflecting in the river.

And, on the bridge, Mr Lomax was waiting, with one foot resting on the low wall and his eyes cast thoughtfully down toward the water.

Dido excused herself hurriedly and ran forward to meet him, holding out her hands and turning her face up to his with affectionate concern.

'Your enquiries are not prospering?' she asked anxiously after a hurried greeting.

'No,' he said, turning towards her with a sigh. 'I have not been able to trace the chaise beyond the first toll gate on the Bristol road. Beyond that the tolls and the staging posts arc too busy – nobody was able to distinguish one carriage from another. And no one at the school in Taunton was able to even guess at where the young lady might be – if she is not with Mrs Hargreaves. Everyone seems to be agreed that that would be her most likely recourse if she left her guardians.'

'I see.' Dido was sorry to have so little information – and sorrier still for the pain his failure caused him. His eyes were so dark she thought he must not have slept at all since their last meeting. 'And were you able to discover anything about the lady's character?'

'Yes – a little.' He frowned upon the water and Dido stepped closer so that she might look up into his face in an attempt to read his thoughts. 'There was general agreement,' he said, 'among both teachers and pupils, that Miss Verney is unlikely to elope.'

'She is an amenable, docile girl?'

'Oh no! Nobody seemed to doubt that she has *spirit* enough for an elopement. But everyone is in agreement that she is not sufficiently *romantic*. Miss Verney, I am told, thinks too well of herself and her fortune to throw herself away.' He smiled. 'As you may imagine, her teachers are inclined to call her sensible – while her fellow pupils condemn her for being too worldly.'

'Ah!' said Dido with a smile. 'The distorting effect of youth!'

'I prefer,' he said gravely, 'to think that age and experience may also distort a little, and that the truth lies between the two extremes.'

'Very well. We shall agree that Miss Verney is rather sensible – and just a little bit worldly. But,' she added with a shake of her head, 'the conclusion must be that she is unlikely to have run away to Gretna Green.'

'That was my conclusion,' he said. 'Until, just as I was leaving, one young lady – a Miss Garnett who had been the most voluble in condemning her fellow pupil as mercenary – stopped me. She told me that, just before she left the school, Miss Verney had said something to her that was a little odd.' He paused. 'It was very odd,' he admitted. 'I know not what to make of it.

'It seems that Miss Garnett had been chiding her friend for coldness, telling her that she would never be happy in marriage if she did not truly love her husband – it is not difficult to imagine the eloquence of nineteen upon such a subject. And it seems Miss Verney laughed at the tirade; she laughed, and she said: very well, she would give romance *one trial* – and if nothing came of it then she would settle for a worldly union.'

'Oh!' cried Dido, laying her hands upon his arm. 'I wonder what she meant by that. Is it possible that this running away is the trial she spoke of?'

'Perhaps it is. Miss Garnett could tell me nothing about the "trial". She said only that it sounded like "one of Letitia's mad schemes". But, as to the worldly union – she had more definite ideas about that. She believes that there is "an old man" that Miss Verney has known all her life. A man her guardians wish her to marry. Miss Garnett did not know the name of this poor decrepit old fellow, but—'

'But,' Dido finished for him, 'it is almost certainly Mr Lancelot!' As she spoke she turned instinctively to the place where she had left that gentleman. And much to her surprise, she found that he was still standing in the shade of the trees.

He was glowering in their direction and his look of disapproval made Dido uneasy. Lomax had followed the direction of her eyes and he also seemed to notice the frown, for he immediately drew Dido's hand through his arm with an air of protection and possession.

Fenstanton's face clouded. He kicked irritably at a tree root.

The couple turned away towards the village. But Mr Fenstanton stood still for several minutes. He appeared to be lost in the contemplation of new ideas which the scene had suggested to him.

Chapter Twenty-Two

Old Charcombe village was small and poor – and rather honest; it did not rise to the dignity of possessing a gaol. It had instead a little stone-built chamber commonly called 'the lock-up'. Besides accommodating drunkards, vagrants and wrongdoers awaiting trial, the lock-up earned its keep by housing a dismantled pillory and the parish bier on which the people of Charcombe were carried to their graves. The building stood in the centre of the village, beside the stone bench from which the fishermen sold their catches every morning and, being so conveniently placed, it frequently contained a basket or two of ageing mackerel.

The place stank – as gaols are supposed to do, though not perhaps in quite the usual way.

The gaoler who conducted Dido and Mr Lomax down a short, sloping passage to the single cell was an enterprising man: he worked upon the fishing boats and was sexton of the church when he was not guarding the felons of Charcombe. He was a big hearty-looking fellow with weather-beaten cheeks and a knitted cap, and had neither the shuffling gait nor the blackened teeth which Dido's reading of novels had led her to expect of a turnkey.

Though he did not lack a keen eye to his own interest.

It had cost Mr Lomax a half-guinea to get them thus far – and another shilling when he had insisted upon a stool being brought so that Dido might be seated during the interview.

'Five minutes,' the gaoler declared as he opened the cell door. 'I can't be allowing y'more than that. For it's right against the rules y'being here at all. And if I'd not got such a soft heart . . .'

'You would be a good deal poorer,' Mr Lomax finished for him.

'Aye, that I would!' The gaoler laughed delightedly, pushed open the creaking door and set the stool down inside the cell. 'Five minutes,' he reminded them as he stepped back for them to enter.

Dido suspected that his notion of five minutes was vague – for she doubted he possessed a watch, and she fervently hoped that his ideas erred in the right direction, for five minutes would certainly not settle all the matters she wished to discuss.

The cell was not well lit, but sufficient light fell through a grille in the door and a narrow barred window for Dido to make out Tom, with his legs in irons, crouching upon the edge of the bier which would seem to be serving as his bed. He presented a sorry sight. His coat was gone, his shirt was torn open at the seam of the shoulder, his smooth buckskin breeches were grimy at the knees, and his cheeks were crusted with two days' growth of beard.

He sat up straighter as the gaoler withdrew, rattling the long chain which ran from his leg irons to a bolt in the wall. 'Have you found the girl?' he demanded.

'No,' began his father, 'there is no trace—'

'You must find her,' Tom interrupted. 'It is the only thing that can save me. For she can tell everyone that I've got nothing to do with her disappearing and so I had no reason to put a bullet into the old man.'

Mr Lomax looked as if he were struggling for a calm reply. His eyes travelled round the damp little chamber with a kind of disbelief that he should ever find his son in such a place.

Keenly aware of the *five minutes* ticking away, Dido took it upon herself to continue. 'How well acquainted were you with Mr Brodie?' she asked briskly.

'I was not acquainted with him at all,' said Tom, turning to her with a sneer.

'But you passed the evening in his company.'

'Not from choice. But you know how it is at inns. In April there are never any fires lit above stairs and one must sit with other fellows in the parlour or else perish with cold.'

Dido sat down upon the stool so considerately provided. 'Did you know that Mr Brodie intended to pay a visit to Charcombe Manor?'

'No.'

'He did not mention any . . . information he intended to convey to Mr Fenstanton?'

'No,' cried Tom, his voice echoing about the stone walls. 'I tell you I know nothing about the man!'

Mr Lomax looked grave. 'There are witnesses, Tom – people at the inn – who heard you arguing with Mr Brodie.'

Tom was uncomfortable for a moment but then gave a

short, bitter laugh. 'That was no more than a disagreement over a card game.'

'A gentleman does not argue over cards,' said his father coldly. 'If a man has not sufficient cash to cover his losses, he ought not to sit down to the table.'

'Good God! The same old cry! You care for nothing but money. Well sir, you need not concern yourself about me any longer. The hangman will rid you of me soon enough.'

Tom folded his arms and leant against the damp wall, his bristling jaw set as if determined against speaking another word. Dido turned to his father and, to her dismay, saw a similar determination, a similar setting of the jaw; a pale, settled anger.

She could scarcely believe their stupidity. Were they, for pride's sake, willing to squander the dearly bought minutes in petulance? She waited a moment, but neither of them spoke.

'Perhaps,' she ventured quietly when it began to seem that the whole visit might be wasted, 'perhaps, Mr Tom Lomax, you would tell us anything you know which might help us to find Miss Verney.' She looked very directly at him. 'Do you know – have you any idea where she is? For if you do, you had better tell it. As you say, your best chance of deliverance lies in our finding her.'

'I have told you. We parted at the gate. I watched her walk into the house.'

'And why did you part at the gate? Why did you not accompany her into the house?'

'Oh!' Tom shrugged up his shoulders. 'She would not

have me do so. And neither was I very eager to encounter the disapproving looks of her friends.'

'Did you meet anyone on your walk – did Miss Verney stop to speak to anyone?'

'No. We saw no one at all – except just before we left Miss Gibbs at the gate, the groom rode up from the village with letters from the post.'

'Letters?' said Dido sharply. 'And was there any letter for Miss Verney?'

'No. For she called out to ask him, but he said there was nothing.'

'But she was expecting to receive a letter?'

'Perhaps she was. I don't know.'

Dido put this consideration aside for a time when she would have more leisure for it. 'And the young lady was not unwilling to walk alone with you?' she continued. 'She did not think it improper?'

'No,' said Tom sulkily. He turned his eyes up to the low stone arch of the roof and seemed to study the little cushions of moss which grew there. 'She did not think it at all improper,' he continued quietly, 'to take a walk with the man to whom she is engaged to be married.'

'Engaged!' Mr Lomax's cry echoed so loudly about the cell that Dido turned anxiously to the grille of the door. But the gaoler did not appear to be listening.

Lomax struggled for composure. 'Engaged?' he repeated with less force but no less incredulity. 'You claim to be engaged to the young lady?'

'Yes,' said Tom with a pretence at bravado. 'We have been engaged these past five months. While we were in

215

Worcestershire, Miss Verney . . . did me the great honour of agreeing to be my wife.'

'You are a fool if you think her friends will ever agree—'

'All that,' interposed Tom quickly, 'can only be decided by Bailey himself – and since he is in the Indies no one here can know his mind. Fenstanton and his confederates have no say in the matter – for all they might wish they had.' He hesitated, ran a finger round the chafing iron on his leg. 'That,' he said, 'is why I have written to ask for his consent. So that I may have an answer from him before any of his friends here can poison his mind against me.'

Mr Lomax let out a cry of impatience and spun about on his heel, meaning no doubt to relieve his feelings by taking a turn about the room. But he had forgotten where he was. The cell allowed for no such freedom and he could do no more than take one small step before he came against the wall, where he stood for a moment staring out of the barred, unglazed window. The cell was beneath the level of the street and all he could look upon were occasional feet hurrying past – and the scarred face of a stray cat who was gazing hopefully into the fish-scented prison.

Meanwhile Dido was struggling to reconcile this new information with everything they had been told of the young lady's caution and worldliness. And she could make no sense of the business at all.

'You are engaged?' she repeated in a puzzled voice. 'The lady has consented? You have gone so far as to seek her guardian's permission?'

'Why should I not?' said Tom.

And there was something defensive in his tone which

prompted Dido to ask: 'Does Miss Verney know of your application?'

'No.' Tom looked sulky; he drew up his legs and touched his sore ankle tenderly. 'I did not tell her that I had written. Letitia's plans were more . . . romantic.'

'Romantic?' echoed Dido and Mr Lomax together. They exchanged puzzled looks.

'Did Miss Verney favour elopement?' said Dido.

Tom nodded.

'But, of course, elopement would not suit your plans, would it?' mused Dido as she struggled for understanding. 'For though you would gain the lady, you might lose her fortune.'

'That is a vile insult,' protested Tom. 'You will take it back this minute.'

'No!' shouted Lomax, turning abruptly. 'You will mind your manners, sir. Miss Kent spoke nothing but the truth. And if you cannot bear to hear the truth there is no hope of us ever getting to the bottom of this business.'

Tom looked mutinous, but held his tongue.

'Does anyone else know about this engagement?' his father asked.

'Letitia has told Miss Gibbs. She must have betrayed us.'

'You think that your engagement is known about at Charcombe Manor?'

'By God, yes! That is the root of this whole business. They have got Miss Verney away from me and they are trying to blacken my name.'

'That would be a very . . . remarkable conspiracy,' observed Dido. 'Why should—?'

'Why? So that they can marry her to the lord of the manor, of course!' cried Tom impatiently. 'Do you not see? That is why Mother Bailey brought Letitia to Charcombe. I'll warrant Fenstanton has been trying for it for years.'

'Yes,' cried his father mockingly. 'And I do not doubt he has killed this unfortunate Mr Brodie for no other reason than to spite you!'

This remark seemed to catch Tom off his guard. 'No,' he said, just a little too quickly, 'Brodie has nothing to do with it.'

Mr Lomax only cast up his eyes in exasperation, but Dido could not escape the conviction that Mr Brodie did in fact have *everything* 'to do with it'.

'We have not much time,' she reminded them. 'Can you tell us a little more about the events at the inn? The proprietor says that you and Mr Brodie left the building together at about midnight. Is that correct?'

'We did both leave the inn about that time. But we did not leave *together*. I walked out on my own – onto the green before the inn – just to escape from Brodie and get the better of my temper. But, within a few minutes, he followed me.'

'And your dispute recommenced?' suggested Dido.

'No, it did not,' Tom said with emphasis. 'The fellow did not speak to me at all. He turned away to the back of the inn and hurried off – as if he had business to attend to.'

'But there was no one else about – no one who can confirm your account?' asked Mr Lomax.

'No, there was not! No doubt it was very remiss of me

not to obtain a witness; but I did not know that I was to be accused of murder.'

'Well, if you had not become engaged in a tavern brawl . . .'

Tom gave a great cry of impatience.

'Where was he going? What is there behind the inn?' Dido asked quickly. 'Was he going to meet someone perhaps? Did Mr Brodie speak of knowing anyone in Charcombe?'

'There was that doctor fellow. He played a few hands with us.'

Dido shook her head. 'Mr Sutherland tells me that he had never met Mr Brodie before that night.'

'Does he?' said Tom.

But his father was looking anxiously towards the door; he had heard the approach of the gaoler's steps. 'Was there no one else that Brodie knew in this neighbourhood?' he asked hurriedly.

'No one in the town,' said Tom. 'He only spoke of "a friend out at the manor".'

'And we still have no idea of who that "friend" might be,' said Dido.

'Do you think that is significant?' asked Lomax.

'I think it may be. For I know of one thing which is to be found behind the new inn at Charcombe. There is the track which leads over the downs – straight to Charcombe Manor.'

Chapter Twenty-Three

'It is possible,' said Dido slowly, 'that Mr Brodie left the inn to meet his acquaintance from the manor.'

'And, you believe,' said Lomax, 'that that acquaintance might . . . have been responsible for his death?'

They were standing now upon the little bridge which spanned the stream in Old Charcombe. Around them crowded the low thatched eaves of cottages, sheltering children and dogs from the glare of the sun. Ducks drifted on the slow, weed-choked current below.

Dido was engaged to join the rest of the company at the inn within the half-hour, in order that she might look upon Mr Brodie's body; but she was unwilling to leave her companion. He appeared stunned, his faculties almost overpowered by the horror of Tom's situation. He was standing again with one booted foot resting upon the low parapet of the bridge, a hand to his brow, his eyes downcast.

'Yes,' Dido declared stoutly. 'I believe that that *is* the most likely explanation, for we *know* that your son is not guilty.'

'I do not say that he is guilty,' he said, with his hand obscuring his eyes. 'I cannot believe that he is. But there is such an appearance of guilt! He has – by his own admission – entered into a secret engagement with the young lady; and if Mr Brodie intended to expose it . . .'

'But everything we have learnt about Miss Verney makes such an engagement improbable. I cannot make it out.'

'It is odd; but I see no reason why Tom should claim the engagement exists if it does not.' He sighed and continued to stare distractedly at the water. 'I fear there is more cause to suppose Tom guilty of this murder than anyone else. I am sure there will be no doubt in the minds of the judge and jury.'

'Oh! No! I cannot agree,' cried Dido with energy. 'There is not a soul in Charcombe Manor against whom a suspicion cannot be raised. Mr George Fenstanton is getting money unfairly from his sister, besides having cause to wish Miss Verney out of the way so that Mr Lancelot may marry his daughter. And then there is Mrs Bailey . . .' she held up her fingers and began to count off her fellow guests, her words tumbling eagerly over one another as she attempted to convince him. '. . . Mrs Bailey seemed *very* conscious when Mr Brodie's name was first mentioned. And Mr Lancelot *ought* to have ridden northward in pursuit of the fugitive, but he has not. And then you know there is Miss Gibbs who is not telling something, but I know not what it is—'

'Miss Kent, please!' He held up a hand to stop the torrent of ideas. 'You begin to sound as if you suspect the entire world.'

'No, I only suspect that portion of it which will persist in behaviour that merits suspicion. But people will behave so very odd! Do you know, Mr Lomax, I have a great idea that *everyone* has a secret to hide? Why even little Miss Emma is up to *something* . . . Though I think I begin to understand what that is. I must have a talk with Miss Emma at the earliest opportunity . . .'

'No!' Lomax shook his head and looked grave. 'I beg you will make no more enquiries.'

'But there is a great deal still to be discovered.'

'I do not doubt it. But I shall investigate alone.'

'Oh! Would you start the old argument against me? Would you charge me with impropriety?'

'No.' He held up a hand against her indignation. 'Please listen to me. This is by no means the old argument. It is one of much greater force. My son stands charged with a terrible crime; he – and his family – are under a cloud of shame. And it begins to seem that . . .' He stopped himself and spent a moment collecting his thoughts before continuing with great determination. 'I cannot allow you to have any part in that shame, or be tainted by the report of a crime, which will soon be the talk of the entire neighbourhood. You must not be seen to associate yourself with us, or with our cause. Such an association would very seriously injure your credit in the world.'

'And do you believe that such a base consideration would deter me from performing the office of a friend?'

'I believe everything which is most honourable to your good nature and compassion. And the belief makes me very uneasy indeed!'

She made no answer.

'Miss Kent, consider how I should feel if your reputation was damaged by this business. How should I answer to your brother for allowing it to happen?'

'I am surprised to find that you value my brother's good opinion more highly than my own!'

'Oh no! I shall not be drawn into disputing with you. It is too dangerous. I am decided. I shall pursue Tom's cause alone.'

'Well,' she said, turning abruptly from principles to particulars, 'how do you intend to pursue that cause? You cannot even visit the manor openly. You are in no position to question the people there. But I am very conveniently placed and have already begun to find things out.'

He looked at her uneasily and she knew that he was longing to ask about her discoveries. She smiled invitingly, but he turned away and looked down at the ducks.

She attacked upon another front. 'Well, I need not be seen to *associate* myself with you at all, if you do not wish it. For Mr Fenstanton has positively invited me to take an interest in the business of Miss Verney's disappearance and, since that cannot be investigated without some attention being paid to Mr Brodie's death, my particular interest in your son's welfare need not be suspected.'

Lomax ran a hand across his brow, tortured by so many sensations and contradictory anxieties that he hardly knew how to reply. At last the concern of the parent prompted him to put aside for a while the scruples of the lover. 'Have you found out anything which might lead us to Miss Verney?' he asked.

'Yes,' she said, endeavouring not to sound triumphant. 'I have found out several things. And if you will only consent to *associate* yourself with me as far as the new inn, I shall tell you everything.'

Lomax looked about him at the sleeping dogs, at a

housewife dipping her bucket in the river, at two little boys standing knee-deep in water, hands submerged, still as herons, as they waited to trap the slow brown trout in the pool beneath the bridge. He seemed at last to decide that no one here was likely to take much notice of their conversation. 'I shall,' he said very carefully, 'walk with you as far as the beginning of the new town – but no further.'

He would not, however, allow even the little fishermen, the housewife and the dogs to see him paying any particular attention to her; he did not offer his arm as they turned onto the rutted track and began to walk slowly towards the new town.

Dido tried not to be hurt by the empty space which yawned between them and turned all her thoughts to business. She gave him a clear and faithful account of her odd conversation with Martha Gibbs and of her discoveries in the east wing. But she kept to herself the theory she had devised in the library that morning. It was fragile – untested – and she would not share ideas which might yet prove false.

As he strode along beside her, there was a great deal of comfort to be found in sharing her thoughts: a kind of pleasure in watching his fingertips come together as they always did when he was considering deeply. Every familiar gesture was dear to her and she did all that she could to prolong the conversation. As they neared the edge of the town her feet slowed between the fragrant gorse bushes. She fell silent and looked to him for a response.

'This chamber with the barred window appears odd, I grant.' He put his chin upon his fingers as he considered.

'But I cannot see why it should have any bearing upon the murder.'

'Do you not? Do you not think that it suggests some secret being hidden? And if there is a secret to be hidden, might that not furnish a motive for murder?'

'It *might*,' he admitted.

'At the very least it suggests that not everyone at Charcombe Manor is telling the truth.'

'Ah!' said Lomax, as if her words had struck some chord with him. He dropped his hands to his sides and walked on in silence for a little way, forcing Dido to hurry after him. 'Miss Kent,' he said, turning troubled eyes upon her. 'It is very painful for me to have to say this . . . But I am afraid it is by no means certain that *Tom* is telling the truth.' His face coloured as if it were his own dishonesty he was confessing. 'It is possible that he is lying about the engagement; though I cannot guess at his motive for doing so.'

He looked so unhappy that Dido longed to cry out a polite and reassuring contradiction.

But there was something pressing heavily on her mind and they had now almost reached the paved road of the town; she could feel the stiff breeze blowing in from the sea. 'I confess,' she said, 'that I had thought the same. And there were two other points upon which I thought Mr Tom Lomax was perhaps . . . less than truthful: when he spoke of Mr Brodie having nothing to do with Miss Verney's disappearance – and when he claimed the argument was about nothing but a card game. It seems a very . . . *slight* cause for a violent quarrel.'

'Perhaps,' he said doubtingly. 'But you are probably

not aware of how very passionate such disputes can be – if a man is found to have wagered more than he can pay. And Tom certainly had no money. The constables found only a few shillings in his pockets when they took him – besides some snuff and a couple of racecards.' He gave her a very thoughtful look. 'But you believe their quarrel had another cause?'

'Mr Brodie knew something about Miss Verney,' she reminded him. 'Something which he intended to communicate to Mr Fenstanton.'

'And you believe that was the true cause of the dispute?'

'Perhaps. Tom *said* that he knew nothing about Mr Brodie's intention of visiting the manor, but—' she broke off. 'Of course,' she added hastily, 'they might have argued only about the reckoning at cards. But I think we should make enquiries upon the subject. It is possible that someone at the inn overheard their quarrel.'

He agreed to it. 'And,' he added, 'I shall also make enquiries among Tom's acquaintances to discover whether there is any knowledge or suspicion of his being engaged.'

But even as he spoke, he was turning away. For they were now at the beginning of the town's promenade – and the dowagers were visible once more, seated upon their bench and alert for anything of interest which might be passing in the vicinity.

'How shall I talk with you again?' she asked quickly. 'How shall I be able to hear what you have learnt – or tell you of anything I have discovered – if you are so very determined not to be seen with me?'

He hesitated. 'I shall call again upon Fenstanton –

very early in the day. He is a decent man. He will allow it, I am sure – and he will not speak of it.'

'Call tomorrow,' she said urgently. 'I hope that by tomorrow I shall have a great deal to tell you.'

He agreed, bowed hurriedly and left her without even a touch of the hand. She stood bereft in the cold wind blowing in from the sea. And this, she thought, was how it would be for ever if Tom was condemned. Lomax's sense of honour would not allow her to be the friend – much less the wife – of a man whose son was hanged . . .

Chapter Twenty-Four

Dido was determined to discover the true cause of Tom's dispute with the dead man and intended to begin enquiries among the inn servants directly. But she was past her time when she arrived at the inn. She found the manor chaise drawn up on the carriage drive, beside the London coach, and regretfully decided that her enquiries must be postponed.

As she hurried into the porch, she almost ran against the brilliant waistcoat of Mr Isaac Mountjoy. 'A thousand, thousand apologies, fair maid!' he cried, drawing back and sweeping off his hat.

Dido politely assured him that not even one apology was required and would have gone on her way. But he detained her with: 'May I be so bold as to enquire whether you are of the party come from Charcombe Manor?'

'Yes.'

'And,' with a magnificent wave of his hand, 'is all that company still gathered within the portals of this hostelry?'

'I am sorry, sir, I do not know.'

He bowed again and she continued on her way – with only one admiring backward glance at the waistcoat.

In the parlour she found Mr Parry waiting for her – and only Mr Lancelot Fenstanton and Mrs Bailey remaining from the manor party: the others having all been conveyed home in Mrs Manners' chaise. Fenstanton quickly assured her that not one of their number had recognised Mr Brodie. 'So unless you can supply an answer, Miss Kent, we are no nearer to knowing who the fellow was.'

'Oh dear, how very strange.' Dido's gaze was fixed upon Mrs Bailey who was sitting in the sunlight by the inn parlour's tall windows; she held her red shawl tightly about her, the rouge was stark against her pale cheeks as she stared out at the people on the sweep, and she was unusually silent. There seemed to be a look of guilt or anxiety about her. Had she in fact recognised the corpse and was she now lying about it?

Dido would have liked to stay a little longer in the parlour to observe the lady more closely, but Mr Parry was very eager to have the business concluded. Mr Fenstanton offered her his arm and she had no choice but to accompany the two gentlemen to the room in which Mr Brodie had been laid.

'I hope you will not find the sight of the corpse too distressing,' Mr Lancelot said as he and Dido followed the magistrate up stairs which were so new built they smelt still of planed wood. 'There is a quantity of old blood. But he has been made decent – and from his face you would not suspect that he had not died the most peaceful death imaginable.' He touched her hand and searched her face. 'You are not afraid are you, Miss Kent?'

'Oh no, not at all.'

'Capital!' But he continued to rest his hand upon hers.

At the top of the stairs Mr Parry turned away from the grand front of the building and led them along a low-ceiled passage with drugget on its floor and a faint atmosphere of boiled fowls; they passed a flight of backstairs and came at last to a small door in a lathe-and-plaster wall.

Mr Parry paused with his hand on the latch. 'There is no occasion for you to approach the corpse, Miss Kent. You need only stand by the door and look upon his face.'

'Oh! I do not mind taking a closer look,' Dido assured him and, before he could protest, she walked boldly into the room.

It was a small room with bare floorboards and clean white walls marked only by a small square of sunlight thrown in through an open window, which also admitted the clatter of hooves on cobbles and the unmistakable odour of stables.

The man lay on a low cot, eyes weighted with pennies, jaw decently bound up with a handkerchief. His coat was stained brown almost all over with blood – and his face was entirely unknown to Dido.

She shook her head and Mr Parry held open the door for her with a look of dignified impatience, but she stepped closer to the bed.

The man who lay there was slightly built with extremely tanned skin. He was elderly – perhaps seventy or so. His sunken cheeks and prominent chin were frosted over with silver stubble which filled and accentuated every crease and fold of his skin. His head was bald and an old-fashioned grey wig lay beside a broad-brimmed hat and a pocket watch on the pot cupboard beside the bed.

His face was creased. Little fans of lines spread from the corners of his eyes – suggesting many years of squinting into strong sunlight.

'I think,' she said, 'that he has lived a long time in a hot climate. Indeed, from his complexion, I would think he has but just returned to England.'

Parry looked at her with disapproval. 'Miss Kent, there is no occasion at all for you to study the body so minutely.'

But Mr Fenstanton showed a great deal more enthusiasm for her ideas. 'Ha!' he cried, 'I thought the same myself. And the landlord confirms it. He says the fellow spoke of being abroad for almost thirty years. But just returned, he said, and making for his old home.'

'I do not think we need trouble the young lady with the details of this unpleasant business,' protested Mr Parry.

'Oh, it is no trouble,' Dido assured him, and pretended not to see that he was still holding open the door for her exit. 'And, I think,' she continued, looking down at the sunken face, 'that Mr Brodie was an ill-tempered, perhaps a disappointed man.'

Mr Parry said something very dignified in which was included something about not permitting any daughter of his . . .

But his words were lost in another great bark of interest from Mr Lancelot. 'Now why should you think the fellow was bad-tempered?' he asked standing close to Dido and looking upon her as if she were a prodigy.

'Because of these very deep lines between his brows.

231

Do you see – here, just above his nose? They are made by frowning.'

'Are they?' To try out the idea, Mr Fenstanton formed his own cheerful features into an exaggerated frown and put his fingers to the furrows on his forehead. 'I believe you are right. That's very interesting, ain't it, Parry?'

'I do not believe the man's disposition is of any significance . . .'

'And what else can you tell us about the fellow, Miss Kent?' cried Mr Fenstanton.

'Very little, except that he favours the fashions of his youth.' She pointed to the long waistcoat, the loose, braided coat, waved her hand towards the wig upon the pot cupboard. 'And his clothes are old and neglected. I do not think he was a wealthy man.'

'Ha! There was not a great deal of money in his pockets!'

'And was anything else found upon his person?'

'No,' said Mr Parry firmly.

'Only this.' Mr Lancelot drew a piece of paper from beneath the wig. 'It was in his coat pocket.'

The paper was heavily stained with blood. Dido took it carefully by a clean corner and carried it into the light of the window in order to make out the words which were written on it. It was a list of places.

Plymouth, Charcombe, Bristol, Birmingham, Manchester, Kendal, Gretna Green.

'It is perhaps a list of the main stages on the journey he was making,' she suggested.

'We think remarkably alike,' cried Mr Lancelot, 'for that was my own thought exactly! And you see he is heading northward.'

'To Gretna Green.'

'Aye. Parry has sent a message there to find out if anyone knows him. It seems likely it is his home.'

'How very . . . odd,' said Dido. That the man should come from the destination of eloping lovers seemed as if it ought to have some significance – but she could not determine exactly *what* it might imply.

She handed back the stained paper and looked about the room for anything of interest.

Poor Mr Parry held open the door and coughed meaningfully in vain. Even when he suggested that his friend should escort the young lady back to the parlour, the young lady affected deafness.

Her eye had fallen now upon a small valise with a heavy travelling coat neatly folded on top of it. On the toilette stand beside it lay a comb, and a razor with its leather strop. All three items meticulously aligned with one another.

'Are these all his possessions?' she asked.

'Yes. He had little enough.' Mr Lancelot obligingly opened the valise for her inspection. Inside there were two shirts and a pair of stockings. Poor, threadbare old things, but arranged with all the care that a duke's valet might bestow upon his master's possessions.

Dido frowned and turned back to the man upon the bed. She studied those parts of his coat and breeches which were not stained by blood and detected several missing buttons – and candle grease upon a sleeve. She looked at the thick brown hands crossed upon his broken breast; the thumb and forefinger of his right hand were stained with ink, the knuckles of both hands dusted with soot.

'Now that is a little odd,' she mused. 'Mr Fenstanton, have the clothes in the portmanteau been rearranged? Or the items on the dressing stand made tidy?'

'I don't believe so, have they Parry?'

'No. It is not my intention that *anyone* should interfere with this room.'

'Why do you ask about it?' said Mr Lancelot, smiling encouragement.

'Because the arrangement of Mr Brodie's possessions seems to argue for a meticulous, tidy character; but the state of his person declares the opposite.'

She leant closer to the bed, searching for an answer to this puzzle. Searching for clues as to who and what this man had been in life. But, close to the body, the smell of death and dried blood was overpowering. She turned away abruptly and, making a hasty excuse, almost ran from the room.

Mr Parry breathed a sigh of relief as she passed him.

Dido hurried along the dim passageway and onto the landing where there was fresh air blowing in through the inn's main door. She stopped and drew in several deep breaths. The wave of sickness retreated.

'Damn me! But you're mighty sick!' cried Mr Fenstanton as he hurried to join her. 'I fear that looking at the corpse distressed you more than you thought of.' He took her hand solicitously.

'It is nothing. It is over now.'

He was standing rather closer than was strictly necessary.

'You are very collected,' he said admiringly. 'And your observations are damned interesting.' Dido paid rather less attention to his words than the fact that he still retained her hand. The rail of the stairs was at her back; it was impossible for her to move. But his proximity was not, exactly, unpleasant.

'You must not mind old Parry being so short with you,' he continued. 'He's a dry old stick and he don't know how to appreciate a clever woman. But,' he said, sinking his voice and searching her face with handsome brown eyes, 'I do, I assure you.'

Dido smiled . . . And then the ordinary, common sense part of her mind, which had been oddly silent since his taking her hand, raised a protest: reminding her abruptly that she was standing a great deal too close to a gentleman to whom she was not related, and that his attentive manner in such a situation – and in the wake of the scene just past – was rather indelicate. 'You must excuse me,' she said, 'I am in need of air – I shall walk out to the carriage.'

'Yes, yes, of course.' He stepped away immediately. 'I must consult with Parry over what is to be done with the body. I shall join you in a few minutes.'

Dido turned away to the stairs and, as she did so, she was almost certain that she caught a glimpse of Mrs Bailey's scarlet shawl in the hall below. She blushed uncomfortably, and hoped with all her heart that the little scene just past had not been witnessed by that lady.

Chapter Twenty-Five

There was no Mrs Bailey in the hall when Dido reached the bottom of the stairs, only the very small pot boy in his very long apron carrying an empty ale jug away from the parlour.

The sight of him provided a welcome distraction and reminded Dido of her need to discover more about Tom's meeting with Mr Brodie. She called out to the boy as she reached the bottom of the stairs, and he stopped in the middle of the hall, swinging the jug back and forth in his hand.

He did not appear at all surprised when she began to question him about Mr Brodie's last evening at the inn, for the topic was upon everyone's lips. He was very happy to tell everything that he knew – and probably a great deal that he did not know but which he had now persuaded himself that he knew.

'Oh yes, yes,' he cried eagerly, swinging the jug more widely, and wiping his free hand upon his apron. He had heard 'the gennlemen' arguing in the parlour that evening. And very angry they had been, he was sure. Shouting and carrying on in a terrible way! He did not know that he had ever heard such another terrible quarrel in his life! They had seemed so very angry that he wondered they did not start out fighting straight away . . .

It was clear that – in the mind of the pot boy at least – the dispute had taken on all the force of a murderous rage. And Dido feared that, by the time his evidence was put before a jury, it might be almost enough to hang Tom Lomax on its own.

'And do you know what their disagreement was about?' she asked.

The boy frowned and peered down into his empty jug. 'Just their game of noddy, miss. Until they started to play they seemed friendly enough. Young Mr Lomax, he kept calling for more whisky and pressing it upon Mr Brodie, very friendly like. "You need it," he said, "to keep the English damp out of your bones." It was only after they sat down to cards that the trouble started.'

'You are quite sure it was the game they disagreed over?'

'Oh yes.'

'Nothing else? Mr Brodie was only angry because Mr Lomax lost and could not pay what he owed?'

'Oh no! It weren't like that!'

'Was it not?'

'No, the young gennleman had won. He'd won and very pleased he was about it. But Mr Brodie was in a great rage. He swore he'd been cheated. "You've robbed me," he shouted again and again. "You've robbed me of everything I'd got."'

'Mr Lomax had won?'

The pot boy nodded vigorously. 'Won pretty handsome, I'd say.'

How odd, thought Dido as the boy hurried away to refill his jug. Why had Tom allowed them to believe that the argument was occasioned by an unpaid debt?

She turned away to the inn's door, but she had not gone far before another thought struck her with great force. If Tom had won 'pretty handsome', then what had become of his winnings? Why were there only a few shillings in his pocket when the constables seized him?

Outside, the sun was shining brightly on the inn yard and the London Mail was gone. A stable lad was whistling as he cleaned the gravel and raked out the wheels' tracks. The manor coachman was holding his horses' heads and jealously guarding the gleaming varnish of his carriage against the approach of seagulls.

Mrs Bailey was sitting within the carriage and, to Dido's surprise, Mr Mountjoy and his colourful waistcoat were in attendance upon her. The gentleman had one foot upon the step and an arm resting upon the open door – and he was leaning into the vehicle in a very familiar way.

Dido was not, of course, so ill mannered as to attempt to hear their conversation – at least, not until she, quite accidentally, caught a word or two. 'A friend sent me to you,' the gentleman was saying. 'She told me where to find you . . .'

This was too strong an invitation for Dido. She halted her approach.

Mr Mountjoy leant a little closer into the carriage; Dido stood still and strained to hear.

'Can I not prevail upon you, my dear Augusta,' he was urging in a low voice. 'While your husband is sojourning in foreign climes, will you not take pity upon your humble servant.'

Dido smiled thoughtfully; she believed she was beginning to understand Mrs Augusta Bailey rather well . . .

'The too, too fortunate Mr Bailey,' continued Mr Mountjoy, 'need never know. If only you will be kind to me, *nobody* need ever know about our connection.'

Dido gave a little cough to announce her presence. Mountjoy turned, saw that he was observed, and immediately took his leave.

Mrs Bailey was seriously discomposed and blushing furiously. 'You must not mind my friend Isaac, Dido,' she said as the gentleman kissed his hand to them both and bowed himself off. 'He is a very old acquaintance and he is inclined to allow himself liberties. He says the most shocking things!'

'If he is a nuisance to you,' Dido suggested, enjoying her discomfort, 'you had better ask Mr Fenstanton to talk to the host here and have him sent away from the inn.'

'Oh no! It is nothing. I beg you will not speak to anyone about it.'

'Very well, if you do not wish it.' Dido was too much preoccupied with other thoughts even to torment Mrs Bailey. She took her seat in the carriage; gradually the colour faded from the cheeks of her companion and an uneasy silence ensued.

They watched Mr Mountjoy striding away to the inn. There was a small thud as a seagull landed on the carriage roof – followed by a furious croaking as the coachman tossed a piece of gravel at it.

A little conversation upon light and indifferent subjects was required to dispel the air of embarrassment in the coach. But all the subjects presently in Dido's mind were heavy – and far from indifferent. If Tom had won at the card table, she thought, why was the money not in his possession when the constables seized him? Where could it have gone? A few shillings, racecards and snuff – that was all that had been found in his pockets . . .

'My dear Dido,' broke in Mrs Bailey, who had now regained her composure and was watching her companion narrowly, 'I hope you will not mind my remarking that you seemed a little distressed just now – when you returned from looking at poor Mr Brodie. I hope you are recovered from the shock of seeing the corpse.'

Dido made as slight a reply as she could. She was by no means pleased to find that Mrs Bailey *had* been in the hall to witness the scene between herself and Mr Fenstanton. Her own feelings about that little encounter were still confused; she did not wish to contemplate how it might have appeared to a looker-on.

'Dear Lance!' cried Mrs Bailey with another shrewd look which she quickly softened into her usual expression of condescending goodwill. 'He seemed so very concerned about your distress.'

Dido made no reply, for her mind had returned once more to the inexplicable emptiness of Mr Tom Lomax's pockets. It had occurred to her that there was something else, beside his winnings, which should have been in them . . .

'This business of Letitia running away,' sighed Mrs Bailey, 'is a very great worry to poor Lance. And now Mr

Brodie is dead and he must put himself to trouble over that. He is so *conscientious.*'

'I am sure he is.'

'Lance always wishes *everybody* to be happy,' continued Mrs Bailey tilting her head to one side and watching Dido closely. 'He is so very attentive to *everybody.*'

She spoke with such particular meaning that Dido must give her a little attention. 'Mr Fenstanton seems to be a very kind gentleman,' she hazarded.

'Oh, he is! I have a very great regard for him – and so has Mr Bailey. And that was why I was so very happy when—' Mrs Bailey stopped herself and put her hand to her mouth with a look of great consciousness. 'I declare! I was upon the point of speaking out of turn! I beg you will forget entirely what I just said, Dido. Being unguarded is one of my greatest faults. My friends are always rebuking me for it. "Augusta," they say, "you are so very unguarded. You are insufficiently cold and reserved."'

Dido only smiled and thought how obliging it was of Mrs Bailey's friends to be always discovering such very attractive faults. She returned to the vexed question of Tom Lomax's pockets . . .

'No, no!' cried Mrs Bailey holding up a hand. 'I must insist that we say no more upon this subject! I declare I have gone as red as my shawl. I beg you not to press me.'

Dido looked out of the carriage window and considered whether there was any way in which Tom could have removed something from his pocket and concealed it before his arrest . . .

'Oh dear!' cried Mrs Bailey. 'I can see that you are

wondering at my breaking off so sudden. I *know* that you are offended.'

'No, not at all . . .'

'Oh! I cannot bear to be suspected of incivility.'

'I assure you—'

'Well then, if you insist upon it, I think I must explain myself. I was,' she whispered, seizing both Dido's hands, and quite forcing her to pay attention, 'upon the point of saying that I was pleased to find Lancelot so very much in love with Letitia.'

'In love?' repeated Dido. She had not expected this to be the secret which her companion was so very determined upon *not* concealing. Nor could she quite understand why Mrs Bailey should wish so particularly to convey the information to herself. 'Mr Lancelot is in love with Miss Verney?'

'Oh yes. He is over head and ears!' Mrs Bailey assured her. 'Of course, he has said nothing about it. But knowing him so very well, I cannot doubt it. My friends tell me that I have quite a talent for detecting these things.' Her sharp eyes seemed to be watching for the effect of her words on her listener. 'And though the Great Bard tells us that "the course of true love never did run smooth", I do believe that in this case . . .' The rest was all sunk in a convenient silence and a knowing smile.

Dido murmured a polite wish for the gentleman's success with the lady, but her heart was not in it. She was distracted, for all at once she was seeing in her mind the moment of Tom Lomax being seized: his attempted escape, his stumbling against the stones, and his careful replacing of those stones . . .

'My dear,' said Mrs Bailey in a gloating voice, 'you seem upset. Have I said something amiss?'

'Oh no, not at all.' But Dido already had one foot upon the step of the carriage. 'It is nothing – a slight headache only. A little air will set me to rights. Please be so kind as to tell Mr Fenstanton that I shall walk back to Charcombe Manor.'

'Very well, and I hope you are soon recovered, my dear,' Mrs Bailey called after her. Her face leant out of the carriage window, yellow curls blowing across her eyes, her startlingly red lips parted in a look of ill-natured satisfaction.

Dido paid her no heed as she hurried down the grassy bank before the inn and started along the terrace. Her thoughts were all fixed upon the benches in the mall – and the heap of stones which lay beside them.

She must investigate those stones without delay.

Chapter Twenty-Six

As she hurried forward, the brisk wind from the sea lifted Dido's pelisse and set it flapping, obliging her to hold it with both hands. She reached the bottom of the bank and came onto the main terrace which, she was pleased to see, was deserted. The dinner hour was approaching and all the widows and half-pay officers had returned to their lodgings to dress.

Down upon the sands a single bathing machine was ploughing out through white-crested waves, the tail of its horse streaming in the wind, the water foaming about its wheels. It would seem that Mr George Fenstanton was setting a good example to Charcombe's visitors and taking his daily dip.

Shivering at the very idea, Dido hurried on towards the place where the green benches stood and, as she came close, she fixed her eyes eagerly upon the stones: a grey pile, almost as high as the bench beside it.

Tom Lomax had hidden something in that pile of stones.

She was sure of it. He had hidden something which he did not wish the constables to find in his possession. That had been the cause of his sudden movement, even though he must have known that escape was impossible.

Perhaps it was the money he had won from Mr Brodie which he had hidden – or perhaps it was something more dangerous . . .

She paused as she reached the bench upon which Tom had been sitting, and she recollected the scene. He had been lounging with his legs stretched across the pavement; one hand had been resting on the head of his cane – and the other hand had been holding a letter. *He had been reading a letter.*

Yet there had been no letter discovered when the constables made a search of his person.

Dido stooped down in the biting wind beside the stone heap. It was comprised of broken rock and fragments of dried mortar, each piece about the size of a fist. She peered into the gaps, but could see no edge of paper, no scrap of white among the grey. She closed her eyes in an effort of memory. Before the men seized him, Tom had been replacing stones on the very top of the pile.

Tentatively she began to remove the topmost stones, trying not to care too much about the staining of her gloves with dust, the scratching of the soft kid. The wind whipped her cloak and bonnet ribbons in all directions, and cut at her cheeks. The stones tumbled about her hands, trapping and bruising her fingers. She fervently hoped that nobody would pass by and see her engaged upon such a strange task. But she had not moved more than a dozen pieces of stone before she was rewarded with a glimpse of white paper. She began to work faster and a minute later she had the letter in her grasp.

Smiling in triumph she sat down on the bench and turned her prize over in dusty hands. The letter was so very stained, its edges so much torn, that she suspected it had been far from fresh even before it was immured in the workmen's rubble. The seal of blue wax was broken roughly as if the letter had been torn open without the aid of a knife.

She looked hastily about her to be sure she was alone on the terrace before reading the direction written on the letter's cover.

Lancelot Fenstanton esquire, Charcombe Manor, Devonshire, England.

There was a great sinking of the heart as she read the words. Though she could not immediately determine why they should fill her with such dread . . .

That the letter was not addressed to Tom Lomax was a surprise and the question of how – and why – the letter came to be in his possession must arise. She folded her arms tightly about her and shivered in the penetrating wind. The answer which suggested itself was not at all welcome.

And now she faced a new difficulty. The only right, the only honourable, course was to hand this letter, unread, to the man to whom it was directed. But what would be the consequence of such an action?

Tom had been most anxious to conceal this letter from the forces of justice. Why? Did it provide evidence against him?

She took the folded paper in one hand and tapped it restlessly against the other. Her heart beat fast with the need to know what was written within . . . And the seal was already broken. When she delivered the letter to Mr Fenstanton he would not know whether she had read it or not . . .

She blushed with shame and found herself remembering a time about a year and a half ago at Belsfield Hall, when she had rebuked Tom Lomax himself for reading what was not addressed to him. She had then been as determined against benefiting from information so dishonourably gained as any well-bred woman could be. Had she changed in the intervening eighteen months? Perhaps the interest she had recently begun to take in mysteries and injustices had weakened her principles, corrupted her mind. Perhaps all her busyness in these causes was no more than an excuse for that impertinent meddling in other people's lives which is so frequently derided in ageing spinsters. Perhaps Mr Lomax was right to condemn.

But the very thought of that gentleman brought her moralising to an abrupt halt, and turned her mind instead to his suffering in the face of his son's danger. And all she could think of was that the paper in her hand might reveal something about the case . . .

In a moment the letter was open upon her lap and her eyes were rapidly devouring the words – as if the severity of her transgression might be lessened by speed.

Hebron Plantation, Antigua. 17th January 1807

Dear Lancelot,

I would have this letter reach you with all possible speed and so, rather than wait upon the packet, I am entrusting it to James Brodie who sails tomorrow in a private vessel bound for Plymouth. God knows! I would find a better messenger if I could; but the fellow says he knows Charcombe. He says he plans to visit the place on business in the course of his journey home. And, dispatch being of the first importance, I must take my chance with him – though I have not known him a week.

I trust you will pardon me, old friend, for not making all those remarks upon my own health and enquiries into the health of all our acquaintance which a fellow is supposed to put in his letters. Consider everything said that is proper, I have not time for it. To the point –

I would have you take hold of young Tom Lomax and tell him that he is a damnable villain. Tell him that if, upon my return, I find him within twenty miles of my family I shall put a bullet through his brains, or else have Jack Smith take the gelding iron to him.

Lance, what will you say when I tell you that the wretch has had the impertinence to raise his eyes to Letitia? Or I should rather say he has raised his eyes to Letitia's fortune. For all his fine words I do not believe there is any real affection in the business. The whole world knows Tom Lomax is all to pieces and his father barely holding off the creditors. And John Harris gave me a hint more than a year back that the fellow was set upon marrying well. But I thought little of it. For I never thought Letitia would be foolish enough to be taken in.

But I tell my tale ill. I have not said that I have had a letter from young Lomax, who, thinking I know nothing of him, has the audacity to 'beg for my consent'. He and Letitia are 'so very much in love and she has done him the inestimable honour of agreeing to be his wife'.

He takes me for a damned fool! He thinks to have the

matter settled while I am at a distance and hopes I know nothing about his character. But you may tell him, Lance, that he has wagered on the wrong horse this time. Tell him that if he marries the girl without my consent he shall not see a penny of her fortune . . .

I cannot write any more now; Brodie rides for the port within the hour. He is waiting in the next room. Dear God! But I can smell the rum on him from here! If only there were a better messenger to be had.

I know that you will not fail me, Lance. I know you will act as soon as this comes into your hands.

The horses are at the door now. I must finish in haste. Yours ever in trust and friendship.

Reginald Bailey.

Dido found that she was shaking uncontrollably; shock and fear were chilling her to the bone. She stood up hastily in the biting wind, folding up the paper and wishing that she might throw it out into the sea. She wanted rid of it. Its touch seemed to freeze her hand.

Tom's possession of this letter, together with its import, would be damning evidence in the eyes of any assize court jury. She doubted there were to be found twelve men anywhere in the country who – when the evidence was placed before them – would not conclude that Tom had killed Mr Brodie in order to get this letter from him.

It was such a very *reasonable* conclusion.

She crossed her arms about herself as a new horror occurred . . .

It was such a very reasonable conclusion that a part of her mind was almost believing it to be true!

249

Never before had she doubted Tom's innocence. Every fibre and sinew of her being had been bent on finding the truth; not simply for the truth's own sake, but because she was sure that the truth would acquit him.

But now, for the first time, she faced the possibility of guilt; a guilt which, if proven, would destroy for ever the happiness of the man she loved.

And for several minutes she was overpowered. She stood, not knowing what to do, in the piercing wind which tore at her pelisse and bonnet, exposing her arms and whipping her hair about her face. She turned blindly first one way and then another; the wind and her wretchedness drew warm tears from the corners of her eyes which chilled immediately upon her cheeks.

But at last she exerted herself, forcing reason upon her terror. She must act. She must find out whether this worst of all fears was founded upon fact or only appearance.

She turned with growing resolution in the direction of Old Charcombe and began to walk. Tom Lomax himself was the only person who could answer the questions which were now raging in her head. She must talk to Tom directly.

She did not know how the gaoler was to be persuaded to admit her, and she preferred not to consider the impropriety of the visit. But she knew that she was bringing a world of trouble upon her own head; for even if no word of her going unprotected into a gaol was to get back to Charcombe Manor, her continued absence from the house would bring sufficient disapprobation from her aunt.

Let all that be as it may. She must speak with Tom. She walked on resolutely towards the village.

Chapter Twenty-Seven

It took every penny in Dido's reticule to gain her entrance to the lock-up 'for a minute. I can't allow more'n that,' declared the gaoler. 'It ain't proper you being there alone with him.' And there was no stool provided this time. Perhaps, she thought, her sitting down would render the visit even less proper.

When she entered the cell, Tom was standing beside the window, watching the passing of feet and attempting to tease the stray cat – which was, however, too clever for him and was contriving to tease *him* by keeping constantly beyond his reach.

He turned as the door opened and looked past Dido – expecting to see his father. He began upon an exclamation of surprise but she cut him short by telling him immediately that she had found the letter.

He stopped with one hand against the window's ledge and turned wary eyes upon the paper in her hand. He licked at his lips as if they were suddenly very dry. And, as the gaoler's steps retreated and her own eyes grew accustomed to the prison's gloom, she saw the raw fear in his grimy face.

'And what do you intend to do with it?' he asked.

'I intend to deliver it to the gentleman to whom it is

directed.' She folded up the letter and put it away in her pocket.

'You mean, in fact, to put the noose round my neck!'

She said nothing, only watched him closely.

Tom looked sly. His eyes slid about furtively, the whites of them showing very bright amid the dirt of his face. 'Why have you come here?' he said. 'Why are you not on your way back to Fenstanton?'

'Because I wish to hear your explanation of how this letter came to be in your possession – that is, if there is any explanation other than your shooting Mr Brodie in order to obtain it.'

'I did *not* kill the fellow!'

She waited in silence.

'Very well,' he burst out. 'I will confess that I got the letter from Brodie.'

'That much is impossible to deny! I saw you hide it. I found it still there among the stones.'

'Damn you and your interference!' He stared up at the clammy roof of the cell. 'I thought you had undertaken to help me. Not find more reasons to hang me.'

'I have undertaken to find out the truth,' said Dido as steadily as she could. 'And you have assured me that the truth will prove you innocent.'

'It will.'

'Then why do you prevent my discovering it?' she cried, trying – and failing – to keep the anger from her voice. 'Why did you lie to me? Why did you tell me that you knew nothing about Mr Brodie, or his proposed visit to the manor house? You knew, did you not, that this was the news of Miss Verney which he intended to convey to Mr Fenstanton?'

'Oh, very well,' he said sulkily. 'I knew. And I . . . persuaded him to give me the letter.'

'No,' said Dido, who had been thinking the matter over as she walked from the town. 'I am quite sure you did not persuade. I believe you won the letter at the card table.'

'How do you know that?' he demanded abruptly, and his look of shock confirmed the idea.

'Because the boy at the inn assured me you had won "handsomely", and yet there was no money either upon your person, or hidden among the stones. There was only a letter – a letter which is of considerable value to you.'

He stared at her for a minute, as if assessing just how dangerous she was. 'Very well, I won the letter from him.'

'That was very fortunate for you,' she said and turned briskly to the question which had taken possession of her mind as she walked. 'But how did you *know* that he was carrying something which was of such great interest to you?'

Tom returned his gaze to the roof stones. 'I cannot recall,' he said. 'I suppose he mentioned it.'

'Oh!' cried Dido tested beyond endurance. 'Will you give that account to the judge? Do you suppose he will believe it?'

Tom licked again at his dry lips as he faced the vision of trial and execution which she had conjured into the cell. 'What do you wish me to tell you?' he said.

'I wish you to tell me about your acquaintance with Mr Brodie.'

'I did not—'

She held up her hand. 'I give you warning. If you repeat the lie that you met Mr Brodie by chance at the inn, I shall leave immediately and assume that you no longer desire my help. I will *not* believe that you met by chance the very man who had in his possession a letter upon which your fortunes depended. You met by appointment, did you not?'

'Very well,' he sighed. 'Yes. Brodie had sent a message to me. He had begun enquiries after a Tom Lomax as soon as he landed at Plymouth.'

'So Mr Brodie had already opened Mr Bailey's letter?'

'Of course he had. Reg Bailey was a great fool to trust the fellow. Brodie would have sold his own grandmother's love letters if he could have found anyone willing to buy them. He had come back to England a poor man and was determined to mend his fortunes.'

'He offered to sell Mr Bailey's letter to you?'

'At a price much higher than I could afford. So . . . we drank a little . . . played a hand or two . . .'

'You mean that you plied him with drink and won all his money from him.'

'The man was no more clever than he was honest.'

'And so, finally, when he had nothing left, you offered one last wager, I suppose.'

'It was a fair offer,' said Tom, 'generous, in fact. I said I would return everything I'd won from him, if he would play one last game – with the letter as his stake.'

'And was the game as fair as the offer?'

'Miss Kent! If you were a man I could call you out for that remark!'

'If your only argument for the game's fairness would be to put a bullet through my head, then I am quite certain that you cheated.'

'By God!' said Tom quietly. 'You are taking pleasure in this!'

'No!' Dido recoiled.

'Yes. For once the little spinster has power over a man and she is determined to make the most of it, isn't she?' His grimy, unshaven face broke into a grin and his teeth gleamed as white as his eyes. 'I pity my father! The old man must be in his dotage if he thinks he can ever be happy married to such an interfering, unfeminine little harridan!'

'Allow me to observe,' said Dido struggling for mastery of her voice, 'that it is a little unwise to insult a person whose help you wish to enlist.'

'But you will help me whatever I say – for the old man's sake. And for your own sake too,' he added with a sneer. 'I know my father and his unreasonable sense of honour. If I hang, he'll cut himself off like a hermit, and you . . .' he pointed a dirty, broken-nailed finger, 'will have lost the last chance you are likely to get of not dying an old maid.'

Every impulse of wounded pride demanded that she walk out of the cell without another word. But affection held her rooted to the spot. She forced herself to speak calmly. 'For your father's sake—'

'The best thing you can do for *him*,' interrupted Tom

255

with a sly look, 'is to burn that letter you've got in your pocket.'

'You know I cannot do that.'

'Good God! It is a pretty kind of love which has such scruples!'

Dido was prevented from defending herself by the sound of a key rattling in the outer door, followed by the gaoler's footfall.

'I shall deliver the letter to Mr Fenstanton,' she said. 'But I shall also convey your explanation of how it came into your possession.'

'Christ!' Tom kicked at the wall. But then as the footsteps neared he said urgently, 'There is something else I must tell you. Sutherland was lying when he told you he didn't know Brodie.'

'Lying?' Why ever do you say so?'

'I have been thinking the matter over.' He leant forward eagerly and winced as the iron chafed his leg. 'Sutherland and Brodie *had* met before. I am sure of it.'

'Why? How can you know?'

'You can always tell by the way fellows play cards whether they have sat down together before. They know each other's little tricks and weaknesses. I'll swear to it that Brodie and Sutherland had played one another before – and played often too.'

'Hmm.' Dido turned away as the heavy door behind her swung open to reveal the gaoler's ruddy face.

'You don't believe me?' cried Tom angrily, starting forward so that the chain on his legs pulled tight, almost overbalancing him.

'Oh yes,' said Dido calmly. 'I believe you understand all about tricks at the card table.'

'If you were a man—' shouted Tom.

'If I were a man you would be obliged to blow my brains out.' She turned towards the door. 'But, as I am a woman, you may leave them in my head where they might, possibly, be of some use to you.'

Chapter Twenty-Eight

Dido almost ran from the gaol – along the village street, over the bridge upon which she had stood with Mr Lomax, and into the shady lane, where Mr Fenstanton had delayed her. It seemed an age since she had come this way; her thoughts were now so different.

In her head she heard still the insults of that sly voice: 'interfering, unfeminine little harridan.'

Her spirit had risen against him in the moment; her tongue moving quickly to her own defence. But now she felt the wound – and felt it deeply. She was doubting her own motives for pursuing Tom's cause, doubting whether she was justified . . .

Tom's cruel words had given her such a very ugly picture of herself as she could hardly bear to look upon.

Her feet flew along the road, obeying the prosaic tyranny of the dinner hour and her aunt's displeasure; conveying her back to the measuring of medicine, the placing of cushions and all the other proper occupations of an impoverished niece and sister. But she knew that her mind had been straying very far from these womanly obligations from the moment that she heard of the murder. There had been from that moment an urge to protect, an impulse to activity which might – in one light – be considered 'unfeminine', an intrusion upon the territory of man.

And no woman who is sincerely attached would wish to appear 'unfeminine'. Was she, in her very efforts to secure a future with the man she loved, rendering herself unlovable? Was she becoming such a woman as any man of taste must turn from in disgust?

'Unfeminine', 'harridan'. Try as she might she could not silence the clamour of the words in her head.

She slowed her steps as she came within sight of the manor gates. Tired and worried, she was inclined to concede that it would be a great deal more *pleasant* to be as 'feminine' as she could: to do nothing – to sit in a bower like the ideal heroine in an old romance, passively waiting to be claimed by her loyal knight . . .

Until, happily, she recollected that she had no bower, and the heroines of old had not to contend with brown medicine and cushions – much less the likes of Doctor Prowdlee and his pew and a half full of children. No, she concluded, a certain degree of activity would seem to be *necessary* in a modern woman.

Femininity, like everything else, must adapt itself to the times. And, since philosophers seemed to be in agreement that 'moderation' should be the watchword of the present day, it followed that even femininity was to be indulged in only moderately . . .

She had reached the stone gateposts now and, breathless with haste and emotion, she must pause a while to collect herself before entering the house. It would be as well to decide now what was to be done next – for, once she walked through the door, there would be little opportunity for thought. Her aunt would, no doubt, have a great deal to say about her lateness.

But there was much to be done – she must be 'getting on'.

The letter must, of course, be delivered to Mr Fenstanton, though the very thought of it turned her heart cold. The evening would furnish little opportunity for private conversation with her host; but she must seek an interview early tomorrow morning. And once that was over, Tom's situation would be . . . *desperate*. She could think of no better word to describe it. But it was too painful an idea to dwell on long.

She turned instead to the bad character which Tom had given Mr Brodie – and the acquaintance he suspected with Mr Sutherland. What, she wondered, had been the business Mr Brodie had claimed to have in Charcombe? Had he come only to deliver – or sell – Mr Bailey's letter? Or – she tapped her hand thoughtfully against the stone pillar – had he other interests to pursue?

She found herself remembering the note which Mr Brodie had written to Mr Fenstanton. In it he had spoken of *papers* which were of the utmost importance. She was sure it was 'papers' not 'a paper'. Yes, he had certainly used the plural. Perhaps he had some other business to transact – business which might be connected with his acquaintance among Mr Fenstanton's guests . . .

This was a useful notion for it must strengthen her suspicions against the inmates of the manor house, and her mind rapidly recurred to her patchwork of the morning . . .

All at once her resolution was taken and she could see

her way forward. Some more penetrating questions must be put to Miss Emma Fenstanton without delay.

She smiled as she started down the carriage drive. Miss Emma's clandestine reading might provide some very pertinent insights into 'femininity', but – what was of greater consequence – she might be made to confess that she too harboured suspicions against one of Charcombe's residents . . .

It was whilst the company was at loo that evening that Dido seized upon her chance of talking with Miss Fenstanton.

She certainly had no place at the card table. They were playing too high for her and, besides, Mrs Bailey had been so good as to observe to Aunt Manners that she did not suppose 'your little companion will join us'. And Mr George Fenstanton, without even waiting for a reply, had dealt only five hands.

She was not sorry to be excluded – though she had pride enough to wish she had been consulted. She had already observed the quiet exit from the room of Miss Emma – with the little Tunbridge-ware workbox under her arm. And, as soon as everyone's attention was fixed upon the cards, she rose quietly and followed her.

The hall was silent and empty, lit only by the glow of one large log lying in a deep bed of ash on the hearth. But the light of candles showed around the door of the library which was standing ajar.

Dido approached cautiously, stepped into the room as quietly as she could, and came to a standstill immediately, arrested by the scene before her.

On a table near the centre of the room there were candles and the workbox stood beside them with its lid thrown back. But Emma was not by the table, she was kneeling upon the floor at a little distance. A small bundle wrapped in a grease-stained napkin lay beside her; one hand was raised and resting against the wooden panelling of the wall.

As Dido watched, Emma leant closer to the panel and began to talk in a low, reassuring voice. 'Do not be afraid . . .'

But at this point Emma looked about her – and saw Dido. She jumped up and stepped in front of the bundle to hide it from view.

'No! No!' Dido smiled, but spoke with firmness. 'You cannot conceal anything from me, Miss Fenstanton. I know what you are about.'

'Oh?' Emma clasped her hands behind her back and returned the gaze with an odd mixture of defiance, laughter and anxiety. 'And what am I about, Miss Kent?'

'You have come to bring food to your friend who is hidden here in the library.'

'Hidden? Here?' Emma raised her brows in playful surprise. 'Can you see anyone here?' She looked about in a great pretence of wonderment.

Dido merely shook her head and looked towards the panel. 'That is the door, is it?'

'Door?'

'The door to the priest's hole.'

'Who told you about the priest's hole?' cried Emma in genuine astonishment. 'No one here knows about it – except, perhaps, Lancelot. Letitia and I discovered it years ago when we were children, but told no one.'

'The Elizabethan lady in the long gallery told me,' said Dido. And when Emma only looked more puzzled, she explained: 'The lady was, quite clearly, a Catholic – for she holds a rosary, and a rosary is no part of Protestant devotions. And yet she lived in staunchly Protestant times. Therefore, her devotions must have been performed in secret; and, since she seems to have used this room as her chapel, I concluded that there might well be a hiding place behind the panels in here. It was a usual convenience in Catholic homes – a place where the priest could be concealed if Queen Elizabeth's men came calling.'

'How very clever of you to think of it!'

'Thank you. And then I remembered Mr Fenstanton's ghostly tale. A hidden child crying and no one able to find him.'

'Crying? You heard crying?' Emma spoke lightly. Her eyes danced about elusively. 'Do you suppose it was the ghost?'

'No, I do not,' said Dido firmly. 'Though I think it likely that you and poor Lady Fenstanton hit upon the same hiding place.' She took a seat beside the table. 'I first heard crying last Sunday night. And that same night I saw somebody coming in secret through the garden door into this room.' She paused. 'Somebody who appeared to be carrying something concealed beneath a cloak.'

'Oh!' Emma sat down and faced Dido across the table. 'You say that you believe I have a friend concealed here, Miss Kent. Who do you think that friend is?'

'The character which you gave yourself the other day first alerted me to the identity. You said that you could never bear to see anyone condemned unjustly. So I had only to look about me for such a being. Who in this house might have been condemned to an undeserved fate? And I realised that I had seen you pleading for such a cause with Mr Lancelot Fenstanton on my very first day at Charcombe.'

Emma smiled and turned her eyes upon the table. She did not seem very much afraid of Dido's deductions – but neither was she willing to give away anything which might be concealed. Secrets were delightful to her.

'I recalled that on that occasion you had come from the direction of the stables. I also remembered that, after you had failed in your pleas to your cousin, you attempted to come in here. I think you meant to look into this hiding place which you remembered from your childhood – to ascertain whether it would suit your purposes.'

'Miss Kent! You see a great deal too much – and remember too well!'

'Perhaps I do, for I also recall the scratch upon your hand that day – a scratch which had certainly not been got from gathering roses.'

'And how had I scratched myself?'

'I regret to say that it was your friend herself who had injured you. The friend for whom you steal food – food which you sometimes leave in a bowl beside the garden door.'

'But we have been very careful! Mrs Matthews takes the dish away every morning.'

'But the mark which it makes in the moss remains – and also the slugs which are drawn there by the meat.'

'Oh.'

'But perhaps I should speak of *friends* rather than *friend*. For besides the lady herself there is a baby, is there not? A baby who cries when he is left alone.'

Miss Fenstanton tilted her head to one side. Her cheeks dimpled. 'You do not mean to expose us, do you?' she said. 'Lancelot has been just too cruel!'

'No, I shall not expose you; but . . .' She was stopped by a little scratching from within the library wall. Emma turned anxiously towards it. 'I think your friend is hungry,' said Dido. 'You had better deliver her dinner.'

Laughing Emma jumped up and went to the wall, feeling along the edge of the panel until she found just the right place, then pressing firmly. The panel swung inward, forming a door no more than three feet high.

Beyond the door, Dido could see a dark, dusty space and, laid upon the stone floor, an old flannel petticoat. Standing on the petticoat and stretching herself was a small, thin, very worried-looking black cat; and, curled beside her, were three fat, sleeping kittens. The cat ran out, writhed gratefully about Emma's ankles and turned towards the napkin. Emma unfolded it and the cat set to work upon the slice of mutton within.

Meanwhile a little black kitten with white paws had woken and raised himself onto unsteady legs; his mouth opened in a tiny pink wail. Emma scooped him up, hushed him and planted a kiss upon the top of his head.

'You will not betray them will you?' she begged. 'You would not see the little ones drowned?'

The kitten, seeming to recognise the gravity of the

265

situation, fastened anxious blue eyes on Dido and opened his little pink mouth again in a completely silent cry. A little dust from the hiding place adorned his ridiculously long whiskers, and his tiny paws rested upon one another as if folded in supplication. It would have required a harder heart than Dido's to give him up to his persecutors.

But, for all that, she could not give her silence for nothing. She *must* condition.

'If I agree to keep your secret, Miss Fenstanton, will you, in return give me a little information?'

'Information?' Emma sat down upon the floor by the priest's hole, stroking the kitten in her lap. 'What sort of information?'

'The sort of information which might save a man from hanging undescrvcdly.'

'I have told you, I don't know anything . . .'

'But, I believe you do. You know something which suggests Mr Tom Lomax is innocent of the charge laid against him. That is why you have been so anxious to exonerate him.' Dido leant towards her, speaking low and urgent, trying with every inch of her being to force seriousness upon the elusive Miss Emma. 'I know it was on Sunday night that you removed the kittens from the stables – for on Monday morning I saw the stable lad searching for them so that he might carry out Mr Lancelot's sentence.'

'Yes, it was Sunday night . . .'

'And that was the night on which Mr Brodie was murdered.'

'Was it?' Emma bent her head over the kitten. 'I had forgotten.'

'No. I believe it has been very much upon your mind.'

Emma said nothing.

'I believe you saw something that night while you were creeping about on your errand of mercy. I believe you saw something which connects someone in this house with the murder.' She paused, but Emma would not look at her. 'Please tell me what you saw, Miss Fenstanton. Did you see one of the inmates of this house stirring? Did you see the murderer returning from the crime?'

'No!' Emma's head jerked up. 'No! I saw no one. I give you my word I saw no one. It was nothing . . . It probably meant nothing at all.'

'And yet it was enough to make you doubt Mr Lomax's guilt.'

Emma's pale little hand flew back and forth on the kitten's black fur. 'I did not see a person,' she insisted. 'And what I did see was nothing . . .'

'Then there can be no harm in your telling me about it.'

'Oh, very well! I saw a horse in the stables, that is all. I saw a horse that was hot and tired – from being ridden, you know. It appeared to be but just returned.'

'At one o'clock at night?'

'Yes. I thought it odd. But there might be a hundred innocent explanations.'

'And do you recall which horse it was? Do you know to whom it belongs?'

'No. I know nothing about horses. I declare they all look the same to me and cousin Lance has so many in his stable!'

'I see.' Dido sat, lost in thought for several minutes.

'There, I have told you everything I know – and you promise not to say anything about the kittens?'

'Oh, yes.' Dido's voice was calm; but her eye did not fail to note the look of exquisite relief on her companion's face. Emma had been fearful of more penetrating questions.

But in fact there was no need to press her further. For Dido could guess which horse it was that had been heated with exercise on Sunday night. It was the horse which had been found to be lame on Monday morning – the little grey mare.

And a simple question put to Charlie had already informed her that the grey mare belonged to Mr George Fenstanton.

Emma had given just the information which Dido had expected – and wished – to hear. And, all in all, the day ended more hopefully than the terrible events of the morning had seemed to anticipate. Here, at last, was solid evidence of a murderer within the house.

And all suspicions must now turn upon Mr George Fenstanton.

His horse had been ridden on the night of the murder; he and Mrs Manners shared a secret; and it was . . . *possible* that that secret concerned Mr Brodie.

This last point – the likelihood of Aunt Manners being the person in Charcombe Manor who knew Mr Brodie – was one of which Dido would dearly love to be certain. It had not been far from her thoughts for the last two days and it came to occupy her entirely that evening as she attended upon her aunt and settled her into her bed.

'If only I was sure that you knew Mr Brodie, Aunt,' she whispered quietly to herself as she put away the slippers and the dressing robe. 'If only I was *sure*. Then I could begin to build my case against Mr George.'

She turned back to the bed and stood for a moment watching the sleeping figure. The room was quite chilly and the air smelt of the woodsmoke which a rising wind was blowing back occasionally from the dying fire. The wind was also throwing thin snatches of rain at the windows and rattling the old leaded frames; the only other sound in the room came from Aunt Manners herself: a rhythmic little wheeze – the precursor of outright snoring.

As Dido looked at the little white face in which every little crease and fold had, through enforced attendance, become as familiar as her own reflection, it seemed all but impossible that there could be secrets or mystery hidden here. But she was too much a pupil of human nature to doubt the possibility . . .

She moved insensibly towards the bed where the slight figure lay, silent and stately. The fragile little fingers were arranged neatly as ever along the sheet's edge. They appeared oddly naked now, with only the white marks in the flesh bearing witness to the lost rubies and diamonds. And the one remaining ring did little to relieve the stark appearance of loss, for it was a plain, narrow thing of pale, poor-quality gold.

Why, wondered Dido again, should any woman give up all her valuable rings to a brother she despised? Was it possible that it was because of an acquaintance with the dead man which must be hidden at any cost?

Was it possible that George Fenstanton had killed the man to preserve a very valuable secret?

She stood at the bedside consumed with the desire to know . . . to know for sure . . .

And, as she hesitated, her eye fell upon the bottle of brown medicine which stood on the table beside the bed. Her aunt had drunk freely of it this evening, and it was impossible not to remember her own words to Eliza . . . the method of gaining information which she had – half in jest – started.

A few nights ago, under the influence of brown medicine, Mrs Manners had been induced to answer a question she would not answer in a sensible state. A question of which she had – most conveniently – no memory the next day.

If Dido spoke now quietly to her aunt, was it possible that she could obtain an answer from within that strange half-sleeping, half-waking world?

It hardly seemed honourable . . . but the temptation was very great.

The wind rose to a howl outside, the window rattled and the old crewel work curtains swayed in the draught.

Dido stepped up to the bed and knelt down to bring her face close to the sleeping woman, her cheek rested on the cool linen sheet. 'Aunt?' she said tentatively, still uncertain whether to make the attempt.

There was no reply, but the lids lifted with promising slowness. The eyes fixed themselves upon an unseen distance; the lips moved, forming no words but making a little dry sound.

These were symptoms too good to be wasted.

'Aunt,' whispered Dido, 'what do you know of Mr Brodie?'

The eyes rolled to right and left, the fingers tightened about the sheet. 'James Brodie?' she said, speaking quite distinct. 'He is not to be trusted – that is what I always said, and I was proved right. He stole from us.'

Chapter Twenty-Nine

'And so, you see, *my aunt* was acquainted with the dead man.' Dido turned her eyes up anxiously to Mr Lomax's face as she finished the account. 'It is a material point, is it not?'

She was earnestly willing her companion to be heartened by the news, for she must soon tell him of Mr Bailey's letter – and that would be a heavy blow.

He had called very early in the day and they had walked out as a further precaution against his being seen. They were seated now in the wildest, least visited part of the manor's grounds, on a bench beside the stew pond, where the trailing branches of a willow hung down into the still green water.

The sun was just gaining power over a garden sparkling from the rainstorm of the previous night. Shadows thrown by the willow twigs moved across Mr Lomax's brow as he listened. A pair of doves from the nearby dovecote murmured in the branches above them. It was an exquisite relief to talk to him. He caught her ideas so very easily. There was no one else in the world to whom she could have conveyed so much in so few words. He always understood – but he did not always agree . . .

'This theory of a secret shared by your aunt and her

brother is ingenious,' he said with a doubting smile. 'But I wonder whether it does more credit to your lively imagination than your reason. What do you suppose the secret to be?'

'I am not sure,' Dido admitted. 'But I *think* it has to do with Miss Francine – the sister who died thirty years ago. Mr Lancelot himself has told me that Mr George was a harsh guardian to his young sister, and that my aunt believes his unkindness was an aggravation of her sickness.'

He shook his head. 'But that will not do. Why should Mrs Manners pay her brother to keep secret his own ill doing? Why does she not denounce him? It is certainly no cause to share her riches with him.'

'But I have been considering that locked door – the barred window,' Dido continued slowly, glad to sharpen her own thoughts against his intelligent opposition. 'And I am inclined to think . . . Supposing Miss Francine's illness was one of the mind!'

'Madness?'

'Now, Mr Lomax, you need not look at me as if I were suffering from that malady myself! It is *possible*. And – if it were the case – my aunt might well wish her brother to continue to keep the secret.'

'Perhaps . . .'

'Or,' she pursued, 'it may be that the sickness was love.' She was speaking her thoughts as they arose and the ideas were pressing so hard upon her that she could not comprehend them until they were released into the world. It was as easy, as natural, as thinking aloud. 'Love for the wrong man. Mr Lancelot says that his father and uncle were anxious for their sisters to make good marriages. Maybe . . . maybe there was an attachment to—'

'Mr Sutherland?'

'You are there before me! You too think it possible?'

'No,' he said cautiously. 'I think that *you* think it possible. You are remembering the fishwives, are you not? Reasoning that when they spoke of an elopement from Charcombe Manor – one which Mr Sutherland knew about – they were remembering an old rumour.'

'Exactly so! You agree—'

'No, no! You are mistaking comprehension for assent. I am unconvinced by the argument of love or madness. For, no matter what the young lady's illness, I *cannot* believe she could be simply shut away from the world in a barred and bolted chamber. Her neighbours would notice; her acquaintances would demand to know where she was.'

'I do not agree at all!' cried Dido with feeling. 'All this might be true of a man; but a woman – an unmarried woman – has no business to fix her in the world, her presence is *essential* to no one. Consider how little trouble it has taken to account for Miss Verney's absence from Charcombe. She is visiting friends! An unmarried woman may always be supposed to be with friends; to be bearing some cousin company, or nursing a sick aunt. I assure you, Mr Lomax,' she finished with a sad shake of her head, 'we disappear very easily indeed.'

'You need not be so very desponding,' he said gently. 'For *I* should certainly notice if *you* disappeared.'

She looked up into the solemn grey eyes, delighting in the affection she saw there, but almost immediately the suffering in his face swept everything else from her mind – even the ideas and suspicions which had begun to form so promisingly.

William Lomax was a great deal too well bred to distress his friends by any neglect of his person; but that loss of sleep and indifference to meals which result from constant worry were taking a toll upon him. His cravat was as well tied, his face as neatly shaven as ever; but his cheeks were thin and hollow, and there was a settled look of fear which wrung her heart.

Dido's hand crept involuntarily to the letter which still encumbered her pocket – and her conscience. The moment of communication could be delayed no longer; she was trifling with his misery by concealing the whole truth. 'There is something else I must tell you . . .'

She began awkwardly upon her tale, struggling against every horrible word. She found that she did not wish to admit that the letter was still in her possession – nor that she had read it. So she proceeded very cautiously, endeavouring to give the idea – without ever stating outright – that she had delivered it promptly and that Mr Fenstanton had revealed its contents to her.

Lomax's expression became more and more wretched as he listened, and she looked away to prevent herself from seeing the increase of suffering which her tale produced. She spoke with her eyes fixed upon the kitchen garden beyond the stew pond where beanpoles marched in orderly ranks across the freshly turned earth and a scarecrow lolled against a brick wall with the air of a dissolute man-about-town.

Her hand strayed again to her pocket – and the letter

which would in all probability confirm Tom's guilt in the eyes of his judges. The tips of her fingers touched its worn edge and she seemed to feel its danger burning against her skin.

As she completed the account he let out a groan and she turned to him fearfully. His head was bowed, his face covered by his hands. 'It will hang him for sure,' he said, and stopped, unable to say more. A tremor ran through his shoulders.

She had never before seen him so overpowered. The desire to put her arms about him in comfort was shockingly powerful and, had she only been more secure of their not being discovered, she doubted she could have resisted. She took one hand and drew it away from his face, pleading, half coherently, against despair.

'I am sorry,' he said, exerting himself. His eyes sought hers; the sun drew out darker flecks in the grey, and the terror which he was endeavouring to keep from his voice shone out, heartbreakingly clear. 'I shall be more composed in a moment. I do not mean to distress you. But . . .' his hand clutched at hers '. . . he will hang, I am sure of it. To contemplate a child's death . . . in such a cause . . .'

She held his hand and they sat in silence for several minutes; he struggled for control and she laid her free hand once more upon the letter in her pocket. Thin shreds of mist twisted up from the dark surface of the pool; the rising sun turned the larches on the hill below the summer house into brilliant green flames. And, in her heart, Dido felt all the corrupting power of love.

Until this moment she had been wretched in the

prospect of delivering the letter to Lancelot Fenstanton, but she had never doubted that it was what she should do – what she *would* do. The time only of that delivery had been uncertain. But now she looked at Mr Lomax; at his bowed shoulders, his shaking hand, his eyes filled with visions of suffering and shame.

She looked – and that sense of duty which had been urging her to deliver up the letter to its rightful owner lost all its potency. Propriety, she found, counted for nothing at all; even the principles of honesty instilled in her nursery days were beginning to seem of little value.

The overwhelming need was to save him from pain.

She drew the tattered paper from her pocket and laid it gently in his hand. He stared down at it, reading the direction and gradually comprehending what she had done. 'You have not . . . ?'

She shook her head, turned her face away. 'I wish you to take it,' she said quietly, 'and do with it whatever you think fit.'

She looked towards the house where folk were beginning to stir; watched smoke rise from the kitchen chimneys as the fires were stoked within. There was a rattling of a well bucket. A little maid was hurrying to the poultry houses with a basket on her arm . . .

'Miss Kent?' He was struggling. The words seemed difficult to form.

She would not – could not – look at him.

'Dido?' The name, which he had never pronounced before, brought her eyes immediately to his.

He took her hand and held it firmly between both his own. 'Do you know . . . do you understand the seriousness of the step you take in passing this letter to me? Are you aware of the consequences in law if it were known that you had had in your possession an important piece of evidence – and disposed of it in such a way?'

'Yes, I understand . . . that is, I know nothing of the law, but I cannot suppose it would acquit me. You may be sure I understand entirely what I am doing.'

'No, I cannot believe that you do.' He replaced the letter in her hands, folded her fingers gently around it and resumed the warm pressure of his grasp, enclosing her hands entirely so that she could not release the document. 'I cannot,' he said firmly, 'I *will* not allow you to do it. You must take this to Fenstanton now – without delay.'

She met his eyes in a steady challenge. 'Why? Would you have done so? If you had found this letter, how would you have acted?'

Just for a moment his gaze flickered from her face; but he shook his head. 'There is nothing to be gained from considering that,' he said. 'The fact is that *I* did not discover the letter. *You* did. Whatever crime I might have been tempted to commit for my son's sake is of no importance. All that matters is that you shall not commit a crime for *my* sake.'

'But you cannot prevent me! You cannot compel me to deliver the letter.'

'No, I cannot.' He raised her hand, which still held the fateful paper, and pressed her wrist to his lips. He kissed her again and again, moving slowly from wrist to fingers. 'I do not believe I could ever compel you to do anything.

And it is that which makes you so very, very dear to me. But I beg you to do as I ask on this occasion.'

'No, do not ask—'

'I must. Your offer is a proof of your kindness, your generosity and – if I may presume so far – a proof of your regard for me. I cannot but be deeply grateful. It is a gesture which I shall always remember with tenderness. But if I were to accept, the very memory would be tainted. The . . . friendship which has grown up between us has given me more happiness than I have ever expected, or deserved. But Tom's actions – the terrible cloud which is gathering over him – *must* bring our friendship to an end. After today I shall not seek you out and I beg that you will . . .' he faltered '. . . not quite forget me, I hope, but cease to think of me with any particular regard.'

'No!'

'My dear, *please* listen to me. Just for once do not argue. Do as I ask. Let my memories be pure – uncorrupted by guilt.'

She tried very hard for speech but it was impossible. Neither her brain nor her mouth were capable of forming words. She could only look at his face, cut clean and clear against the blue of the morning sky; notice the way a single muscle moved constantly in his hollow cheek as he fought for control of his emotions; and feel still upon her hand every single place that his lips had touched.

Slowly he got to his feet.

'Don't leave me!' she cried.

'I must. And you must go to Fenstanton. Give him the letter – and try not to concern yourself about what becomes of Tom and me. You have done your best to help. You have acted like a true friend.'

'I have acted,' she cried desperately, 'like a woman in love.'

He stopped upon the very point of turning away; indeed it seemed as if the whole world stopped, as if the very birds ceased singing in order to listen.

'It is true,' she said with an air of defiance. 'I love you.'

Afterwards she could never be certain whether pleasure or pain was most obvious on his face as he took in her words, for, in a moment, he stepped back and bent over her.

'Then I know you will not fail me,' he said. 'I know you will do as I ask.'

'No! I cannot.'

'Dido, please! I shall never ask anything of you again. Please promise me that you will take the letter to Fenstanton – *now*.' His eyes held hers.

'Yes,' she whispered, feeling that the word would choke her.

He put a warm, unsteady hand to her cheek – and then he was gone.

Chapter Thirty

The company was gathering in the breakfast room when Dido returned to the house. But, as luck would have it, she met Mr Lancelot almost as soon as she entered the front door. He was just crossing the hall from his business room and called out a hearty greeting.

'But Miss Kent,' he said hurrying forward. 'You look quite done up! You should not be about so early in the day. I am sure you are putting your health at risk.'

She could not even raise her eyes to his. The promise weighed heavily upon her – like the curse of a witch in a fairy tale, compelling her to act against her will. With her gaze fixed upon the freshly swept flagstones, not daring to give herself a chance for second thoughts, she held the letter out to him.

He stared at it as he took it and she began upon a hurried explanation of its discovery – and Tom's account of his possession. Her voice sounded harsh and unreal in her own ears. It seemed to echo too loudly about the high walls of the hall, although she spoke as quietly as she could. Phrases jarred in her head like notes struck too loud upon an instrument. 'Hidden in the stones . . . won at the card table . . . I believe he is telling the truth . . .'

'I am sorry,' she finished hastily. 'I should have

delivered the letter to you yesterday, but I have had little opportunity.'

He looked concerned. Dido longed for escape.

He began upon a reply, but they were interrupted just then by Mrs Bailey hurrying down the stairs and seizing the arm of her host. '*Mon cher*, Lancelot,' she cried, ignoring Dido entirely and compelling the gentleman to walk with her towards the breakfast parlour. 'The girls and I are quite determined to take a *long* walk today. We shall go out across the downs to the sea and walk on the sands. And I *insist* upon your accompanying us. No, no, do not talk to me of business, I shall not listen to a word of it. You *must* accompany us.'

Dido drew a long breath of relief at being alone and turned away to the great window. The ground seemed to heave a little beneath her feet. There was a feeling of everything having slipped away from her, of everything now being beyond her power. She hated the sensation. She liked to have control over events . . . And now that the letter was given up she was uncertain . . .

In the very moment of surrender there had been doubt – an agonising uncertainty. And, as she stood in the morning sunlight, she forced herself to recall the vow which had propelled her into action; the promise that bound her . . .

The letter was given up. It was done and could not be undone.

But, she reminded herself, she had promised only to deliver the letter. She had made no other undertaking. When Mr Lomax spoke of her ceasing to concern herself over Tom's danger, she had agreed to nothing . . .

282

Her face burnt, she put out a hand to the cold stone of the window frame for support, as she recalled what she *had*, in fact, said . . .

She had told him that she loved him! She had all but shouted the words at him!

That Dido Kent should at last make the irrevocable declaration of a woman's life in a cry of defiance was perhaps not to be wondered at. Other women might whisper the decisive words in tones of tremulous modesty – but tremulous modesty had never been a part of Dido's character.

Her hand tightened on the cold stone and a small smile lit up her face. The words were spoken, and she would not recall them if she could . . .

And, oddly enough, the memory of those words had the power to stop the ground from lurching beneath her. There was strength here. It was as if she had discovered a new power of resolution by openly acknowledging a truth she had prevaricated over so long.

And matters were not, after all, beyond her control. She could think. She could act. Tom's situation was more perilous than ever – but that was a spur to action, not an excuse for despair.

There were evidences pointing to guilt within the walls of Charcombe Manor. Someone here had been astir on the night of Mr Brodie's death; the dead man was intimately connected with the secrets of this house. There was also motive aplenty here for wishing Letitia Verney out of the way . . .

There was a great deal to be discovered. And only two days before the judges arrived for the Devonshire assizes . . .

Dido turned from the window with a new air of resolve and determination. And, as she walked towards the breakfast room, the floor of the hall lay firm and still beneath her feet.

In the breakfast room she found Mr Lancelot (with the letter still unread beside his plate) manfully resisting Mrs Bailey's attempts to enrol him in her scheme.

'I have matters to attend to at home,' he was saying, 'but . . .' as Dido entered the room '. . . I am sure Miss Kent will be very glad to join your walking party. She is too pale this morning. A little of our sea air will set her up famously.'

'Oh! Miss Kent!' cried Mrs Bailey with her shrill laugh; and she looked about, as if she must remind herself just who this insignificant creature was. 'Why, I had not thought of little *Miss Kent* coming with us. I am sure her *duties* will not allow it. She will be a great deal too much employed with Mrs Manners. She had much better stay here where she is wanted.'

'No, no,' said Mr Lancelot firmly, 'I quite insist upon her joining you, Augusta. She is too much in need of refreshment. And as for Mrs Manners. Ha! She is my aunt too! This morning I shall play the part of dutiful nephew. I can measure out medicine and place cushions, you know. Though I doubt I can do it as prettily as Miss Kent does.' He smiled kindly at Dido – and she could not but be grateful for his attention.

So, in the end, Mrs Bailey began upon her Long Walk in a state of profound dissatisfaction – resenting Dido's presence and feeling the loss of the gentleman acutely.

'Dear Lancelot, he is so very devoted to his aunt,' she remarked loudly as they left the house.

'No he ain't,' whispered Miss Gibbs, drawing close to Dido. 'He is much more devoted to *you*.'

Dido coloured and hastily put the idea aside. She was by no means sure what she thought of Mr Lancelot's gallantry and she preferred not to investigate her feelings.

She was, however, very glad to be at liberty from her aunt. Walking was a great relief and she was in hopes that the excursion might produce some very convenient opportunities for conversation.

She was particularly anxious to talk alone with Martha, but at first that was impossible, for Mrs Bailey was in full flow about another scheme she had just devised.

'I have decided,' she said as they all crossed the high road and entered the ride which provided the shortest route to the new town, 'that we shall form a little exploring party to the cliff tops on Saturday. It will be the simplest thing imaginable. We shall dine *al fresco* – as the French say.'

Emma smiled and tried to catch Dido's eye to share the joke, but Dido resisted.

They walked on under yellow showers of hazel catkins, and Mrs Bailey continued to detail the rustic simplicity of her delightful scheme. There were to be pigeon pies and cold hams and tea and wine laid out upon a table in the shade. There was to be but one man to wait upon the company and only hothouse fruit and jellies for dessert. It was all to be done with the greatest simplicity!

'It sounds mighty pleasant,' said Martha. 'Quite like a Gypsy party.'

'Why yes!' Emma's dimples flashed into being. 'I believe we had better give Mr Parry warning – else he might have his constables arrest us all for rogues and vagabonds.'

This time she succeeded in catching Dido's eye. But fortunately they were come now to a set of stepping stones which crossed a small stream and for several minutes everyone was occupied in their delicate negotiation. When they had all safely reached the other side – with a great deal of arm waving and a wet foot on Miss Gibbs' part – Dido dawdled a moment and allowed Mrs Bailey and Miss Fenstanton to walk away.

'Miss Gibbs,' she said quietly, taking possession of that lady's arm, 'Mr Tom Lomax has told me that he is engaged to Miss Verney – and that your friend has confided in you. Is this true?'

Martha stood quite still for a moment, her mouth a little open. Dido waited, glad to let their companions move away. The soothing sound of birdsong and running water wrapped itself around them, bringing a very welcome privacy to their conversation.

'Yes, of course it is true,' said Martha at last. 'Why should it not be?'

'Well, everyone speaks of Miss Verney as being a cautious young lady, and unlikely to enter into a secret engagement.'

'But if she is in love!'

'Yes, of course, that would make a great difference.'

Martha looked sullen – as if determined against communication.

'Mrs Bailey,' said Dido, 'believes that there is a degree of regard between Miss Verney and *Mr Lancelot*.'

'Well, you know,' said Martha, 'the engagement must be kept secret. Letitia don't want people suspecting her real feelings.'

'Yes. I see.'

They stood for a moment on the mossy stones of the stream's edge. The cool, damp breath of the water was upon their faces, but overhead bright sunlight played through the newly opening leaves.

'Miss Gibbs,' began Dido very seriously, 'do you know of any plans which Miss Verney and Mr Lomax have made for their future?'

'They are determined to be married.'

'Yes, but how is that to be accomplished?' She watched Martha's face closely as the light and shadows played across it. 'Do you know whether Mr Lomax has applied to your friend's guardian?'

Martha looked shocked. 'Mr B would never agree to it.'

'So what are they to do? Elope?'

'It is the only way. And so I told—' She stopped talking and swung about her reticule.

'You advised Miss Verney to elope?'

'No . . . But . . .'

She stopped again and looked down sullenly at the sunshine sparkling on the stream. Dido said nothing, allowing the silence to stretch out until poor Martha could bear it no longer.

'But there ain't no other way for them to be together, is there?' she said, half pleading. 'And if they *love* one another . . .' She withdrew her arm and began to walk on after the others.

'But,' said Dido as she followed, 'I confess myself to be a little puzzled. When we spoke last on this subject you seemed to be very sure that the cause of your friend's disappearance was *not* an elopement.'

'I *know* she has not eloped.'

Dido looked at her sharply. Why was she so sure on this point? And why was her account of her friend's behaviour so very much at odds with everybody else's ideas? Again she felt the certainty of Martha knowing more than she would confess.

They had come now to a place where a spring ran into the ride, making it too wet and muddy for pedestrians. A narrow footpath climbed the bank on one side, through a carpet of bluebells and primroses, to follow a higher route. Martha took the opportunity of hastening up this path as if she wished for escape.

'But why are you so certain?' persisted Dido, ducking her head beneath the low branches and hurrying after her.

Martha said nothing.

'I beg you,' said Dido, 'if you know where Miss Verney is, to tell it.' She laid her hand on Martha's arm and they stood together a moment. Mrs Bailey's soliloquy was fading away through the trees, leaving them alone with only the insistent singing of the birds. 'I am becoming increasingly concerned for your friend,' Dido continued urgently. 'This morning Mr Fenstanton told me he has received word from your connections in Worcestershire – from Mr Hargreaves. He says Miss Verney is not in his house.'

'Oh Lord! But is he sure?'

'Why, I think a man may be trusted to know about the guests in his own house! I have seen his letter myself and there can be no doubt. He complains . . . I mean he *remarks* that the house is, as always, full of his wife's friends; but he is quite certain that Miss Verney is not among them.'

Martha plucked a tight green hazel bud and ground it between her fingers. 'Mr Hargreaves don't like Melia's friends,' she said.

Dido looked at her keenly. 'And might that discourage Miss Verney from going there?'

'No, it would not. She would go to Melia, for sure.'

'But she has not and we know not where she is. I beg you to consider your friend's danger—'

'But I can't help her!' cried Martha, 'I don't know where she is!' And Dido saw now that there were tears forming in her eyes and beginning to roll down her cheeks. 'You do not understand! Oh, I wish I dared explain.'

Dido drew out a handkerchief and gave it to her companion, then watched quietly for a minute or two while she struggled for composure. 'I think you might confide in me, Miss Gibbs,' she ventured at last. 'There is clearly some secret weighing upon your mind which I make no doubt it would be a relief to share.'

'I do not know,' said Martha, twisting the handkerchief about in her hands. 'I do not know what I should do . . .'

The signs were all very promising. Dido sensed that

Miss Gibbs was a little adrift without her friend to guide her, and would dearly love to find someone else to rely upon.

'If only I could be sure—' Martha stopped short, her head raised, listening. Her face was suddenly pale.

It was a moment before Dido could discern the sound which had alarmed her. Then she made out the clatter of a horse being ridden along the lower track. She looked down but could discern nothing through the hazel thickets.

However Martha's mind was made up; she called out to Miss Fenstanton who stopped and waited for her to catch up.

Greatly vexed at having lost the opportunity of discovery, Dido remained where she was, struggling to get the better of her disappointment and straining her eyes and ears towards the sound of hooves. It was probably a stranger riding down there upon the track; but Miss Gibbs had feared an eavesdropper – a secret follower. Who did she think it was?

The trees here were coppiced and grew very thickly. It was impossible to see the ride below. And then, after a moment or two, the horse was halted. It was standing with only an occasional restless movement of its hooves and the small tuneful sounds of harness. Dido considered turning back in an attempt to discover the rider, but doubted she could move quietly enough. If the horseman wished to remain unseen it would be the work of a moment to turn his mount and hurry off. He could be out of the wood entirely before she regained the lower track. Better to continue and let the pursuer – if he was a pursuer – believe himself undetected.

She walked on after her companions, and soon saw that the path and the ride were drawing back together. They would meet at a stile just a hundred yards ahead. When she reached that point she would be able to look back along the track and see the mysterious rider.

Chapter Thirty-One

The whole party stopped to rest at the stile, Mrs Bailey taking possession of the most comfortable seat upon its step, and the others all standing about her. Ahead were the open downs: gorse and wild thyme, and grass kept short by sheep, stretched away to a wide expanse of cloudless sky with a single buzzard hanging motionless in the clear air.

Beside the stile a gate closed off the end of the ride and Dido and Martha turned together to look over it. There was nothing remarkable to see; just a dim tunnel under the arching hazel boughs, a track so awash with water that it seemed to be half a stream, and high banks covered with moss, primroses and white windflowers. It was possible to see no more than fifty or sixty yards along this tunnel before a turn obscured the view. If the horseman was still in the ride, then he had stopped. He was staying back, determined to keep out of sight.

Martha peered and peered, and twisted her locket about in a growing state of dread.

'Perhaps the rider does not wish us to see him,' said Dido quietly, while the others were shading their eyes to watch the bird of prey.

Martha gave a great start and edged herself away. And,

when they all began to be in motion again, she took care to place herself as far from Dido as possible.

Dido walked slowly at the rear of the party as they made their way across the downs, looking back frequently to the stile and the gate beside it. Each time she did so she hoped to see a rider emerging from the trees. But she saw no one, until they came to the highest point on the path and all stopped for a moment to sit upon a large stone and catch their breath.

The air was very still and the rock was warm to the touch. The sun was so bright that it was already difficult to see the stile and the path into the wood. Dido drew down the brim of her bonnet to protect her eyes as she gazed backward – and thought that she discerned a slight movement. She narrowed her eyes.

Her companions were moving on now but she held her place, struggling to see. There *was* a horse down there, standing just within the shelter of the trees in the shifting light and shade. The horse was brown with a blaze of white down its face. And she was almost sure that the rider wore a green coat. She waited a moment longer, but the horse did not start towards her. It remained where it was. Perhaps its master was watching the walking party.

Suddenly Dido felt very much alone – and was immediately angry with herself for it. Why should she be so discomposed by a fellow sitting upon his horse and watching her? If he was indeed watching her. It was more likely that he was pausing to admire the view of the downs, or else to decide upon his way.

But she was suddenly keenly aware that by attempting to save Tom from the accusation of murder, she was threatening a real murderer with discovery. And a man who had killed once might have little compunction in killing again to save his own neck . . .

In the past she had laughed when Mr Lomax suggested that her passion for uncovering secrets might place her in danger. So why should she now feel so very exposed, so very lonely? Perhaps it was because he was not by to reprove her. Perhaps there was comfort to be had from criticism born of concern. And now, separated from Mr Lomax, she was truly alone, without the annoyance – or the safety – of a man's censure.

She jumped up from the stone and determinedly turned her mind to purely rational thoughts. Rational thoughts which soon reminded her there was only one man in Charcombe Manor who habitually wore a green coat – and that was Mr George Fenstanton.

Once they arrived at the sands, Dido hoped for another opportunity of talking with Martha Gibbs. She had come very close to discovering Martha's secret and was quite determined to win it before the end of the day.

But, unfortunately, when the descent to the beach had been made and the party paused – as all visitors to the sea must pause to take in its beauty and health-giving atmosphere – Mrs Bailey stepped forward to claim Dido's arm and attention.

And it soon became clear that, during the course of their walk, Mrs Bailey had formed a resolution of action. The affront which Mr Fenstanton had given in the breakfast room was not, by any means, forgotten.

'Well now,' she said quietly as they all turned away

from the town and began to walk along the sands, 'I have been quite worried about you, my dear, since your suffering so badly with the headache yesterday.'

Dido began to protest that she was entirely recovered, but Mrs Bailey only tightened her hold upon her arm. The grip of her fingers was steely.

'I am afraid, Dido,' continued Mrs Bailey, 'that you are exerting yourself too much in this business of poor Letitia's disappearance. I fear Lancelot is imposing upon your good nature.'

'Imposing, Mrs Bailey?' Dido stopped and looked directly into her smiling face. 'Why, I am sure Mr Fenstanton has done no such thing.'

'Oh! I know that he does not mean to be unkind. But the dear, dear man is so *very* worried about Letitia. He is so very attached. I fear that he will stop at nothing to find out what has become of her.' Another sidelong look to see how her words were affecting her listener. 'I fear that he may be attempting to enlist your support – using his charming manners to persuade you to help him. For he is an excessively charming man, is he not?'

There was no mistaking the meaning of all this. Mrs Bailey was jealous – on her ward's account – and it would have been the work of a moment to silence her. Dido had only to assure her that she did not suspect anything *particular* in the gentleman's attentions towards herself. It would only require a word or two.

But there was in Dido a contrary spirit – upon which Aunt Manners frequently remarked. She had a great dislike of being manoeuvred into saying what was expected of her. And she saw no reason to oblige Mrs

Bailey now. She turned her face away to watch the long waves rolling in across the sands. 'Mr Fenstanton,' she said demurely, 'is a . . . *delightful* gentleman.' There was a sharp intake of breath from her companion. 'I find his society very pleasant indeed, and I am happy to give him any assistance within my power.'

Dido enjoyed discomposing Mrs Bailey; but, as they walked on in hostile silence, she found that she was more than a little discomposed herself. For there was no denying that Lancelot Fenstanton *was* a delightful man – and she could not help but notice it. Which she found a little odd and inconvenient. Since her affections were now most decidedly fixed, she had supposed that she would cease to notice the agreeableness of other men; but it seemed that was not the case. And whatever was one to do about it? While there was the *possibility* of falling in love, then appreciation of a handsome man seemed allowable; but to appreciate when one's heart was already engaged elsewhere did not seem quite *proper*.

This little conundrum – which most women are compelled to contemplate long before they reach the age of six and thirty – kept Dido silent for some minutes.

And meanwhile Mrs Bailey's brows were gathering into a look of deep consideration. 'My dear,' she began at last, in a dangerously gentle voice, 'there is another little matter which I feel I must just mention to you. I hope you will not take offence.'

'I am never offended when no offence is intended, Mrs Bailey.'

'Well then, I feel that I should just mention that your aunt is unhappy about your behaviour. Yesterday, when you were so very long in returning from Charcombe, she complained to me of your absence. Naturally I attempted to soothe her. I represented to her how much more pleasant it must be for you to walk out – to mix in society – suggested that you were perhaps a little weary of being confined to attendance upon an invalid.'

'It was very kind of you to draw those little matters to her attention, I am sure.'

'But I regret to say,' continued Mrs Bailey, pursing up her lips, 'that she did not seem soothed at all.'

'Did she not? How very . . . remarkable.'

Mrs Bailey drew her cloak about her shoulders with an air of satisfaction. 'If your . . . preoccupation should continue, Miss Kent, if you should continue to pursue Letitia's case and neglect poor Mrs Manners, I fear it may become quite difficult for me not to draw these matters to her attention.' Mrs Bailey smiled and, to be quite sure that her refined little threat had found its mark, she added, 'It would be a great shame, would it not, if the dear lady was so displeased as to settle her fortune away from your family? But dear me, I cannot promise to hold my tongue! It is in my nature to say what I think. "Let me have no lying", as the Great Bard says, "it becomes none but tradesmen".'

For several minutes Dido was too angry for speech and – since they had now come to a place where the sea ran in across the sands, almost to their feet – she stopped walking, withdrew her arm, and stood looking down upon the white curve of foaming water. Retaliation was, she felt, beneath her; but it was a great temptation and she certainly had the means of a very powerful counter-attack. Mr Mountjoy's words in the inn yard yesterday had confirmed a little suspicion which had been growing upon her for some days . . .

She watched the lacy foam dissolve into the sand as the wave drew back.

Yes, she decided, retaliation was in fact *necessary*. Her investigations must continue. She certainly could not allow herself to be bullied into inaction.

She looked about to be sure their companions were not near. But Miss Fenstanton was stooping down to search for fossils higher up the beach, and Miss Gibbs was a long way back, almost under the cliffs.

'But curiosity is in *my* nature,' she began in a light conversational tone. 'I thank you for your concern, Mrs Bailey; but you had better cease worrying about my enquiries. I am as I am, and . . .' she turned her eyes upon her companion '. . . as the Great Bard says, "Things without all remedy, should be without regard".'

Mrs Bailey coloured suddenly, and one hand twisted rapidly in her scarlet shawl.

But, before the hand was quite hidden, Dido noted with satisfaction that its fingers were crossed. She bent down and dug out a shell from the hard, damp sand. 'In point of fact,' she said, brushing sand from the shell and running her finger thoughtfully along its curving ridges, 'although I have not yet solved the entire mystery of Miss Verney's disappearance, I am satisfied that I already understand one or two very material points.'

'Upon my word,' cried Mrs Bailey with a brittle laugh. '*Vous est trop* . . .' she faltered, flapped her hand about a little '. . . *inquisiteeve,*' she finished hopefully.

'Yes, I daresay I am. And one of the points I now understand is why you do not wish Miss Verney to be found.'

Mrs Bailey said nothing.

But a sideways look proved to Dido that her companion was biting anxiously at her lip. 'You do not wish me to pursue my enquiries,' she continued, 'because you believe that the young lady might not wish to return to Charcombe Manor; you fear that she would be angry if she were brought back against her will; and her anger might be turned against you. You cannot countenance an angry Miss Verney, can you, Mrs Bailey? She would be too dangerous to you.'

'Dangerous? Why this is just too ridiculous for words!' trilled Mrs Bailey valiantly. 'I am sure I do not know what you are talking of. Why ever should you suppose I fear my ward?'

'I suppose it because you have, of late, become quite incapable of checking her behaviour,' continued Dido seriously. 'It seems you can deny her nothing. You did not wish her to remain at the manor to meet Mr Lomax on the day she disappeared – but you could not prevail upon her. You do not approve her friendship with Miss Gibbs, but you cannot prevent it.'

'This is nonsense! Why do you suppose Letitia is so very terrible to me? Why must I always give way to her?'

'That is a point which puzzled me for some time. But then I remembered that your acquiescence originated in the visit to Worcestershire last autumn. And I considered Miss Gibbs' account of that business – the circumstances under which the matter was decided.'

It was Mrs Bailey's turn to look about to be sure they were not overheard. Her yellow curls bobbed about her red cheeks as she turned this way and that.

Dido obligingly lowered her voice to a whisper. 'I recalled that your consent to the Worcestershire visit was given after an evening at a *theatre*.'

Mrs Bailey said nothing, but insensibly pressed together her hands as if pleading silently.

The gesture assured Dido that she was coming at the truth. 'And it occurred to me,' she said, 'that there is something of the theatre about you, Mrs Bailey. It is in your manner – your gestures. And then you know so much of the *Great Bard's* work. You frequently quote his words.'

'A lady ought to be well read, I'm sure!'

'But I have noticed something else. There are some extracts from Shakespeare which you do not like to hear. Miss Fenstanton's remark that the sleeping and the dead are like pictures was not at all to your taste. Nor was the line which I quoted just now.' She smiled and tossed the shell out into the sea. 'And those lines, I have discovered, come from *Macbeth* – a play which is generally held to be unlucky – by *actresses*.' She turned a look of great meaning upon her companion.

Mrs Bailey let out a kind of yelp at the word. She laid an anxious hand on Dido's arm. 'You will not say anything, will you?'

'No. We shall trust one another to be discreet, shall we not? I shall not mention that you earned your living upon the stage before your marriage, and you will say nothing about my behaviour to my aunt.'

'Oh yes.'

Dido smiled in triumph – and then pressed a little further. 'But I hope you will oblige me by explaining just one little detail.'

'What do you wish to know?'

'Well, I can understand that Miss Verney may have discovered your past that evening at the theatre . . . Perhaps you met with an old theatrical acquaintance?'

'It was Isaac,' Mrs Bailey explained hastily. 'Isaac Mountjoy. Letitia overheard him talking to me. Isaac wishes me to return to his company.'

'And I understand that with such power over you, Miss Verney would be able to do pretty well as she wished. But . . .'

'What is it?' Mrs Bailey's voice was sharp with worry – Miss Fenstanton was now making her way towards them across the sands.

'When Mr Mountjoy spoke to you in the inn yard,' said Dido, 'I heard him say that "a friend" had told him where to find you. And I cannot help but wonder whether that "friend" was Letitia.'

'Yes,' admitted Mrs Bailey quickly. 'It seems that after she ran away, Letitia sent a note to Isaac – at the theatre in town. To spite me.'

'And do you know of any reason why Miss Verney should particularly wish to make trouble for you just now? Had there been a disagreement between you just before she left Charcombe Manor?'

'No, there had not.' Mrs Bailey's brow contracted so that there was a great danger of the paint cracking. 'I was surprised to find that she had gone away in such anger

301

against me. Since that time in town I am sure I have done my utmost to accommodate the ungrateful girl.'

'And yet it must have been something very particular which prompted her to take such an action as sending Mr Mountjoy here to cause you embarrassment before your acquaintances,' mused Dido. But Miss Fenstanton was within earshot now and she was obliged to abandon the enquiry.

Mrs Bailey gratefully seized her opportunity of escape, claimed Emma's arm, and walked off.

Dido could not look upon her stout figure hurrying away across the sands – pink bonnet ribbons and red shawl fluttering – without feeling a little triumph at her discomfort. But she earnestly wished that she might have had a moment longer to pursue her success.

Well, enquiries in that direction must now wait. And, in the meantime, she could not afford to stand idly by here on the sand watching the long waves roll ashore their burdens of foam and weed. At the top of the beach Miss Gibbs was still loitering alone beside the cliffs. This was undoubtedly the best chance of persuading that young lady into a confidence; here, upon the open beach, even the most suspicious mind need have no fear of eavesdroppers.

She hurried up the hard wet sand and made her way towards the cliffs.

As Dido approached it seemed that Martha was also in search of the fossils for which Charcombe's shore is famed; she was walking slowly with her eyes downcast among the rocks and pebbles which had fallen from the cliff face.

However, as Dido came closer, she saw that it was misery rather than geology which was bowing down the poor girl's head. There were fresh tears upon her cheeks; she was twisting one hand in the chain of her locket and crying quietly.

Dido stopped, reluctant to intrude upon such patent distress. Should she attempt to force a confidence? Would it be too unkind?

Martha had come to a standstill now in the shadow of the cliffs. The dark rocks looming over her figure gave her a small, vulnerable appearance.

As Dido hesitated, a single pebble rattled down the cliff and two seagulls started noisily into the air; their movement drew her eyes up the face of crumbling rock to the gorse that grew atop . . .

And there she saw a brown horse with its rider standing beside it – so close to the cliff's edge that he seemed to be actually *in* the gorse bush. She had only time to note that he was standing immediately above Miss Gibbs, before the rocks began to fall.

Chapter Thirty-Two

At first it was no more than a few pebbles that fell – rolling and bouncing in little clouds of dry earth, mingled with tufts of grass. But in a moment there were larger pieces of rock falling, rolling down the cliffs with a terrible noise which echoed and re-echoed. Martha looked up and seemed to watch them for a moment without comprehending her danger. Then she screamed and began to run. And there was a horrible appearance of the stones being alive and wilfully pursuing her. They bounded down the cliff and out across the beach, moving with alarming speed through a rising cloud of dust. For a while there was nothing but noise and dust and fear.

Dido found herself foolishly holding out her hands and urging haste as if the tumbling rocks themselves were not encouragement enough to the terrified girl. Then, just as it seemed Martha had outrun the landslide, she stumbled, half fell, put one hand to her ankle. Dido started forward, seized her arm, and dragged her clear.

And, as she did so, through the cloud of dust and the grit in her eyes, she saw the man up on the cliff remount his horse and ride rapidly away across the downs.

Martha clung to Dido's arm with both hands, her fingers rigid, her whole body shaking. The dirt was in their eyes, their noses, their mouths; it had settled in their hair. A few last stones rattled down the cliff and came to rest at their feet. Their companions were running towards them.

'There was a man,' Dido whispered hastily, brushing the dust from her lips. 'He was on the cliff top. He made the rocks fall.'

'Where?' Martha looked about fearfully, her eyes appearing very white in her dusty face. 'I can see nobody on the cliffs. There is nobody there.'

'He is gone now – but I swear to you he *was* there. Who is he? Why did he do it?'

'I can't!' Tears were making clean streaks through the dust now. 'I just can't tell you . . . You mustn't say a word about it.'

Martha broke away and joined the others in exclaiming upon the terrible accident. They were all agreed that it was a very terrible accident indeed and no one could find words adequate to describe how they had felt upon first seeing the rocks falling. But it was a mercy that Miss Gibbs had looked up when she did, was it not? If she had not, the accident might have been a great deal worse . . .

Martha was consoled, her face cleaned with a handkerchief; her ankle was discovered to be only twisted, not broken; Emma undertook to hurry on to the inn and send word for the carriage to be brought – and Mrs Bailey offered a great deal of advice.

And still no objection was raised against the word 'accident'. Martha did not contradict it and, after a little consideration, neither did Dido. She needed to think a little about it all before she could determine what to say or do.

As the others began to move away she loitered behind on the deserted beach, looking at the debris spread across the damp, hard-packed sand: earth and pebbles and grass, bushes torn up by their roots, and the clean fractured rock from the heart of the cliff – angular fragments veined with grey and red. There was even the ragged remains of a bird's nest with one pale egg lying within, miraculously unbroken by the fall.

Cautiously Dido picked her way back towards the cliff through the smell of damp rock and disturbed earth. The voices of her companions were fading into the distance, Mrs Bailey still declaring that she had never, never been so frightened in her life. For she was not easily frightened; her friends frequently remarked upon her steady nerves. But, upon her word, she could not describe how she had felt when she first turned and saw those great stones tumbling down . . .

The dramatic tones trailed away and were replaced by the cries of returning gulls, the crash and sigh of distant waves.

Dido gazed up the cliff, with its raw red scar, loose pebbles and hanging tufts of grass, to the place where the man had stood. Half of the gorse bush was now fallen away. The ground up there was certainly unsafe; the cliffs seemed to be formed of crumbling rock and soft red earth. From his position, the watching man could have easily set the slide in motion by kicking away at the edge.

She did not doubt he had done it. His hasty escape

confirmed his guilt. But why had he done something so very dangerous?

From his vantage point he would have been able to see Dido approaching Martha. Had he feared the girl would be persuaded into telling the secret which weighed so heavily on her mind?

Dido shrank from that thought – it was horrible to suppose that her own search for information had imperilled Miss Gibbs . . . But it also produced the certainty that Martha's secret was of the utmost importance.

She sat down upon a rock and gazed across the wet, shining sands to the white shimmering line of breaking waves. The sudden sense of danger twisted painfully in her breast; but weighed against it there was swelling indignation. Someone was so determined to keep Miss Gibbs silent that he was prepared to endanger her life. Someone was attempting to prevent her – Dido – from discovering the truth!

And that was not to be borne. Not when the life of an innocent man was at stake.

She rested her chin in her hands and tried to reason calmly. The man on the brown horse had followed them through the wood and across the downs – so he had almost certainly come from Charcombe Manor. And who else could it be but Lancelot or George Fenstanton? The figure had been too distant for her to distinguish . . . though the green coat argued for it being Mr George.

But what could Martha's secret be that it should make him so determined to prevent her from speaking?

She turned her thoughts back to the conversation in the wood – and its tantalising interruption. Martha had been very certain of Miss Verney's affection for Tom Lomax. And yet she had repeatedly denied the possibility of elopement. 'I know she has not eloped,' she had said. But why was she so certain? How could Martha know that Letitia had not eloped? And why had it been so very dangerous for her to explain herself?

Was it because the explanation could expose a murderer?

Dido felt as if an answer to at least some part of this puzzle was there, almost within her reach, in the salty breeze. Something suggested by a dozen small hints and clues and contradictions – a word spoken here, a look there . . . She tried hard to grasp it, but still it eluded her . . .

At the other end of the beach, Mrs Bailey was now assisting Miss Gibbs up the steps to the town. Dido watched Martha climb painfully, her head bowed against the wind. The poor girl must not be put into danger again – and yet her secret must somehow be obtained, for without it there was no way of reaching a proper understanding of either the disappearance or the murder.

She rose and began to make her way back across the beach; but, as she did so, her eye was caught by the gleam of something among the scattered rocks and debris at her feet. She stooped down, pushed aside some pebbles and a large tuft of grass, and found, half covered by the fallen nest, a gold chain. She carefully drew out Martha's necklace – the necklace in which her hand had been twisting just before the landslide began. The chain had broken, and the locket had sprung open as it fell.

Dido ran the chain into a little golden pool in the palm of her hand – and looked at the miniature portrait contained within the locket.

The sly, handsome features of Tom Lomax sneered back at her.

And it was as she held that treacherous smile in the hollow of her hand that some inkling of Martha's great secret began at last to form in her head.

Chapter Thirty-Three

. . . Eliza, I think I begin to understand at last how Miss Verney disappeared from one side of a door and never appeared upon the other.

It is a strange theory, though – a fantastic creation which rather puts me in mind of Lady Lorton's pictures worked in 'curiosities'. Do you remember them – great landscapes made up of shells and feathers and moss and butterfly wings and I know not what? Well, so is my solution made up of bits and pieces I have found about me – my 'curiosities' being nothing more than glancing looks and ideas half spoken; a visit to Worcestershire; a portrait in a locket; the contradiction of a cautious and worldly young lady entering into a secret engagement with a handsome and penniless man; and the time upon the stable clock . . .

The clock, I believe, is the very centrepiece of my design. It is just the right piece of feather or moss or withered turnip to make up my picture!

But I am not quite satisfied with my completed landscape. I am not sure that I would wish to have it framed in mahogany and hung upon the dining room wall. I am as hesitant to display the work of my genius as we agreed Lady Lorton ought to have been.

I must put my ideas to the test, and I can think of no

other way of doing so than by applying to Martha. Only
she can tell me whether my suspicions are correct. And yet it
must be a secret conference. I would not have anyone see us
talking together for fear of putting her in danger again.

And that is why I am not yet abed, though the clock
down in the hall struck one a quarter of an hour ago. Aunt
Manners is snoring and the old house has at last creaked and
groaned itself into silence. I intend to go now to Martha's
chamber. Even rousing her from sleep will be kinder than
exposing her . . .

'Lord! Miss Kent, I have told you, I don't know no better
than anyone else where Tish has got to.' Martha Gibbs
stared at Dido in bewilderment. She had scrambled back
into her bed after cautiously opening the chamber door
and was sitting now with the covers drawn up to her
chin over bent knees. Curl papers twisted from under
her nightcap and her face was greasy with some kind of
lotion. 'I only know that when I returned to the house
that day she was gone.'

'I do not suppose that you understand *everything*,
Miss Gibbs. But I know that there is something of great
importance which you will not tell.'

'I *cannot* tell it.'

'But you know that Mr Tom Lomax was deceived,
do you not? And you know why he believes that he saw
Miss Verney return to the house. You know *how* she
disappeared, even if you do not know where she is now.'

Martha's eyes rolled wildly. But Dido continued
to regard her steadily and, at last, she essayed the very
slightest of nods.

'But there has been a threat made, has there not? You have been told that you must not reveal what you know.'

There was another small nod.

'May I ask how this threat was made? Has someone in this house spoken to you on the subject?'

'Lord! No! No one has said a word to me.'

'You have received a message, then? A note?'

Martha tried very hard to give no answer. But silence is not easily maintained. Every well-brought-up miss is taught to fear silence – it is a rudeness, an embarrassment. And anyone who has ever paid a morning call knows that silence is a great provoker of unguarded speech. Dido had known many a young lady make an unsuitably confiding remark simply to fill an intolerable silence which was threatening the tranquillity of the tea board.

She waited.

'Yes,' Martha burst out at last. 'Yes, I got a note. A very nasty note.'

'And this was on the day that your friend disappeared?'

'Yes. It had been pushed under that door.' Martha's eyes strayed to the door of the chamber, as if she expected to see the nasty note still lying beside it. 'I found it when I came up here to dress for dinner. Not a proper posted letter, you know. But a note – folded and with my name writ very clear on the outside. It said I had better hold my tongue about what I knew. There would be great trouble if I did not, it said – great trouble for me – and "for everyone you care about." That is what it said.'

'Do you still have this note?'

'No, I burnt the nasty old thing.'

'I see. But was there a name – a signature – upon it?' It

was, of course, a forlorn hope. She was not surprised by Martha's shake of the head. 'Do you know from whom it came?'

There was no answer.

Dido said nothing for a while. She was keenly aware of Martha's hands gripping tightly at her knees, the fingers clenching until they were white; but she continued to gaze about her and allow the silence to do its work.

'I think,' Martha said at last, 'it was Mrs Bailey.'

'I see.' Dido was determinedly calm. A lady should never seem surprised when a companion blunders into confidence – certainly not if she wishes the discourse to continue flowing. 'You believe that Mrs Bailey knows your secret?'

'Yes, and she wants me to hold my tongue because she don't want Tish found.'

'But you wish Miss Verney to be found, do you not?'

'Yes. Of course I do.'

'And she may *never* be found if you do not tell what you know.'

'But I cannot!' cried Martha in great alarm. 'I beg you will excuse me . . . What happened on the beach today was just too horrible for words and I don't doubt it was her – Mrs Bailey, I mean – that sent the man to push the stones down on me!'

Dido shook her head. She reached out and laid her hand over Martha's hot, trembling fingers. 'I do not think,' she said gently, 'that it is Mrs Bailey who wishes you to be silent. I saw the man upon the cliff – and I believe that it was Mr George Fenstanton.'

Martha stared in confusion and pressed her hands to

313

her face. 'But why?' she whispered through her fingers.

'I am not sure. But I promise you that if you will only tell what you know, I shall do my utmost to discover the whole truth.'

'But I dare not.'

Dido jumped impatiently to her feet. 'What would you say, Miss Gibbs, if I told you that I know your secret? I know – at least, I think I know – why Miss Verney seemed to vanish during the course of her walk along the carriage drive. I only want you to tell me if I am correct. You need only say yes or no.'

'Oh.' Martha seemed unable to say more.

Dido watched her closely. The difficulty would lie in determining whether she was telling the truth when she spoke her yes or no. 'I believe, that the stable clock provides the answer,' she began quietly.

'The clock?' cried Martha with a frown.

'Yes. When you came into the hall on the day your friend disappeared, you said that its being slow had made you late for dinner.'

'Yes.'

'And you are quite sure that the clock was slow?'

'Yes.'

Dido smiled. 'Well! Therein lies the explanation of the little magic trick! Miss Verney seemed to walk along a drive and pass through a door; but she never arrived upon the other side of that door. Now that, of course, is impossible . . . unless one small detail is not as it seems; unless the eye and the brain are deceived in one small matter . . .'

Martha looked blank for a moment. Then: 'Yes!' she

said. 'Mr Lomax was wrong as to the time! He too was calculating by the stable clock . . . And so . . . so it was not five o'clock when he saw Miss Verney walk into the house – it was later.'

'And if that was the case,' Dido pointed out, 'Miss Verney could have passed through the hall unnoticed, after the company had all repaired to the dining room.'

'Yes,' said Martha, 'Quite so. It is just as you say. If you but change one detail it all becomes as clear as anything!'

Dido watched her face with interest – and was satisfied. 'Was that the deception practised upon Mr Tom Lomax?' she asked. 'Is that the secret you must not divulge?'

'Yes.' Martha blushed and looked down upon her hands which were twisting up the edge of the sheet. 'Yes,' she said again. 'Yes it is.'

Dido watched for a minute or two as the silence worked on Martha; watched her hands writhe, her feet shift under the coverlet. She consigned every detail of the girl's manner to memory – remembering that this was how Martha behaved when she told a lie.

Then she walked to the window, pulled aside the edge of the heavy curtain and looked down upon the gardens – and the fateful carriage drive which gleamed palely, lit by a fragment of moon. The only movement in the cold silver world was the occasional lope of a rabbit feeding on the lawns. 'Well then, that part of the mystery is solved.' She spoke quietly without turning back into the room. 'But it is very strange.'

'Strange?'

'Yes, it is very strange indeed.' She turned and found Martha regarding her with a look of fear. 'Because,' she

315

said, 'Mr Lomax came only to the manor gates when Miss Verney returned – and it is not possible to see the clock from the gates.'

'Oh!'

'And furthermore, if Mr Lomax *did* derive his idea of the time from that clock, he would in fact have received a fairly accurate impression.'

'No, he would not,' protested Martha. 'The stable clock is slow.'

'For the greater part of the week it is, yes. But, as you will recall, it was just a week ago – on a Thursday – that Miss Verney left Charcombe. And the stable clock is at its most accurate on Thursdays – because it is corrected every Thursday morning.'

'Oh, but . . .' Martha's eyes rolled about '. . . everyone talks of the stable clock being slow . . . I have heard about it again and again . . . I did not know about it being put right on a Thursday . . .'

'Of course you did not – or you would not have blamed it for your lateness when you returned that day.'

Martha simply stared.

'You have said that you accompanied your friend and Mr Tom Lomax to the gates that day, and then turned aside. Where did you go?'

'To the summer house.'

'You passed the entire afternoon in the summer house?'

'Yes.'

Dido paced restlessly across the room to the toilette table and sat herself down upon the low hair-brushing stool. 'I do not believe you,' she said quietly.

'Why?' Martha fixed her gaze upon her own hands

which were now wrapped up tightly in the sheet.

'Because the stable clock can be seen very clearly from the summer house. If you had passed the afternoon there, you could not have failed to notice that it was now telling the right time – you would certainly not have blamed it for your lateness.'

Martha frowned and bit at her lip.

'And if you were not in the summer house that afternoon, where were you? What were you so busy about that made you late for the dinner bell? I do not believe you were here in the gardens at all.'

'I was! I was!' cried Martha, wringing her hands together. 'I did not go anywhere. *Please* believe me.'

'I wish that I could. I wish with all my heart that I did not have to torment you with these questions. But Miss Verney's safety and a man's life depend upon the truth coming out.' Dido turned away from Martha and peered into the dark mirror on the toilette table. Her own face, pale with weariness, stared back: eyes seeming overlarge and haunted in the poorly lit reflection. 'The truth is that after you accompanied your friends to the gates, you did not turn back at all, did you, Miss Gibbs? You continued on the walk.'

'Lord! What are you saying?' The mirror showed that Martha had risen up in the bed in great agitation. 'Do you think I would lower myself to follow them? To spy on them? Do you think me so mean-spirited and nasty?'

'No,' said Dido gently. 'I do not believe you mean or nasty at all. But I do believe you to be in love with Mr Tom Lomax.'

Martha put her hands to her face and Dido drew the

317

necklace from her pocket. She turned and held it out. 'I found it on the beach,' she explained quietly. 'The locket was open – I could not help but see the picture within.'

Martha took the locket in a shaking hand, tears starting to spill down her long cheeks. This was one point which she could not – would not – deny. And for that Dido honoured her.

'It explains a great deal. You have always admired and trusted Mr Lomax, but your friend did not. She was cautious; she suspected him of mercenary motives—'

'But she was wrong!' Martha burst out. 'He don't care about money. I told her he don't. But she was horrible cold and suspicious.'

'It is in her nature. It is the character which everyone gives her. And in her caution, I believe, lies the explanation for her seemingly impossible disappearance. You see, I believe this engagement with Mr Lomax came about through a kind of trick – or perhaps "test" would be a better word. Miss Fenstanton tells me that Miss Verney is fond of "testing" her suitors.'

Martha stared fearfully at her interrogator. 'I did not want to be part of it!' she said wretchedly. 'From the first I did not like it. But Tish had got her heart set on it, and Melia said it would be a great laugh.'

'Ah yes, Amelia – Mrs Hargreaves – played an important part, did she not? It was in her house that the scheme began. And a very fine scheme it was! Such a very clever "test". One which would try the motives of any suitor. A way in which to discover whether they were disinterested, or mercenary—'

'But she should not have been so cold and suspicious!' cried Martha. 'Not of *him*.'

'You mean Mr Tom Lomax?'

'Yes.' Martha released her hold of her legs, threw aside the covers and knelt up on the bed – her cap was askew and the curl papers writhed from under it; the light of the candle made the lotion on her nose gleam. 'He ain't got a mercenary thought in his head,' she said earnestly. 'He told me he don't care about the fortune one little bit. Oh, Miss Kent, if you had but heard him yourself, I know you would believe him! His feelings, he said, was as fixed as the stars. And if there was no money it would make no difference at all, he said – he would still love me . . .'

She broke off, put her hands over her mouth and sat back among the pillows. But, above her linked fingers, her eyes shone out with a look of confused defiance. Silence filled the room.

Dido closed her eyes and knew a moment of pure pleasure in the discovery that her calculations had been correct, before her mind moved to much more sober considerations.

'He said that he would still love *you*?'

Martha bit her lip and hung her head. But her hands dropped and lay motionless in her lap. They did not writhe about as they did when she told a lie.

'It is you that is in love with the gentleman, is it not? You to whom he became engaged?'

Martha nodded.

'And this is how it was possible for a lady to pass through a door and never appear upon the other side of it. It all becomes simple if one small detail is changed. And

319

that detail is not a time – it is a *name*. This is a possibility which has haunted me ever since Miss Fenstanton's extraordinary book taught me how easily a title may be changed. Mr Lomax watched *Miss Verney* walk along the drive and pass through the door. But *Miss Gibbs* appeared upon the other side of that door.'

Martha covered her face. 'He thinks,' she whispered miserably through her fingers, 'that I am Miss Verney.'

'Because that was the trick played in Worcestershire, was it not? This was the "last trial" of romance which Miss Verney meant to make before resigning herself to a loveless match with Mr Fenstanton. At your friend's house – in a country where neither of you were known – you and Miss Verney changed names. There you appeared as the heiress Miss Verney, and she took the part of the penniless Miss Gibbs. If any man courted her in that guise she would know that his motives were pure. That was the purpose of the trick, was it not?'

'Yes.'

'But it was not Miss Verney that was courted – it was you. And you consented to the engagement.'

'Because I love him so much! But I swear I meant no harm. I did not mean it all to end like this. Tish was not supposed to disappear. We had agreed that I should walk with Mr Lomax that day; she would turn back and come straight back here to our chamber. She was to hide here until I returned. I swear to you I don't know where she is. When I got back and found her gone I didn't know what to do . . . And then there was the note . . . and that man was found dead . . . and poor Mr Lomax . . .' Martha covered her face and began to cry in earnest.

Dido went to her and took her hand. 'I am sure you meant no harm in the deception of Mr Lomax and you are innocent of everything but wishing to oblige your friends. But you must help me find out the truth. Because for some reason, which I cannot yet understand, your girlish trick has cut across the much darker schemes of someone else in this house – and placed you, Miss Verney and young Mr Lomax in very great danger indeed.'

Chapter Thirty-Four

The sun had not been half an hour over the horizon when Dido, hot and breathless, gained the highest point of the downs and threw herself upon the wide, flat stone which marked the summit. From here she could look in one direction over the woods in the valley where the rising sun was touching on the new leaves and calling forth the ruddy autumnal tint which is peculiar to oak woods in spring. In the other direction she could see the muddled buildings of New Charcombe and the grey, restless sea beyond. The sun was warm on the stone, but a great bank of cloud was gathering over the sea, threatening a storm.

She was weary, for, after returning from Martha's room, she had passed the night curled upon her narrow bed endlessly reviewing the difficulties which beset her. And dawn had found her crouching in the thin grey light from the window, endeavouring to order her thoughts into a letter.

. . . the scene has changed entirely, she had written. *It would seem that Miss Verney did not take her leave of Charcombe Manor when she walked out with Tom Lomax; nor did she mysteriously vanish before the young man's eyes upon her return.*

In fact, she disappeared from this house during the time which Tom and Martha spent walking upon the downs. Something happened during her friend's absence; something which resulted either in her fleeing the house – or else being removed from it; something which has endangered Miss Gibbs; something which, I believe, has also resulted in murder.

And there is another consideration which I hesitated to mention to Miss Gibbs: the possibility of Miss Verney having another secret – one which she has not communicated to her friend. Why was she taken with the strange fancy of putting her mirror in the darkest corner of the room?

Her lowness of spirits since returning from Worcestershire is explained, I think – for it must have gone hard with her to find herself neglected when she was thought to be poor. But it seems unlikely that her disappointment would result in a dislike of her own reflection . . .

She had stopped and read through the letter; but this morning there was not the usual comfort to be found in the orderly lines upon the page. They did nothing to clear her weary brain. And the breaking dawn had reminded her that another day was gone without the identity of the murderer being uncovered; that she was come another day closer to the time when the assize judges would parade with all the pomp of authority through the crowded streets of Exeter to dispense justice – and judicial death.

I have been considering, she had continued miserably, *how the case now stands against Tom Lomax. And, since I at last have some proof that he did not abduct Miss Verney, I might* hope that the jury would look favourably upon him, _if it were not for the existence of Mr Bailey's letter_.

But, regrettably, the letter is still damning. The jurymen may think that Tom is a fool to be deceived into courting the wrong lady. But I doubt they will think him an _innocent_ fool. For the fact remains that he _believes_ himself engaged to an heiress, and the letter from Antigua cuts across all his ambitions.

The letter alone will probably hang him, unless I can discover the whole truth about Mr Brodie's death . . .

It was upon reaching this point that Dido had decided escape from the house was essential. But fresh air had done little to improve her ideas and now she sat upon her stone wishing that she might remain here for ever, facing nothing more complicated than the vagaries of the weather. She wished she could run and run on the downs, scream aloud like an unruly child . . .

Though, when she considered the matter rationally, she could not see how such an indulgence would actually help in the present case. It would not bring her any closer to an understanding of Charcombe's mysteries – nor would it restore Mr Lomax to her . . .

The separation from Mr Lomax was complete. And, after a sleepless night, Dido had no power to resist despair.

The trouble in which Tom now stood would make every acquaintance draw back from his father, and there was not a member of her own family who would not cry out against her attachment if it were known to them.

And now, when it was certain that he would never again ask her to be his wife, the 'yes' rang out clear and true in her head. Yes, she would do anything, bear any shame for the privilege of being with him. Yes. She spoke the word aloud into the empty air. If only she had spoken it months ago and publicly joined her fate to his – then she could now claim it as a duty to share in his disgrace.

And this, of course, was the very worst of it. There are few miseries known to mankind which cannot be made worse by the knowledge that a simple action of our own might have changed everything. There is more wretchedness contained within 'what if' than there is in any other two words of our language.

Dido was so absorbed in wretched thought that she did not see the man on a tall bay horse ride out of the wood below; and the sound of hooves did not intrude until horse and rider were almost upon her. She sat up, hastily brushing away tears, and saw that the rider was Mr Lancelot Fenstanton.

She had had no opportunity for private conversation with the gentleman since she had put Mr Bailey's letter into his hands, and, as he dismounted beside the rock, she eagerly searched his face for signs of anger or reproach.

But the suntanned face with its eyes narrowed against the light gave little away and she realised that Lancelot Fenstanton's countenance might not be an easy primer to decipher. The expression of good humour and gentle self-mockery was so very unvarying.

He bowed a greeting, threw the reins onto the horse's back and stood for a while looking down upon her in silence. His smile had questions in it. And there was rather less of the bewildered boy about him this morning; he looked more knowing.

'I wished to talk to you alone,' he said. 'About the letter, you know.'

'I am sorry to put you to the inconvenience of riding out.' She looked away towards the sea. 'How did you know where to find me?'

'My gardener informed me that you had set off in this direction.' He tapped his riding whip against his boot. 'In his own house, a man is pretty well placed to spy upon his guests.'

'I am sure you do nothing so discourteous, Mr Fenstanton.'

'Ha! I admit it freely. Though,' he added, 'I confess I am a little uneasy when one of my guests repays the compliment and begins to spy upon *me*.'

'I am sorry,' she said, catching immediately at his meaning. 'It was unpardonable of me to keep your letter from you – and to read it.'

'Well, well, I did authorise you to pry into anything you wished, did I not?' He smiled easily; his manner was calm – but for the powerful forefinger which continued to tap his whip against his boot. 'Perhaps I should have been more cautious. But I did not quite expect you to be so very *thorough* in your investigations. Nor, if you will permit me to say, quite so prejudiced. You seem determined to prove young Lomax innocent. Innocent of abducting Letitia – and innocent of murder too.'

Dido was extremely uncomfortable, but her consciousness of having concealed the letter would not allow her to deny him an answer. He had every right to question her behaviour. 'I am by no means convinced that Tom Lomax is the author of either crime,' she said cautiously.

'And why are you not convinced? Upon my word, Miss Kent, it seems like the damned fellow's guilty to everyone else in the world!'

'Oh, but—' she began eagerly enough, but was brought to an abrupt stop. She had little enough evidence for Tom's innocence and the little that she had, she dared not yet communicate.

'Why are you so determined to prove he didn't do it?' persisted Fenstanton. And then, when she still remained silent, he added quietly, 'Of course, young Tom is a very handsome fellow. Got that kind of way about him I fancy all women like.'

'No, you are mistaken!' she cried, with a blush. 'I have no particular regard for Mr Tom Lomax. I believe I have as low an opinion of his general character as anyone at Charcombe – it is only murder I believe him incapable of.'

'Indeed!' he said. She heard the continued thoughtful tap of leather on leather. 'So it is not on the young man's account you'd have the name of Lomax cleared of suspicion.'

She suspected he was guessing at her true motive, and dared not look at him for fear the truth might be written too plain in her eyes. They remained in silence for a while. The dark shape of a lark swung up across the downs and mounted to the sky. The horse shuffled restlessly, then, seeming to resign herself to waiting, settled to a breakfast of grass.

'Well,' he said at last, 'I'm in a fine fix, ain't I, Miss Kent? Damned if I know what I should do! For I ought to be on my way to Parry right now with that letter of Bailey's.'

Dido's head lifted at that. 'You have not yet shown the letter to the magistrate?' There was a kind of hope in her voice – though she did not know quite what it was that she hoped for. 'Why did you not take it straight away?'

'Why?' he said looking very seriously at her. 'Because it's as plain as the nose on my face that your little heart's set against such evidence getting to the court.'

She stared up into his smiling face. Her heart was beating violently and it seemed all but impossible to draw breath. If only she could find the right words. If only she could snatch from the warm, thyme-scented air the words – the argument – which would persuade him to destroy the hateful document.

'Well now,' he said. The whip tapped faster against his boot. 'Whatever am I to do?'

'It is,' she said with great care, 'a very powerful – a very dangerous document. It is sufficient, perhaps, to convict young Mr Lomax, even if he is not guilty.' He nodded at that. 'A man's life is in your hands, Mr Fenstanton. What . . . what do you suppose is the *right* thing to do?'

'Ha! The right thing? I'm damned if I know what that would be. You see this letter is what the lawyers like to call *evidence*. So I'm sure a fellow *ought* to hand it over. I'll tell you what – there's very likely a law to say a fellow *must* hand over such a thing. But . . .' He laid his arm along his horse's neck, patting her thoughtfully. 'The fact is, you don't want Parry to see the letter. And I cannot believe it would be right to break the heart of such a charming lady.'

'You are very kind.' She spoke with painful care – fearing every moment to say the wrong word – the word which would determine him upon disclosure. 'I confess I should be sorry to see Mr Parry . . . misled by the document. But . . .' she attempted a smile '. . . you would no doubt claim that I am influenced by prejudice.'

'Well, well, ain't we all prejudiced, Miss Kent? Come now, don't look so sly! I know you have been watching us all at Charcombe Manor. You've found out that we are all hiding secrets, have you not? You know we're all ploughing our own furrow, so to speak! Why, you've scared dear Augusta almost out of her wits with your cleverness in fathoming her. And let me say I honour you for that.'

'You did tell me that I was free to enquire . . .'

'Yes, yes, of course I did! And I don't mind it one little bit. Why, it's kept me better amused than a whole month of good shooting, seeing how you've gone to work on 'em all. But I can't suppose that with all this investigating carrying on, you ain't taken the measure of me too.'

'Oh, I would not presume so far, Mr Fenstanton! You, I believe, are not so easily understood as your guests.'

'Ha! But are you really ignorant of my guilt – have you not fathomed my secrets?' He put up a foot on the rock and planted his hands on his bent knee. With eyes narrowed against the sun, he searched her face. 'No! You cannot be ignorant of what I am up to. For I know you have been asking little Miss Gibbs about my reluctance to ride after our fugitive. You know that I ain't behaved quite honourable.'

Dido hesitated over a reply. He seemed close to a confession, and to insist upon ignorance might make him withdraw. 'I have made some observations,' she said, 'but my conclusions are not quite complete.'

'Are they not?'

'Perhaps you would sit down here with me and explain a little more?'

'Why, that'd suit me very well, Miss Kent! For that's what I've rid out here for, you know. I want to explain myself to you.' He looped the reins more securely about the saddle and sat down on the rock beside Dido, holding the whip across his knees with both hands.

She waited.

He looked into her face and then out towards the sea.

'Why have you not pursued Miss Verney?' she prompted.

'I ain't pursued her,' he said, 'because I don't want her back at Charcombe – not yet.' He looked sidelong with his puzzled little boy expression. 'Because the fact of the matter is, Miss Kent, I've got myself into a bit of a scrape over Miss Verney.'

'A scrape?'

'You see everybody is expecting me to marry her. No definite engagement, you know. But one of those growing understandings that everyone – women in particular – set such store by.'

'And . . . is it not . . . ? I mean, why do you call it a scrape?'

'Because it ain't what I want . . . That's the truth of it.

330

Not now.' He rubbed at his brow, threw another sidelong look. 'I thought Letitia and me would suit well enough. I've known her all her life. And Reg and Augusta believed it would be a fine match. She's a pleasant girl, and I will not deny that her fortune was an inducement. But, the long and short of it is, Miss Kent, I don't love her. I thought I liked her enough to marry her; but I don't. I know that now.' He finished with a shrug of his broad shoulders, looking more bewildered than ever.

'I see.'

'Ha! Do you, Miss Kent? Do you understand that when a fellow's got to two and forty without falling in love he thinks it ain't ever going to happen to him? So then, why should he not marry a pretty girl with twenty thousand pounds. It seems it'll do well enough, until . . .' He stopped and looked very directly at his companion, his eyes wide, his smile disarmingly open . . .

There was silence between them in which could be heard the distant surge of the sea and the cry of a whinchat. Dido gazed into the earnest brown eyes and, at last, guessed at exactly what her companion had followed her out onto the downs to explain.

He reached out and took her hand. 'It will do well enough until a fellow really falls in love,' he said. 'And then, you see, he knows a pleasant girl he likes ain't enough at all. Twenty thousand pounds ain't enough. Because the only thing that'll make him happy is to spend his life with the woman he's set his heart on.' He bent his head and pressed his lips to her hand.

Dido stared, quite unable to speak.

'Miss Kent, will you do me the honour of becoming

my wife? No!' he held up his hand. 'I don't want an answer straight away. But say you'll consider, I beg you. Don't turn me down out of hand.'

Dido's reeling mind struggled for words. She reached out for every convenient phrase which can help a lady at such a moment: she was flattered; she was astonished; she had never suspected that he thought so very highly of her; he did her too much honour. The words poured out. They seemed to be no part of her; it was as if she was listening to another woman providing the perfect reply.

And, in the minutes which it took to complete the speech, there seemed to be an almost infinite amount of time for thought; time to consider – as she looked sidelong at the sturdy knees beside her, the strong square hands clasped about the whip – how would it be to be married to him?

The idea was vague – for he was little more than a stranger to her. And yet many of her friends had married upon just such a short acquaintance.

The world, if it ever heard of the match, might cry out in amazement over the union of Miss Dido Kent ('six and thirty, you know, and her brothers can give her nothing') and Mr Lancelot Fenstanton of Charcombe Manor ('a *very* fine estate, and the family settled there for centuries'); but the slightness of their acquaintance would not figure among the causes of wonder. It was the fate of many a woman to place her future happiness into the hands of a man she scarcely knew . . .

Meanwhile his eyes were following her eagerly through her speech and he seemed relieved that there was no outright refusal contained within it. 'You will consider my proposal?' he asked when she fell silent.

'Oh! Y-yes,' she stammered, wanting nothing but to be alone; to clear her mind; to *think*. 'Yes, I will consider.'

He pressed her hand and smiled. 'And, I'll tell you what – if you say yes, I'll give you that letter of Bailey's. A gift to mark our engagement.'

Chapter Thirty-Five

. . . I cannot accept him, of course, Eliza. It would be very wrong, would it not, to accept a man while loving another – no matter how hopeless that other attachment is?

But it is such a very remarkable proposal!

He declares that he loves me; and how can I doubt it? For there are no other inducements – I am not rich; I am not beautiful; I can furnish him with no useful connections; I am not even young. No, I cannot suppose that he would pursue me without love.

But then, you know, men with large estates do not fall in love with poor women – unless the poor women are young and very beautiful. It is a principle which one so rarely sees violated it seems almost a law of the land.

And altogether I do not know which is more unlikely: that the gentleman should love me, or that he should marry me without love.

Oh, what am I to do?

It must be a negative, of course. I ought to have spoken it straight away, but the shock of the offer seemed to take away my wits entirely. I hesitated over inflicting the pain of refusal – and then he mentioned Mr Bailey's letter . . .

He would keep that promise I am sure, Eliza. For a man would wish to save his bride from the pain of seeing a friend suffer. And besides, the shame of the connection would be his too, if he were my husband . . .

Oh! Would marriage be such a high price to pay for dear Mr Lomax's peace? Or would it be so very wrong to pay it? Women — when all is said and done — marry for a great variety of reasons. It is not always love, and many moralists would have us believe that love matches are not the best foundation — that they do not produce the greatest happiness . . .

And Mr Fenstanton is a fine man. I esteem him highly. And admire him. He is very much the gentleman; there is no objection to be made to his person . . . there would be no <u>unpleasantness</u> in being his wife. In fact, Eliza, if there had been no Mr Lomax in the case — if I had never met that gentleman — I believe I might have been favourably inclined towards Mr Fenstanton.

And that consideration brings me to a <u>very</u> great dilemma . . .

For, if my only cause of refusal is love for Mr Lomax, then how paltry, how very selfish must that love appear! What manner of love is it which condemns its object to a lifetime of shame and misery rather than endure a union with another man? This is <u>false</u> delicacy; <u>false</u> affection.

Mr Lomax and I are divided now. We cannot be together. So why should I hesitate over marriage to another? The man I love can never be more lost to me than he is now. The consequence of my marriage would not be to divide us further — but only to save him from wretchedness.

Eliza, I believe that love directs me to accept the

offer . . . And duty demands that I make Mr Fenstanton content with his choice. I must give up every thought of Mr Lomax – learn not to love him. And learn instead to love my husband . . .

She stopped writing at this point, for her own arguments had produced a conclusion from which she could not help but recoil. The course of the future which her pen had just mapped out was bleak and painful; and yet the logic which had brought it there was unassailable.

She looked up from her writing desk, glancing about with a kind of desperation – as if she hoped to find in the surrounding scene some argument against the terrible reasoning on her page.

She was sitting in the window of the great hall and the sun was now high in the sky. Out in the garden Mrs Bailey was gathering flowers, Miss Gibbs was slowly pacing the gravel walk beside a high yew hedge which divided the lawns from the meadows beyond, and Miss Fenstanton was curled upon a sunny bench avidly devouring the last pages of . . . *Blair's Sermons*.

The two Mr Fenstantons were discussing business in the Mr Lancelot's room. Mr Sutherland and the electrical tractors were in attendance upon Mrs Manners, and Dido was free for an hour or so to pursue her investigations. But she was not 'getting on' as she ought. The extraordinary proposal had set up such a tumult in her brain that it had been absolutely necessary to confide the whole business to her sister.

And now the sun's position in the sky declared another day to be nearly half gone. Tomorrow the assize court judges would arrive. It seemed almost possible to hear the approaching hooves of their horses . . .

Well, Mr Fenstanton need not be given an answer yet – and, in the meantime, everything must be done to make acceptance unnecessary. She must find the murderer. It was perhaps an unusual alternative to marriage: but she must not give it up.

With a great effort of will she put away her letter and turned her attention to the figure of Miss Gibbs, just visible in the shadow of the yew hedge. There were still more questions to be put to that young lady.

Martha was walking slowly beside the yew hedge, looking down upon something in her hand. And, as Dido drew close, she saw that it was the locket that she held and Tom Lomax's insinuating features that she was studying.

She hesitated to interrupt. But Martha happened to look up – and made no attempt to hide the portrait; she looked steadily at Dido.

'Have I been a fool to believe he loves me?' she asked abruptly. 'Have I been deceived?'

'You are certainly no fool,' said Dido, stepping into the deep, cool shadow of the yew. 'It is not foolish to be trusting. And as to deception . . . Well, you will soon know about that. It must all depend upon how the gentleman behaves when he knows the truth.'

'Yes,' said Martha quietly. 'You are in the right.'

Dido waited for more, expecting excuses and arguments in the young man's favour. But none came. Martha pressed together her lips, as if she had determined upon keeping her own counsel. There was a new dignity.

It seemed almost as if the girl had grown closer to being a woman in the course of the night just past. And the look suited her – it gave to her long, heavy features a kind of distinction. Perhaps, thought Dido, losing the constant companionship of her friend had been to Martha's advantage, and the deficiency might now be supplied, not by a new confidante, but by a greater reliance upon her own judgement.

She took Martha's arm and, by unspoken consent, they began upon another turn along the gravel walk.

'You want to talk more about Tish going away, don't you?' said Martha.

'Yes. I have been thinking over your account of the day Miss Verney disappeared – and there are one or two points I particularly wish to ask you about.'

Martha sighed. 'Upon my word, I have scarce thought of anything else since we talked. But I am sure I don't know any more than what I have told you.'

'At what time did you set out on your walk?'

'It was half after two. I remember hearing the clock chime the half-hour as we was walking down the drive.'

'I see. And,' said Dido pursuing a thought which had occurred during the restless hours of the night, 'what did Miss Verney plan to do while you were absent from the house. She would have had to remain hidden, would she not? For she was the one who everyone supposed had walked out onto the moor. I believe you said that she meant to hide in the bedchamber which you shared?'

'Yes.'

'But that is rather odd. I did not think of it when you first told me, but now it appears a little strange.'

Martha looked puzzled.

'How was she to get to the bedchamber?' asked Dido. She stopped walking and turned towards the house, drawing her companion with her. 'Look.' Across the sunny lawn the ancient house front faced them: with its grey stones; its green creeper, starred here and there with the first pink flowers; its steep, mossy roof; its thicket of twisted, irregular brick chimneys; its old porch that fronted the great hall.

Miss Gibbs looked and shook her head.

'Look at the drive and the door,' said Dido giving their joined arms a little shake. 'Do you see the difficulty? To return to your chamber, Miss Verney must walk back along the carriage drive and into the house. Through the main door there.' She indicated the jutting porch. 'And *through the hall*. Where – you will remember – the gentlemen were talking.'

'Oh! Yes.'

'There is, of course, a back door and backstairs. But I have observed that the back door of this house leads directly into the kitchen. She certainly could not have entered there without a dozen maids and men seeing her.'

'But I swear, that that is what she said she would do – she said that she would go to the bedchamber and wait there for my return.' Martha's look of worry deepened. 'Oh dear, Miss Kent, do you suppose the gentlemen saw her – and guessed at our scheme – and were so angry about it that Tish ran away?'

Dido shook her head and they walked on slowly. 'I can see no reason why the gentlemen would be much in anger about your scheme to deceive Mr Lomax. Nor why the discovery should make Miss Verney wish to escape the house. But, if we are to come at the truth, I believe we must discover exactly what she did after she left you at the gates.'

Martha rolled her eyes about as her habit was when forcing herself to think deeply. 'She stood beside the gates, I remember, watching us as we crossed the highway. And then we started along the track to the downs . . .' Her eyes rolled frantically. 'When we was a little way down the track – almost to the stream – I looked back . . .'

'And Miss Verney was still by the gates?'

'No. She had turned about and was walking down the drive. That was the last I saw of her.'

'She was walking towards the front of the house?'

'Yes.'

Dido stopped and turned once more to look across the lawns to the house. Again the drive and front door presented themselves uncompromisingly to her view . . . But then her eye was drawn away into the shadow of the creeper. 'Oh!' she cried, staring in momentary bewilderment.

'What is it, Miss Kent?'

'There is,' she said slowly, 'another door.'

Martha followed her gaze with a puzzled frown. 'But that,' she said at last, 'leads only to the library. If Tish had gone in that way she must still have crossed the hall to the stairs – and the gentlemen would have seen her returning.'

Dido's only answer was to withdraw her arm from Martha's and snatch her hand instead. She began to run across the lawn, drawing Martha after her.

'Whatever is wrong?' cried Martha as she was propelled past a disapproving Mrs Bailey, who was pressing her hands to her breast in a vast gesture of alarm – and scattering flowers about the lawn.

'I think,' said Dido breathlessly, 'that I understand now why Miss Verney moved the toilette table.'

Chapter Thirty-Six

Dido did not stop until they reached Martha's chamber and there she dropped down upon the bed, facing the hearth.

'I remember,' she said, gasping a little, 'Mr Lancelot claiming that this was your friend's favourite room. That she had had a fancy for sleeping here ever since she was a little girl. And I believe that is because she knew something about this room.'

'But what?'

'Something which is quite clear to see if one sits here and only looks closely at what is before one.'

She turned to Martha, but there was no sign of understanding: she sat with flushed cheeks staring uncomprehendingly, the bonnet falling back awkwardly from her head, the precious locket still clutched in one hand.

'What do you see directly ahead of you, Miss Gibbs?'

'A fireplace.'

'And to your left?'

'Nothing, just panelling.'

'And the place in which the toilette table stood when you and your friend took possession of this room?'

'Yes.'

'And what do you see to the right of the fireplace?'

'A closet.'

'Exactly so!'

Miss Gibbs shook her head.

'If,' said Dido, pointing her finger accusingly at the innocent-seeming wall, 'there is space for a closet on the right-hand side, why is there only a flat panel on the left-hand side of the chimney? I knew there was something amiss with this room! It made me feel uneasy the first time that I entered it!' She jumped up and put her hand against the panelling on the left-hand side of the fireplace.

'What are you looking for?'

'I am looking for the reason why Miss Fenstanton's little cats have been disturbing your sleep continually, while troubling no one else in the house.'

She ran her hands along the oak panels, pressing as she had seen Emma do in the library below. And at last – just as she was beginning to doubt her own genius – the wood shifted beneath her hand. There was a creak and the panel moved inward, revealing itself to be a very cleverly constructed door.

Martha screamed.

And even Dido must hesitate a moment. There was something too closely akin to a horrid novel in the creaking open of a hidden door. She could not quite escape the idea that there were skeletons and torture chambers to follow; and it was several minutes before she could reason herself into exploring the space beyond the panel.

But there were no skeletons, only a little dusty space the size of a convenient closet – and, within it, the head of a narrow stone staircase. A chill musty draught of air was blowing up the steps, bringing with it the reassuringly mundane sound of cats.

Martha crept pale-faced to the door, as if all the horrors which had occurred to Dido had now possession of her brain. 'That is why Tish wanted the table moved. So that she could come at this secret door.' She peered anxiously into the space. 'But where do you suppose the stairs lead?' she asked tremulously.

'To the library,' said Dido with conviction. She turned back into the hidden room; but the stairs were an inky-black well and all the reason in the world could not prevent a shudder as she stepped forward.

'Is it safe?' asked Martha.

'Oh yes,' replied Dido with more assurance than she felt. She made her way down the first two or three narrow steps. The air struck a chill through her and her footsteps echoed; below she could dimly see a stone staircase twisting down, as in a castle tower. 'Yes, it is quite safe.' She brushed away a spider's web which had attached itself to her face and continued downward. 'Miss Fenstanton and Miss Verney discovered the priest's hole and the stairs when they played in the house as children. It was their secret.' She stopped and held out her hand to Martha who had begun to follow her cautiously. 'But it would seem that upon this visit, they both decided to make use of the secret for their own purposes. Oh, take care! There are kittens here near the foot of the stairs.' There was a crack of light ahead, and it showed three puzzled little furry faces; three little pink mouths opened in protest.

Dido made a hasty explanation of the kittens' presence,

stepped past them, ran her hand along the panelling, and found a tiny catch. It clicked softly and, a moment later, the two women were ducking their heads and stepping, out of the dark, dusty little priest's hole into the bright ordinary world of Mr Lancelot's library.

The black kitten with white paws toddled out after them, blinking delightedly and looking about for adventure.

Miss Gibbs brushed dust from her white muslin gown and stared at Dido. 'Tish *knew* about the hidden stairs?' she said, struggling for understanding.

'Oh yes. And that, you see, was how she intended to return to your bedchamber. She planned to come in through the little garden door, to the library, and then once here she could slip up the hidden stairway.' She looked about at the room, the shelves of books, the watching portraits, the door into the hall which stood ajar. 'But I believe something happened while she was on her way to the bedroom. Something which made her leave this house—'

She stopped. From the hall came Mr Lancelot's hearty voice.

'It ain't no good arguing with me, George,' he was saying. 'My mind's made up and I have already spoke to the lady.'

Dido stepped cautiously to the door and looked out. The two gentlemen had stopped as they crossed the hall in the sheltered corner where a table stood in the shadow of the gallery.

'Spoke to her?' George Fenstanton was bouncing with rage – like a small terrier snapping at a hound. 'Why, I cannot believe it! You have asked a penniless little old maid to be your wife?'

'Ha! Mind what you say, please! Remember you are talking to a fellow in love.'

Martha giggled and turned an expressive look on her companion, but Dido hurriedly closed the door and leant her back against it. 'That,' she said quietly, 'is our answer, I think. Miss Verney *overheard* something, just as we did now.'

Martha began upon a question, but just then both women were distracted by a pitiful wail. The kitten had found the library steps and begun to climb them with enthusiasm – only to discover that coming down was a great deal harder than going up. He was now on the fifth step, clinging desperately with all four paws and crying for assistance.

Dido lifted him down and returned him to the priest's hole.

Martha pushed closed the panel and turned about with eyes full of questions. 'What do you suppose Tish overheard?'

'I am not quite sure. But anyone at the table in the hall would think themselves safe from prying ears *so long as they supposed the library to be empty*. The gentlemen were talking in the hall that morning. And I would guess that they were sitting at the table under the gallery.'

'They were, but it was only business they were talking about – no one would care a jot about Tish overhearing it.'

'Oh, I cannot agree. Business was their subject, and so was *money*, was it not?'

'Lord! Yes, but it was only how they was to get enough money for the new town. No great secret.'

'Oh! But I think there might have been a very great secret under discussion,' said Dido thoughtfully. 'For Mr George has a scheme for getting money which I do not think he would wish to be generally known.' She stopped as another idea took hold of her mind. She turned away and began to walk about in great agitation, attempting to arrange her thoughts into a satisfactory shape.

Miss Gibbs watched anxiously.

'The note!' cried Dido turning suddenly to her companion with a look of enlightenment. 'The note which you found in your bedchamber when you returned from your walk with Mr Lomax. What did it say?'

'It said, "You must not tell what you know. It will be the worse for you, and everyone you care about, if you do."'

'Miss Gibbs, that note was not about your deception of Mr Lomax.'

'Was it not?'

'It was not even meant for you.'

'Oh it was, you know. For it had my name writ upon it.'

'But that was only because the gentlemen believed *you* were the one to have returned to the house. Do you see?'

'No.'

'They thought that Letitia had walked out with Tom Lomax.'

'Yes.'

'It was *you* they believed to have stayed close to home. After you had both left the house, I think they fell into rather particular discussions – discussions which they would not wish anyone else to hear. They felt secure because they thought the house was empty. But they were wrong: the house was not empty. Miss Verney was making her way back through the library. The gentlemen perhaps heard a sound – feared that their scheming had been detected. Now they would immediately think that it was *you* creeping about the house. Not Miss Verney, because they believed her to be out on the downs with Mr Lomax. So the note was written to you, telling you not to tell what you had overheard.'

Martha's eyes rolled about as she absorbed the new idea. 'And so you think it was the note which made Tish run away?'

Dido took a rapid turn across the room. 'No,' she said at last. 'I do not believe she read the note. Why should she? It did not have her name upon it. No, I do not think she needed any threat. The secret she had heard was enough to frighten her in itself. I believe it shocked her so badly she decided she must escape.'

Martha stared. 'But what could it be that was so shocking?'

'That,' admitted Dido, 'is something which I do not yet entirely understand . . . But I believe I almost have it.' She put a hand to her head. 'It is all to do with my aunt's jewels, and some letters cut in stone . . . and the directions on some letters and Miss Fenstanton's book of sermons . . .'

Miss Gibbs looked bewildered. 'What do you mean to do?' she asked rather fearfully.

'I mean,' said Dido, 'to make a small experiment.' She turned briskly towards the hall door.

But Martha called her back. 'Miss Kent,' she said slyly, 'may I wish you happiness upon your engagement?'

'As to that,' said Dido pulling open the door, 'apply to me again in two days' time. I shall tell you then whether your good wishes are needed. But I sincerely hope that they will not be.'

Dido ran across the hall and up the stairs, her heart beating fast. She sped along the gallery and paused briefly outside her aunt's chamber. She set her ear to the door. From within came the low, comforting voice of Doctor Sutherland. 'You may rest now,' he was murmuring. 'There is nothing to worry about.'

Satisfied that she would not be needed for a while, Dido hurried on to her own room where she took her penknife from her writing desk. Then she set out with an air of great determination for the east wing to make her experiment.

If the outcome of that experiment was as she expected, then, she believed, everything would begin to make sense . . .

Chapter Thirty-Seven

The experiment was decisive.

Dido stood beside the little barred window at the end of the east wing staring out, half seeing, onto the bright spring green of the lawns where the company had begun upon a game of bowls; Mrs Bailey's pink silk bonnet bobbed about beside Miss Fenstanton's white straw and the scarlet shawl had been laid aside with a parasol upon a bench.

At last, she thought, she understood why Mrs Manners gave money to a brother she despised; and why the secret which they shared was so important as to have cost Mr Brodie his life.

She studied the window ledge. The afternoon sun was lighting up the grey stone and the old carved letters; the slanting light deepened the cuts, giving them a distinction they had not had in the early morning. She ran her finger over them, and then turned her attention to the new carving which she had just completed – untidy scratches, ill-formed letters; but a very practical proof of her theory.

There was but one doubt remaining in her head – though that was a substantial one. How was the truth ever to be made public? For it must all depend on Mrs Manners confessing. And, even if Dido could find the courage to confront her aunt, she lacked the authority to enforce compliance. What was she to do?

There was a great temptation to do as poor Miss Verney had done and run away from the wretched complication of guilt which was the rotten core of Charcombe Manor. But that was not possible; the peace and safety of others depended upon her actions.

She folded her penknife, slipped it into her pocket and turned towards the half-open door of the prison room. But as she did so, she became aware of a creaking footstep in the passageway beyond the bedchamber. Someone was walking slowly and cautiously; but the ancient floorboards were defeating the attempt at stealth and crying out so loud that only Dido's preoccupation could have kept her deaf to them so long.

She looked out through the prison bars into the colourful ordinariness of the garden – counted the bowlers. There was Mr George, and Miss Gibbs – with her locket still clenched in her hand – and Mr Lancelot. Miss Fenstanton was just putting off her shawl and stooping down to roll a ball, and Mrs Bailey was in a great flow of inaudible words.

Unless one of the servants had broken the injunction against entering this part of the house, then the footsteps were certainly those of Mrs Manners – come again to visit this room which held such terrible memories . . .

With rising panic Dido looked around at the dusty floor, white walls and narrow bed. There was no hiding place here. The footsteps came on, hesitated at the door of the outer room, and then began to cross the bedchamber.

The door was pushed open – niece and aunt faced one another in silence.

'What, pray, are *you* doing here, miss?'

Dido groped behind her, pressed her hands for support against the cool stone sill. The scene which she had most dreaded was forced upon her without any opportunity for thought or preparation. But it must be gone through; there are some matters which must transcend respect and deference.

'I am waiting for an answer.' Mrs Manners crossed to the table and sat down slowly on the narrow little chair, with the air of a queen taking her place on a coronation throne. 'I insist that you tell me what you are about.'

'Aunt,' Dido began, striving against the tremor in her voice, and determined to get immediately to the heart of the matter. 'I believe I know why Miss Verney left this house.'

'Letitia?' cried Mrs Manners with a look of great astonishment. 'You know what has become of her?'

'I believe I do. And I hope that you will not blame me for investigating the matter. For you have yourself been most anxious that she should return to her friends. The idea of an elopement has made you extremely uneasy.'

Mrs Manners sat very straight in her chair. She had an air of fragile dignity in her black silk gown, with a mass of grey curls piled upon her head, prettily set off by a tiny white lace cap. 'And am I to suppose that *that* is the cause of your impertinent intrusion upon this room?'

'I have not meant to be impertinent.'

Mrs Manners waved aside the protest. 'Very well, miss,

I daresay I can guess at what you have found out. Letitia has run away to marry young Lomax, has she not?'

'No, I do not believe she has. The reason for her departure was quite different.'

'Oh?' There was a steely challenge in the single word. It seemed intended to remind Dido of her aunt's power – her consequence in the family; the necessity of pleasing and placating.

It cost her a struggle, but Dido continued quietly, intent on getting the worst over as quickly as possible. 'Miss Verney left this house – she ran away – because she heard Mr Lancelot and Mr George talking about money; and she heard something she should not have heard.'

The words were a blow to Mrs Manners; it was detectable – not from any sign of pain, but rather from an increase of dignity. Her back straightened, her head lifted and poised itself as if the pile of grey curls was a heavy burden which must be carefully balanced. 'And what was it that she should not have heard?'

'I believe she heard Mr George Fenstanton's scheme of getting money from you. The reason why you have been giving him your jewels.'

'That is enough, miss! I insist that you say no more. I am not accustomed to such impertinence. You will say no more about the affairs of my family. We shall have no more of your disgusting *investigations*.'

'I am sorry for taking such a liberty, Aunt. But it is necessary.'

'Necessary? I know why you think it necessary. It is for the sake of young Lomax. Are we all to be allowed no privacy on *his* account?'

'I do not believe that he should pay with his life for your convenience,' cried Dido with spirit. 'And,' she added more calmly, 'I can neither stop my enquiries – nor cease to know what I have already discovered.'

Mrs Manners caught at the danger in this speech. 'And what have you discovered? I insist that you tell me about it immediately.'

'I doubt it will please you.'

'I doubt it very much, miss. But you will tell me none the less.'

Dido looked about her – at the bolted door, the barred window. 'Miss Fenstanton has told me,' she began quietly, 'that your sister, Miss Francine, had a chamber in this wing.'

'Yes. She had.'

'Knowing so much, and observing that Miss Francine is always spoken of as "sickly", I could not help but wonder whether it was her illness which called for the means of restraint which are still to be seen here.'

'Francine was not mad!' Mrs Manners' little hand struck the table.

'No, she was not,' said Dido quietly. 'I understand that now. There was no madness. This room was made into a prison for another reason entirely. It's purpose was to break the spirit of a young woman who was determined to marry for love rather than the convenience of her family. She was shut away here until her brothers had gained their point.'

Mrs Manners face remained impassive. She folded her little hands neatly upon the deal table.

Dido longed to know the thoughts behind the soft,

faded prettiness of that little face. Because everything must depend upon a confession. And not only a confession spoken in this secluded place, but repeated to the world – to the assize court.

'Pray go on,' said Mrs Manners quietly.

'Doctor Sutherland,' continued Dido, introducing the name rather fearfully, 'was Miss Francine's medical advisor. He was a constant visitor to this house.'

'Yes.'

'Constant visits produce a kind of intimacy within the family – intimacy which can lead to affection.'

Mrs Manners stared down at her hands.

'Affection which would certainly not have been approved by two brothers determined upon their sisters making grand alliances. A plan of elopement to Gretna Green would be a natural recourse.' Dido stopped and looked upon her aunt; she had bent her head a little now, as if desirous of hiding her face. 'There *was* an elopement thirty years ago, was there not? There is still a rumour of it remembered in Charcombe village.'

In the silence that followed, Dido could hear the laboured breath of her aunt. She watched the slight tremor of the thin little shoulders in their black silk and reproached herself for unkindness. She was breaking every code of behaviour. Here was insolence where there should be deference; honesty where there should be polite dissemblance. But she would not – could not – retract.

'It is a very old tale,' said Mrs Manners quietly at last. 'It ought to be forgotten. Common delicacy ought to make you shrink from mentioning it.'

'But I must. I am sorry to cause you pain, but there is a higher good to be served here.'

'A higher good! Upon my word, this is modern cant! When I was a girl, young ladies did their duty and were not so immodest as to concern themselves with *higher goods*. Why must you recall it? The escapade was short-lived; my brothers had it all smoothed over. There is nothing to be gained from remembering it.'

'But your brother has a great deal to gain from remembering it. It is his threat of publishing this old tale which puts your jewels into his hands . . .' Dido paused, then added very quietly, 'Why?'

Mrs Manners raised her head; the little white face looked like a child's in the slanting sunlight, the burden of hair almost too great for the fragile neck to support. 'Why?' she repeated. 'Are you so lost to all natural feeling that you cannot guess my reason? Naturally I wish to protect my sister's reputation.'

'At such a high cost? Thirty years after her death? Indeed, Aunt, I think you might let Mr George do his worst. I doubt anyone would care about the old story now. Why, even the women selling fish in the marketplace seem to know it already!'

'You do not understand, miss! You know nothing about family loyalty.'

'But I think I do understand why you must pay so dearly for your brother's silence.' Dido turned away to the window sill. 'The explanation lies here. In these initials cut into the stone.'

'Initials?' The word was a little cry of fear. The chair on which Mrs Manners had been sitting scraped back, toppled over and crashed to the floor. She was on her feet now, beside Dido. 'They are not still there? There is nothing which can still be read!' She peered short-sightedly at the window ledge. 'I can make out nothing.' She waved an imperious hand at Dido. 'Fetch my spectacles,' she said – the ingrained habit of command surviving even the extremity of the moment.

'I cannot supply your spectacles just now, Aunt, but I can tell you what the letters seem to be.' Dido ran her finger along the clearest of the carvings. 'FF,' she said.

'Oh!' Mrs Manners held out a shaking hand and touched the letters with the kind of searching gentleness a blind woman might employ upon a loved face. 'Francine Fenstanton,' she said.

Dido waited, hoping that she might continue; hoping that the rest of the tale might be taken out of her own hands. If only Aunt Manners would tell it herself. She searched the little white face for any sign of weakening; for a sign that true feeling – old feeling – might triumph over the rigid mask of dignity and propriety which had been worn for thirty years. But, after that one burst of emotion, the mouth and jaw were set firm once more.

'Francine Fenstanton,' said Dido reluctantly. 'That is the interpretation which occurred to me. But now I have examined the letters more closely. And I have also carried out my own experiments in stone cutting.'

Mrs Manners threw her a look which accused her of officiousness, but she said not a word.

'And, I am quite sure that *this* . . .' Dido ran a finger over the first letter '. . . is not an *F* at all.' She did not look at her aunt, but sensed her emotion. 'It is an *S* written long and straight – in the old-fashioned way.'

Mrs Manners turned away unsteadily. Dido hurriedly retrieved the chair and righted it. Her aunt sat down and folded her shaking hands in her lap.

'You still write your *S*'s in that style, Aunt. It – and your rather careless handwriting – bewilders the poor postmaster and turns the word Bristol into something resembling Beef-tea. To a modern eye your *S* looks very like an *F;* there is only a slight difference in the cross-stroke.'

'What nonsense!'

'No, I do not believe it is nonsense at all.'

'Oh, but it is, miss!' cried Mrs Manners with renewed spirit. 'For all the world knows that when it forms an initial letter, *S* is never written long.'

'No, in general it is not. And that is why it took me so long to properly decipher these initials. But then I remembered the many scratches – the unsuccessful carvings – which surround the finished letters. And I made my experiment.' She laid a hand upon the window ledge. 'This stone is very hard; and, using only a lady's penknife – the implement with which I believe the letters were made – it is *impossible* to form a curled *S*. Curves are the very hardest thing to cut. I believe the person who made these initials—'

'Oh very well, very well, miss,' cried Mrs Manners impatiently. 'I have had enough of your boasted cleverness. I know what you are about! You mean to accuse and humiliate me. You mean to say that the initials are SF, for Selina Fenstanton.'

'I am right, am I not? You carved these initials.'

Mrs Manners said nothing.

But Dido interpreted the silence as consent. 'I see now,' she continued, 'that I misunderstood Miss Emma's information. She spoke of the east wing not being used since Miss Francine died, and immediately afterwards she said, 'those were my aunts' rooms.' I misheard. It is a deficiency of our language. One is not able to *hear* where a possessive apostrophe falls. With Miss Francine in my mind I heard Miss Emma describing the whole of the east wing as belonging to that lady. But, of course, I was wrong. She said "aunts'". It was a plural. In fact, this particular room was not Miss Francine's at all. It was yours.'

There was a long silence. Mrs Manners stared down upon her own linked fingers where the white, dented flesh still spoke of the rings lost to her brother's greed.

And, at last, Dido thought it best to continue, for she suspected that strength and courage might soon fail her. 'I believe,' she said, 'it was you, not your sister that fell in love with Mr Sutherland during his visits to this house. And it was you that ran away with him. I have wondered for many days at your knowledge of the road to Gretna Green. When your mind wanders under the influence of physic you recall every detail. You have travelled that road, have you not? You eloped and your brothers brought you back. They shut you away and forced you to give up your lover – and marry my uncle instead.'

The look of pain deepened on Mrs Manners' face, her hand formed itself into a fist upon the table. There was such a silence in the room as admitted the little sounds of wood hitting wood out on the bowling green – followed by a little smattering of handclapping. Mrs Manners drew a long breath and raised her head proudly. 'It is an old story,' she said. 'Why must you torment me with it now?'

Dido felt no triumph in this oblique confession; only a horrible confusion of guilt. Every word she had said was a violation of duty which even her belief in her own cause could not make her forget. 'I do not wish to torment you, Aunt,' she said wretchedly. 'I only do what is necessary, because this old story – and your brother's abuse of the knowledge he possesses – all this I believe has resulted, not only in Miss Verney's removal from the house, but also the murder of Mr Brodie.'

'The murder?' Mrs Manners shook her head. 'No,' she pronounced, with all the authority of a woman whose word has been law for thirty years, 'it has *nothing* to do with the murder.'

'But I believe that it has.' Dido dropped to her knees before her aunt, gazing up into her face. 'Your brother has been so very determined to keep the business secret that he has threatened poor Miss Gibbs, whom he believes to know about it. And he has attempted to injure her by causing rocks to fall on her at the beach. There is great danger here and I can neither prevent its continuance, nor reveal the true cause of Mr Brodie's death, unless you authorise me to publish this old story. Unless I can present all the facts to Mr Parry he will never believe that young Mr Lomax is innocent.'

'And I am to be made a subject of gossip, for Mr Tom Lomax's convenience, am I? I am astonished that you should even suggest it. George's . . . unkindness to me has nothing to do with the killing of the unfortunate man at the inn and I cannot, I *will* not, have it made common knowledge. The tale is thirty years old, I will not have it revived. It is too painful.'

'My dear Aunt, I understand that you have suffered, but—'

'No, miss, you do not!' cried Mrs Manners with sudden passion. Her hand struck the table. 'You understand *nothing* about the demands of duty, decency and family loyalty. You care about nothing but having your own way. Why, *you* believe yourself to be in prison because you have not every minute of every day at your own disposal! Oh yes, miss, you need not look so surprised. I saw the complaining letter which you discarded.'

Dido blushed and turned down her eyes in confusion as she remembered the intemperate words which had burst from her when she had first written to Eliza after their arrival at Charcombe.

'But *I* learnt my duty many years ago,' continued Mrs Manners. 'And I have never swerved from it. I know what it is to be confined – confined by my obligations to others, to my family. I have remained a prisoner . . .' Her voice faltered. 'I might have thought, when I was released from this room that I was free . . .' She stopped. Her hands clutched at one another, enforcing stillness. 'That does not matter,' she said with a great effort. 'I have nothing with which to reproach myself.'

Dido looked up at the dignified little black figure with its heap of grey curls, and was suddenly reminded of a fanciful painting she had once seen of the French queen in her tumbrel. And a strange thought slipped into her head: She speaks true, she *is* still a prisoner. She never escaped . . .

'Well, well, it is an old story.' Mrs Manners had recovered herself and was rising to her feet. 'It is of no consequence to anyone.' She turned towards the door. 'We shall forget all about it, Miss Dido. You will not mention it again – and I shall not mention to your brother and sister how extremely displeased I am with your behaviour towards me.'

Dido scrambled to her feet in terror. Another step would take her aunt beyond the door and everything would be lost. She *must* be stopped.

'But the old story is of the greatest consequence!' she cried desperately. 'I know that it is. I know the whole truth.'

Mrs Manners pulled open the door, she was on the point of hurrying out into the bedchamber beyond.

'It is of consequence, because you know the *entire route* from Devonshire to Gretna Green.'

The black figure froze in the doorway.

'If one looks closely at the carving on the window ledge,' Dido continued, forcing herself to speak calmly, but hearing a treacherous tremor in the words, 'it becomes plain it is not SF at all. It is the same letter repeated. SS.'

Slowly Mrs Manners turned back to face her niece. Her face was white, her hand was clenched for support on the latch of the door, her knuckles pale and bloodless.

'Selina Sutherland,' said Dido, speaking quietly in the great silence that filled the room. 'It was carved, I think, as an act of defiance. A declaration of your true name.'

A tiny noise disturbed the silence. It was the rattling of the latch beneath Mrs Manner's clutching hand.

'It is true, is it not? Your brothers brought you back, but they were too late. You and Mr Sutherland had already reached the blacksmith's shop – a marriage had taken place.'

'You cannot prove it,' said Mrs Manners at last.

'No, I cannot,' said Dido slowly as she took in the full import of her aunt's words. 'But you believe that Mr George Fenstanton *is* able to prove it. That is what gives him power over you. Your fortune is at his disposal, because you believe he is able to prove that you have no claim to it. The prior marriage makes your union with my uncle unsound. You were never legally his wife – and have no rights in his estate.'

'That is enough, miss! I shall listen to no more.' Mrs Manners released her hold upon the door. She turned away.

'Please, Aunt, wait! The life of an innocent man is at stake . . .'

'I have told you: this business has nothing to do with the murder.'

'But it *has*,' cried Dido. 'Mr Brodie knew of the marriage, did he not? His home is in Gretna Green and I believe . . .'

But the little black figure was retreating, rigid, dignified, taking with it all hope.

'Please, you cannot run away from me . . .' Dido clutched at the table's edge. 'You cannot run away from this room,' she cried. 'I know that it still holds you prisoner.'

The retreating figure stopped.

Dido's fingers tightened on the table until they were all but numb. 'Aunt Manners,' she stammered, 'I *do* understand. Though I have never suffered the confinement, the unkindness that you received at the hands of your brothers, I understand why you are still a prisoner. I know the power which has held you, long after the bolts were drawn on this room, long after you seemed to walk free from this prison.'

Mrs Manners turned, poised with brittle dignity. 'What do *you* know about that, miss?'

'I know the power of "what if",' cried Dido desperately. 'The terrible haunting of the mind. The knowledge that I might, by my own decisions, have made everything different. That is why you are still a prisoner, is it not, Aunt? You have never been able to escape from the thought that you might have held out against your brothers; that you might, in the end, have won your way back to the man you loved.'

Dido leant against the table. She knew that she had played her last card; that there was no retreating from this point. She could never return to a state of polite accommodation. She had, in an effort to touch her aunt, delivered the final insult.

Very slowly Mrs Manners walked into the dressing room, pulled back the chair with an unsteady hand and sat down. For a moment she looked upon her niece with the kind of startled recognition which a traveller in savage lands might turn upon the speaker of an English phrase. '*What if*,' she repeated quietly. 'So, Miss Dido, you suppose that you understand . . .' She stopped herself, shook her head and turned her gaze upon the barred window. For several minutes there was silence in the wretched, dusty little room. Dido began to hope . . .

'No,' said Mrs Manners at last, as if speaking to herself; then, more loudly: 'No. You do not truly understand the decision I made. You have not yet learnt all there is to know about duty to your family.'

'Aunt Manners, please. You must help me bring about justice . . .'

'No. You shall receive no help from me.' She was recovering herself now; the moment of weakness was passing. 'I have said, this murder is no concern of mine. And you will hold your tongue about my business, because you can prove nothing. You will not get a word from me – and George will certainly say nothing while I continue to pay him. You may forget all about it.'

'But I cannot forget,' cried Dido, tormented by the look of determination on her aunt's face. 'And if you will not help me, then I must find some other way to prove my case.'

'I am not afraid of you,' said Mrs Manners calmly. 'Even if there is proof to be found, you will never bring it to a court of law.'

'I shall!'

'No, miss, you will not. I promise you that within four and twenty hours you will have changed your mind entirely. You will no longer wish to expose this old story. Before the sun sets tomorrow you will be pleading with me to keep everything hidden.'

She stood up slowly and Dido watched her in mounting panic and confusion. She knew not what to say. She could not believe that she would ever cease to seek the truth – but her aunt's odd conviction was disturbing.

Mrs Manners paused in the doorway. 'You suppose now,' she said, 'that you understand the decision which was forced upon me thirty years ago. You think you know all about obligation and duty. You know nothing of it – not yet. But soon you *will* understand – I shall ensure that you do.'

Chapter Thirty-Eight

Mr William Lomax looked angry, concerned – and very uncertain of what he should do.

He stood, stiff and straight beside the Venetian windows of the new inn's busy parlour and looked down upon the eager little figure who had sent a waiter to summon him from his apartment. A muscle moved in his hollow cheek. He swallowed hard. 'Miss Kent, I cannot speak to you.' He glanced about uneasily at the passengers of the Plymouth coach who were drinking tea – at a gay party of ladies and gentlemen who had just arrived in a pair of open carriages. 'We agreed,' he continued quietly, 'that we should meet no more.'

'Oh no,' said Dido. 'I remember your expressing an opinion on the subject, but I do not believe we *agreed* upon anything other than my delivering the letter.'

Anger seemed to be getting the better of it in his face. 'I *cannot* talk to you. Good day.' He bowed stiffly.

'If you walk away from me,' she said quickly, 'I shall call you back. I shall call so loudly everyone in the room will hear.'

'You would not!' said he indignantly.

But Dido was desperate. 'I would,' she said with great feeling. And it was true. In fact if he attempted to leave her, she believed it would be impossible for her to hide her distress. She would certainly call him back – she might even break into hysterical tears. The judges were perhaps already arrived in Exeter. There was little time left for the gathering of evidence and she could not proceed without his help. She needed him to act in ways which were all but impossible for her; but most of all she needed him to listen. She needed to check the riot of her ideas against his steady reason. 'Please sit down with me,' she said. 'And we will talk as quickly and as quietly as we may.'

He hesitated, looked about at the many witnesses, then back at her face, where he met an expression of great determination. 'Very well,' he sighed and gestured her towards a chair. 'But I cannot imagine what has happened to make you so very . . . contrary.'

'Oh, I have read a rather shocking book,' she said as she sat down and folded her hands demurely over her reticule, 'and I fear it may have corrupted my mind.'

'Indeed!' He drew a chair close to hers and studied her face.

'No, I assure you it is dire necessity which has brought me here. You see there is evidence – at least, I believe there may be – and you must find it. It is our only chance.'

He looked confused. 'Evidence of what?'

'The marriage, of course!' she cried impatiently, but checked herself before his startled expression. Communication with him was so natural, so easy, that she must sometimes remind herself that it was, after all, *necessary*; that he did not immediately know everything that was in her own head. She gave a hasty account of the old elopement.

Lomax shook his head several times in astonishment as she talked, but he wasted no time upon futile questions. As she concluded, he pressed a hand to his brow; his grey eyes narrowed above the painfully prominent bones of his cheeks; and he immediately took up the most important point. 'You believe that there is evidence of this marriage still in existence?'

'Yes. And my aunt believes that her brother holds the evidence. I am sure of that because she fears him. She does not fear my knowledge for she knows I can prove nothing. But she fears Mr George so much she supplies him with funds for his new town.'

'And what do you suppose this evidence to be?'

'Well,' she said thoughtfully. 'I know that marriages in Gretna Green's famous blacksmith's shop are perfunctory: there are no banns called, there is not even a proper clergyman to officiate; but I cannot believe that the ceremonies are entirely undocumented – after all, proof of the married state must generally be wanted by the lovers resorting there.'

'They are not undocumented,' agreed Lomax. 'A certificate is provided – often at preposterous expense.'

'And there must be witnesses to the ceremony, must there not?'

'Yes, generally some local men drawn in by the promise of payment—' He stopped, catching at the meaning of her raised brows. 'You believe that *Mr Brodie* was such a witness?'

She nodded. 'His home would seem to be Gretna

Green. By your son's account, he and Mr Sutherland were already acquainted when they met here on the night of the murder. And he is known too to my aunt; she believes him unworthy of a trust placed in him – she claims that he stole something.'

'The certificate?'

'Yes. At least I think it may be the certificate . . . I hope that it may be.'

'And now Mr George has got it from him?'

'Oh, I sincerely hope he has not! For if he has I do not know how we shall ever recover it. I believe that our only hope lies in Mr George Fenstanton being a liar. I think it possible that he has convinced his sister he owns a proof which he does not.' She thought a moment. 'Yes,' she cried at last, so loud the laughing ladies from the open carriage party turned to look curiously at her. 'I think there is a chance here, Mr Lomax! For why else was Mr Brodie killed?'

He looked about anxiously and made a little gesture with his hand to quiet her, for her voice was rising with her certainty. But he could not keep excitement entirely from his own voice as he said, 'This you believe was the motive for the murder?'

'Yes! All Mr George's schemes for getting money would be spoilt by the arrival of the man who actually held the certificate of marriage. He would be quite desperate to get the document from him. And besides,' she added as a new idea occurred, 'Mr Brodie had boasted of possessing it! I am sure he had!' She clapped together her gloved hands.

'I cannot understand why you should be so very certain.'

'There is the evidence of the folded shirts and the tidy razor to be considered.'

'I beg your pardon?'

'Someone else had searched for the certificate. When I looked into Mr Brodie's chamber I was surprised to find that, although his person showed signs of carelessness and neglect, his possessions were meticulously ordered. I thought it very odd; but now I understand the cause. The shirts and the razor were, in fact, arranged with just that exactitude which *Mr Sutherland* applies to everything he touches.'

'Sutherland had searched the room when he was called to inspect the corpse?'

'Yes – and that means that Mr Brodie must have talked of the certificate in the course of their meeting. He had, perhaps, offered to sell it to the doctor. After all, he was the bridegroom, he would have an interest in it. Though I think it most likely that Mr Sutherland's intention was to return the document to my aunt.'

'But he declined to buy the paper from Brodie?'

'I doubt he could afford the price set on it. Mr Brodie was a greedy man – returning poor from the West Indies, where many unscrupulous men go to seek wealth. He was determined to mend his fortunes and no doubt believed he could get a high price for the certificate at the great house. Perhaps he was as foolish as your son believes, for he was courting danger by turning his threats in that direction.'

'But,' said Mr Lomax with a doubting shake of the head, 'we cannot be sure that he made any such threats.'

'Oh, but we can!' cried Dido. She leant forward eagerly

371

and wished very much that she might get up and take a turn about the room. A little exercise would certainly make her thoughts flow more freely. But she dared not attempt it – their earnest discourse had already attracted more than one look of curiosity and she was very grateful that Mr Lomax's growing interest rendered him a little indifferent to the damage which their 'associating' might be inflicting upon her reputation. 'We can be sure that he made those threats,' she said, 'because *I have read them myself.*'

'There has been a threatening message sent to Charcombe Manor?'

'There has indeed. For I see now that that is exactly the character of the note Mr Fenstanton received. The note which he read to the entire company over tea on Sunday. It was all threats and insinuation from beginning to end! Mr Brodie wrote of an elopement and secret marriage – of the danger connected with them. He spoke of being intimately connected with someone at the manor. All this would have been instantly comprehensible to anyone familiar with the events of thirty years ago. And then he spoke of *papers* in his possession, before ending with the darkest threat of all – a suggestion that it would be dangerous to ignore his demands.'

'But how could he know that the threat would meet its mark – that Fenstanton would read the letter aloud?'

'He could not, of course, be certain. But by mentioning the acquaintance, he was inviting Mr Lancelot to ask his guests whether they knew the sender. And do you see what he was about? He had more than one document by which he meant to profit at Charcombe Manor. Besides Mr Bailey's letter, he had the old marriage certificate.'

'You may be right,' he mused, 'but I do not see much hope of evidence in all this. If George Fenstanton killed Brodie to preserve the secret of his sister's marriage then he almost certainly secured the proof of that marriage.'

Dido closed her eyes at this terrible idea which must be the destruction of all their happiness. 'Perhaps he did,' she admitted, 'but we must hope that he did not. And we must act upon that hope. We must put our faith in Mr Brodie having learnt his lesson. He had already lost one of his valuable papers to your son – let us hope that he was more cautious with the second and that he did not take it with him to his meeting behind the inn. I do not doubt Mr George Fenstanton searched the corpse – but it is possible that he was disappointed.'

He studied her face as if trying to catch some inkling of this hope from her expression. His own haggard features showed only the same, immovable terror, reined in by an almost superhuman effort of will, and a kind of yearning to believe in her words.

'And there is just one other small cause of hope,' she said, fixing her eyes upon his. 'When I examined Mr Brodie I observed that there was soot across the knuckles of both his hands.'

'And what might that signify?'

'Nothing perhaps. But I cannot help but wonder at it. For he had not been mending the fire in his bedchamber. Your son told us that there had been no fires lit above stairs – that was the reason he gave for being forced into the parlour and Mr Brodie's society. And it also occurs to me that a cold, unused fireplace might provide a very useful—'

'Hiding place! You think that the marriage certificate may still be in the chimney of Brodie's room!' He seized both her hands and, indifferent to wondering looks, raised them to his lips. 'You are right! It is a chance we must investigate immediately.' He recollected himself and released her hands. But, sitting back hastily in his chair, he could not help but smile at her. 'You are a truly remarkable woman!'

'Remarkable but contrary?'

'Yes.'

She was content with that. It was highly desirable that he should be able to acknowledge her faults and still smile upon her.

'I shall contrive a means of getting into Brodie's chamber straight away,' he said. 'And if I find the document I shall take it directly to Parry.' He stood up with an air of decision and determination, and she was delighted to see that the fear in his eyes had given way to just a little spark of hope.

Mr Lomax was so emboldened by hope as to accompany Dido onto the steps before the hotel and, despite all the business that lay ahead of them, they were both a little reluctant to take leave. The sun was shining, small white clouds scudded over the sea, driven by a warm breeze. Two barouches and a very smart curricle were to be seen driving along the mall. On the green before the inn two little boys were capering about in delight as they flew their kite and an elderly half-pay officer was waving his walking stick and hallooing encouragement.

Everything spoke of spring and of hope and, though their troubles were by no means behind them, both Dido and her companion could not help but feel refreshed by the scene.

'Do you return directly to the manor house?' asked Mr Lomax as they paused at the top of the steps.

'No, for we are to picnic on the cliffs this afternoon and I shall walk there to meet with the others.' She looked beyond the town as she spoke, towards the woods and meadows and the sandy road which looped about in a leisurely route to the cliff top. There was already, ascending the road, a wagon from the manor laden with tea kettles and trestles and rugs, baskets filled with cold fowls and bottles of wine, china cups packed up in straw – and all the other necessary accompaniments of a simple, rustic meal. 'It is a scheme of Mrs Bailey's which rather inclines me against it; but the whole company will, I think, be gathered there and there is a little matter which I may conveniently settle in the course of the afternoon.'

'Miss Kent,' said Mr Lomax, anxiously laying his hand on her arm. 'You do not mean . . . you will not endanger yourself by speaking directly to Mr George Fenstanton? You must not approach him until either I or Parry are present. If I can find the document, I shall urge Parry to send the constables straight away, and come to you myself as soon as I may. But you must not go near him. Nobody must know of our suspicions until we have the evidence in our hands.'

'Oh, you need not be concerned. My business this afternoon lies with the nephew, not the uncle.'

He still looked anxious. 'You have business to discuss with Mr Lancelot Fenstanton?'

'Yes. He has asked me a question. And I think I must answer it soon.' She hesitated and the day became a little less bright as she recollected that the answer to that question was still uncertain. The evidence she sought was not in their hands, and it might yet be necessary to become Mr Fenstanton's wife. 'However,' she finished, her eyes fixed upon the kite as it swooped earthward, 'before I can supply an answer, I must first discover just *why* he has asked the question. That is another little mystery which I am quite determined to get to the bottom of.'

By the time this faltering speech was complete her companion was looking upon her very anxiously indeed; searching her face for meaning. But before he could satisfy himself, the smart curricle turned off the mall and came to a standstill at the foot of the hotel steps.

The driver was none other than the gentleman they had been talking about. 'I am come to drive you to the picnic, Miss Kent,' called Mr Lancelot.

And Mr Lomax was obliged to accompany Dido down the steps and assist her to climb up into the high carriage. He leant forward as she mounted the step and whispered urgently, 'Ask him whether his uncle is to be at the picnic – we need to know where the wretched fellow is.'

Dido settled into her seat with pleasure – a drive in an open carriage was a rare treat and she was quite determined upon enjoying it, in spite of everything. 'Is our whole party joining in Mrs Bailey's excursion?' she asked Mr Fenstanton.

'Ha! Yes, she has compelled us all to it. Though George will, of course, be a little late – he cannot postpone his dip on any account.'

'Oh!'

Mr Lomax bowed and turned away up the sunny steps. He was satisfied; but, all of a sudden, Dido felt as if everything had slipped a little – as if ground which she had supposed to be firm and solid was quaking.

She looked anxiously at Mr Lancelot. 'And he takes his dip at three, does he not?' she asked, speaking with some difficulty for her mouth was rather dry.

'Yes.' He took up the reins. 'You might put your watch right by him. George never misses his daily swim.'

Dido pressed her hand to her brow. 'He has *never* missed?' she asked in an unsteady voice.

'Not once in over two years.'

She made a little noise which might almost have been a suppressed scream and looked towards the hotel steps. Mr Lomax was hurrying away on his mission. He was at the top of the steps – a waiter was holding open the door for him.

She longed to call him back; but she dared not. Their plans must remain secret – no one from the manor must suspect.

The carriage was beginning to be in motion, but she felt none of the anticipated pleasure in the drive. For she saw now that there was a flaw in all her recent deductions. A terrible, dangerous flaw . . .

She watched the sandy track and the grass and the

gorse bushes blur with the speed of their motion. And she thought:

If Mr George Fenstanton swam *every* day, then he had done so on the day that Letitia Verney left Charcombe Manor. In order to keep his appointment on the beach at New Charcombe at three, he must have left the manor almost immediately after the walking party quitted it at half after two . . .

And that meant that Mr George Fenstanton could not have been the person who detected an eavesdropper and wrote the threatening note to Miss Gibbs. He had had no time in which to do so much.

Dido turned her head fearfully towards the gentleman beside her.

It was only Mr Lancelot Fenstanton who had remained behind in the hall that day . . .

Chapter Thirty-Nine

'Have you considered my proposal, Miss Kent?' Mr Fenstanton asked as they left the town behind and started along the sandy road.

Dido looked at her companion, almost as if she had never seen him before.

The hair was blowing back from his face, his square jaw was set in a look of determination, one powerful hand controlled the reins, the other idled on the whip. Outdoors, with his boots and his greatcoat and his horses, Lancelot Fenstanton was in his natural element, at ease with himself – much more the man of property and lord of the manor, less the eager little boy.

She wondered again whether she quite understood this man. Was it possible that he was involved in his uncle's dark schemes? Because Lancelot Fenstanton *must* be the person who had heard a sound in the library and issued the horrible threat against Miss Gibbs. There had been no one else in the house to do it . . .

Her companion had turned now and was looking for an answer. And the question of just *why* he wished to marry her took on a new urgency.

'I am very sorry to keep you in suspense,' she began cautiously, trying with all her might to sound as if a proposal was all that she had on her mind. 'But any offer of marriage is a very serious matter. And this one, I think, is particularly difficult to decide upon.'

He smiled sidelong at her. 'Am I such a very difficult prospect to consider?'

'Perhaps you are.' She cast down her eyes, for, after all, a lady is allowed to be bashful when an offer of marriage is under discussion. 'I confess it is the letter – Mr Bailey's letter – which makes me hesitate.'

'No need for you to worry about that, my dear,' he said promptly. 'I'll put it into your hands the moment you consent to marry me.'

She fixed her gaze upon her own small feet which were swinging an inch or two above the floor of the carriage; but out of the corner of her eye she could see his booted feet and the tip of his riding whip, which was just beginning to twitch and tap against one foot.

'But,' she pursued, 'it is that which makes me uneasy, Mr Fenstanton – your promise to give me the letter *after I have agreed to be your wife.*'

'Ha!' he threw her a quick, assessing look.

'You see, I cannot help but feel that I am being . . . manoeuvred into marriage. That my consent is being enforced.'

He frowned and seemed for a moment as if he would not answer. But she waited in silence.

'Don't they say,' he remarked at last, 'that everything is fair in love as it is in war?'

Dido continued to look down. His whip was still tapping on the high leather boot. 'But I would wish to know,' she said, 'whether this is a case of love or of war.

In short, are you making love to me or threatening me?'

'Why, I'm making love, ain't I?' he cried. She looked up and saw that he was trying for a smile. 'I have told you that I admire you – and, by way of proof I'm offering to do you a service.'

'But the service is conditional upon my acceptance of your offer?'

He threw her another troubled, sideways look, then turned his attention back to his horses. Clearly he had expected only a 'yes' or a 'no', not this lively interrogation.

'I cannot allow myself to be threatened and tricked into marriage, Mr Fenstanton.'

'Threatened? Why, what nonsense!' He laughed and urged on the horses. 'I only mean to *persuade*. Marriage is a manoeuvring business. It is the way of the world.'

Whether Mr Fenstanton was embarrassed, or only anxious to reach his destination, he was driving the horses harder and harder and they were now travelling at a speed which was not entirely comfortable. Dido held to her seat with both hands and studied the profile of her companion. His jaw was set, he had a look of determination. But what, exactly was he determined upon?

And was his pursuit of her some part of the other mysteries?

The motion of the carriage whipped blood into her cheeks, made her heart beat fast – and emboldened her to ask: 'And what do you hope to gain from the manoeuvring, Mr Fenstanton?'

'Why, I hope to gain you, of course,' he answered, and tried to laugh.

'I am a bad bargain!'

'You are a great deal too modest!'

'No, an excess of modesty has never been a part of my character,' said Dido. She put up one hand, attempting to catch her bonnet which was being blown from her head. But she found that both hands were required to prevent her being shaken from her seat. She gave up the attempt, allowed the bonnet to be carried back onto her shoulders and held hard to the seat. 'My failings lie elsewhere,' she said.

'I am sure you have no failings,' insisted the gentleman – but impatience was beginning to break through his gallantry.

'Oh, but I have! I am poor and I am not young. Those, I think, would generally be considered my greatest weaknesses of character.'

He shook his head in exasperation. 'This is an extraordinary way to talk to a fellow that's made you an offer of marriage.'

'It is an extraordinary offer.'

'Damn it!' he cried suddenly and urged the horses to greater effort. 'Why must you argue?'

'Arguing,' said Dido – speaking loud to be heard above the noise of the wheels, 'is generally considered to be my third great fault. And, all in all, I cannot help but conclude that I am a bad choice for a wife.'

In reply he pulled the horses to a sudden, slithering halt and turned towards her – his brown eyes were earnest, a little frown of puzzlement was gathering on his brow. All at once he was the bewildered boy again. 'But what if a fellow has fallen in love with you?'

'Ah!' she said as the quiet afternoon settled about them

and the sounds of the sea and the circling seabirds reasserted themselves. 'If that were the case, it would, of course, change everything.'

'But, I tell you, it *is* the case! Why must you doubt me?'

She turned her eyes directly upon him, 'Because of the means by which you have sought to win my consent. I grant that marriage may often be a manoeuvring business, Mr Fenstanton. But,' she said with great firmness, 'there is no manoeuvring when there is genuine affection in the case. Love is open and honest, and it seeks to promote the welfare of its object without cavil or condition.'

He frowned, drew the reins thoughtfully through his fingers for a moment or two and looked down at his boots on the splashboard. 'You speak very decidedly about love,' he said quietly. 'You seem to know a lot about it.'

She blushed at that. 'I know,' she said, as composedly as she could, 'that there has been very little of love in your behaviour towards me. If you had burnt the letter as proof of your esteem and *then* sought my hand, I might have believed that you cared for me. But to make conditions – to inflict the pain of decision – that is not the behaviour of a man in love.'

'Good God!' Fenstanton closed his eyes a moment and seemed to struggle for control of himself. 'If you argue so, it is no wonder you have never married.'

'You are not the first to express that opinion,' Dido assured him. 'But I cannot consider a proposal unless I understand *why* it is being made. I am not rich, I am not well connected. I am neither young nor beautiful. And you certainly do not love me; I am quite sure that you do not, for, quite apart from your behaviour over Mr Bailey's letter, there is the little matter of when your passion for me began.'

'When it began?'

'Yes. You have told me yourself that your affection for me was the cause of your not pursuing Miss Verney. But your reluctance to ride after the fugitive was apparent to her friend on the very day of the disappearance. And that was *the day before* my aunt and I arrived at your house. No, Mr Fenstanton; the vainest woman in the world could not believe that you conceived an overwhelming passion for her a full four and twenty hours before any meeting took place.'

He said nothing.

'I repeat: why do you wish to marry me?'

But he remained sunk in his own thoughts. Dido pulled the bonnet back onto her head, secured the ribbons and waited for a reply in determined silence. From the cliffs above them came the voices of their companions and the faint rattle of teacups being set out on the board. After a moment or two Mr Fenstanton set the horses in motion and they started slowly up the hill. His eyes were fixed upon the road ahead. But one hand still tapped the whip against his boot.

'I'm damned if I know what to say,' he admitted at last. 'You see, I'm not supposed to tell it all, unless I have to.'

Dido was becoming more uneasy every minute. She was sure now that this proposal went deeper than she had thought. She studied the easy laughing lines of his face. She had always supposed that there were no ugly lines there because there were no ugly thoughts. But it occurred to her now that a smooth brow might indicate a lack of proper care and concern for others.

'My brother Edward,' she began slowly, 'won a medal for debating at Cambridge; and he told me once about logic – how, by putting together two propositions, one might come at an unassailable conclusion.'

Fenstanton shook his head in bafflement.

'In this case,' pursued Dido, 'the two propositions might be: first, Mr Lancelot Fenstanton is so troubled by debt that he *must* marry for money; second, Mr Lancelot Fenstanton is seeking to marry Miss Dido Kent.'

'Ha! And the conclusion?'

'The conclusion,' said Dido – a little shocked by it herself, 'the conclusion must be that Mr Lancelot Fenstanton expects to enrich himself by marrying Miss Dido Kent. It is a matter of pure logic; it cannot be escaped.'

But still she looked at him – expecting him to offer an argument against such a nonsensical conclusion.

'Your brother is a very clever fellow. Though I ain't sure he was so clever to put logic like that in the hands of a woman.'

'My conclusion is correct?'

'Yes.'

They rattled on a little way, turning at the zigzag which rendered the assent easier on the horses. The picnic in all its glory came into view. White cloths and sparkling glasses and steaming urns, surrounded by bracken and gorse bushes and the black, staring faces of a dozen or so bemused sheep. The manor party was elegantly disposed about it: Miss Fenstanton and Miss Gibbs in new white muslins and Mrs Bailey in unbecoming puce; and Mrs Manners in uncompromising black, seated regally upon a chair beneath a gay parasol, hands clasped upon the head of her walking stick – looking with marked approval towards the approaching carriage.

'It is my aunt!' cried Dido.

He only shrugged up his shoulders under the many capes of his riding coat and slapped the reins needlessly along the backs of the straining horses.

'My aunt,' she repeated more quietly, for they were now almost within earshot of that lady, 'my aunt has promised to settle money on me!'

The words were shrill and frail in the warm salty breeze and they sounded so foolish when spoken aloud that she was ashamed of having uttered them. Her companion began to laugh. He pulled the horses to a standstill on the grass beside Mrs Manners' chaise.

'Ha! Your logic gets you but halfway there,' he said. 'She ain't promised to settle money.'

'No, I did not think it possible . . .'

'You see,' he explained hurriedly, 'dear Mrs Manners don't like the way her whole family is after her fortune. We don't give her any peace, she says. And she don't see how she can satisfy us all. So she wants an alliance between the families of Manners and Fenstanton. She has promised that if you marry me, she will keep only the money settled on her at her marriage – and make you heiress to your uncle's entire fortune.'

Chapter Forty

As she stepped down from the curricle, the picnic closed about Dido with all its noise and business – and there is a great deal of noise and business when ladies and gentlemen have determined upon taking refreshment without the walls of a dining parlour. Every cup of tea is drunk with a sense of something achieved; the eating of every slice of cold meat, every spoonful of jelly, in a safe and elegant manner is an accomplishment.

With a mind so burdened, Dido would have been very glad indeed to have been excused eating entirely. She would have liked nothing better than to be left alone to consider just *why* her aunt should make such an extraordinary offer. Mr Lancelot's explanation had shaken her badly and she longed for an hour or so of quiet reflection . . . But that, of course, was not permitted. The purpose of the party gathered on the cliff top was to eat – and eat with elegance. She immediately found herself attacked with pigeon pie and a dressed cucumber and a wine glass – which she could find nowhere to stand.

But she was at least able to escape from Mr Lancelot, thanks to the kind offices of Mrs Bailey who laid claim to that gentleman's attention as soon as he set foot from his carriage. She was fortunate too in finding a seat at a little distance from the main party, on a rug beside Martha Gibbs – who proved a very kind and sympathetic listener.

'Lord!' cried Miss Gibbs when the startling cause of Mr Lancelot's proposal had poured from Dido's lips. 'Fancy you being an heiress and not knowing it! And do you mean to have him?'

Martha was smiling in that manner peculiar to discussions of matrimony, and her look made Dido cautious. The immediate need to communicate her news had been overwhelming, but now she exerted herself to think rationally – and remembered that the proof they needed was still not found; that an acceptance of the proposal might yet be necessary. 'Mr Fenstanton,' she said – seeking for a place on the grass which might accommodate the troublesome glass – 'appears to be a very agreeable, respectable gentleman . . .'

'Oh! But Miss Kent, do you love him? Do anything rather than marry without affection!'

Dido smiled sadly at the commonplace saying, considering what the 'anything' was in her case. She said nothing, but Miss Gibbs seemed to catch at her expression.

'You think me foolish and romantic, I know,' she said, reddening. 'You think me taken in by Mr Lomax. But you know, I am not so very stupid. I have been thinking a great deal these last two days, and it seems to me that a woman can only be safe if she is poor.'

'I beg your pardon?' Dido looked at her companion with sudden interest. Something in her words had struck a chord . . .

Martha's face was flushed but calm, her pale eyes

solemn as she gazed down at the ham rind and bread crust on her plate. 'I believe a woman can only really be *sure* that a man loves her if she is poor. Else you know she will always wonder whether his motives are unworthy. Or,' she glanced up, 'or else *other people* will always be doubting him and that, you know, must make a woman uneasy. Lord, Miss Kent, I'm sure no one can be happy when there is suspicion.'

'Why,' said Dido with increasing respect. 'I believe you are in the right!'

'And so,' Martha continued hurriedly, 'I mean – just as soon as we are sure Tish is safe – I mean to write the whole truth to Mr Lomax and release him from our engagement.' She paused, and put her hand to a little constriction in her throat, but continued with determination. 'Then, you know, if he really loves me, he will seek me out and . . .'

Her words faltered and stopped; but Dido was busy with her own thoughts. 'Your reasoning is very sound indeed, Miss Gibbs,' she cried. 'In point of fact, it is so sound that I cannot help but wonder whether someone else has found her way to exactly the same conclusion!'

'Someone else?' Martha looked bewildered. 'Who?'

Dido was pretty well bewildered herself. 'Someone,' she replied with a shake of her head, 'that I had certainly not set down as "romantic". In fact, the last person among my acquaintance who I would ever suspect of making a disinterested gesture.' She jumped to her feet. 'But I believe you may have explained the reason for my aunt's extraordinary behaviour! Please excuse me. I must talk to her directly.' She turned towards the laden picnic table where Mrs Manners sat in state – then hesitated.

She turned quickly back to Martha, whose eyes were once more downcast as she bit at her lip, lost in her own thoughts. 'And remember, Miss Gibbs,' she said gently, 'if, when he knows that you are poor, Mr Tom Lomax does not seek to revive the engagement, then he is unworthy of your love. You may forget him and find a more deserving man.'

She laid her hand in brief encouragement on Martha's shoulder, then made her way towards the dignified black figure beside the fluttering white cloth.

Mrs Manners sat alone beside the picnic table under a large parasol. The rest of Mrs Bailey's intrepid exploring party was seated at ease on rugs spread about among the gorse and sheep. But Mrs Manners held to her chair – as erect as if she had been at a court banquet.

A little exploring party of wasps had already established itself about the cold meat and the cakes on the table and the footman was constantly employed in walking up and down flapping his hands at them. They rose each time at his approach – and settled again when he was past. Except for one particularly angry wasp which had become trapped in a wine glass and kept up a constant drone of fury.

Dido took a seat opposite Mrs Manners who looked upon her suspiciously. 'Well, miss,' she began, 'and what have you to say for yourself?'

'Just this: why do you wish to give away your fortune?'

'That, miss, is my own affair.' Mrs Manners folded her hands about the fan in her lap and turned her face away to the sea.

Dido waited a while, hoping for more. She watched her aunt in silence across the crumbling pies and melting jellies. The wasp in the wine glass droned furiously. Mrs Manners' face was shaded by the vast brim of a sun hat which obscured her eyes entirely – leaving visible only lips drawn tight and a chin lifted in determined silence.

'It is a test, is it not?' said Dido at last. 'A test of Mr Sutherland. That has been your plan from the beginning. You came to Charcombe to find him out; to give him the opportunity of a reunion – if he chooses it. But the fortune might be a barrier between you. A village doctor might well hesitate to approach such a very wealthy widow.'

Mrs Manners continued to watch the distant waves.

'You do not deny it?'

'No,' she said at last. 'I do not deny it.'

'Well!' Dido sat for several moments in astonishment. 'I am all amazement!' she said at last. 'You, who have always spoken so firmly of duty . . . of family obligation . . . That you should make such a gesture of affection! Here is greater inconsistency of character than I would have supposed possible!'

Mrs Manners turned slowly to face her. Her eyes, still heavily shaded by the hat, were difficult to read, but they fixed themselves in a steady stare. 'No, Miss Dido! I do not recant a single word I ever spoke. I only advocate the need for duty in the *young*. But I,' she struck the table with her fan, 'I am no longer young. *I*, miss, have done my duty for thirty years. I have earned the right to act for myself – to think only of my own interest.'

'And you will act like an impulsive girl of sixteen!'

'That is no concern of yours! I shall act as I please – for the first time in my life. I think you had better consider how you are to act yourself.'

Dido's thoughts turned abruptly from wonder at her aunt's romantic gesture, to her own danger. 'You consider that I am yet young enough to be constrained by duty?'

'Oh yes,' pronounced Mrs Manners firmly. 'But I do not need to tell you that. You know your duty. That is why I have chosen you from among all my husband's nieces. I know that every little attention you pay to me is done for the sake of duty; you do not court me for selfish motives, it is all done for the sake of your family, is it not?'

Dido coloured. 'I hope,' she said, 'that my behaviour has never seemed grudging or reluctant.'

'Oh, it has seemed very grudging and reluctant indeed!' cried Aunt Manners. 'And I honour you for it! But,' she folded her fan with a sharp snap and pointed it at her niece, 'what I wish to know – what I have set out to discover – is how dutiful you will be in greater matters. I knew from the beginning that you might need a little persuasion. When your sister-in-law told me you were determined to refuse the widowed clergyman, I wondered about you, Miss Dido. How unexceptionable would an offer of marriage have to be to overcome your romantic scruples? I was, I confess, surprised to hear that you had hesitated over the proposal of such a very eligible man as the master of Charcombe Manor. But then,' she reached across the fruit and broken loaves on the table and tapped her fan against Dido's wrist, 'Lancelot told me of your attachment to Mr William Lomax – and I began to think that perhaps you must know the whole truth before you would do your duty.'

'And,' said Dido in a rather unsteady voice, 'you would claim it is my duty to marry Mr Fenstanton?'

'But of course it is your duty. Just as it was my duty to marry your uncle. Think, Miss Dido!' she smiled knowingly. 'You would be a rich woman – able to assist your brothers, able to save your sister from poverty. You could reward the family who have supported you. Think how they would all cry out against your refusing so advantageous a match.'

'No!' answered Dido immediately. 'My sister would never speak a word against my refusal. Eliza would teach in a school before she would let me marry a man I do not love! And as for my brothers . . .' she hesitated a moment here. 'I cannot believe . . . I *will* not believe that my brothers are as selfish and unprincipled as yours proved themselves to be. And if they are so corrupted as to sell their sister's person for worldly advantage . . . then their disapprobation can be of no consequence to me. I care not what they think!'

Mrs Manners narrowed her eyes in disbelief and studied her niece. Dido endeavoured to meet her stare calmly, but her heart was beating so hard it was difficult to keep her hands still upon the table. The brilliance of the sun-spangled sea hurt her eyes and the picnic smell of sweet jellies, vinegar and bruised grass seemed oppressive; her breath caught and ached in her breast.

'Do you mean to refuse Lancelot?' asked Mrs Manners at last – and it was spoken in much the same way as she might have asked whether Dido intended to cease breathing, or place her hand into the fire.

The stark question threw Dido's mind into turmoil. She swallowed back the instinctive 'yes' which had risen to her lips. She thought of the damning letter now in Mr Lancelot's possession; the relentless reasoning which had brought her to the conclusion that she *must* accept Mr Fenstanton's offer; the call of a higher, more compelling duty which her aunt could not even suspect. 'I do not know,' she stammered. 'I have not yet reached my decision.'

'Ah!' cried Mrs Manners with great satisfaction. 'I did not think your pretty notions would stand out long against the claims of hard cash. Did I not tell you yesterday that in four and twenty hours you would have changed your mind? Now that my fortune is in your hands, I doubt you are so very anxious to publish an old story which would throw doubt upon my claims!'

With a great effort of will Dido kept silent. She must be cautious. She looked beyond the table spread with it's fine linen and glass and broken pies, to the town of Charcombe lying in the great, white-laced curve of the bay; but most particularly she looked to the sandy track which led up from the town to the cliffs. She fixed her eyes upon that road with a longing so intense it might almost manufacture the sight she wished for – the approaching figure of Mr Lomax. Surely, she thought, he must soon come to her. Soon she would know whether he had secured the document which could free her from Lancelot Fenstanton's claim upon her future . . .

And these thoughts brought Dido abruptly back to all her doubts over her solution of the mystery; and she was able to turn from feeling to reason.

She looked at her aunt's gloating face. 'Before I can say yes or no to Mr Fenstanton's offer,' she said, 'I feel I must know a little more about his character. In particular I would like to know whether he has taken any part in Mr George Fenstanton's scheme to get money from you?'

'No!' cried Mrs Manners indignantly. 'Of course he has not taken any part in it! He knows of it. I have told him myself. But he would never be a party to such an outrage. Why do you ask such a ridiculous question?'

'Because, Aunt, I believe I have made a mistake. When I spoke to you in the east wing, I said that Mr George and Mr Lancelot had been overheard in discussion by Miss Verney. But I realise now that that cannot have been the case.' She explained her reasons for believing that Mr George Fenstanton could not have detected Miss Verney in the library, that it must have been Mr Lancelot himself who had been so discomposed by her presence as to write the threatening note to Miss Gibbs.

Mrs Manners flicked open her fan with a frown of disdain. 'This is nonsense,' she exclaimed when the account was finished. 'Complete nonsense.'

'No—'

'Oh, but it is! You think yourself so clever, Miss Dido, but a child could see the weakness in your argument! If George was gone away to take his dip in the sea, then Lancelot was *alone* in the hall. He could not have been talking to anyone, so there was nothing for Letitia to overhear.'

'I cannot quite make it out,' conceded Dido. 'But I am sure *something* must have occurred while he was alone in the hall and Miss Verney was making her way back through the library . . . And,' she continued thoughtfully, 'there can have been no meeting – no confrontation – for he did not know that it was her; he thought it was Miss Gibbs.' She shook her head, determined to puzzle it out. 'It *must* have been an overhearing. I can think of no other explanation.'

'Nonsense! I have told you, there was nothing to hear! Gentlemen do not talk to themselves.'

'Oh!' cried Dido in great excitement. The words had called forth a memory. A memory of her first day at Charcombe, the arrival of the messenger with Tom Lomax's letter. She remembered sitting in the darkness of the hall and watching Mr Lancelot on the sunny step *talking to himself.* 'This gentleman does,' she said through lips rendered almost immovable by shock. 'Under one particular circumstance, Mr Lancelot Fenstanton does talk when he thinks no one is listening.'

Her companion continued to look disdainful.

'Mr Lancelot reads aloud,' Dido explained. 'He reads his letters aloud, even when he believes himself alone.' Her mind was racing now, all manner of ideas sliding into place – and forming a very alarming picture indeed.

'You believe he received a letter?'

'But of course he did! I remember now that Mr Tom told us the letters were coming from the post as he set off upon his walk with Miss Verney.' Dido jumped to her feet. 'I believe I know who that letter was from,' she cried as she began to pace about. 'And I know why its contents made Miss Verney run away!'

Chapter Forty-One

Dido was on her feet because she could sit still no longer. She must move. With her, exercise of the body and of the brain were all but the same thing. She walked away from her aunt to the edge of the cliff, where bushes of gorse and juniper grew so thickly as to form a hedge, and a steep narrow set of steps led down to a rocky little beach. She stood here for several minutes watching the green glass walls of the waves shatter into shards of foam on the rocks below; and she thought about Lancelot Fenstanton. She considered everything that had passed between them since her first coming to Charcombe. Then she turned back and looked again with longing towards the town.

She felt quite unequal to continuing without Mr Lomax. The whole business had taken such a turn as made her doubt she should proceed alone. She kept her eyes upon the track and willed him to appear. He must come soon. It was almost a prayer in her head . . .

But she had judged ill in leaving the protection of a companion. For now the whole party was putting aside its plates and glasses and turning its mind to the next great business of the day – the admiration of fine prospects. And Mr Lancelot had taken advantage of the general movement to seek her out.

'I fear,' he said, approaching her so quietly that she started and almost fell into a bush of juniper, 'that I must press you for an answer to my proposal, Miss Kent. Our aunt is eager to have the business settled. And besides, I am sure I need not remind you that the assize judges arrive in Exeter today.'

She looked up at him hastily – then back to the sandy track. Still there was no movement upon it.

'I . . . I need to consider,' she said. He was standing too close again; and now she found it most decidedly unpleasant. She wished he would go away. And she wished too that she had been a little wiser herself. A little less easily flattered. Too late she suspected that her recent behaviour towards him might have been interpreted as *encouraging*.

She began to walk away, but he pursued her and drew from his pocket a tattered paper which she immediately recognised for Mr Bailey's letter. She stopped.

He looked from the letter to her with an air of innocent puzzlement. 'Now, what shall I do with this? Shall I deliver it directly?' The breeze blew the loose black hair into his face and he blinked like a little boy. 'You would not wish me to do that, would you, Miss Kent?'

The pretence of innocence was more than she could bear; all at once, anger had the better of her. 'You are mistaken,' she cried, 'if you think such ungentlemanly behaviour can prevail upon me.'

He laughed. 'Now, take care what you say, my dear. Remember everything that is at stake.'

'Oh,' she said. 'I understand exactly what is at stake. And that is why . . .' She fought for control – but it was control of her voice, not her temper. She could feel caution blowing away on the warm sea breeze. Her eyes had ceased to search the track for the approach of assistance. She could not help but act for herself – and speak what she thought. She knew that she might regret it in a moment, but the words would not be held back. 'I thank you for your offer, sir, but I cannot marry you,' she said, turning to face him. 'I cannot marry you because I have reason – good reason – to doubt your character.'

'My character?'

The air of surprise was a further provocation. Her anger was rising with every moment. His very expectation of compliance was an insult – and a shameful reminder of how weak and foolish her own behaviour had been. 'Yes, sir,' she cried, the words almost bursting from her lips. 'I could never marry a man who is so lacking in consideration for the feelings of others, and who has no respect for the rights or possessions of his fellows! Nor,' she added after a moment's thought, 'could I accept a man who is so remarkably irreligious.'

Fenstanton took a step back, almost as if her words were blows. 'Ha! Now, I think you had better explain yourself. A fellow can't have such accusations thrown at him without wanting to hear an explanation, you know.'

'You shall, by all means have my explanation,' she said, but was forced to stop and collect her powers.

It required all her strength to form rational, comprehensible words when she only wished to scream and rail against him. They had come now to a place where a small but rapid and noisy stream ran down between banks crowded with curls of young bracken and pale-pink cuckoo flowers. She stood for a moment watching the clear water swirl and chatter around the stones, then drew a long breath and raised her head.

When she spoke her voice was tolerably calm but it had still the edge and tremor of extreme emotion. 'You have shown how very indifferent you can be to the sufferings of others by your cruel treatment of Miss Verney. You had pursued your interest with her, led her to believe in a "growing understanding", but did not hesitate to give her up when a more favourable alliance fell in your way.'

'I daresay she will not be too badly hurt by it.'

'Oh no, Mr Fenstanton, she has been very badly hurt. It was your defection which made the poor girl quit Charcombe Manor. I had not understood that until today . . . I have been foolishly blind and thought it was your uncle's crimes which frightened her away. But now I understand the truth. Miss Verney was in the library on Thursday last when you read aloud a letter in the hall.'

'Ha!' he cried as her words struck home. 'Now what are you at? What are you saying?'

'Miss Verney disappeared the day before my aunt and I arrived at Charcombe. And it was on the day before our arrival that you received my aunt's letter giving notice of our visit.' She began to walk slowly along the stream bank, trailing her hand across the bracken fronds. She did not wish to look at him. 'That was the letter you received when you were alone in the hall – the letter you read aloud, as your habit is.'

'And what if I did?'

'The letter also contained an explanation of the "arrangement" my aunt wished to make with you, did it not? In point of fact, you knew how valuable I was to you *before* I came here. That is why you were willing to let Miss Verney run to Scotland if she pleased.'

He pursued her and caught her arm, his face flushed red at first, then bleached white with a cold, settled anger. 'Now then,' he said. 'I don't like the way this is going, madam.'

'Neither, sir, do I. I find it extremely distasteful. But these are facts which cannot be ignored. For after you had read the message – and, I don't doubt, betrayed by your very manner of reading your enthusiasm for the scheme – you suspected yourself overheard and made a threat against poor Miss Gibbs whom you believed to be the eavesdropper. A cruel, horrible threat! But you were mistaken. It was Miss Verney herself who had heard that you meant to throw her over for a more advantageous match.'

'Letitia heard?' He was shocked now. She watched him struggle for comprehension of everything that would follow from this one fact. 'No,' he insisted at last. 'She cannot have heard. Letitia had walked out with young Lomax.'

'As it happens, she had not. Miss Gibbs had accompanied the young man; it was Miss Verney herself who had returned to the house – just in time to hear you exulting over my aunt's letter. The effect of your treachery upon that very spirited young lady was to determine her upon discomposing you by disappearing. A trick which she knew she could accomplish very effectively because of a particular arrangement which had been made between her and her friend.'

'I am not certain that I quite understand . . . How can you know that Miss Verney heard any such proof of what you term my "treachery"?'

'Because she was determined to punish not only you, but also the guardian who had so assiduously promoted her marriage to you. Miss Verney clearly felt that Mrs Bailey had betrayed her too. After she left the house she took a very cunning revenge upon that lady. She sent an old theatrical acquaintance here to cause her embarrassment.'

Fenstanton kicked at the pebbles by the stream as he considered, stirring the clear water to muddy brown with the toe of his boot. 'And so Miss Gibbs knew nothing of the matter?' he asked at last.

'No. She knew nothing at all,' said Dido quietly, her eyes fixed upon his brooding face. 'You need not have pushed down the stones upon her.'

She waited, hardly daring to breathe. The sunlight threw shimmering reflections up from the water onto his face. They glimmered across his tanned cheeks and the little fans of lines at the corners of his eyes. Dido remembered how she had once thought all the creases of his face caused by good humour. She had been deceived. Selfishness might very effectively inoculate a man against trouble; by always getting his own way and never concerning himself with the pain of others, a man might keep his countenance open and unravaged.

'Now what,' he said at last, 'makes you suppose that I pushed the rocks onto Miss Gibbs? Did you see me perform the act?'

'No, for you took great care to keep at a distance which

made recognition impossible. I saw only a horseman in a green coat.'

'Ha! But I don't possess a green coat.'

'But that would be no obstacle to you, Mr Fenstanton! For that, you know, is my second cause for disapproving your character. You have no respect for the rights of property. I do not doubt that you appropriated your uncle's coat to deceive me.'

'And so I am a thief too, by your calculation!' He stood solid and angry before her. His face was pale and his voice loud. But the walk upstream had gained Dido a little height and, beyond his broad shoulder, she could once more see the road from town – and there were the solid forms of Mr Parry and his two constables hurrying up the hill. But outstripping them by many yards was Mr Lomax – he was already nearing the summit.

'Yes, I believe you might be described so.' She folded her pelisse about her, driving her fingers into her arms in an effort to prevent herself trembling with emotion.

His head was thrown back, a powerful hand clenching and unclenching continually as if there was also passion in him which only the proximity of others prevented his acting upon.

'His coat was not the only thing you took from Mr George Fenstanton.' She could not keep the tremor from her voice now. A part of her brain was wondering that she dared speak this at all – but indignation drove her on. 'You also appropriated his horse.'

'No!' He took a step towards her. 'Damn you!' She began to walk back towards the picnic party. But he pursued her and caught her arm in a bruising grip. 'You will explain yourself, madam! What is all this?'

Across the meadow she could see Mr Lomax. He had gained the top of the hill and was beginning to run past the table towards her, quite disregarding the consternation of the picnickers. Mrs Bailey was staring; Mrs Manners had risen from her seat and raised her stick in protest; Mr George Fenstanton was beginning to trot after him. His faint protest of 'Now then, now then . . .' reached Dido on the breeze.

She raised her eyes to Mr Lancelot's furious countenance. 'This,' she said quietly, 'is my answer to your proposal. I thank you very much for the compliment. I am keenly aware of the honour you do me in asking, but I cannot marry you, sir, because you are a murderer.'

'Ha!' His grip tightened for a moment, and then he released her. 'This is madness, no one will believe you. You have imagined it all.'

'Oh no. My weakness has not been imagination, but rather slowness of comprehension. I was foolish enough to assume that Mr Brodie's killer had ridden his own horse to the crime. But I should have known better. The stable boy had told me something very different – if only I had listened to him. In talking to the mare he said "some great lump has ridden you". The horse had been injured by someone other than her usual rider; someone who was too heavy for his mount.'

'No!' He raised a hand and let it fall again, uncertain what to do.

'Miss Kent!' The cry had come from Mr Lomax who

was hastening forward with a look of extreme anxiety on his face. 'You must come with me immediately.'

'Oh yes, Mr Fenstanton,' she said hurriedly as Lomax approached. 'I understand it all now. It was you. There was no one in Charcombe Manor with better cause to wish dead the man who could prove my aunt has no rights in my uncle's fortune. For you are the one who meant to gain the whole. You understood very clearly Mr Brodie's threats – despite your seeming innocence. You went to meet him at the inn on Sunday night, and, when you could not persuade, you killed him.'

As Mr Lomax reached her and seized her arm, Dido turned to find a scene of chaos and consternation. Mr Parry and his constables were now arrived and were hurrying across the spread rugs with a look of determined business about them. Mrs Bailey had succumbed to hysterics and the two young ladies were attending her. Mrs Manners continued to brandish her stick. In the confusion, a cloth had been dragged from the table and a pair of gulls were already squabbling over a shattered pie, while an upturned red jelly wobbled in a gorse bush.

Mr Lomax was half leading, half carrying her away towards the edge of the cliff, she leant gratefully upon him, for a moment quite beyond thought or action. But then her head cleared a little. 'Oh, but you do not understand,' she gasped. 'I was wrong. It was not Mr George . . .'

'I know,' he said calmly and continued to walk. 'I know that Mr Lancelot Fenstanton is the killer. That is why I am removing you from him. My mission at the inn

405

was more successful than we hoped. The old marriage certificate was indeed in the chimney piece. But it was not the only document which Brodie had concealed there.'

Dido stopped walking abruptly and pulled him to a standstill. 'The note!' she cried. She turned shining eyes up to his face. 'The other document which you found, it was a hurriedly written note, was it not? A note written in pencil!'

'Yes it was . . .'

'I knew it!' she cried in delighted relief. 'For that was my third argument against Mr Fenstanton's character. He is lacking in religious devotion.'

'I beg your pardon?' He was looking down with an expression of utter bewilderment on his flushed face. She noticed that there was soot still upon his hands – a smudge of it on his cheek.

'In church last Sunday I saw Mr Lancelot writing during the sermon. And I supposed that he was noting down the beauties of the discourse. But such piety is certainly not a part of his character. In fact, his mind was upon other matters entirely. He had received the letter from Mr Brodie before he entered the church. I saw the boy deliver it to him. And during the service he wrote a reply. The reply changed the time of his meeting with Mr Brodie. He suggested that instead of the gentleman coming to Charcombe Manor next morning, they should instead meet behind the inn at midnight.'

'He did indeed.'

'And that was the note you discovered in the chimney?'

'Yes, and it is very powerful evidence against him,' said Lomax in a voice of great relief. 'Together with the

marriage document, it will suffice to get Tom released.'
They had reached the cliff's edge and the hedge of gorse
now, and they turned together to watch the destruction
of Mrs Bailey's delightful little exploring party.

The boots of the constables had left a trail of mud
and broken pie crust across the rugs as they made their
relentless way to the arrest. But they had passed Mr
George by entirely; he was still at liberty, bouncing and
voluble.

The men were hurrying instead towards the shocked,
unmoving figure of Mr Lancelot Fenstanton.

Chapter Forty-Two

Mr Lomax – anxious to protect Dido from distressing sights and the need of painful explanations – began to lead her away down the steps which led through the gorse to the little beach.

The sound of upraised voices faded away behind them and was replaced by the crash of waves on the rocks below. The steps were narrow, and ran between a variety of spiked and hostile bushes; they were obliged to walk close, and she leant heavily upon him. Soon there would be all manner of questions to be answered, a hundred explanations to make. But, for now, she only wanted to be with him.

As they walked he attempted to express his gratitude for her help in saving Tom. The phrases were broken. To a grammarian they would have been quite unintelligible; but to Dido they were eloquent of appreciation and affection.

The steps led them to a little cove of deep pools and large irregular rocks ranked with cormorants gravely watching the foam of an incoming tide. And they stood for a moment, as still as the birds, watching the bright sea framed by the dark curving arms of the headlands.

'Miss Verney might be sent for now, I suppose,' said

Mr Lomax quietly at last. 'For we may be sure now that she is in no danger.'

'Yes. You know where she is, do you not?'

He nodded. 'Like you, I have known it ever since we learnt the story of the altered identities. She is with her friend, Mrs Hargreaves, I do not doubt. For Mr Hargreaves' information to Mr Fenstanton was only that there was no *Miss Verney* in his house. I suppose if he was asked about a *Miss Gibbs* his answer would be different.'

'I am sure it would.'

They stood in silence a little longer and – like a general regrouping his forces after a hard-won victory – Dido arranged her straggling thoughts.

'My aunt will feel the loss of her favourite nephew acutely,' she said at last. 'But that is her only loss. No doubt her family and their lawyers will now claw away her fortune and squabble over it in the courts. But, since her wish is only to be becomingly poor in Mr Sutherland's eyes, I hope that, in time, she will be reconciled with the way I have acted.'

'I hope it too. But you must not be hurt if she is not reconciled. You certainly have nothing with which to reproach yourself.'

'Thank you for saying it. But I should like to have my aunt's good opinion. I find that I value it more highly than I supposed. She and I are rather alike, I think. Though I never suspected it before, and if anyone had suggested it just two weeks ago I should have laughed in his face.'

He smiled and offered no contradiction.

'I hope that Mr Sutherland will satisfy her hopes,' Dido continued. 'Perhaps a love match may even cure her of those illnesses which her marriage of convenience caused.'

'Perhaps it will. Everybody in the town assures me that he is a very clever doctor!' He paused. 'And a man of honour too, I think,' he added more seriously. 'He seems to have acted with integrity throughout this business.'

'I confess,' said Dido, turning to a more troubling notion, 'I am rather disappointed that the law has no power over Mr George Fenstanton. For, though he is no murderer, his behaviour is such as *ought* to be punished.'

'Well, he may escape a noose and a prison,' said Lomax, 'but I think that after all he will not go unpunished.'

'By the loss of his sister's money and the calling in of his debts?'

'Yes, and that, of course, will entail the loss of all his ambitions for his new town. That I believe will be the heaviest blow – New Charcombe is very dear to him.'

Dido considered and her sense of justice was appeased. 'And besides all this,' she added with a brightening smile, 'there is another suffering preparing for Mr George. His daughter has just that spirit of independence which can bring misery to a self-seeking parent! She will have her own way with her life in spite of him.'

She stood for several minutes, watching the sun dart and sparkle on the sea and the sombre cormorants stretching out their wings to dry in the warm breeze. She wondered just what might be achieved by a woman twenty years her junior setting out upon a life of defiance . . .

But then her mind turned to a very different young lady and her smile faltered. 'It is Miss Gibbs I grieve for most,' she said. 'There will be no justice for her. She is guilty of nothing but a trusting heart, and yet her punishment will be severe. Your son will reject her when he learns the truth – and she will suffer acutely. She talks bravely of releasing him from their engagement, but I am sure she more than half believes that he will stand by her.'

'It will be a blow, I do not doubt. But it is to be hoped that the pain will be of use to her. It may make her a little more cautious in future.'

'Oh,' she cried. 'I am sure that is all very sound and moral! But I wish there was something I could do to help her.'

'You have done enough,' he said gently, taking her hand. 'You must be satisfied. You cannot hope to solve every difficulty of everyone around you!'

She sighed, began upon an objection, but then, looking up into his face she was silenced by the wonderful relief that she saw there. His easy look sent her heart soaring.

Despite all the business which lay ahead of him, despite his concern for the scene enacting on the cliffs above, Mr Lomax was happy. He was more free from worry than she had yet seen him since his coming to Charcombe. His face was still hollow, but the look of dread had lifted; his grey eyes shone calm and clear as ever.

She drew out her handkerchief and, with her hand on his arm, reached up to wipe away the smudge of soot from his cheek.

He smiled at the attention and looked searchingly into her eyes. 'There is one small matter I still wish to be explained,' he said quietly.

'And what is that?'

'The question which Mr Lancelot Fenstanton had asked you: was it a proposal of marriage?'

'Yes, as it happens, it was.' She recalled the interview just past and blushed. 'My reply – my reason for refusal – was a little unusual. I do not suppose that many suitors are rejected on the grounds of murder.'

'I doubt they are! But, if he had not been the guilty man and . . .' he hesitated '. . . and if I had failed to find the certificate – in short, if Tom had remained in danger, would you have accepted Mr Fenstanton?'

'There is nothing to be gained by considering so very many ifs,' she said firmly. 'Mr Lancelot is a murderer. I could not accept him. There is nothing more to be said.'

'But you did not know he was guilty until the last hour. When we talked at the inn you were quite sure that his uncle had done the deed. An hour ago you held Mr Lancelot Fenstanton in high regard – and it is not unreasonable to suppose that your answer might have been very different.'

Dido thought for a long time, watching the waves boil and tumble about the rocks.

'No,' she said at last. 'I do not believe I could ever have brought myself to acceptance. Some instinct would have made me draw back, I am sure.'

'An instinct which informed you that your suitor was a murderer?'

'No. An instinct which, I believe, has protected me ever since I was sixteen years old – continually warning me of the great danger to a woman in marrying a man she does not *know*.'

She smiled and began to pick her way across the slabs

of rock towards the sea. 'I believe,' she said as he followed her, 'that a lack of real knowledge is, after all, the great difficulty which exists between men and women. I think that Miss Wollstonecraft, for all her revolutionary ideas, has come at but half the truth.'

Lomax took her hand to steady her as they approached the sea and the rocks became treacherous with damp. 'You believe that the sexes have insufficient knowledge of one another to form successful alliances?'

'Yes. We are, generally, so separated our intercourse before marriage is limited to trifles and compliments. It is impossible for the real character to be known.'

'And so there is a great danger that unthinking young ladies may marry murderers?'

'I grant that few women marry to find their husbands guilty of killing in cold blood, but a great many unfortunate women discover faults which are almost as dangerous to their peace.'

He began to laugh. 'And what remedy would you advocate for this great social evil?'

She turned a smiling face up to his. 'Argument,' she said with great conviction. 'Constant argument. Dispute should be the very foundation of courtship. Young women should be taught not to paint landscapes and play upon the pianoforte, they should be taught to express their ideas.'

He laughed louder and she loved the sound as it echoed about the damp rocks and sent the cormorants flapping out over the sea on slow, black, ponderous wings. It seemed an eternity since she had heard him laugh.

'Perhaps,' she suggested, 'I shall write a shocking and

revolutionary book of my own upon the subject of how young women should be prepared for the world!'

'It would be a remarkable book,' he said. 'It would make Miss Wollstonecraft's *Vindication* appear like an etiquette manual in comparison!'

'Do you advise me to write it?'

'No.' He stopped laughing and looked very seriously upon her. 'I advise you instead to marry me; marry me and prove to the whole world what a very happy union a man and woman may argue themselves into.'

She thought for the space of time which it took two waves to break upon the rocks. Then: 'Yes,' she said, 'I should like that much better.'

'Yes?' he repeated, not daring to believe he had heard aright.

'Yes,' she said with quiet decision.

He laughed aloud and seized both her hands. His intention perhaps was to raise them to his lips. But she happened to step towards him, and she happened to turn her face up to his. And, for one reason or another, the kiss fell full upon her mouth.

PREVIOUSLY IN THE DIDO KENT SERIES

'Beautifully written. Characters one cares about immediately and a mystery which becomes more urgent with every page'
Anne Perry, author of the Inspector Pitt novels

'Delightful . . . fascinating . . . this is a beautifully written, skilfully crafted novel and a very enjoyable read'
Historical Novels Review

'It's the world of Jane Austen and Charlotte Brontë . . . Charming, utterly charming, and totally good fun!'
Books Monthly

―◇―

To discover more great historical crime and to place an order visit our website at
www.allisonandbusby.com
or call us on
020 7580 1080